MW01514779

Just One Summer

By
Nicole Deese
Tammy L. Gray
Amy Matayo
Jenny B. Jones

Copyright—Just One Summer

This book is a work of fiction. Names, characters, places, and incidents are the product of the authors' imagination or are used fictitiously. Any resemblance to actual events, locales, or persons, living or dead, is coincidental.

A Summer Remade—©2015 by Nicole Deese
Waves of Summer—©2015 by Tammy L. Gray
A Painted Summer—©2015 by Amy Matayo
Wild Heart Summer—©2015 by Jenny B. Jones

ISBN-13: 978-1512391343
ISBN-10: 1512391344
Print Edition

Cover Design by Sarah Hensen, Okay Creations
Cover Image by Darren Muir, Stocksy.com

Dedication

To our readers.

The only people crazy enough to spend as much time with our imaginary friends as we do.

We appreciate you all.

Prologue

Ten Years Ago

JOSS SANDERS DIPPED her pink pedicured toes into the lapping water below the dock. A warm breeze swooped through the sun-spotted cove, carrying the melody of the maple and alder trees: a shake, a rustle, a brushing of branches. This was the song of summer on Washington's Lopez Island.

The sassy eleven-year-old watched a boat zip by and tossed up her hand in a friendly wave. Her three best friends were too busy sunning themselves and chatting to notice. Joss thought of all the rising chaos at home and wished for the millionth time she never had to leave the family's summer cabin. This year she'd been allowed to bring her friends, making the vacation spot even better.

Her feet numb, Joss pulled them from the chilly cove water, took off her sunglasses, and regarded her friends.

"I have an idea."

Sydney straightened her ponytail and sighed. "If this is about your plan to get Tyler Martin to ask you to the fall dance, we've heard it."

"And we still don't think stuffing your bra with tissue paper will end well," Avery said.

"It isn't about either of those," Joss said, crossing her arms. "But I still don't see why he hasn't asked me. You think I should use socks instead?"

Darby popped her gum, completely ignoring her. "Your ideas always end up with at least one of us in trouble."

Avery nodded. "Like the protest you organized in P.E."

Joss's mouth fell open. "Running should be optional. Sweating has to violate some kind of right."

Sydney smiled. "Then there was the time you set all of your neighbor's dogs free."

Joss thought perhaps she should be a tad more annoyed with her friends, but there simply wasn't time. They only had two days left on the island. Her best summer ever was coming to a close.

"Back to my idea. Let's make a promise that we come back every summer."

Darby rolled over on her towel to give equal time to the back of her legs. A girl couldn't have an uneven tan. "That's your idea?"

"Yes, and it's a good one. We're gonna get older and things are going to get complicated."

Avery put down her book and sat up. "Who says?"

"One of my mom's magazines." Joss eyed the three friends who meant the world to her. "I say no matter what's going on—problems with our parents, catastrophes with boys, summer camps, college—we find a way to get back to this cabin."

"So every summer we come here together and soak up the sun, watch old movies, eat ice cream, and giggle until we fall asleep?" Darby asked. "Count me in."

"Me, too," Sydney said.

"My mom all but packed my bag for me," Avery said. "You know I'm up for it."

"Let's promise." Joss stood and extended her hand. "Assemble formation."

The three other girls stood and placed their hands on Joss's.

"I'm not spitting this time," Darby warned.

"Girls, do you solemnly swear on our friendship that you will do everything in your power to return to this cabin with me every summer?"

"We do," they chimed.

"Even if it means we have to lie to our parents, hitchhike on the back of a pickup truck, or walk backwards the whole way to get here?"

"I would never hitchhike!" Darby said.

Joss rolled her eyes when the other girls nodded in agreement. "You're missing the point," she said. "Now, do you swear or not?"

"We swear," they agreed again in unison.

"Then I now pronounce us best friends, sisters, and vacation buddies for life." Joss threw her arms around her friends and pulled them into a sticky group hug.

"Together forever," Avery said.

Sydney laughed. "Nothing can stop us."

"So I'll see you next summer," Darby said.

Joss grinned at her three best friends. "And every one after that."

A Summer Remade

By

Nicole Deese

Chapter One

*O*NE HOUR.

I've been on the phone with my mother for sixty straight minutes, and I've said approximately six words. Most of which are one syllable; half of which could be replaced by a *hmm* or even a caveman-like grunt.

The signal to my phone has dipped in and out, but no worries because no matter how long the gap of silence lasts, she's still there.

Still talking.

The Bluetooth in my car is both a blessing and a curse.

I jam the clutch into the floorboard of my faithful Corolla and shift into fourth. The last ferry to the San Juan Islands leaves in just twenty-three minutes, but thanks to the pokey *Golden Years* tour bus, I might not make it aboard the punctual sea vessel. My only hope to salvage the worst summer of my life.

"...Your dad and I have also agreed on the holidays. We want to make this as easy as possible on everyone. We're thinking you can spend Thanksgiving break with your dad since Grandma Sanders would be heartbroken if you didn't show up for her big hoopla...and well, you know, she's only going to be around for so long. And then you'll be with me for Christmas."

If I don't speak now, I may actually vomit. "With you where, mom?"

"The condo."

The condo. Two words that shouldn't elicit a visceral reaction. Yet they do.

I need air. Right this second.

I crack open the window and a rush of salty air calms my restless gut.

"I thought you liked it," she continues in a tone that borders on hurt.

"I don't really remember it." That's not exactly true. I remember one wall, painted to match the ominous clouds of a coming storm. The backdrop to my nightmare come true.

I'd hoped the request to meet them at the model high-rise condo in Seattle would be the announcement of a fresh start, a new beginning, a decision based on the advice of their long-time marriage therapist.

But only one of my parents is moving to Seattle.

"Joss, you just saw it last week. Of course, I can add my own touches to it, make it homey."

But nothing about that place would ever be home to me. It was as cold and sterile as the stainless steel appliances crowding the pocket-sized kitchen.

"And the den can double as a guest room, for when you stay with me."

Taking a deep breath, a familiar mix of ocean, rust, and seaweed fills my lungs. I roll my neck and visualize the promise that awaits ahead.

A foghorn blasts in the distance.

"Joss? Where are you?" My mom's voice has morphed into the robotic staccato of a dying phone signal. I couldn't have prayed for better timing. The call cuts short. The second I'm stopped, I shoot her a quick text and then power down my phone.

Parking on the lower level of the ferry, I take my keys from the ignition, climb the nine white steps marked with faded caution tape, and push against the heavy metal door to the open deck.

And just like that, I'm free and going home. Not to the house I grew up in, but to the cabin that holds every treasured memory from my childhood. The same cabin I've visited every summer with my three closest friends.

Except for this one.

Sydney's playing bridesmaid for her mother's wedding—again. Darby has a once-in-a-lifetime audition in L.A., and Avery's about to leave for a summer-long culinary internship.

But no matter how legit their reasons, this summer is one broken promise after another.

Thus the theme of my life as of late.

The ferryboat shudders to life and I grip the railing, a rumbly vibration under my feet. Dark water churns below, pushing and pulsing against the walls of the massive ship. I exhale, my breath lost to the cutting wind, and lift my eyes to the horizon.

This is the one view on earth that has the power to right wrongs, rewind time, and glue all the broken pieces back together again.

The white-capped Olympic Mountains that surround the San Juan Islands off the coast of Washington State are but a faint backdrop against today's overcast sky. But their presence, their fortress-like protection which encompasses the Puget Sound and beyond, offer a breathtaking invitation to come closer. An invitation I accept.

The islands are a combination of rolling hills and fertile valleys, luscious green forests dominated by evergreen and pine, and patches of sandy beaches that border a rocky coastline.

And it's this beauty, this mesmerizing wonder of my childhood summer home on Lopez Island—the heart of the San Juans—that stirs a belief in me that I can go back in time.

To a life before.

Before the fighting, and the packing, and the leaving.

A life before change.

Because the only chance to escape my future is to find comfort from my past.

"HOLY MOSES." AN odor so foul it could double as a torture device, rocks me back on my heels as I unlock the front door.

I yank my hoodie up over my nose and take a cautious step inside the cabin.

Rubbing my palm along the bumpy wall, I feel for the switch that will kill the darkness and shed some light on the cause of this rancid smell.

Click.

Nothing.

I flick the switch again. And again.

No. Way.

My hand fumbles for my phone in my back jean's pocket, as if this tiny piece of technology holds the same protection as a military-grade arsenal. I bring up the flashlight app and aim. Instantly, the kitchen to my left is basked in a florescent glow.

Clutching my phone like a shield, I walk toward the fridge, its door slightly ajar. A box of old pizza, a tub of sour cream without a lid, and a shelf oozing with greenish-brown slime—

"No!" My foot slips and my phone smacks against the floor, skittering across the linoleum.

Along with my body.

I'm flat on my back, fridge door banging against the top of my head and sloshing yet another dose of nastiness into my hair. Peeling myself from the floor, I grip the counter and curse the liquid green vegetation leaking from the bottom of the kitchen's largest appliance. Obviously my parents had just cause for firing their property management company. If I were a random vacationer and not their only daughter, I'd sue.

Ignoring the ache in my lower back, the throb in my right elbow, and the squish in my shoes, I zombie-walk toward my phone.

I freeze.

Eyes—reflective, beady little eyes that guarantee certain death—stare back at me.

A guttural war-cry wrenches from my throat.

And then I run.

Down the hall, past the kitchen, and onto the front porch.

Slamming the door closed behind me, my chest heaves in unison with my pounding heart. "This isn't happening, this *can't* be happening."

A frantic glance around the heavily wooded darkness might cause a lesser person vertigo, yet my fear doesn't make time for that. Ages ago I used to pretend this place was Snow White's cabin, and right now, I'd give anything to have the Seven Dwarfs stumble out of the trees and tell me what to do.

The back of my wet shirt has suctioned itself to my bra, but I won't let myself think of the toxic waste seeping into my pores. Instead, I close my eyes and will my mind to focus. Because if I don't, I'll crumple into a pathetic heap right here in these less-than-fairytale-like woods and never get up again.

And then I see it. The storage shed, the one that houses my bike. The same bike I used to ride to the Culver's house as a young girl.

The Culvers.

Pat and Shirley Culver will help me. They live on this island year-round. And they are two of the most generously hospitable people I know.

I sprint to the shed, tear open the metal doors and find that my pink Huffy bike—equipped with rainbow tassels and boy band stickers—is still here. Right where I left it.

Finally, something is how it should be.

I'm huffing, peddling down the path toward the yellow Victorian house. I know this path well. Even in the dark.

Several branches whip across my cheek, snag my hair. But I don't stop peddling.

An old tire, suspended like a pot-bellied ghost in the moonlight, is tethered to the Culver's large oak tree out front. Yet my eyes focus on the house behind it.

The very dark house.

Four feet from their driveway, I squeeze the hand breaks, slide off the seat, and allow my Huffy to fall to the ground. Along with my hope.

I kick the bike. Hard.

"Stupid! Stupid! Stupid!"

The magenta hunk of metal from my youth doesn't deserve this kind of abuse, but I know the second I stop kicking, the second I stop fighting, the second I stop running, I'll hear their words again. *"We're getting a divorce."*

Only the deeply male voice I hear next belongs to neither of my parents.

"Can I help you?"

I whirl around, lungs seizing from my bike-killing exertion.

A half-naked man who looks like he could grace the cover of *Surfer* Magazine, stands in front of me.

I have no words.

Seconds ago, I was on the verge of a full-fledged panic attack, and now I'm on the verge of wishing I could crawl under those porch steps and never come out.

The shirtless man, whose chest muscles jump and glisten in the moonlight, blinks. Twice.

"Joslyn?"

Chapter Two

*W*HAT THE—I take a step back. "How do you know my name? Do you work for the Culvers? Do you know where they are?" My ability to speak has magically reappeared.

His laugh has a bounce to it, a lighter-than-air quality, but it doesn't last long enough to put me at ease. I cringe as his gaze travels from my wildly sticky brown mane, down my growth-stunted, five-foot-two frame, and parks on my green-gooed sneakers.

My dignity and self-preservation are at war with each other.

"I'm Drew." The man-boy says as he rests his hands on defined hips.

Drew. I don't know a Drew. "How do you know me?"

Shaggy, sun-bleached tresses tease the tips of tanned ears. My eyes follow the imaginary line leading to the center of his face: a Roman nose, a squared chin, a pair of perfectly parted lips.

He's smiling.

It's this feature, this stunning, radiant smile that cuts my breath short. I blink myself sane, only his smile doesn't fade. Not when the standard be-nice-to-a-woman-in-distress timeline has passed. Or even when a giant drop of ooze falls from the end of my ponytail and splatters near my feet.

"You don't remember me?" He tilts his head as if that gesture alone might pinpoint his face on my Handsome Stranger Inventory. It doesn't.

I shake my head and the sour-tip of my ponytail lands inside my open mouth. I spit it out.

It's fair to say the likelihood of making a good first impression is no longer in the realm of possibility.

"Why don't we go inside. You look like you could use—"

"A bathtub full of bleach and some hard alcohol to forget this day ever happened?"

He laughs again. "Something like that."

He turns toward the porch steps, as if I'm the type of woman who would just up and follow his amazingness inside a dark empty house.

Only I'm not. No matter how badly I wish I could claim otherwise, this guy is a stranger. I force myself to spell out the word, letter by letter, inside my hormone-crazed brain.

S-T-R-A-N-G-E-R.

"I'm not going inside."

His steps halt. He looks over the top of one very muscular shoulder and throws another one of his electric-current grins my way.

I clear the weakness from my throat. "Stranger danger and all that."

I glance down at the bike at my feet and remember the dark cabin and the hideous smell and the rabid eyes.

He hops down from the second porch step and walks toward me again. "Joslyn, I'm Drew Culver. Pat and Shirley's grandson."

My head snaps up to search his face.

I stare unabashed as a dusty memory crowds the forefront of my mind. "You're Doo-Doo Drew?" And then the visual of a round, chunky boy running from the dock with mud caked on the butt of his jeans plays out before my eyes.

His laugh is a boom that shakes something loose inside my chest.

"But you were like...a foot shorter than me and...and you were uh..." Pudgy. Chubby. Liked the ice-cream a little too much.

"I grew up." He shrugs as if those three little words could explain a transformation like his, swipes a t-shirt from the banister, and tugs it over his head. "Guess I'm not a stranger after all." He holds out his palms to face me. "No danger to be had here. Promise."

I bite my bottom lip to keep from grinning like a circus clown.

"Alright, well, I think I might need some help."

His gaze drifts down the length of me once more. "I think it's safe to say you need *a lot* of help."

⌒◠

DREW IS BENT at the waist, sucking in air like a cracked vacuum cleaner. "Wait—what were the eyes like again?" He's actually crying. Real-life tears.

Hands on my hips, I shoot him my meanest glare. "This isn't funny. I almost died."

He tries to sober himself, tries to appear the ever-compassionate neighbor. He fails.

Two things I've learned about Drew Culver in the last ten minutes: 1. He loves a good story. 2. He's a terrible actor.

"But it didn't come after you? This uh, this creature of the night?"

I throw my arms out wide. "I didn't stick around and wait for the attack!"

He leans back against the sofa I wish I were sitting on. But I'm much too aware of the nastiness that coats my body to do that to sweet Mrs. Culver's furniture.

What I wouldn't pay for a shower right now. And a hairbrush. Oh, good glory, a hairbrush.

"I think you should take a shower."

I blink several times in a row, and my skin heats from a slow-rising simmer to a blistering boil.

He must re-hear his words, because for the fist time, Drew looks less than sure of himself. "I just meant...you obviously can't go back there tonight. It's dark and we won't get anything accomplished until we have light. So, if you want to, you're welcome to stay here. There's a bed in my grandma's sewing room at the end of the hall. Unless you have another option? Someone else you should call?"

At this, I curl my hand into a fist and punch my thigh. My phone. My stupid, stupid phone is inside the cabin with the freaky-eyed monster.

"No," I say in a volume that would barely register above a whisper. "I don't have another option." Because trying to book a hotel room on the island during the height of tourist season is like trying to reach Santa Claus on Christmas Eve.

"Okay, then." Drew stands and walks toward the hallway. "Stay here. I'll be right back."

Humiliation burns through my veins as Drew's footsteps grow faint. If he hadn't been here tonight, what would I have done? Slept in my car? The first ferry out doesn't leave until after sunrise tomorrow.

The thought makes my vision blur and my airway constrict. Pinching my eyelids shut, I swallow my ever-rising anxiety. Even if I caught the ferry back tomorrow, where would I go then? My dorm's undergoing a complete renovation during summer break, and home is not home right now.

"Uh...I'm sorry in advance. I don't think my grandma owns a pair of pants that aren't elastic waist and polyester. This is the best I could come up with."

I open my eyes.

Drew holds out what can only be described as a 1950s housecoat. It's pale pink and sprinkled with white fluffy kittens. And, by the length of it, will reach just above my ankles. If there was even the slightest bit of sexual attraction between the two of us, this nightgown has murdered it. And buried it six-feet.

Without another word, I walk toward him, take the muumuu, and lock myself inside a mauve-colored bathroom.

⌒⌒

THE SHOWER HAS long-ago turned cold, but at least my hair is clean (I only had to wash it three times.) I open the lacy curtain. It's safe to say I can claim *human* as my species again.

The pink housecoat buttons to my chin and its ruffled bell sleeves hang past my wrists. The hem brushes against the top of my ankle bones. I remind myself to be grateful. Because at least it's something to wear while I launder my foul-smelling clothes.

Drew stifles a laugh when I walk out of the bathroom. Surprisingly, he manages to swallow it. Somebody's taught him well.

"Want something to eat? Drink?" he asks.

I'm *starving*, but—

"I have Pop Tarts."

Like a faraway dream, I see the Culver's portly young grandson headed down the bike path to share his Pop Tarts at the shoreline. With me and the other summer island kids.

Back then it was a peace offering; now it's a testament to good character.

"Sounds perfect."

Drew reaches into the pantry, and one by one by one, he displays seven boxes on the countertop. *Seven.* You can take the chub off the boy, but...

He leans onto the yellowed Formica, his biceps flexing. "Take your pick."

The gown swishes around my calves. I point to the box on the far right. "Brown Sugar, please."

Drew grins, his teeth a perfect shade of baking soda white. "My favorite, too."

I pull out a chair at the little oak kitchenette dining table and sit. It feels odd to be served by a guy I haven't seen since I wore braces and played hide-and-seek, but then again, nothing about this day or night feels normal. Maybe there is no normal.

Maybe someday I should give up the hunt.

I take a deep breath, the scent of honey, cinnamon, and cloves baking in the air. "So, where are Pat and Shirley?"

Drew's eyes flick to mine over the steam of the toaster. "Gran's visiting my aunt for a few months in Maryland. But my Gramps..." Drew shakes his head. "He's in a home now—Alzheimer's. I'm housesitting. For the summer." His voice sounds flat, a deflated balloon.

Drew and his grandfather used to be close. Just like the Culvers used to be a staple part of the island community.

I hate how time robs us.

I decide to move onto a safer, less invasive topic. "You in school?"

His focus remains on the ancient press-and-hold toaster. "Senior at University of Washington. Business major."

"That's cool." But what I really want to say is: Why do you look like *that* if you're a business major? Why are your arms the size of my thighs? Why is your back shredded like some sort of WWF champion? But I keep my mouth shut because the way he stands now is more like a fortress than a gate. If there's more behind his summer island stay, he doesn't want to discuss it. At least, not with me.

"What about you?"

"English." I chose that major when I was ten and simply wasn't brave enough to try anything else, steer off course. "A junior at Western Washington." Because then I could drive home often and arrange family dinners so my parents could sit awkwardly around a silent table while I tried (and failed) to come up with new and exciting ways to get them to converse.

Drew shifts his weight, catching my attention again. "You seemed pretty upset earlier—kicking your bike and all."

I cringe inwardly. Oh, how I'd hoped he missed that bright and shining moment. "Um, I just…"

"I get it. Today must have really sucked for you." There's no judgment in his tone.

I curl the plastic map of America placemat in front of me into a funnel. "It really did."

The first set of Pop Tarts spring from the metal toaster. And in a style that's totally unique to Drew, he pinches the corners and tosses each tart on a plate. Obviously, he's a pro.

He sets the dish in front of me. "Here you go. Dinner is served."

I thank him, and he slumps in the seat across from mine. "You still friends with the Gossip Girls?"

I laugh only because I don't know what else to do with my sudden onset of nervous energy.

"Yes, I'm still friends with Sydney, Darby and Avery. They're my best friends, actually."

Though I'd made friends in college, none compared to the friendships I'd found in these girls long ago. They are like sisters—the only siblings I would ever have. Maybe our bond had originated early on due to our common ground as only children. But it's become something so much deeper now.

Which makes keeping my most recent life events from them feel even more reproachful.

But I wouldn't beg them to come to the island. I wouldn't beg them to keep their summer promise to me, not at the cost of breaking another one. A more important one.

I wouldn't become a burden to my friends—not in the way my parents had become one to me.

"Ah, yes. Darby—she's the redhead, right?"

"Yep. Hair like an open flame." Darby hated that reference, but it fit.

"I don't remember much about Avery," he continues, "except for her nasally laugh. But Sydney..." He shakes his head, chuckles. "Man, that girl had a mouth on her. I *definitely* remember that."

I take a slow guilt-filled breath and pinch my lips closed. Of course he remembers Sydney. It was Syd who came up with his nickname after he slid down the muddy hill, the same hill we told him to hike so we could all hang out and go whale watching together. Only we never met him.

Instead, we watched him hike the hill from the trees below. Watched him look for us, listened to him call our names with nothing but an echo in reply. And then, we watched him trip and slide all the way down the hill on his backside.

But Sydney wasn't the only one to blame. She was just the loudest.

The truth was, we'd all chanted the nickname. We'd all sang it to the tune of "Mary had a Little Lamb." And we'd all made sure he'd heard it as we canoed past him while he sat alone on the Culver's dock.

The summer between our eighth and ninth grade years might have been a long time ago, but we were old enough. *I* was old enough. Old enough to know the value of being included.

That was the last summer I saw Drew Culver on the island.

A layer of shame sticks to the back of my throat. "They've really changed a lot. I think you'd be surprised if you could meet them now." They were supposed to be here. "They're all chasing after some pretty big dreams."

"What about you? What are you chasing after?" His focus has returned to me.

I blink and force myself to swallow, wishing the extra seconds might allow me to concoct a more normal college-girl response. But the only word that comes out is, "Hope."

Drew lifts his eyebrows, a curious flicker of interest in his gaze, yet he doesn't act on it. Doesn't prod. Doesn't take more than what I'm willing to offer tonight. And I decide right then and there that I like him even more than I did an hour ago.

Neither of us speaks for nearly a minute.

I break off two corners of my Pop Tart, blow on the scorching-hot sugar filling, and take several tentative bites. "You have an older sister, right?" My second attempt to veer away from the awkwardness.

"Yep. Sara. She married an engineer. Two kids."

"Wow."

"Yeah, it's crazy how time changes everything."

His statement is my life's thesis.

Drew leans back, his eyes ever-focused on my face. "Things were starting to get pretty boring around here, until you showed up tonight."

I chew another piece of warm, sugary goodness. "I think I would have preferred boring to my unexpected arrival. I'm a mess." I meant to say *I was a mess*, as in past tense, as in my nasty hair, my stinky shirt, my soaked-in-spinach tennis shoes. But given the look on his face, Drew doesn't miss my verbal slip.

His gaze holds steady, strong. I break the connection.

"How long do you plan to stay on the island, Joslyn?" He stands up from the table and walks toward the sink, pulls a glass from the cupboard above the ancient dishwasher.

"Actually, I go by Joss now," I say without taking a breath. "And I'm not exactly sure." Because, so far, nothing has gone according to plan.

He hands me the cool glass and winks. "Well, *mi casa es su casa* for as long as you need it."

Drew may not realize what he's offering. But I do. Because until I make that cabin livable again or until I'm brave enough to face my parents or until my life stops spiraling out of control, I'm homeless.

Chapter Three

I PACE OUTSIDE the bedroom door I believe Drew sleeps behind. Not because I'm afraid to go back to my cabin alone, because I'm not afraid. I'm petrified.

Sure, he'll probably think it's a silly request, but even if he pokes fun at me the entire way there, moral support is moral support. And right now I need moral support almost as much as I need a strong cup of coffee.

Pressing my ear to his door, I listen for a soft snore, or the squeak of a bed frame, or any possible indication he might be inside—

"Morning."

I jump and clutch my heart as if it were glass on a shelf and Drew a seismic earthquake. Somewhere in my subconscious I register his face, yet the scream that escapes me can't be stopped. "Why aren't you in there sleeping?" The octave my voice strains to reach is on a scale only dogs can hear.

"In where?" Drew asks, his face glistening with a layer of sweat far more appealing than should be allowed at eight in the morning.

"In *there*." I point to the door I've been stalking for the last fifteen minutes.

The twitch of his chin indicates my level of idiocy.

He turns the knob, opens the door, and reveals a linen closet stuffed full of perfectly-folded sheets and towels. "Call me crazy, but I prefer something a tad roomier, Joslyn."

Here we are again. A repeat of last night, only this time I'm slime-free.

Drew's fresh scent of endorphins and damp Crossfit chest draw my gaze back to his.

Only he's not looking at my eyes. He's looking at my freshly laundered—and lavender scented—outfit. Thanks to Mrs. Culver's dryer sheets.

"No more pink housecoat, huh? I really think you could have started a trend at the dorms. You looked pretty cute last night."

Why I would blush at this comment I can't possibly know, but my ears and cheeks are a scalding fire.

I clear my throat, stare at the lopsided laces of my shoes, and don't bother correcting him on the use of my full name. "I was wondering…"

"What time we should head over to the cabin?"

I lift my eyes to his. He said *we*, right? I didn't imagine it?

He takes a few backward steps down the hall. "I'll drive us over—I just need to grab a quick shower first."

I lift my shoulders in a light shrug, as if I'm not totally thrilled by his suggestion. "Only if you don't have anything more important to do today."

I'm such a girl.

"Nope." He winks. "Believe me, you're the most exciting thing that's happened since I've been here."

I turn my face away a second before my grin reaches the explosive level. "Hey, does Gran Culver have coffee?" Please, Dear Lord, let her have coffee. It's my one addiction—after romance novels and before liquid eyeliner.

"Yep. Second cupboard to the left of the stove."

I swing back in time to see Drew toss his shirt on the bathroom floor. I exhale sharply and spin around. "Should I make a pot to share?"

"Nah. Don't like the stuff. I'll make a protein shake before we leave."

In my book, declining coffee, especially when born and raised in the Northwest is a blatant form of blasphemy. It's only due to Drew's voluntary offer to help today that I don't point this out.

I round the corner into the kitchen.

The distinct screech of a shower curtain being tugged across a metal bar echoes down the hall.

Coffee. Focus on the coffee.

⤫

MY PLAN IS simple: Drew locates the creature, compliments my die-hard courage, and thus redeems any and all crazy-girl-moments since our reintroduction.

He takes the porch steps up to the far-from-innocent white cabin two at a time. The cottage looks like any other home on the island—slightly weathered by the salty ocean breeze with a need for some TLC around the perimeter. Shrubs, bushes, weeds have grown up around the edge of the house, and the roof has a few missing shingles. But still, it's charming, quaint…familiar.

My parents had hired a rental company to manage the property for the last few years, opening the doors to a few carefully selected families who wanted a summer get-a-way, but apparently, the property management company was not committed to excellence. Or even sub-par living conditions.

If I were talking to my parents, I'd let them know they made the right choice in firing the crooks.

As Drew turns the knob on the front door, I back up several yards on the unmowed lawn. Though I'm confident my dragon slayer can take the creature down, I'm not confident the slaying will happen inside the house. I prepare myself to run.

He steps through the doorway, and I cup my hands around my mouth. "Be careful!"

Drew slows and releases a low chuckle.

I'm on my tip-toes, my lips pursed, my fingers pawing the bottom of my clean t-shirt.

It's not until my calves begin to cramp that I hear it.

Not a shriek or a howl or even a ferocious roar.

A scrambling of footsteps—*Is he being chased?*

"What's happening in there?"

No answer.

"Drew? What's going on?"

Less than ten seconds later, my slayer moseys out onto the porch. He's carrying a cat.

A cat? No, that's not possible.

I point at the feline. "That's *not* the creature I saw last night." This is far from the sanity redemption moment I had envisioned. "The eyes I saw were definitely from a wild animal."

Drew leans against the front door jamb and stares at me, eyebrows raised. "Well..."

I open my mouth to ask about raccoons and opossums and other possible varmints. Where there's one there's bound to be more—an infestation of uninvited fur balls.

"There's a litter of kittens under the house, outside the back bedroom. She was probably looking for food when you scared her last night."

I scared her? Did he actually just say that?

He strokes the gray and white cat nestled into the crook of his elbow.

I close my eyes and count to five. I don't actually believe I'll disappear—or that Drew and the cat will disappear—but somehow this sad, old habit still helps me feel in control. Or in this instance, less like a hopeless loser.

If only this coping mechanism worked long-term.

"Joslyn?"

I open my eyes, blink.

"You're right about the mess in the kitchen. And the rank smell. I checked the breaker box in the laundry room too. Electricity's still out." He pauses until I meet his gaze. "But I promise, there's nothing living inside this cabin that will attack you."

His grin is slow, slight, easy.

I wait for the punch line. But Drew doesn't capitalize on this moment. Not to point out my tendency toward the overdramatic, or even to repay me for a summer of snobbery long ago when I had three close friends at my disposal, and he had none. He simply steps back inside the dimly lit cabin and invites me to follow.

And I do; I follow him inside.

Because right now, I'm the one who's desperate for a friend.

Chapter Four

I'VE BEEN ON hold for nearly twenty minutes with the island's utility company—and that's twenty minutes I've spent daydreaming about a certain island boy who lives just a short hike away. I stare out the picture window in the front room, let the sun's rays soak into my skin through the smudgy glass, and try not to die from inhaling the stench steaming from the kitchen.

My phone vibrates against my ear. A text. From my mother.

> **Mom:** *Are you on the island? I thought your friends couldn't make it. We need to talk.*

There's more of course, but now is not the time for another mom lecture. I've listened to plenty of those lately. I tap the screen and darken her words.

"Mrs. Sanderson?"

"Yes?" I answer the man who speaks as slowly as paint dries. "It does appear your account is current, but there seems to be an issue with the main line."

No kidding. "Yes, so how do I go about getting that checked out?"

"I'd have to make an appointment for someone to come out and take a look."

Was that not what we were just doing?

In the same amount of time I've been on this call, Drew made two runs to the Culver's house for box fans, disinfectant, paper towels, and candles.

He stands in front of me now, head cocked to one side.

I roll my eyes and point to the phone. This call is a joke. My whole life is, really.

"Looks like we can have someone out there..." he pauses, "Tuesday."

"Tuesday?" Might as well be next Easter. "But today is Saturday."

"Yes, it is." The man drawls. "Weekends are reserved for emergency-status only."

I contemplate chucking my phone out the window just as Drew grabs it from my hand.

"Drew," I squeak.

He turns his back to me and drops his voice an octave. "Hello? Yes. I'm Mr. Sanderson, and we'd really appreciate someone here sooner than Tuesday. We've been on the island for over twenty-four hours now without electricity, and I've checked the breaker box and perimeter outside thoroughly. That constitutes an emergency in my book, especially since our account hasn't lapsed." Drew pauses, listens. "Yes, that's right. Okay, we'll wait for your call then. Thank you." He ends the call.

A huff of air passes through my lips when he faces me again, and he shrugs at my unspoken question. "Worked in a call center freshman year. Terrible job, but I learned a few tricks."

"I guess so." He places my phone in my palm. "When are they coming?"

"Hopefully tomorrow, if not, first thing Monday morning."

"Thanks." It's sooner at least, yet it still means camping indoors for longer than I'd hoped. Which is roughly a minute past never.

"You know..." Drew scratches the back of his head. "It doesn't make sense for me to have that big old house all to myself, indulging in modern conveniences, while you're over here in the Stink Pit."

I turn in a full circle, arms out. "What do you mean? This place is like a mini-paradise."

At that exact moment, the mop I left propped on the hallway wall keels over, splashing dirty, sudsy water onto the living room carpet.

Wet carpet, yet another awesome smell to add to the mix of spoiled food and cat poop.

"It's a vacationer's dream house, really," Drew deadpans. "What was I thinking to offer you an alternative?"

I giggle, the kind synonymous with notes passed on a playground, "yes" boxes checked.

Seconds pass before I realize he's waiting on me. For an answer.

I tap the toe of my shoe against the living room rug. I should decline with a gracious, *"I'll be fine, really."*

Drew watches me, a steadiness to his gaze, a cool sort of confidence in his stance. "No need to over-think it. It's pretty simple. I have a house. You have...well, this." He gestures toward the spilled mop bucket. "Seems like a no-brainer, Joslyn." His smile is annoyingly free, a seemingly-permanent fixture on his well-balanced face. And then it hits me: Drew's like one of those positivity posters in the waiting room of a therapist's office. *Keep your head up. Tomorrow's a new day. Be a glass half full to the half empties around you.*

Surely, between the two of us, I'm the glass half empty around here.

I tilt my head. "You know, that name you keep using is *twice* as many syllables as the one I prefer to be called." Obnoxiously, I clap the difference to prove my point. *"Jos-lyn. Joss.* See? So much easier."

"I've never been one to go for easy."

For the second time today, my cheeks ignite. I glance at the puddle on the carpet. "Okay."

"Okay?"

"Okay, I'll stay with you—but only until the electricity comes back on."

He nods and points to his group of supplies next to the kitchen table, as if my declaration was the expected solution. Only he was the one who expected it, not me. At least, not so easily.

"And once the electricity comes on, we can use the box fans to help air the place out. For now though, I'll get the windows open so we can at least get a good cross breeze going in here."

I don't miss his use of *we*. As if he's planning on sticking around a while. Which, I'm not in any way opposed to.

"Well," I sigh heavily. "The nasty floor beckons."

Drew holds up his fist, waits.

Tentatively I form one of my own and then tap it to his.

"That had to be the weakest fist-bump in the world."

Without warning, he grabs my hand, molds it back into a fist, and does a re-bump.

"Better. Now, let's get to work, roomie."

⌒○

MOP IN HAND, I slide its wet ropey fingers over the last smear of green goo tacked on the kitchen floor. Pausing mid-swipe, I twist at the waist and sneak another peek at Drew.

He spent a good thirty minutes prying open the painted-shut dining room windows with a screw driver, and now he's removing the dusty sheets from the sofas in the living room. With his back to me, he raises his left shoulder, and rotates it forward. Twice.

I can't help but watch.

Drew has a nice back. No, a spectacular back, one that's chiseled into a mountain range of muscles and tendons and—

He turns and points to the far corner of the living room. "What's in that old chest?"

"Err...what?"

"The chest. What's in it?"

Pieces of my soon-to-be past.

"I'm not sure." The lie slides over my lips easily—out before I can think of a better reply. Or an honest reply.

"That's some gorgeous woodworking."

Drew walks toward it and my heart beats wildly against my ribcage, a cold knot forming in the pit of my belly. *Please don't open it.*

He rubs his palm over the top of my dad's first anniversary present to my mom. A carpenter since before I was born, my dad's always shown his love through his art. Frames, shelves, even a set of bunk beds for when my friends stayed over on the weekends.

I swallow a mass of unshed tears and blink my way back to the present.

"I'm hungry." The blurt is quick and loud and completely unladylike, but I had to say *something* before Drew fingered the lock or, worse, lifted the lid.

Drew stands and brushes the dust from his hands onto the thighs of his jeans. "Want me to grab some take out from Luck's?"

"I think we could both use a break from this place, and the least I can do is buy you lunch for all your help today."

Drew's bottom lip has a life of its own. As does his dimple—the one that indents the middle of his right cheek when he talk-smiles. "You can try."

I swipe my purse off the table, only as soon as it's in my hand, I know I can't go anywhere with him, not until I clear my conscious and offer the apology I should have given him years ago. It's time.

He's waiting for me on the front porch when I call after him. "Drew?"

"Yeah?"

Suddenly the bold prompting in my head dims to that of a timid whisper. "I uh, I wanted to say sorry. For that last summer on the island together. We were horrible to you. *I* was horrible to you—"

He steps toward me, grips my shoulders in a way that makes my words fall away on a lost breath. "That was a long time ago. Let's just be grateful neither one of us is thirteen anymore."

Certainly he's not—not with that Olympian physique he's got going on.

He winks and jogs down the porch steps. "I've got to make a quick call before we head out. I'll meet you at the car."

I spare one last glance at the old chest in the far corner of the living room.

The reason I came.

And then I tug the door closed and turn my key in the deadbolt.

If only my heart were just as easy to lock-up.

Chapter Five

THIS ENTIRE LUNCH conversion has been entirely unbalanced. One-sided.

Drew is casually munching on his fish and chips at Pacific Winds Diner, while I answer question after question. Nothing deep, or ultra-personal has been asked, but still, Drew hasn't given me a second to breathe, much less turn this question and answer time on him.

As he reaches for another fry, I snatch his basket away.

"Hey now—" He throws his hands up, and I wish I could guess his wingspan—if only to report it to Darby. She's a sucker for good arms.

"It's *your* turn. The ratio is way off here. I've answered everything from my dorm dimensions to my favorite trilogy. You can earn one fry back for every question you answer."

Though I know Drew could swipe the basket from my pathetically short reach, he leans back in his chair, wipes his mouth with a napkin, and concedes.

"One question, one fry?" he repeats.

I nod and try to keep a round of awkward giggles from leaking out. I *never* get to win this easily. My friends would have tackled me to the ground before going along with one of my "special social games," as Sydney calls them.

I can practically see Avery's epic eye roll now.

"Yep. Okay." By the look on Drew's face he'll play along—at least for a few fries. Five if I'm lucky.

I better choose my questions wisely.

"So why do you look like that?" Okay, that didn't exactly come out as planned.

His neck crawls with a shade of crimson, but his lips, of course, are turned up in a grin. "Like *what?*"

He's playing with me now. Everyone within a quarter mile radius of Drew knows "like what?"

There's *in shape*. And then there's Drew Culver. If I worked out full-time, made a career of strength training, lived and breathed the inside of a gym, I couldn't do to my body even *half* of what he's managed to do with his.

"I row."

"You what?"

He demonstrates the motion by using his fork to part the air. "You know, *row*."

At this, I lose it. I snort-laugh as Drew, this tall, masculine anomaly, role-plays his own unique rendition of "Row, Row, Row Your Boat" for me.

Finally, he sets his fork down, eyes gleaming as he says, "I've been on a rowing scholarship for three years at UW."

I toss him a fry; he catches it in his mouth.

I like this game a lot.

"I've never met a rower before."

"Well then, I hope I exceed your expectations."

You already have, Drew. You already have.

Questions two, three, and four are spent uncovering the secrets of life as a rower.

"But aren't you freezing out there? I mean, it's Washington. Not Florida."

"The goal is to *not* get wet."

Cheeky. He earned two fries for that answer.

"And you've been all over the U.S.?"

"Yep. Been on a lot of lakes."

"Are you close with your crew?"

Drew's smile dips slightly, his gaze reaching into mine. "The closest. They're my brothers."

This I understand. Not in a team spirit kind of way. In an I-understand-the-irreplaceable-value of true friends kind of way. Because, like Drew, my friends are also my closest family.

"So you don't have any—what do you call them? Races? Meets?— that you're supposed to be at this summer?"

Drew opens his mouth and his phone dances a jig across our table. He reaches for it as if to mute the vibration, but his hand pauses as he reads the contact name. I read it, too.

Coach Carson.

"Sorry, I have to take this." Drew scoots his chair back and walks out onto the patio.

Every female eye in the diner follows him.

Drumming my fingers on the tabletop, I slide my own neglected phone from my back pocket and scroll through a half-dozen texts.

> **Sydney:** *Did you make it to the island okay? I'm still waiting to hear about the "big talk" on the homestead. Oh, and if you want to see my bridesmaid's dress, Google "Housewives of the Rich and Tacky." Call me.*
>
> **Darby:** *You will never believe where I just got hired. Like never ever ever. Call me.*
>
> **Avery:** *I hate flying. I think I'd rather walk to Arkansas. Is that a possibility?*
>
> **Mom:** *Did you get my text? Call me.*
>
> **Mom:** *Just talked to your dad, he hasn't heard from you either. Please call me.*
>
> **Mom:** *I'm officially worried. You don't get to text me saying you're headed to the cabin after everything we've talked about and then not answer my calls. NOT okay. Call me.*
>
> **Dad:** *Call your mom.*

Head in hands, I groan. The walls of my pseudo-freedom are about to cave in. I pinch my eyes closed, beckoning a calm to cover my anxiety.

"Hey, you ready?"

I sit up, turn my head to face Drew—or rather, to face his abdomen.

"Oh, hi. Is…is everything okay?" I point to the phone in his hand. Why is it always easier to ask someone else what you should really be asking of yourself?

"Yeah, just checkin' in." Drew tosses a twenty on the table, then grabs my hand when I reach to throw it back at him.

"I'm paying. It's done. Now, let's go finish up what we can at the cabin before it gets dark."

With Drew's hand still latched to mine, he leads me through a maze of tables and chairs. Once in the parking lot, he opens the passenger door for me. "Sorry we had to cut the game short."

The game, the game….oh! The Fry Game.

I buckle my seatbelt. "Maybe we can play it again sometime. With Pop Tarts."

"Deal."

⤳

THE SUN SET hours ago, and I was ready to give up the second the last sliver of light disappeared behind the horizon. But Drew Culver doesn't give up—not for darkness or bad odors or even moldy refrigerator shelves. I'm starting to understand why he looks the way he does. He set the goal that we'd finish the cleaning tonight, and it's been impossible to deter him.

Several times during tonight's clean-fest, Drew's stopped to stretch his back, roll his neck, and tug on his left shoulder. And several times, I've stopped whatever I was doing to watch.

Random groupings of tea lights and holiday candles line the countertops and tables, and it's safe to say that every single surface of this one-story residence has been scrubbed and disinfected—except for the carpet in the master bedroom at the back of the house. That is the room that holds the worst of the cat smells.

I'd conquer it some other day. For now, that door can remain closed.

The good news: I can finally take a breath without the urge to rip one of my five senses from my face. I'd say that's pretty impressive progress.

Walking onto the gleaming kitchen floor, I wince-cringe as I see Drew bent over the sink, scrapping away a science project's worth of mold from a refrigerator shelf. A job I had planned to save for tomorrow. Because out of all the chores we've tackled thus far, this task is likely the most gag-worthy.

At least I caught him before he got too far into it.

I fake a loud yawn, stretch my arms above my head. "Wow. I think I could fall asleep standing up. You've got to be exhausted. You were up way before I was this morning. Let's call it a night, head back to your place. I can tackle those shelves tomorrow." In other words, please stop scrubbing. You've done more than enough for me for one day. Or a lifetime of days.

"Good thing we have a short commute, then. And even better that I drove." He continues scrubbing, soaking his hands in grime and suds. "This is the last shelf. I'm almost done."

Awesome. Just awesome.

Drew shuts off the water at the sink. But before he can search for a dry rag, I rush into action, two steps ahead of him.

I grab a yellow sunflower-printed hand towel from the drawer next to the stove and grip the end of the fridge shelf. He may have started this yucky project, but *I* should be the one to finish it. "Here, I've got this. Please go take a break."

Drew doesn't take a step to the side like I anticipate. Instead, he stays put, our hips a hairsbreadth apart.

There've been many words exchanged between us today, many joke-filled conversations, yet this moment between us feels oddly different, as if charged by our close proximity.

He lets me take the shelf, but still, he doesn't move away.

"So your friends, they aren't joining you here?" he asks.

In a wax-on, wax-off motion, I continue to dry the glass as if it were my only goal in life. To create a streak-free refrigerator shelf.

I feel his eyes search the side of my face with the kind of curious intensity a child has when he's sent to hunt for hidden treasure. Only there's no treasure to be found here. The only thing waiting at the X is a lonely girl pretending she can escape her future.

At twenty-one, I've become a sad sort of cliché.

"No. Not this summer."

"What about your family, then? Are they coming up for the Fourth?"

The pulse beat in my throat constricts my voice box. "Nope."

He lifts the shelf from my hands and sets it onto the counter. He faces me, his fingers curled around the counter edge. They're my focus point—his hands, both strong and reliable.

"So you're like what, a summer squatter?"

In typical Drew-style, his happy-go-lucky charm pulls me out of my introspection. I blurt out a laugh. "I guess that's exactly what I am. A squatter."

He angles his head, nods. "I thought so—you have the look."

Based on first impressions alone, *squatter* is a compliment.

A lull spans between us, and I wonder what Drew sees when he looks at me the way he's looking at me right now. Because it's this look that makes me want to spill my sorrows, trust him in a way I've yet to trust myself.

I open my mouth—

"The island's a great place to sort out whatever needs sorting," Drew says.

Even in the dim lighting, the sincerity of his eyes matches the kindness in his tone.

And though I'm certain my parents felt the exact opposite was true, Drew's words washed me in calm and filled me with courage. "I'm glad you think I can sort from here because you might be the only one."

"What about you? What do you think?"

I have no idea what I should think. This particular topic of running off to the island to escape my family drama hasn't exactly been opened up for discussion with my friends. Sure, I could say there wasn't time to call them before I left, or that I didn't want my problems to interfere with their busy schedules, but neither of those excuses is the truth. My friends would make time for me. I just simply hadn't asked them to.

Drew's thumb slides across the back of my hand and a shiver waltzes slowly down my spine.

"I think you're brave—coming out here on your own." He exhales and shifts his weight from one leg to the other, and then tucks his hands into his pockets.

The absence of his hand on mine feels like cold disappointment.

"I wish I *felt* brave."

"Feelings rarely tell us the truth."

The candle closest to the sink flickers. Then, in an instant, we're standing almost entirely in the dark, relying only on a candle a room away, on the dining room table.

But I'm not scared. Not with Drew here.

"What do you mean?"

He shifts his body again, only this time I can't tell where or how.

"Feelings aren't concrete—they're fickle, easily swayed by circumstance." He exhales, his breath sweeping across my cheek. "If you let feelings drive you, you'll run out of steam before you ever reach the finish line. They lie to you—cheat you from seeing what's real. Sometimes we have to outsmart our emotions in order to deal with our junk." I think he taps his temple before bumping my shoulder with his.

Then he pushes away from the counter. "Let's head out. I have to catch the ferry first thing in the morning."

"You do?" I hate the needy whine that exits my throat, but I hate even more that he won't be around tomorrow.

He reaches back for me, offering his hand, as if to guide me through the dark house.

I give it to him.

"I'll be back by dinner. Hope you can survive that long without me," Drew says.

"Har har."

But little does he know I'll be counting down the hours.

Chapter Six

J-

Don't do anything crazy today. See you later.

Drew

I TUCK THE note inside the back pocket of my jeans, lock Grandma Culver's front door, and Huffy-bike-it-up to my cabin. The sun is shining, the breeze is crisp and light, and all in all I feel as if Drew Culver's Secret To Positivity is within my grasp.

Whether he's aware of it or not.

I practically bounce up the porch steps into my cabin, then pull back all the curtains the moment I'm inside. The scent of pine, lemon, and mold-killing bleach still hangs in the air, yet not even the aroma of clean can overshadow the inviting comfort of home.

This. This is the place I remember.

Room by room, I check our work from the day before, and room by room, I add another course to the repayment dinner I plan to make for Drew. Hopefully, I'll be able to cook it here at the cabin, but that will require a visit from the utility company, and I've yet to receive an update as to their timeline. On second thought, given the gleeful dose of serotonin to my brain, I'd make him dinner over a campfire if need be.

Nothing's going to derail me today.

I stand in the middle of the living room, stare down the hallway at the master bedroom, and make a declaration. One I dreamed about last night after Drew's little pep talk on feelings and goals.

Well, I have one now. A goal, that is.

And it's not to eat cold pizza every night and cry into my pillow.

This little cabin was once the epitome of family. My dad built that kitchen table, my mom knitted that afghan draped over the back of the sofa, and I dented that wall next to the bathroom with my pink Barbie jeep.

If I can fix this old neglected house, then maybe, maybe I can fix my broken family too.

⌒৹

THE MORNING STARTS off with a humbling, yet happy, selfie that I send to my mother. Sure, I haven't been the best at communication since "the talk," but as my new plan continues to morph into a masterpiece, being on both of my parents' good sides is non-negotiable.

Mom's reply to my picture: *Nice to see you smiling. Cabin looks great. Still need to talk to you. Soon.*

I text back, *I'll call you tonight,* and continue with my slightly overzealous task at hand.

Sweat trails the side of my face as I yank the frayed edge of carpet from the tack strip in the corner of the master bedroom. It smells like a litter box in here, one that hasn't been changed in a year or two. But thanks to my impeccable memory, I remembered the hardwoods underneath.

My parents only had this room carpeted due to my mother's pet peeve of cold floors in the morning. Well, if she had the choice now, I'm sure she'd choose chilly feet over potty stains.

I yank the carpet corner back again—harder. By the ripping sound, you'd think I'd just peeled back an entire houseful of carpet. But, in truth, I've only managed to lift a few feet.

Carpet tack removal has to be a chore that originated in Hades.

Huffing as if I just ran the perimeter of the whole island, I lean against the wall. "There's got to be an easier way."

I stare at the mess: the furniture pushed to one side of the room, a quarter roll of carpet and pad uprooted and curled, and a few dozen tack strips (which I hadn't realized were a part of this whole deal until after I started tugging) cling stubbornly to the floor's perimeter.

"Time for Plan B." I wipe my forehead with my sleeve, then tiptoe out of the room and close the door behind me. "Shopping."

❧

ON MY WAY back to the cabin from Trash Or Treasure, my favorite little reuse and recycle shop in town, I stop off at the local hardware store—which is also a food mart and pharmacy—and pick up tonight's grocery list.

And several rustic shades of paint.

Freshly painted frames lie drying on every surface of the house by late afternoon, and it's safe to say the last half of the day has been highly productive. At least more productive than this morning. As I glance around the room at the rearrangement of furniture, my heart warms. I can't wait to show Drew. I may not have the photos chosen yet, but these frames will look fantastic in the cabin. Fresh, inviting, homey.

I sweep a final stroke of Tiffany Blue onto a squared canvas I purchased for only three dollars and then hear a buzzing. Followed by a pop.

Lights! They're on!

I throw open the front door to thank the person responsible, but all I see are the taillights of an old white service truck.

No matter. I wave and shout my gratitude anyway. I'll take this unexpected turn of events as a sign I'm on the right track.

Back inside, I plug in all the box fans Drew brought over yesterday, prop them up on the windows sills and turn them on. The circulation of air not only adds a nice cross breeze to regulate the mid-eighties heat outside, it also blows in another fresh bout of motivation.

Soaking the wet paintbrushes in the sink, I dry my hands on the back of my jeans, and prepare my mind for yet another round of Joss vs. Carpet.

I've been in this bedroom for so long that I can't even remember the last time I inhaled without carpet fibers filling my lungs. I've backed myself into a corner—literally. Pushing the queen size bed from one wall to another, it's now propped on its side across the open doorway. My t-shirt sticks to my damp torso. I huff and pull my hair up into a messy bun. I'm pretty sure I could fill a swear jar with pennies for how many times I've sworn in the last few hours. My fingers are raw, my hands cramped, and my back? Don't even get me started on my back.

I'm ready to quit.

"Joslyn? Are you here?"

Drew! Never have I been happier to hear the voice of another human—especially when that human is Drew.

"I'm in the back bedroom." I twirl around in a circle, as if magically my fairy godmother might swoop in and make this disaster disappear. And, while she's at it, make me cute and presentable, too.

"How in the..." Drew stares from the other side of the mattress. He blinks, mouth open wide.

"I'll slide the mattress over. Hang on."

Easier said than done. The theme of my summer it seems.

I pull at the far end of the propped mattress until there's space enough for a man-body to squeeze through.

Drew steps inside my little project from hell. He looks from me to the floor and then back again. A full five seconds of silence passes, and my skin itches to hear him say something. Anything.

"So, you must not have seen my note this morning."

His note...his note. *Oh.* The one in my back pocket. The one that said *not* to do anything crazy today.

His lips twitch. "What part of this,"—he points to the floor or lack thereof—"doesn't seem crazy to you?"

Avoiding a small pile of carpet tacks, I kick my foot to a successfully rolled heap of stinky carpet pad. "I just thought I could..."

No, if it doesn't sound right in my head, I definitely shouldn't speak it out loud. I slap my mouth shut and bat my eyelashes at him instead.

"Come on, let's at least get the furniture out in the living room. We'll roll this carpet properly, pull up the tack strips, and deal with the rest later. Fortunately, the hardwood looks to be in good shape."

"I think you're my favorite optimist."

The dimple in his right cheek surfaces, and he shakes his head. "And I think you could use all the optimism you can get your hands on."

Was that an invitation?

I grin to myself, grip the back of the mattress and allow Drew to guide us down the hallway.

Chapter Seven

"**S**AY IT." DREW bumps my shoulder with his, and my feet swish frigid ocean water below the Culver's dock.

"Fine. You were right." I double roll my eyes and take a bite of my waffle cone. "This is way better than spaghetti."

I'd wanted to make dinner for Drew tonight, at the cabin, to celebrate my—err, our—house transformation. But he had other ideas and, besides, the frames I painted earlier were still drying on every surface of the cabin. But, he'd made the right call. Ice cream cones at the dock were a perfect way to end such a productive day.

"Ya know," I say, taking another bite, this one packed with a large chuck of Oreo cookie, "we could have our own show."

"A show?"

My heart cartwheels at the sound of Drew's amused tone. I turn my face to his and catch a reflection of the full moon in his eyes just before he blinks. "Like one of those house renovation shows—people watch those."

"You should really come teach a business course at my school sometime. Your whole 'people watch those' approach could be a killer new marketing tactic."

I can't help but giggle as he air quotes my slogan.

I splash his leg with water, even though I know if Drew wanted to, he could soak me in less than three seconds. But something I've come to love about him is the gentle way he treats me, like I'm something special, *someone* special. And even if I managed to push him into the chilly water, Drew is not the kind to get even. He's too much of a gentleman.

He pops the last of his cone into his mouth, then stretches out on the moonlit dock, his feet no longer submerged. Staring at the stars, we're surrounded by serenity—a peace that rests on the water and soaks into our souls, and suddenly, I'm unsure if I should stay.

"Should I…" *Give you some privacy? Leave you alone? Go back to my own house?*

He pats the space next to him; I need no further invitation.

Folding my arms underneath my head like a pretzel, I slide my legs next to his and stare at the heavens. The array of twinkling dots set on a backdrop of inky black, steal my next coherent thought, and the one after that, too. If I had the job of counting stars on Lopez Island, I would be happy for the rest of my life.

Beside me, Drew's breathing becomes rhythmic, so much so that I wonder if he's dozed off, but then, "What happens *after* you fix the cabin up? Get it just how you envision it?"

His question startles me, awakens the hibernating honesty I secretly hoped could remain dormant forever. I take a few seconds to replay his words in my mind, but still, I have no idea how to answer him.

"I…" How can I tell him what I haven't even admitted to myself yet.

Drew turns his pensive, star-gazing eyes on me. "I peeled up your cat-pee carpet, Joslyn. I scrubbed your dirty fridge drawers and even pretended to be your father on the phone to that utility guy." He nudges my knee with his. "And, if that's not enough, I can still re-member you with braces and bangs."

I groan and close my eyes. If only I could evaporate into the waves.

"It's pretty safe to conclude we're passed the shyness stage," he con-tinues.

"Shyness stage?"

"You know what I mean."

I do. I know exactly what he means, but…I turn my eyes back to the vast sky above and take a deep breath. On my exhale, my words rush out. "I guess I hope the cabin might help them change their minds—make them remember what life could be like again."

"Who?" Drew studies my profile, his breathing no longer steady or consistent.

"My parents."

I count the seconds. He doesn't even make it to three.

"Their marriage in trouble?"

Understatement of all time. "Their marriage is a signature on a piece of paper held over an open flame."

Every second Drew stays quiet, the sounds around me amplify. The chirp of a lonely cricket, the bubble-burp of a bullfrog, and the rapid *thump, thump, thump* of my pulse against my throat.

I expect him to say, "I'm sorry," or "Most of my friends have divorced parents," or "Just give it time, you'll be okay." But once again, Drew surprises me.

"How long has it been bad?"

I surprise myself even more when I don't hesitate. "Since forever." The knot in my stomach clenches as I recall the nights I lay awake in bed, listening to their arguments, feeling their claims of unhappiness like bone-deep bruises. I could hide the pain, but I couldn't hide the life-limp their angry words created. "But it's been a lot worse since I left for college."

The knot in my gut morphs into a coil of barbed wire. I close my eyes, breathe, and replay the statement our family therapist made me repeat in her office last fall. "I am not responsible for my parents' marriage."

Only, repeating words you don't believe is like trying to spend Monopoly money at the mall. No bank will back fake cash. And no heart will accept empty truth.

"Where do you go?" Drew's soft voice brushes against my thoughts.

I open my eyes. "What?"

"When you close your eyes like that. Where do you go?"

"I...nowhere."

"You do it a lot. Do you go to a place? Replay a memory? What?"

I sit up. Reflection time over. A few minutes ago I'd been worried I was over-crowding Drew. But now I'm the one who feels overcrowded. Planting my feet on the slatted dock, I reach for my sandals.

"Joss. Wait."

It's not his hand on my arm that stops me, I could easily break away from his grasp. It's the name, the one I've asked him to use since we met. Everything inside me slams to a halt.

I stare at him, my chest rising and falling at a much quicker rate than normal. The heat of his hand radiates through my arm and, with another gentle tug, my shoes *plink* and *plunk* against the dock, and I sit back down beside him.

Drew's face turns pensive, his voice smooth like the glassy water in the bay. "I hated the water when I was a kid. I was afraid of it. I knew *how* to swim, of course. My parents signed me up for lessons every summer until I was ten, but the fear of drowning, the fear of being fully submerged into something I couldn't control, freaked me out."

I dip my big toe back in the seawater and trace a circle, feeling the truth of his words beat against my chest. "How did you get over it?"

He stares into the dark abyss. "My grandpa bought a boat. Said he was gonna cure me." He points to the ocean that fills the nearly secluded cove. "And he did. This place...this dock...is where I fell in love with the water."

"But weren't you still afraid to get in the boat? People drown in boating accidents all the time."

Drew tilted his head to the side, a twinkle in his eye. "You're not very good at glass half full are you?"

I shake my head. Not at all.

"I'd been a slave to my fear for years, but that day..." Drew sighs. "That day my love for what the water could give me finally outweighed what it could take from me." His hand slides down my arm to my wrist and, in one slight move, he cradles my palm on his hand. Every muscle, joint, and tendon relaxes as he continues, "So, when I asked where you go…where you go when you close your eyes, I just wondered if you had a place like mine."

I clear my throat, search for my voice, yet the sound that follows is hardly more than a whisper. "I think your place is better than mine."

"Hey. No stealing places." He leans into me, his closeness like a blanket of peace.

Drew sets our connected palms on the dock between us, the air thick with questions neither one of us knows how to ask.

A motion light at the back of the Culver's house flicks on. Our hands drop.

"It's just a cat," His statement is meant to reassure, only instead it reminds me of the way he looked holding the cat I believed to be a rabid wildebeest on my front porch.

He must recall the scene too because soon we're both lost to a fit of hopeless laughter.

The change in breathing causes me to yawn, and I rub my eyes. "What time is it?"

Drew slips his phone from his back pocket. "Almost one."

I groan. "Guess we should head back." But even as I speak the words, I know it's the opposite of what I want to do. I could stay and talk with him on this dock all night.

I stand, slip on my shoes, and watch Drew do the same.

"You sure you're okay staying at the cabin tonight?"

He's rephrased this question about two dozen times since he got back on the island, which reminds me…"Hey, you never told me where you went today."

We start the trek up the trail to the Culver's house. It's the same trail, that if followed far enough, leads to the back of my cabin.

"You never asked."

"Oh, so that's how we're playing it now? I have to spill my guts open and you get to be all tight-lipped about your mysterious trip to the mainland?"

Drew reaches for my elbow and pulls me over a rocky incline in the pathway. "I'm not tight-lipped."

"Then where were you?" I'm starting to wish I would've dropped the subject several statements back.

"A doctor's appointment I couldn't reschedule. You know how those are." His shrug is simple, yet his face, his face says far more than his words.

"Sure." My mind has already leapt off the cliff of worry.

"It's just routine, Joss. I'm fine."

As Drew says my name, he takes my hand. And that's how we walk. All the way back to my cabin.

Whatever this thing is between Drew and me, wherever it might go, or however long it may last, I'm grateful for it tonight. I'm grateful for him.

After he shuts all my open windows and checks the cabin over again for any stray cats, he instructs me to lock the door behind him. I doubt there's been a single crime on the island for years, but I'll appease him.

"Goodnight, Joss."

With a wink, he's gone.

It's that wink that keeps me from falling asleep, but it's the continuous buzz of my phone that wakes me.

Crap. I forgot to call my mom. Again.

Chapter Eight

"*I* PUT AN offer on the condo yesterday."

This is how our conversation begins. I haven't spoken to my mom on the phone since the day I came to the island, believing all I needed was a little time and space to deal with a word I hated almost as much as divorce: condo.

But I was wrong.

I yank the front door open, trip down the porch steps, and start up the driveway. My chest aches when I pull in my next breath and tug my sweater tighter around my middle. The chilly morning air is definitely fresh, but it comes with a wave of shivers.

"I'm hoping you might help me pick out some furniture before summer's over and you go back to school. You've always had such a gift for decorating."

I push my legs to walk faster up the rocky driveway. Her flattery falls on deaf ears. I don't want to talk about decorating the condo. I don't want to talk about anything that will happen after I leave this island—my safe haven.

Tall, bushy trees shadow my every step. And I don't care that those steps are from my slippered-feet or that my hair looks like a nest of bees attacked it. But I do care that all my mom wants to discuss is a stupid condo. Not my feelings, not my pain, not my emptiness.

She continues without missing a beat, "I just want you to feel a part of this new place. I know how much you hate change."

And yet, somehow, change just keeps smacking me in the face.

My steps halt. If I couldn't breathe before, then I'm about two seconds from keeling over now. The phone slips down my face several inches as I stare at a sign staked into the roadside.

One that points to my cabin with a red arrow.

"Joss? Are you still there, honey?"

Hot, rage-filled tears inch their way up my throat and into my eyes.

"When were you planning on telling me, mom?" Anger cuts out the shape of every letter as I speak.

"Tell you what?"

"The cabin."

Silence. It eats into my ear from the phone.

"Oh." She sighs. "I was getting to that. I didn't want to tell you over text, and you wouldn't call me back—"

"You're *selling* the cabin?" The screech of my last few words echoes in the hollow, tree-lined pathway to the cabin's front door.

I stare at the eighties style "glamour shot" picture on the real estate sign. Dotty Harrison and Associates. I want to kick the cheesy smile off her face.

"We haven't been there as a family in years, Joss. And there are many better vacation rentals on the island than our little shack."

"Don't."

"Don't what?" She sounds confused, though I know she's not clueless. She's in every memory I hold dear at this cabin. She and my father both.

"Don't pretend this place doesn't matter to you. Sure, we haven't been here as a family for a few years, but..." I shake my head so hard my vision blurs. "You can't sell it!"

"Joss, listen to me."

"All I've done is listen to you! I've listened to you fight. I've listened to you complain. I've listened to you tell my father you don't love him. That you haven't loved him since I was skipping around in pigtails. I've listened enough!"

I lift my chin, try to stop the flow of tears by reversing the pull of gravity. It doesn't work. Just like my plan to restore the house. Just like my plan to restore my family.

From the roadway, I have a perfect view of the cabin. But this time, instead of the warm memories it usually provides, I feel nothing but the stab of gut-wrenching loss.

"I'm sorry."

She's crying, but I can't let myself comfort her. Not over this.

She sniffles loudly into the speaker. "We have to sell it, and this prime time to have the cabin go on the market. Dotty says the island gets the best real estate activity during Fourth of July. She called me yesterday, said from looking in the windows the place looked great inside. Really clean. I'm glad you've been able to enjoy one last summer."

I close my eyes, and tears land on my chest. A woman was looking in my windows yesterday? While I was slaving over smelly carpet?

And I never even had the chance to show my parents all my hard work.

I clamp my teeth so hard my jaw throbs.

And then understanding dawns…what my mother's saying without actually saying it at all.

"You need the cabin sale to purchase the condo, don't you?"

Her silence confirms my fear.

⌒⌒

I WALK.

I walk and I walk and I walk. The tread on my slippers is threadbare; the light cotton fabric damp with dew.

And still I don't stop moving. Because I can't stop thinking.

My legs carry me down to the dock, and even though I know the chances of Drew waiting there for me are slim, I search for him anyway.

In less than four days, my ears have grown accustomed to his laughter, to his easy way of speaking, to his dependable optimism that tells me—even without words—that everything's going to be all right.

Even when it's not.

I sigh. He's not here.

Tasting the salty air on my tongue, I kick off my soggy slippers and step out onto the dock. The morning breeze lifts the frazzled ends of my hair and tickles my cheek. Each stride feels purposeful. Daring.

Toes curled around the last cold plank at the ledge, I lean forward to peer into the placid water.

But the tear-stained face floating in the liquid mirror does not reflect a little girl. It reflects an adult. A young woman who's dedicated her happiness to the stability of her family.

"No more." The words carry across the vast water, their meaning resonating in my chest.

In the time is takes a lonely seagull to travel from the shallow end to beyond the horizon's edge, the dutiful child in me disappears.

And Joss Sanders, the Rebel, has surfaced.

Soaked slippers in hand, numb toes and feet, I hike the path back to my cabin. The second I'm inside, I dive toward the junk drawer and yank it open.

And there I find my prize.

A black Sharpie.

Chapter Nine

I WATCH DREW pull in, park, and leap up my porch steps two at a time. All the while, I lounge quietly on the Adirondack chair I rescued from the cobwebs an hour ago.

He doesn't see me as he raises his fist to knock on the door.

I clear my throat. "Morning." I'm the one to surprise him for a change.

Drew hops back a step and glances left, his eyes wide. His gaze free falls from the top of my head to the tip of my Converse-covered toes. "H-hi."

It's the stutter that gives him away. Drew likes what he sees. And *I like* that Drew likes what he sees.

The extra time spent on my hair and makeup this morning after my "little moment" on the dock was apparently time well spent.

I open my mouth to save us both the awkwardness of recognizing that I no longer resemble some kind of island-hobo when he speaks.

"You look really pretty."

Really pretty. The sweet and simple words corkscrew into my heart.

Too many people think boldness is the same as bluntness. But I disagree. Drew's boldness doesn't stem from the need to say everything that's on his mind. No, he chooses his words carefully and lives by the honesty-is-always-the-best-policy rule. Which makes a compliment from him a thousand times more amazing.

His gaze steadies on mine.

I could take flight with the number of winged creatures filling my abdomen.

"Thank you." A swirl of heat rises in my chest, then swims across my shoulders and down into my back and arms. I uncross my legs, plant them flat on the porch, and stand. "Did you want to come in?"

"Uh…not exactly." Drew tugs on the back of his neck. "I was hoping you might be free today."

"Do you mean *free* as in not ripping up soggy carpet, deep cleaning freezers, or rearranging old cabin furniture? That kind of free?"

Drew's light laughter fills the space between us, my heart skipping to a new beat. "Free as in, would you like to come with me into town for the day and—"

"Yes!" I need an adventure—something to take my mind off of…well, everything. An adventure with Drew is a thousand times more exciting than sitting here alone.

"You didn't let me finish. What if I was about to invite you to go garden supply shopping?"

"Then I'd tell you I'll pick out the very best hoe you've ever laid eyes on."

A quirk in his eyebrow followed by a twitch in his bottom lip takes my innocent comment plummeting to a whole new level of Joslyn's Foot-In-Mouth Disorder.

He shakes his head. "Good to know. But I don't want to take you to the Garden Supply Center."

Heat floods my cheeks like a radiator set to high. "So where, then?"

"I need help building a float for the Fourth of July parade."

A buzz of energy zaps through my veins. "Seriously?"

Drew's confident expression wavers. "Yeah?"

I bounce and clap my hands like a three-year-old at a birthday party. "I've always wanted to help with a float!"

Drew holds out his hand to me and winks. "Then I'm honored to be the man who gets to fulfill such a wild fantasy of yours."

Linking my arm through his, we head to his car. As he opens the passenger door, his eyebrows draw inward. "Joss?"

"Yeah?" I say, tugging on my seatbelt.

"Why is there a real estate sign at the top of the driveway with a giant X through it and the word 'Not' scribbled before the words 'For Sale'?"

The heat in my cheeks is back, and it's blazing down my neck.

I shift and sit straighter. "Because I'm not a child anymore."

Three seconds of a solid Drew-stare later, he closes my door. No more questions asked.

⌒⌒

WHEN DREW PULLS up to an old, dilapidated warehouse it's as if I've jumped from Anne Shirley's picture-perfect Green Gables farm into Alfred Hitchcock's *Psycho*.

My sense of adventure may not be the same as Drew's.

This place is a dump. And given the dozen or so full black trash bags stacked in a pyramid at the side of the building, it might actually be a dump.

He shrugs apologetically as I step out of the car. "I know it's not much to look at, but there's no parking out front."

I pinch my lips closed. Unlike Drew, my optimism is much harder to pull to the surface. I'd be willing to bet all four of my appendages that the front of this eyesore is no more appealing than the back.

Drew takes my hand and leads me toward a narrow alley at the side of the building. Half-dead patches of grass and half-eaten dandelions force their way though dirt and broken pieces of concrete.

We turn the corner. Drew stops, tugs on my hand.

I see the signs. They scream at me from every angle of the warehouse's garage-like front. Most are weathered. All are bold, either in word or graphic or color.

"Birds poop every fifteen minutes. How long have you been standing here?"

"Children left unattended will be given to the Circus."

"25 mph. Yes, your car can go that slow."

And my personal favorite:

"In case of a fire. Please exit before tweeting about it."

Drew laughs at my wide-eyed expression. "Impressive, huh?"

I nod slowly as my eyes work to take in the rest of the property. Hundreds of oversized rusty gear pieces, random cut-off pipe, metal, and rebar. "What is this place?"

A three-legged pit bull hobbles out of the open retractable door, bark-wheezing at us.

"You chasin' the devil again, Pete?"

A weathered old man I'm certain could double as a deep sea fishing captain, calls after the mutt. The abrupt halt of the man's shuffling feet and the gasp that leaks from his permanently puckered lips indicate we've been discovered. His wrinkled roadmap of a face transforms in an instant. "Drew Culver."

Drew rushes to meet the old-timer, wraps a strong arm around his back and gives him a man-slap. "Good to see you again, Harve."

Compared to Drew, Harve looks pocket-sized, shrunken and frail, yet his gap-toothed grin cannot be contained. It's the face of joy. The kind carved from a lifetime of experience. The kind that's chosen.

"You made it." Harve says, beaming. "And you brought a lady friend with you."

Harve faces me, and Drew's cheeks brighten to a new shade of pink.

I take a step toward the men and the less than fortunate dog who sits at Harve's feet, watching me through folds of skin. "Hi. I'm Joss Sanders."

I offer my hand. Harve's thick calluses scratch against the inside of my palm. He's a hard worker. Even at his age. Which has to be eighty-five? Ninety-six? A hundred and ten? I've always been bad at guessing games.

"It's mighty good to meet you, Joss Sanders. I've known Drew here since he was toddling around his old pops." Harve grows silent, and it's then I realize the connection between these two unlikely souls. Harve and Grandpa Culver were friends. "I think old Bill started bringing you out here to help with the float, well, what? A decade or so ago?"

Drew's nod is thoughtful, as if he can see each year laid out before him in a colorful calendar spread, each memory, each moment with Grandpa Culver and Harve. His warm, acorn-colored eyes seem to hold a secret, and I hope he'll share it with me.

"I'll show you the supplies I've gathered. It's not much, but I have faith you two can come up with something." Harve pats the outside of his thigh. "Come on, Pete." The pit bull limps after him obediently.

It's hard not to stare at this odd couple of dog and man.

Drew bumps my shoulder and winks. "Probably should have given you a little warning, eh? I forgot how..." His eyes comb over the property again. "Unique this place is."

Unique is one word for it. "No, it's fine. This will be fun." If a lie is small enough, simple enough, does it really count as a lie?

His smile answers my momentary moral dilemma.

He touches my arm, squeezes gently. "I'm glad you're with me. Today would've been boring without you."

Drew turns and follows Harve into the mysterious warehouse, leaving me with no other choice but to do the same.

Chapter Ten

*W*E TRAIL AFTER Harve in the dusty sanctuary of old car parts, gears, trinkets, and signs. Lots and lots of signs. He stops in front of a back room where a giant heap of "supplies" scatter the concrete floor.

"Here it is." Harve nods at the mess as if we're supposed to understand what it is.

Naturally, Drew understands. He walks inside the dimly lit room, leaving me with Harve and his wonder dog.

"Great. We'll get started. Mind if we carry this stuff outside? Better lighting under the pavilion, I think," Drew says, managing one of his mega-watt smiles.

My gaze drifts to the floor. I can't take my eyes off this mismatched pile of materials.

"Fine by me. I don't care where ya choose to assemble it. Help yourself to any tools ya find." Harve folds his arms over his bony chest. "The big parade's only six days from now, you sure you're up for this?"

Drew's confidence is as inspiring as it is unwavering. "Absolutely. Joss is an expert visionary."

Harve flashes me a crumply grin, and I don't know whether to feel flattered or flustered by Drew's unfounded assessment of me.

"I'll be over in the main shop today. Got a lot of tinkering to get done before nightfall. Come on, Pete. They don't need you nosin' about."

"Sounds good." Drew's already dropped to his knees to examine what we've been given.

The second Harve is out of earshot, I lean against the splintery doorjamb. "An expert visionary? Really?"

"Look what you did with your cabin in only a few days. And those old frames you painted. That takes vision."

"Or a few days of cleaning and a few cans of paint."

"Joss." Still hunkered on the ground, he looks up at me, eyes alight with the kind of bright belief I wish I possessed. "I think you're perfect for this project. Now grab some of this stuff, and let's get to work."

⌒〜⌒

FOUR HOURS INTO project Mess o' Metal we are closer to filling a landfill than creating a float to pull behind Harve's old Ford.

I hop up on an old workbench, the unsanded wood scratching the underside of my thighs. "We're in over our heads, Drew."

For the first time all day, he looks a bit, well, defeated. He's rolled his shoulders, stretched his back, and sighed about a thousand times. Not that I've been counting. Everything he's managed to piecemeal together has fallen apart.

Drew lifts the bottom of his shirt and swipes at his forehead. My throat feels stuffed full of cotton balls, and I drink the last few drops of warm water from the plastic bottle beside me.

"I swear this used to be easier." He scratches his head, frowns at the pile.

"Probably because your grandpa knew how to build stuff. He had what? Forty some odd years of float-building experience." I point between the two of us. "We don't."

Drew's gaze narrows. "Who do you think taught me how to build? I could use some help creating a plan, you know." He holds up his palm, halting my next argument before it can start. "And no, explaining why everything I try won't work isn't a plan." There's a defensive quality to his voice, a gravelly accusation. Due to the heat and the mess and the lack of food in our growling bellies, we're far too close to the edge to step back and reassess the danger.

"You're the one who took on this impossible project. Don't get upset at me for being realistic." I swing my legs, prepare to jump off the table top when Drew drops his hammer in the dirt and stalks toward me.

"Realistic?" He laughs, only this isn't the jolly laugh I adore. "Is that what you call yourself?"

The impact of his words hits the center of my chest hard, digs in deep. He shakes his head and speaks to the ground. "Unbelievable."

I raise my chin higher, embrace the hurt, pile it on top of all the other unresolved drama in my life, and resist the urge to cross my arms over my chest and stick out my tongue.

Drew lifts his eyes to mine. The rise and fall of his chest indicates he's thinking, planning, scheming. And then, instead of walking away, he steps closer. His back shades me from the sun's hot rays.

"Harve is a master at taking something meant for trash and turning it into a treasure, a keepsake. It's why he named his store, Trash Or Treasure. He's an artist. A brilliant creative who's been dealt a whole lot of crap in his lifetime, and yet he's used it for good. He sells his art all over the world. He's humble, lives a small life on this tiny island. My grandpa saw a lesson in the way Harve lived his life, in the way he saw the world. He wanted that for me, too."

Harve owns Trash or Treasure?

The kick drum of my heart booms louder, beats a truth into my veins that causes my body to heat from the inside-out. Drew didn't bring me here to save me from boredom. He brought me here to show me what his grandpa had showed him.

I exhale, my throat tight as Drew's hip brushes against my shin.

"Sometimes a fresh start means taking what's already there and making it into something new. Something functional or even beautiful."

My bony kneecaps press into his hard abdomen, our eyes, level, and I adjust for him to step closer. I feel the intake of his next breath, and the one after that.

"I'm sorry for being such a horrible assistant today. You've helped me so much and I…"

"You've helped me too."

I can't quite believe that, not when he's literally rescued me more times that I care to count.

Drew combs a hand through his maple-brown hair, and suddenly my fingers are alive, itching to touch what's felt off limits until now. I don't ask, I just reach. Drew stands stalk-still, like prey targeted by a hunter, his eyes focused on my face, then dipping to my lips. I roll a lock of his shaggy hair between my forefinger and thumb. It's softer than I imagined, sleeker too. But Drew's silence and heavy gaze make me wonder if I've overstepped. Slowly, I lower my hand.

Drew catches my wrist mid-air.

Before I can utter a single phrase, Drew's mouth is a whisper away. The feather-light graze of his lips against mine makes my skin tingle and my toes curl. This kiss is unexpected, but it's not unwanted. Not at all unwanted. I tilt my head to the side, invite him closer.

He reaches around to my back, slides me forward to the edge of the table and—

Drew breaks away from me, the heat between us gone in an instant. He's bent in half, his left arm cradled by his right, his body crumpled in on itself. With eyelids pinched tightly, his face matches my dusty white Converse.

"Drew!" I hop off the bench onto wobbly legs. "What's wrong? What's happening?"

"Keys. Pocket." He grunts out through clenched teeth. "Drive me home."

I fumble instead for my phone. I should call 911 or maybe I should run and grab Harve or—

"Joss! My keys. Just…get me home."

I grab the warm metal key ring from his pocket and run to Drew's car. I pull it up to the pavilion in record-setting time and pop open the passenger side door with my foot. He slides into the seat, a grimace set on his mouth.

Drew's silent, ashen face twists my belly into knots.

"I'm driving you to the medical clinic." The only one on Lopez Island.

He shakes his head, eyes half-shut, head pressed to the back of his seat. "No. To the house, *please.*"

Only a guy like him would say "please" in a moment like this, but it works. He wins. Against the nagging in my gut, I do as he says. I drive him home.

Thirty minutes after popping a white pill from a brown prescription bottle, Drew's color returns to his face, the rigidity in his body relaxing into a familiar ease.

I make him a sandwich, peanut butter and jelly, since the groceries here are slim pickings. But I need him to eat *something*, I need him to show me I made the right decision in taking him home. That he's not about to keel over and die.

"Joss, sit down. I'm fine now."

I don't sit. I stay standing. And then I pace.

"What the heck was that back there? I feel like my heart is still a second away from exploding."

His lips twitch. "Good to know I can affect your heart."

I try my hardest not to give in to his smile, but he knows how to get to me. And right now, I want to hate him just a little bit for that. Nobody outside of my best friends can read me as easily as he does. "I'm serious, Drew."

"As a heart attack?"

"Stop it."

"It was just a bad cramp. Relax."

"I've had lots of cramps in my life, and they've never caused that level of pain."

"It's just an old injury. From rowing. I'm working through it."

Hands on my hips, I want to call his bluff, demand things of him I have no right to demand. But the truth is, we're just friends—albeit, friends who've shared a two second kiss, but still.

I'm not his girlfriend. I'm a summer…fling? That word stings my lungs on my next inhale. I don't want to be Drew Culver's fling.

"Sit. Down."

This time I obey. I sit across from him on the recliner, and my legs bounce with nervous energy.

"We need to make a game plan for the float tomorrow," he says.

I pop right back up. "We are *not* talking about the float right now. We're talking about your near-death experience from kissing me."

I don't mean to say that last part aloud, but as I blurt the words into the room, Drew throws his head back with a laugh. "That was the most memorable kiss of my life to date!"

I purse my lips and put my hands on my hips. "Glad this is all so amusing."

Gradually, he sobers, rests his head against the sofa. "You're more than just amusing." And then he pats the empty spot next to him and sighs. "Fine, why don't we just relax and watch TV for a bit. We'll make a plan later."

I shake my head, raw stubbornness coming to my aid when I need it most. "Nope, sorry. Can't trust that I won't cause you another injury attack."

Drew raises his head slowly. He offers me a smile so devastatingly perfect that it could cripple even the greatest of athletes. And I've never been one to claim athleticism.

"Fine. I'll sit on the opposite side of the sofa." I plop on the plush green couch.

He leans toward me with stealth-like speed and slips his hand around my ankle. With a single tug, he tows me to his side. I'm reduced to a mix of girlish giggles and weak resolve.

Drew kicks his feet onto the coffee table and presses the power button on the remote. In all of five seconds, I'm snuggled into his side, enjoying a rerun of *The Office*.

I'll fight with him later.

Chapter Eleven

OR THE NEXT four days, Drew and I are slaves to his float-building blueprints. The same blueprints he penned while under the influence of prescription pain meds. But this time, I won't be the voice of reason. Or negativity. This time, I'll keep my commentary to myself.

Drew's shoulder cramp never resurges, but unfortunately, neither does our kissing moment. Sure, there've been plenty of spine-tingling glances, double-takes and glass-shattering smiles. But Drew hasn't pinned me to a work bench to kiss me breathless, though there's been ample opportunity to do so. I'm beginning to think his lack of advances has little to do with opportunity at all.

Drew pulls his phone from his pocket. "I've gotta take this call."

He heads out to the open field. He's been taking more and more calls in private recently. In fact, that's all Drew's ever done. Take his calls in private.

I stop my mind from going where it wants to go. To some sorority girl with blonde bouncing curls who cheerleads for him as he rows. I face the giant piece of art we've dedicated our week to, and blink the imaginary girl away. The structure before me is full of raw edges and untrimmed pieces, but even as it sits, waiting to be polished, pride swells in my chest. The gears, dials, numbers, and rusty rods of rebar, finally reveal what Drew knew was here all along. A clock or at least a parade float that resembles a giant timepiece. It's modern, edgy, and one of the most unique pieces of art I've ever seen. Harve made us a sign earlier today that will fit snugly in the center. *Trash or Treasure—*

20% off for a limited time.

Clever.

I take a pic of the float and send it to Sydney. I laugh at her imme-diate reply.

> **Sydney:** *A time machine?*
>
> **Me:** *Surprisingly close.*
>
> **Sydney:** *I miss you. I'm in Crazy Town. What are you up to?*

I hesitate, fingers hovering over the text keys.

> **Me:** *I'm just hanging out. Wanna talk tonight?*
>
> **Sydney:** *I wish. I have a stupid rehearsal thingy until late to-night. But I can text you under the table?*
>
> **Me:** *Haha. Good thing Mrs. Smith won't be there to confiscate your phone.*
>
> **Sydney:** *True story.*

I slip my phone in my back pocket and wonder if planning a text chat with Sydney qualifies as another adult-sized leap forward. Alt-hough not quite as personal or informative as a phone call would be, texting with Syd will allow me a bit more freedom to be selective. Share the good stuff that's happened so far this summer.

My gaze drifts to Drew out in the field. I bite my bottom lip. Be-cause even from a distance, I can sense the delight on his face.

Phone call over, he cups his hands over his mouth and yells, "You ready to go have some fun, Joss Sanders?"

I mimic his hand megaphone. "What kind of fun, Drew Culver?"

Before I can reply, Drew's running full speed ahead.

Together, we race to his car.

⌇

A FEW YARDS out from my driveway, I see her. The "glamour shot" lady, Dotty Harrison, the face on my cabin's real estate sign.

"Slow down, Drew." I tap his arm with far too much vigor. "Actually, just pull over. *Pull over!*"

Drew gives me a side-long glance, but he pulls his small navy Honda off to the right. And, as luck would have it, his car sits perfectly situated behind a row of wild blackberry bushes.

Good news: I can still see Dotty. And that's really all that matters in this scenario, anyway.

Drew exhales loudly, a sigh that's both bewildered and bemused. I poke my head out the window to glimpse a better view of the woman staking a sign in my lawn. One without my most recent of vandalisms.

This is sign number three. She's catching on.

But between float building and spending every possible minute with Drew, I've managed to avoid this coral-lipstick-wearing woman. I mean, really. When has coral ever been a natural lip color?

"Mind telling me what we're hiding from?"

"*Shhhh.*" I wave Drew off, and he catches my wrist to pull me back into the car.

"You know, I've grown accustomed to some of your weirdness. But this? This stretches a little past weird, Joss."

I roll my eyes, lower my voice. "It's the listing agent. She's at my cabin."

Drew is unimpressed with this information. Or maybe with me. I'm not actually sure. "So…your parents are selling the cabin, and you thought your little Sharpie artwork could interfere with a sale?"

"No." Only a crazy person would think that. "I just don't trust her is all."

"Because?"

I don't have time to engage him in a round of Twenty Questions. I pop my head back out the window and gasp when I see Dotty knocking on my front door.

But then I gasp again as Drew fists the hem of my shirt, starts up the engine, and whips out onto the main road.

"Drew!" My squeal is lost to the wind, half my body still hanging out the car.

"Get inside. Or you'll be plucking out blackberry thorns for weeks."

I don't have time to reply because in less than five seconds we're in my driveway, and Dotty Harrison is walking toward us.

"I hate you," I mutter under my breath.

"No, you don't."

Okay, fine, he's right. But I really *want* to hate him.

Drew comes around to my side of the car and opens my door.

"Hello? Hi there, are you Joslyn Sanders?" The plump woman in the paisley sundress asks. She extends her hand as I step out of the car.

"Hi, yes. I'm Joss."

Dotty smiles like she's just found a multi-million dollar asset instead of a soul-searching twenty-one year old. "Well, great! Your mother said I'd find you here, but every time I stop by, you seem to be out."

Maybe because I want to keep *you* out. "I keep pretty busy." I shove my hands into the pockets of my linen shorts.

I don't miss the arch of Drew's eyebrow as I speak, or the way he leans casually against the hood of his car and watches this exchange like he's viewing the latest reality TV show.

"Well, I have several very interested clients. Is tomorrow morning a good time for a showing?"

Did she just hit me? I swear I felt one of my ribs snap. Maybe two. I shake my head, but the words won't fall out of my mouth.

Drew steps in, wraps an arm around my shoulder, and then leans forward to shake Dotty's hand. "I'm Drew Culver, Joslyn's neighbor. What time were you thinking, ma'am?"

"Nice to meet you. I'm thinking ten would be good." She turns her heavily made-up eyes on me again. "Your mother gave me permission to put a lock box on the door, as well, since she's been having some trouble reaching you."

I look past her and see an ugly grey box on the cabin's front door.

"You...you have a key?" I manage to croak out.

"Yes, your mother sent me one after we signed the listing agreement. This time of year is our busiest."

"Wait," I say, her statement jolting me back to life. "I don't want random people walking through my front door. What if I'm in the shower or…or sleeping in?" There's a shake to my voice I hope Dotty can't hear.

"I understand your concern. If you give me your phone number, I can text you when a buyer requests a showing time."

I rattle off my number, and Dotty saves it in her phone. I feel sick.

"It was nice meeting you both. See you in the morning."

She walks away, and I punch Drew in the ribs. Might as well show him how I feel rather than try and explain it.

Marching up to the front porch steps, I open the door with *my* key, and before it can slam shut, Drew catches it.

He barges in. "You really thought you could stop a sale?"

"Go away." My steps are angry as I make my way down the hall toward the back bedroom.

"You realize how that sounds, right?"

I whirl around. "Crazy? Is that what you want me to say? That I'm crazy? That I'm pathetically hopeless because I'm losing everything all at once?"

"Everything?" Drew stops walking, his question an invitation, not an interrogation.

I tick the list off my fingers one by one. "My parents, my family, my childhood, my past….*this home*!"

Drew studies me. "That's a lot."

I know he's trying to trick me into being calm, into being rational, into not being a slave to my feelings. But I've tried his way. And it doesn't work.

The narrow hallway closes in on me slowly. "Yes."

I expect him to say something more. Add some guru words of wisdom. But Drew doesn't say anything. He just stands there, waiting for me to continue.

I rest my hand over my heart. "I've tried…I've tried to kill it, to numb it, to ignore it. But it won't stop." My voice breaks on the word. "This pain…it never stops."

I push past him into the living room, half expecting him to stay put, half expecting him to walk out the front door and not come back. Instead, he sits on the sofa and crosses his ankle over his knee.

I swipe at a rogue tear with the back of my hand. "That…" I point to the hand-carved chest in the corner of the room, "is filled with family pictures. Dad brought them here so mom could scrapbook the last time we were on the island together as a family. But she never got around to it. So there it sits. A chest full of memories. *Dead* memories. Just like their dead marriage. Just like my dead childhood."

Then, my adrenaline is gone. A *whooshing* sound leaves my chest, and I slump against the nearest overstuffed chair and bury my head in my hands.

"Memories don't die, Joss."

I sniffle.

"You get to keep those pictures *and* all your memories. I know what this cabin means to you, but…" Drew's words trail down a long path of silence. "But the sale of this cabin, just like your parents' marriage, isn't in your control. Maybe it's time to stop holding on so tightly to everything that was and try to accept what is."

I know he's right, but whether I'm Joslyn the child or Joss the adult, the pain of that truth is the same.

Drew crouches in front of me. His warm hand brushes over the top of my head and skims the length of my hair. "What are you thinking?"

I lift my face to his, steady my gaze. "That I'd like to jump off the dock. With you."

He pulls me to my feet and hugs me. "You're strong, and if anyone tells you differently, you can send them to me."

I pull back just enough for him to see my face.

"Don't you mean I should go tell 'my neighbor, Drew Culver?'" Not only do I nail the tone and verbiage of his casual introduction to

Dotty only minutes ago, I seem to have struck a nerve.

Drew's almond-shaped eyes sharpen on my face, his gaze blazing a path to my lips. He's not amused by my impersonation.

"You're more than my neighbor, Joss."

"How much more?" I'm baiting him. And by the slight crease at the edge of his mouth, he knows it.

"Enough to wish I could redo our first kiss every time I see you."

Drew's hands slide up my back to cradle my head. The pads of his thumbs rest under my jawbone, my pulse thrumming wildly against them. In mere seconds, the steady current between us sparks like a downed, live wire, flailing with want. His lips brush across mine, as if to test the charge.

Drew takes the risk.

Tightening his grip in my hair, Drew pulls me forward, my hands pressing flat against his chest. His mouth covers mine, his lips urging me to follow his lead, to find a rhythm that's all our own. Knocking hard against my palm, Drew's heartbeat hums the cadence of desire. I lean closer, invite him to take our kiss deeper.

He doesn't hesitate.

Not the setting sun or the buzz of cell phones or even the lure of a legendary dock floating above placid water could pull us from this kiss, this moment.

Because whatever we've discovered, it's something.

And something is significantly more than a summer fling.

Chapter Twelve

*F*LUFFY SPUN SUGAR, chewy caramel popcorn, and every kind of skewered meat that money can buy are the pungent aromas of Fourth of July on Lopez Island.

We were at Harve's warehouse till late last night, applying the finishing touches on the *Trash or Treasure* parade float. Really, there wasn't too much left to be done, but once again, Drew had managed to get me out of the cabin during yet another round of showings. This trick has become a new favorite pastime of his: knocking on my front door with some ridiculous emergency, or a food craving, or a sudden itch to go fishing off the Culver's dock.

Over the course of the last week, a half-dozen families have walked through my cabin. And little by little, showing by showing, the cinched belt around my heart's been adjusting, one notch at a time.

Drew secures my hand in his, and together we walk to the end of the parade route, to Harve's old Ford. The float platform is attached by a trailer hitch, and seeing this huge steampunk-style clock finished in all of its unique glory makes me smile.

We did this.

Drew squeezes my palm as we approach a familiar three-legged dog and his master. "Hey, Harve."

"There you two are," Harve says, clearing his throat. "Thought you should do the honors." He tosses a ring of keys at Drew.

"Wait. You want us to drive? In the parade?" I ask, speaking the confusion written on Drew's face.

"Yep. I've looped that parade route more years than you two have been alive." His wrinkles crease deep trenches on either side on his smile. "Just don't forget to throw the candy. The kids love it."

Pete whimpers near Harve's ankle, and the old timer bends to scratch behind the pit bull's ears. "Let's go get us a bite to eat, Pete."

"You're sure?" Drew calls out to Harve's backside.

Harve lifts his hand and shuffles away. "As sure as the coming rain."

I lift my eyes to the sky. Clear. Blue. Sunny.

Drew chuckles at my expression. "Don't second-guess him."

"Um...there's not a single cloud. It's a gorgeous day."

He nudges my shoulder with his. "I tend to trust the instincts of people who've outlived me by half a century."

And once again, Drew has a point.

A bright spear of sunshine spotlights the bulky buckets of candy in the Ford pick-up. My heart smiles as I think of old man Harve, who just like candy, has a sweet center.

I laugh more in the next two hours than I've laughed in the last six months. My forearm sports a permanent indentation from leaning out the window, tossing candy to hoards of patriotically-dressed children screaming for sugar.

One last time, I reach into the bucket as Drew nears the last corner of the parade route. I toss a hefty handful of candy to a couple of knee-height toddlers waving their miniature flags. They aren't quite old enough to collect the treats that tumble over the curb onto the pavement, so I aim the candy at their feet. The festively dressed woman next to them waves at me, thankfulness in her smile.

Satisfied, I sigh and fall back into the cab. Drew slides his hand onto mine and flips my palm over to intertwine our fingers. Two tiny shivers dance up my spine at the contact of his skin on mine. I could melt into this touch.

"How did I get lucky enough to have a pro candy thrower as my co-captain?"

I lean my head against the seat, the sun's rays kissing my face. "You were the expert parade driver. I couldn't have done it without you."

"Five miles an hour isn't exactly expert-level driving." He slows the truck to a stop and parks under the leafy branches of an oak tree. "I could have fallen asleep at the wheel and no one would've noticed."

As if intoxicated by sunshine, sweets, and celebratory happiness, I rotate in my seat to face him. The words slip through my lips without hesitation. "I would have noticed."

Drew's prominent boy-next-door grin, the one he's worn since my first night on the island, no longer feels innocent. A prickly heat fills my chest.

His eyes linger on mine, a stretching silence that spans the distance of our shared bench seat and pushes us closer, pulls us together. There's no first move, no grand gesture, no spoken invitation. We simply answer the silence.

Our lips meet.

The bright, cloudless sky might prevent the visibility of fireworks until nightfall, but within the depth of Drew's kiss, an explosion of fiery color extends from my head to my toes.

Under heavily lidded eyes and through raspy, uneven breaths, Drew presses his forehead to mine. "Joss."

There's an ache in his voice I've come to recognize. The same desperate plea that's taken a hold on my heart. A tone that carries with it a kind of pleasurable pain that plagues as much as it pacifies.

"I know," is what I want to say, "I'm falling for you, too."

But, instead, my words are lost to a kiss I hope will last until the real fireworks begin.

$$\sim$$

"IT'S SO LOUD. Where are you, Syd?" I cup my hand over my opposite ear and adjust the phone. The phone beeps a warning into my ear. *Low battery.* I step off the blanket Drew laid out for us hoping for a great view of fireworks over the water.

"My mother's ridiculous bachelorette party. Hang on. I'm almost inside. I just wanted to check in with you." The peppered beat of a drum fades, and suddenly I can hear her again. "I haven't heard from you since we texted last week."

I hike my way to the top of the short hill. "I know. I'm sorry." My apology is lame, but trying to come up with an excuse that will satisfy Sydney, or any of my friends, would be even more so.

"When are you headed back?" Sydney asks.

If only "back" were an actual place. "Um...I'm not exactly sure yet." I glance down at Drew. He's entertaining a family of six with card tricks galore. The fireworks show isn't set to start for another hour. "The island's been good for me."

"You mean Doo-Doo Drew's been good for you," she says in a sing-song voice.

"Not funny, Syd." I'm starting to regret telling her about him at all.

She laughs. "Sorry, couldn't resist. I'm sure he's every bit as hot and charming as you claim, but what does Drew have planned when this little summer rendezvous is over?"

The word "rendezvous" punches me in the gut.

"He'll go back to school. He's a senior on scholarship at UW with the rowing team." I swallow the uncertainty that swells in my throat, and anticipate her next question.

"And then, what? Do you think you'll do the whole long distance thing? Or is this just a—"

"How's Myrtle Beach?"

She laughs at my poor attempt to reroute her. "Haven't seen much of it yet. Bridezilla and all. I'm so ready for this wedding to be over."

"I bet." I draw a heart in the sand with the tip of my sandal and pretend I haven't thought about how impossibly hard it would be to watch one of my parents remarry as many times as Syd's mom. Or remarry at all.

"So..."

I stop moving at the hesitation I hear in her voice. Sydney never hesitates. She says what she means, means what she says. "I talked to your mom yesterday, Joss."

"*What?* Why?" The voice that squeaks out is small and tight.

"Because she's worried about you."

I brush my foot over my art in the sand and turn my back to Drew and the pack of goofy kids calling out card games to play. "What did you tell her?"

"The truth. That I've been worried about you, too."

"Sydney!" I slam my eyes shut, search for a tangible calm inside. I find none.

"You disappeared on everyone. No one knows what you're thinking."

"That's not true, Drew—"

"Has known you for all of three weeks. I've known you since fourth grade." She sighs. "Why didn't you tell me?"

The question is so soft, yet it's loud with emotion. "Because then I'd have to face it." I'm shocked I've admitted this so freely, but I shouldn't be. What Drew's helped me come to terms with in the last three weeks could be classified as miraculous.

"Yes, but out of the four of us, I get it, you know? You were there for me when my parents went through their divorce. You made me cards and drew me pictures and invited me to sleepovers at your house constantly. I know we aren't kids anymore, but I can still be there for you. All of us can be, if you let us." She pauses again, and I blink quickly to avoid the spill-over of pooling tears. "I'm glad you've had Drew this month, really I am. But he can't replace a lifetime of friendships. He can't replace two loving parents. And you shouldn't want him to."

She's right; I hate that she's right. My bottom lip trembles as I open my eyes and exhale. "I miss you."

"If I could be there with you I would be. You know that, right?"

"I know it. I love you, Syd."

"Ditto."

I hang up the phone and power it down to conserve the rest of my battery life. Drew waves and I join him again on the plaid blanket he swiped from Grandma Culver's sofa.

"Everything, okay?" He lifts his eyes to mine while two blonde boys, each no older than seven, sit on the edge of our quilted perimeter. Looks like they settled on a game of Go Fish.

I sit, loop my arm through his, and lay my head on his shoulder. "Perfect."

He kisses the top of my head, anxiety leaving me like sand through a sieve.

We stay this way long after the last of the fireworks have exploded. Long after the last family has packed up. Long after the moon and stars have reclaimed the night sky.

On our slow walk back to the Culver's dock, Drew kisses my cheek. The way he's done at least a dozen times since we left the beach. And not even the blisters forming on the back of my heels can kill the joy I feel just by being near him. I'd walk all night long if it meant random kisses from him.

We reach the trail that forks at the Culver's dock. He grips my waist, and I take several calculated steps backward on the path that leads to my cabin. It sits, perched like a lighthouse at the top of the trailhead. Ever since the showings began, I've kept the lights on, hoping to avoid random knocks on the door or peeks through the windows.

"We should say goodnight," I say.

"Go ahead. Say it." He continues walking, hands steering my hips.

We're only a few yards out from the back of my cabin.

"No, *you* say it."

Drew laughs, the curve of his lips teasing me to join in the fun. "Nope."

"You're so stubborn." I stop walking and place both my sandaled-feet on top of his. Drew is not deterred. He continues forward, carrying me with him as he steps. My laughter echoes through the dense forest around us.

"Stop!" I wheeze, clutching his biceps for balance. "You're never going to wake up in time for your run tomorrow." Something cold and wet tracks down my scalp. I hold my palm out to the sky. A raindrop. The old man was right. "And now it's raining!"

Drew kisses my left temple and then my right. "You're worth the lack of sleep. And rain's never bothered me."

"You're crazy," I whisper against his mouth as several more drops land on our heads and shoulders and backs.

"It would seem that way."

He kisses my mouth once more and I sigh into it, wrap my arms around his neck, and wish I could stay like this all night. "Goodnight, Island Boy."

"Let me walk you to the front door."

The rain falls harder, thumping against the ground, releasing the scent of pine and bark and fresh, rich soil. "No, Drew." My meaning is clear. Not tonight. I'm not clear-headed enough to keep him on the front porch.

Drew buries his head into curve of my neck, his damp hair against my skin causes me to shiver. "Text me before you fall asleep, okay?"

"Okay." My heartbeat's in my throat when he lifts his head again to search my eyes. "I'll see you tomorrow."

I slip out from his hold and continue up the path, one slow backward step at a time. I want to see him until the last possible second. Drew doesn't move, not even as the night's drizzle turns into a pounding onslaught of rain.

"Lock the door behind you!" He calls after me.

At the front corner of the house, I turn and scurry up the porch steps.

I dig in my pocket for my key, but before I can grasp it, before I can recognize the sound of a turning deadbolt or notice the parked vehicle that sits off to the right of the driveway, I'm staring into the eyes of my unresolved past.

"Hello, Joslyn. Nice of you to join us."

Chapter Thirteen

I CAN'T HELP but compare the fresh facelift of the summer cabin to the angry scowls of its inhabitants. My parents stand in the center of the living room, arms crossed over their chests, mouths turned down into half-moons. My arms hang loosely at my sides, hands numb and heavy. And for a moment, I forget how to speak.

They're here. Together. At the cabin.

These phrases cycle through my mind a dozen times until my dad's frown morphs into a lecture I can easily recall from my teenage years.

"Why are you getting home so late?"

Only I'm not fifteen anymore, and I no longer have a curfew. I shake my head, willing a boldness into my voice that might over-compensate for the weariness in my limbs. "What are you doing here?" I ask.

"We own this cabin, Joslyn," my mother says, her eyes sleep-heavy, her mascara smudged. "It's after one in the morning. We've been waiting for you for hours, calling you over and over."

But my phone is a dead lump in my back pocket.

My eyes skirt the living room, searching for something that might make their surprise visit feel less like an invasion and more like a homecoming. But the sting of the surreal only intensifies as my eyes hone in on the photographs. There, strewn about the floor, are the snapshots once stored inside a familiar hand-crafted chest.

I can't stop the gasp that escapes from my throat or the tears that burn hot behind my eyelids. All of my childhood memories are on display. Pieces of paper that could easily rip or tear or smudge—all reminders of a past determined as inconsequential by the very people standing in this room.

My dad says something, or maybe several somethings, but the drumbeat inside my ears drowns him out.

"What are you doing with these? Why are they out of the chest?" A rescue mission to reclaim these treasured pictures consumes me as I push past them. Shrugging off my wet jacket, I pick them up, one by one by one. I press the photos to my dry, warm chest.

"Joss, sit down. We drove a long way to see you, and now we're forced to take tomorrow's early morning ferry."

My head snaps up at the use of we. "Together? You drove here together?" I snatch up another collection of photos, of birthday cake wishing and Christmas card posing.

"No. Your mother's car is parked at the ferry dock. I just drove her to the cabin."

Figures. The ride to the cabin from the ferry dock is less than ten minutes. Last time we were all together like this in mom's condo they lasted about twelve minutes before the bickering began.

"Sit down, please." The strain in my mother's tired voice tugs at the child inside me. I obey.

My parents move to sit on opposite sides of the sofa while I refuse to get comfortable. I perch on the arm of a chair across from them. My right foot ticks uncontrollably, my cramped fingers still clutching the hope of my youth.

"This has got to end, Joss." The rational father I've grown up with is back, a calm descending over him despite the charge in the air. "You can't go days or weeks without returning our calls. We need to know you're doing okay. With all of this."

I clench my teeth together so hard my jaw aches.

He continues, "Our divorce isn't about you. We want to make that very clear."

So much for my resolve to stay silent. "Not about me?"

"You know what I mean. This is a choice we've made. It will affect you, but it's not *because* of you."

"Those lines were blurred a long time ago, Dad."

My mother's worn-out eyes find mine. "It may feel like all this happened once you moved out, but the truth is we had problems even before you were born."

"You don't think I know that?" I stand, my frazzled nerves causing me to move. "I might have been young, but I wasn't hard of hearing."

My father's shoulders slump forward. "Then you know this decision has been a long time coming."

If his words are meant to bring comfort, they don't. Instead, they confirm the very truth I've wanted to deny: That all the fleeting moments of happiness and laughter and smiles were fake. A failure.

The ache in my ribcage presses against my diaphragm, my next breath labored and heavy. "Why?" It's all I can get out because the sentences that are meant to follow refuse to be spoken: Why did you ever believe a baby would fix your problems? Why can't you fall in love again? Try harder? Why does following your future have to mean giving up my family?

I peel the stack of pictures away from my chest and hold them out, the image on top shattering my heart one fragment at a time. "Was all this a lie?"

Silence creeps into the space between us as I flash a picture. My parents and I are playing together on a beach. I flick it off the top with my thumb and watch as it falls. I imagine the fluttering paper smashed by an anvil, the weight of twenty years lost. "Or this one? Or maybe this one?"

My first day of second grade.

My dad and I in his workshop.

My mom's fortieth surprise party at her favorite restaurant.

I flick and flick and flick till every memory falls dead at my feet. A littering of lies.

"No..." My mom cradles her head in her hands, her words on the trail of sobs. "We've tried. We've been to four different marriage counselors, attended group meetings, read book after book." She shakes her head, tears falling freely. "We just can't do it anymore. I can't do it anymore. This decision is ours, Joss, and so is the blame." She takes a breath and meets my eyes. "But those pictures, those memories of us as a family, I will always cherish."

I can't remember the last time I saw my dad cry or if I've ever seen him cry. But right now, his eyes are misty and red-rimmed. He stands and walks toward me. "I'm sorry, sweetheart. I'm sorry we've made you question everything, even your childhood. We never wanted to hurt you, but we know we have."

I'm swallowed up in his embrace, and the little girl inside me weeps at the comfort I find in my father's arms.

There's a new touch on my back. Cold, skinny fingers I'd recognize anywhere, rub a circle at the nape of my neck. My mom.

"I'm sorry too, baby. We don't want to lose you. We can't lose you."

I nod into my father's plaid shirtfront, his spicy cologne of cinnamon and cedar drawing out another round of fresh tears.

"We love you, Joss. That's never been up for debate."

I sniffle and wipe my snotty nose on my shirtsleeve. "I love you too. Both of you. But I still hate this." And I do hate it. Yet this decision has never been in my control. Not as a child. And not now as an adult.

I hear the old family therapist's words again. "I am not responsible for my parents' marriage." And this time I believe her.

"I know. I know there will be lots of changes to come, but we're committed to you, even though we're not committed to each other in the same way we used to be," my mother says through tears.

My father kisses the top of my head. "She's right. We'll always be committed to you."

"Then I want a say in holiday plans and family gatherings. I don't want to be some pre-scheduled mark on your calendars. I'm old enough to decide where I want to go, and when."

"Fair enough," Dad says.

"And I'm changing my major to interior design." It's the first time I've spoken it aloud to anyone, the first time I've been brave enough to acknowledge my secret desire. My dream.

I wait for an argument, but neither of my parents appears to be shocked or even...disappointed.

"Good. That's the right choice for you," my mom says.

"It is," my father adds, but as his eyes scan the room of he cabin, I know that's not the last of what he's about to say. There's more.

I take a step back. "What about the cabin?"

"We received a full cash offer today," my mom answers. "That's another the reasons we came tonight. We know you're very attached to this place, and your dad thought it would be best if we didn't tell you over the phone."

I close my eyes. Tears pool at the corners of my mouth. This is the taste of sorrow. This is the taste of letting go. Acceptance is so much easier when it's far away.

"The furniture and appliances will stay, but we can haul anything else you want back with us tomorrow morning."

I pull away slightly, look at them both as a new thought beats into my brain. "When do I have to be out?"

Dad looks at mom, a secret language passes between them. They may have a divorce decree with freshly-inked signatures, but there are some things time can't erase. "Monday night. The inspection is Tuesday morning. We're set to close Thursday if everything goes smoothly."

I do a quick calculation, my foggy brain desperate to catch up to speed. My heart plummets. I have twenty-four hours left on the island.

Drew.

I step back and pull out my phone, turn it on. Sure enough, Drew had texted me goodnight. My fingers itch with the need to text him all that's transpired since our parade driving and rainy kisses, but instead I text a single word: *Night.*

Morning is so far away, yet much too close. I'm not ready to say goodbye to him.

"I think we should all try and get some rest. We have a long drive back tomorrow, and the ferry leaves in just a few hours. I'll sleep with you in the master. Dad can take the spare room."

My dad nods his approval, but my heart is an erratic mess of emotions I can't decipher. With one last round of hugs and promises to stay in better communication, even once I'm back at the dorms, I shuffle into the bedroom with my mom.

Only twenty-four hours left with Drew, and I have to waste the next precious few on sleep.

Chapter Fourteen

MY PARENTS LEAVE the cabin before the sun has a chance to greet the island with a proper hello. The wooden chest full of pictures and keepsakes is on the way back to the mainland too, along with several other sentimental items I begged my dad to take. He did, without so much as a sigh.

The instant his taillights are out of sight, I bolt from the cabin's front porch steps and run down the trail to the Culver's house. I can't wait another minute to talk to Drew.

The back door's unlocked. The kitchen lights are on, a banana peel and empty energy drink are on the countertop.

"Dang it," I say to the empty room.

He's out for his morning run. His phone sits next to his car keys on the small dinette table, the same table we shared our first ever Pop Tart dinner on my first night on the island. I run my finger across the dark screen, touching it because I can't touch him. I asked him once why he doesn't run with his phone, why he doesn't drown the miles in beats and music. His response was typical Drew: "Because I like the sound of nature."

I trace the outside edge of his purple and gold University of Washington phone case. And as I make my second pass, the phone buzzes. I jump back, my chair nearly toppling over.

> **Coach:** *Saw your latest scans. Sorry, son. I don't want to push you, but I need an answer on the Asst. position. The school needs to post an ad if you decline.*

The words float on Drew's screen for several seconds before they disappear. I curl my fingers into my palms, refusing the urge to pick up his phone and reread the text. And even though I know it wasn't meant for my eyes, my mind has already gone to work, piecing together facts of a complicated puzzle. A few words here and there. A few snapshots of time. A few strung fragments of a text message.

The back door swings wide and a sweaty, shirtless Drew barrels inside, jolting to a stop when he sees me sitting at the table. His surprise morphs quickly into an open mouth grin. But I can't bring myself to share a joy that's only surface deep.

"Morning. You're up early, want to go grab some breakfast? Just give me a minute to—"

"Drew." The conviction in my tone sounds more like an overprotective parent than a doting girlfriend.

The light in his eyes dims along with his smile.

"Your coach just texted you." I point to his phone on the table, and as if on cue, the text flashes again on the bright, tiny screen, reminding him to check his missed calls and messages.

He reads the text without moving a single inch closer.

"Your shoulder. It's why you're not rowing this summer, isn't it? Why you can't row. You're hurt." And so am I, that he didn't tell me. That he led me to believe his injury was old and insignificant.

Drew's double blink is the only indication he's heard me.

"All this time, all your mini sermons of not allowing my feelings to get the best of me, of accepting the hand I've been dealt, of focusing on what I can control, and yet you've been hiding from the truth, too."

He turns, faces me dead-on. "It's not permanent. I just need a little more time to heal."

But the way his voice quivers, the way his gaze darts to the table again, tells my heart otherwise. And I wish so badly I could go back to living in the same world Drew lives in. A world of ideals.

But I can't. Because he's the one who taught me to face reality.

I reach for him, but he steps out of my grasp. "He offered you an assistant position—like an assistant *coaching* position?"

"It's not for me," he says gruffly, looking everywhere but my eyes. "I'm one of the crew. I'm a rower, not a coach."

"But if you can't row, isn't the next best option to—"

"I'm not quitting, Joslyn. That team is my life."

The pain in his voice presses hard against my chest. I don't want Drew to hurt. I don't want him to be anything other than the positive ray of light I've known him to be for weeks, but I can't encourage his denial. The same way he's never encouraged mine. A true friend doesn't allow you to live a lie. I soften my voice to just-above-a-whisper, try to give him another chance to explain. "What do the scans of your shoulder show?"

For a moment I think he'll answer me, maybe even pull out a chair and sit down at the table to explain it to me in terms I might understand. But a shadow dulls his eyes, his jaw clenching.

He won't speak it out loud. Because then he'd have to believe it. He shakes his head. "You're not my doctor, and I'm not your patient."

The muscular ridge of his back strains as he takes a step toward the hallway, away from me.

"So, who am I to you, then?" I pause long enough to realize he's not going to answer. "A summer project? A distraction that kept you from facing the truth?"

He stops walking but doesn't turn around.

"Rowing isn't your identity, Drew. Yes, it's a huge part of who you are. But it's not all you are."

He glances over his shoulder, eyes narrow. "I'm done talking about this with you."

I think back to last week, to the words he spoke to me before our redo kiss. "'Maybe it's time to stop holding on so tightly to everything that was and try to accept what is.'" I point at him. "Those were your words. Do you really think I can't relate to what you're going through? Do you really think I don't know what it's like to have my entire life shaken and turned upside down?" I purse my lips, gentle my voice.

"Please, let me help you the way you've helped me."

His shoulders slump forward in a way that makes me think he's about to accept my offer, come clean and tell me the whole truth without patches or holes. But pride is the killer of all reason.

"I don't need help. Not from coach and not from you. I can do this on my own." He rakes a hand through his hair. "Ya know, I should probably stick around here today, get some chores done."

I don't miss the lack of invitation to join him. Of all the goodbyes I imagined, this scenario with Drew never crossed my mind. Not even once. My vision blurs as he waits for me to respond.

"Fine," I say, because like Drew, pride keeps me from saying more, from telling him that goodbye today is likely goodbye forever.

"See ya around, Joss." Drew walks around the corner, disappears.

And then I'm left alone. "No…you won't."

Chapter Fifteen

I CAME TO Lopez Island three weeks ago with nothing more than a suitcase. Yet when I secure the bulging black bag into the trunk of my car, I can't help but feel I've forgotten something. And not the small kind of something that's easily replaced, like a lost article of clothing or a half-empty bottle of shampoo. The kind of something that completes. The kind of something that brightens. The kind of something that fills a lonely heart with anticipation, suspense, and desire.

The kind of something that's actually a someone. Drew Culver.

Pivoting slowly, I face my family's picturesque cabin and take one last mental snapshot. If this summer's taught me anything, it's to appreciate every moment. The small, the big, and the life-altering. I tuck each memory into a cherished pocket of my heart, pull down my sunglasses and slip into my car.

I don't look back.

Five, four, three, two, one. The tires round the corner onto the main drag, and I exhale. Yet the ache that churns in the hollow of my belly doesn't dissipate. Neither does the regret that fills my oxygen-starved lungs.

I haven't memorized the ferry schedule, but I'm willing to risk a wait. Because I tell myself the hard part will be over once I get on board. Once I look over the railing. Once I put the island behind me.

Six over-sized orange barricades block my entrance to the ferry.

The white cardboard clock that hangs from the middle blockade states I just missed the 3:20pm departure. The next one won't be here until 5:00. Exactly one hour and thirty-three minutes from now.

I park under a large oak tree in the deserted lot and decide to stretch my legs by the shoreline. Maybe there'll be a nice distraction out on the water I can watch for two hours or maybe I can recite the alphabet a few hundred times, or maybe—

A crusty-sounding bark echoes in the not-so-far-away distance. I whip around. Pete, the infamous guard dog, hobbles alongside his coverall-wearing owner. The pair stops to rest on a weathered park bench a few yards away, and I wonder if Harve's seen me. If it's too late to duck-crawl back to my car and feign sleep.

"Joss? That you, kiddo?"

Yep. It's definitely too late. I shift my weight from foot to foot and wave.

He holds a brown paper bag in the air, shakes it. Pete stretches tall, as tall as a three-legged dog can stretch, and whimpers.

"Come get yourself some donut holes while they're still hot."

Harve's gruff suggestion sounds more like a demand than an invitation, but I move toward them anyway. Chatting it up with Harve wasn't exactly what I had in mind for my last few hours on the island, but then again, neither was leaving Drew without a goodbye.

Drew.

I erase his name the instant it appears in my mind.

"You leaving us?" Harve asks, opening the pastry sack and shoving it toward me.

I look from him to his dog. Pete glowers at me with the same wrinkly expression of distrust he's worn since we met. And without looking away, I reach into the bag and grab three sticky-warm glazed donuts holes. Pete barks and I can't help but savor my first bite.

The chipping paint on the tabletop scratches the underside of my thighs as I sit and plant my feet on the park bench. "Yep. It's time to get back." The words taste sour on my tongue.

Harve pulls out a donut hole from the bag and tosses it to Pete.

Shockingly, Pete's reflexes for donuts are faster than his well-practiced hobble. He catches it easily, the folds of his skin wagging for a full two seconds after his initial bite. It's both disgusting and impressive.

"Hard to leave a place like this." Harve doesn't look at me, but each syllable he speaks carves a hole in the center of my chest.

"Yeah."

"Especially during the summer months. This weather is a taste of heaven."

"Yeah." Because what else can I say?

"But goodbyes come, no matter if we're ready for them or not."

My eyes snap to his, but still, Harve looks beyond me, through me, to a place I can't reach, to a peace I've never been able to locate.

"What do you mean?"

"Goodbyes are like the seasons. Inevitable."

I scan the trees, searching for evidence of a prank or even an angelic figure with a halo. I see neither, but the hair on the back of my neck stands at attention.

"Thanks for the donut holes, but I should really get going." Where? I have no idea. I scoot to the right and my cotton shorts snag against the tabletop.

He ignores me completely and continues on as if I haven't said a word. "The timepiece float was the talk of the parade. You and Drew make a good team."

Drew's name is like one of those rent-by-the-hour sky banners towed behind a two-seater airplane. The image is impossible to blink away.

I hop from the bench and dust off my backside. "Glad you were happy with it."

Harve focuses on my face for the first time, my words trailing off as his gaze cuts through my I-have-it-all-together veneer. "But just like the seasons, sometimes goodbyes come too soon. And sometimes too late."

The punch to my heart shifts to a permanent stab-throb-squeeze.

"How did you...?" My words stumble, and a gentle smile tugs at the inside corners of his mouth.

I don't understand all the hows or whys, but the erratic beat of my heart tells me his wisdom on changing seasons is much like his prediction of coming rain. Spot on.

How many times have I buried my head instead of facing potential conflict, potential hurt? How many times have I closed my eyes and wished my changing world away?

Far too many.

I bite the tremble from my bottom lip and will myself to be braver than I am, will myself to be a lesson learned. I could stand here and hope that Drew comes to his senses before it's too late. That he shows up like the Neighbor In Shining Armor he's been for me a billion times over in the last three weeks. Or I could go to him.

I could be the one who takes the risk, bets it all. Because he's worth it. "Th—thank you, Harve."

Harve tosses another donut hole at his dog, and then lifts his leathered-palm and waves. "Anytime."

I BURST THROUGH the front door of Grandma Culver's house because naturally Drew's left it unlocked and call out his name. No answer. I run around to the garage, fully expecting him to be in the midst of another insane rowing workout. But he's not there either. My heart pounding hard in my temples, I race down the sloppy hill to the well-worn trail.

I see him.

Drew paces at the end of the dock, his phone in hand.

A happy sob escapes me. "Drew!"

He spins around, and before I can catch my breath to say more, he's rushing toward me. Our bodies collide in the soggy grass where land kisses sea. He tucks me in close and wraps his arms around my waist.

My hands are at the base of his neck pulling his mouth toward mine. I kiss him because I can. I kiss him because I didn't leave. I kiss him because hope is stronger than regret.

Drew's words are filtered through choppy breaths as we break for air. "I thought you were gone."

I shake my head. "The cabin sold. My parents came to the island last night. I was gonna tell you this morning and then—"

"I know. I just talked to the realtor. She told me you took the ferry back with your parents. I'm so glad she was wrong." Drew tightens his hold on me. "I'm sorry, Joss. I shouldn't have said what I did."

"No, I was wrong to push. You have a lot to process, and I never should have made it seem like an easy decision. It's not."

Drew's crescent-shaped eyes are a Grand Canyon of light and dark brown, of amber and copper flecks. "I decided." He answers my next string of questions before I can ask, before I can take another breath. "I've seen four doctors and two physical therapists. All of them are in agreement." The slow shake of his head makes me want to kiss his words away, kiss the truth away. "I drained my savings account for one last opinion, a high-end surgeon near Seattle. That scan was my last hope for competitive rowing, but the tear in my rotator cuff is inoperable. Because of the multiple tears, and the trauma to surrounding tendons, my best hope is continued physical therapy. For normal use function only."

"Drew..." But I have nothing more to add. No words that will ease that kind of blow or soothe that kind of loss.

He kisses the end of my nose and then the middle of my forehead. "I took the job, Joss. You were right. Assistant coaching is a much better alternative than denial. I'm headed back to school tomorrow."

His words are a chiming benediction for us both. Neither of us can stay on the island forever. Eventually summer turns to fall. Eventually all vacations must come to an end.

Drew has one more day on the island; I have one more hour.

"I'm happy for you, Drew." I close my eyes until I find the

strength to speak again. "I told my parents I'm changing my major to interior design."

"Don't forget I was the one who pointed out your mad visionary skills."

I want to laugh, but I can't quite make the sound come out. "I also told them I'd head back to the mainland tonight. I need to spend some time with them both before I head back to school." I exhale slowly. "So, I guess this is our goodbye."

He crushes me to his chest and I nuzzle into his shirtfront, savoring his warmth. My nose tingles with a warning of tears, but I don't care about crying. I care about leaving.

I care about Drew.

I lift my head, pull back slightly to see his face and prepare to answer a question he asked me weeks ago. An answer I've only shared with my closest friends and family. "You asked where I go when I close my eyes."

Drew blinks and then takes my face in his hands. "Yes."

"I close my eyes to escape. To take a tiny break from reality so I can remind myself to breathe and focus on something that calms. Sometimes it's clouds, or water, or even a color. But lately..." I swallow the swelling emotion in my throat. "Lately, whenever I close my eyes, I see you."

Tears slip down my cheeks, and Drew swipes them away with the pads of his thumbs.

"I want to be more than your escape, Joss." He kisses my tear-dampened face. "A lot more."

"You do?"

He leans in closer, his smiling words a whisper in my ear. "This is the part where you say you want that too."

"It is."

Drew holds out his palm to me. "Where's your phone?"

"What?" The excitement I hear in Drew's voice is like a shot of caffeine to my bloodstream. I hand him my phone.

Several quick swipes on my screen later, he turns the phone toward me.

A map. Of the two-hour route that separates our universities.

"What exactly are you suggesting?" The teasing in my voice is outweighed by a desperate hope that he means what I think he means.

"I'm suggesting we become officially more than island neighbors." The curl of his bottom lip relaxes into a lazy grin. Quite possibly my favorite grin on the planet. "And I'm also suggesting you stay here tonight. Let me take you out on a real date. We can catch the ferry together in the morning."

"Tonight? But—"

Drew drops his hands from my shoulders and holds his palms to the air. "You can stay in the sewing room. You can even borrow that pink housecoat you loved so much."

I swat at Drew's arm playfully. My parents can wait one more day. "Deal."

"Yeah?" He steps closer and pulls me against him once again, as if I was made to fit into the contours of his chest, feel the rhythm of his heartbeat, notice every detail of his fresh, ocean scent.

With a single finger, Drew lifts my chin and leans close. His cool lips taste like the open water he holds so dear, the perfect combination of adventure, fun, and freedom. This is not the kiss of a casual island fling. This is the kiss that starts a new chapter, a new season, a new beginning.

This is the kiss that took an unusual summer and made it unforgettable.

The End

About the Author

Nicole Deese is a lover of fiction. When she isn't writing, she can be found fantasizing about "reading escapes," which look a lot like kid-free, laundry-free, and cooking-free vacations.

Nicole is a Kindle best selling author of The Letting Go series and *A Cliché Christmas*, book one in her new Love In Lenox series. She writes clean contemporary romance with an inspirational twist, and lives in beautiful north Idaho with her swoony husband and rambunctious sons.

Other books by Nicole Deese:

The Letting Go series:
All for Anna
All She Wanted
All Who Dream

Love in Lenox series:
A Cliché Christmas
A Season To Love (Feb 2016)

Be sure to sign-up for Nicole's Newsletter!
As a newsletter groupie you'll receive the following:
*Bonus Scenes
*New releases
*Book news
*Cover reveals and sneak peeks
*Exclusive giveaways

You can also connect with Nicole on:
Website: www.nicoledeese.com
Facebook: Author Page
Twitter: @nicoledeese
Instagram: nicoledeeseauthor
Pinterest: nicoledeese
Email: nicole@nicoledeese.com

Keep reading for Sydney's summer adventure on Myrtle Beach!

Waves of Summer

By
Tammy L. Gray

Chapter One

THE NUMBER OF twinkle lights hanging above the makeshift dance floor is enough to super charge a Third World country. But nothing less than flash and sparkle will do for my mother's fourth wedding. Especially since it comes a week before her fortieth birthday.

"Sydney, darling, isn't this the most perfect day you've ever known?" She looks toward the setting sun and then off to the ocean in the distance. Its waves roll against the rhythm of reception music—a sad mix of ninety's pop rock—and crash on the shore.

Perfect setting? Yes. Perfect day? Not so much. "Looks like nature is on your side after all," I say.

She and Richard exchanged vows in the plush back yard of Richard's beach house, despite the thirty percent chance of rain.

So much for this thing ending early. The stars are practically bouncing to the music.

My mom dances a finger along her flawless skin that doesn't look a day over twenty-five. "Well, nature owed me. I spotted a wrinkle yesterday. A wrinkle." The sheer horror in her voice makes me wonder if the apocalypse is coming.

"I'm sure you'll survive. Richard is practically foaming at the mouth when he looks at you." So much so that it's weird.

At least they will be miles away for the next several weeks in Bora Bora on their honeymoon. The thought turns my stomach. Creepy stepdad naked is not a picture I ever want to have.

My mom stares at her new husband flailing his arms while his brown hair flops over his face. "Yes, he is quite a catch." She grins. "Not bad for an aging lady if I do say so myself."

Oh, man, here it comes.

"Now you, beautiful girl, need to get a move on. You're practically my twin, and yet I'd already been married two years by the time I was your age."

"That's because you were knocked up." And I'm not her twin. My eyes are brown, hers an intricate hazel. I crave independence; she craves rich men who pamper her.

She frowns, pats her mane of chestnut hair. "That's not the only reason. Your father adored me." She lengthened adored like it had ten syllables. "You're in your twenties now, my dear. Trust me, your youth won't last forever."

I'm two months shy of twenty-one. But the minute I reached the second decade of life, my mom started buying me bridal magazines. Between her insistence on a husband and my dad's insistence on pre-law, both of which I don't want, I am practically a delinquent in the making.

My mom fluffs my already too high hair and pinches my cheeks. "There. Now, why don't you find that bartender who was asking about you last night? He is very cute. And the perfect distraction until Nathan comes to his senses."

How she remembered anything from last night is beyond me. Open bar. Bachelorette party. Cougar women waiting to pounce. Yikes. I should go find the bartender if for no other reason than to apologize.

Richard's slithery arm around my mother halts the sarcasm on my lips. "My two favorite ladies." His other reaches for me.

I dodge, take a polite step back, and try not to cringe. I only met the guy a month ago.

He ignores my dismissal and rewards me with a sloppy, wet kiss on my mother's mouth. I shouldn't have eaten the shrimp. Those nasty little suckers are poised and ready in the back of my throat to come out all over Richard's two thousand dollar shoes.

"Did you tell her our surprise?" He asks as my mother wipes the skin around her lips.

"You didn't give me time."

Oh no. "What surprise?"

"The beach house. It's yours for the rest of the summer. Stocked and ready to go. We're going back to Charleston after the honeymoon. You should invite those girlfriends of yours. You know, the ones you always vacation with." She innocently blinks her heavily mascaraed lashes as if her last-minute wedding hadn't ruined those exact plans.

We'd made a pact, the four of us. Every summer. Every year. And now, thanks to my mother's impeccable timing, I get to spend the summer alone. Figures. Nothing else in my life is going right. Why should this?

"We've been in wedding mode for weeks. It's not like they can plan their summer around my schedule." Although I wish they could. I miss them. The disappointment is enough to burn my eyes. They're my anchors. My stability. Being separated during summer just isn't natural.

My mother waves off the accusation and wraps a thin arm around her new husband. "All the same. I insist." She eyes the bartender in the corner. "Who knows, maybe some space away from your neglectful boyfriend will get the ball rolling."

"Ex-boyfriend."

"For now." She blows a kiss before walking off with Richard in tow.

I close my eyes, relieved she doesn't know the whole story. If I let them all have their way, I'd be Ms. Nathan Proctor before the end of the year. But I said no, and I meant it. It's the first real decision I've made in years, and part of me hopes this summer is the beginning of many more.

THE PARTY IS finally coming to a close. My mom and Richard's grand exit did little to stop the festivities, but I'm hoping the midnight hour will.

I glance around at the over-turned chairs, broken lights and clear plastic cups lying across the grass. My mom failed to point out that cleaning up her post-wedding trash was part of the surprise package. Yay me.

Sexy bartender hasn't made eye contact all night. For a man who works for the Traveling Rum Hut and wears a Hawaiian shirt that Jimmy Buffet would kill for, he is much too quiet.

He's my mother's pick, so naturally that makes him off limits. Not to mention, he's cleaning glasses and stacking them in three perfect rows. It bugs me. There's too much order. Too much thought and planning over something so insignificant. Yet my gaze drifts in his direction for an annoying tenth time tonight. It's because he's the only guy under thirty, I decide. It's not because he fills out that shirt like a body builder or that his lips are full and kissable or that his eyebrows frame two perfectly-shaped, almond eyes.

I'll just talk to him for a second. Get a much-needed break from the noise and be on my way. I pull at my bridesmaid's dress, closing the thigh-high slit, and walk toward the bamboo structure.

Taste has never been a strength of my mother's, but her choosing a dress that makes me look like a flamenco belly dancer is proof she's completely over the edge. The beaded belt chimes and shakes so much a Zumba instructor would be jealous.

I mash my free hand over the brass chain belt, silencing it. My better judgment says to go to bed. I'm tired and still dealing with Nathan's constant phone calls. I'm half tempted to block his number, but our history keeps me from doing so. Plus, my parents see him as their son, and he would immediately call them.

Ugh. A drink sounds good. A drink served by sexy bartender sounds even better. I need a distraction.

Yet the eye roll I get from Mr. I-want-your-daughter's-number is making me wonder if my mom had been three steps off her rocker when she talked with him last night.

"So, what do you recommend?" I take a seat, offer a dazzling smile and wait.

He glances up at the neon sign. "Rum." The lack of inflection in his voice could be funny if not for the scowl on his face.

"Okay." I draw out the word, offer another dazzling smile, one with a little less confidence this time. "Then a Mai Tai, I guess."

He drops an elbow on the bar, flattens his hand. "ID."

Is he serious? "Excuse me?"

"ID. I don't serve to those under twenty-one. And you." His gaze passes from the tip of my head to my tacky golden shoes. "Are nowhere near twenty-one."

He's wrong, but I learned early a man under-guessing my age should be seen as a compliment. I try a hair flip. This has moved past the initial ego-boost and into challenge territory. "I'm only two months out. But what is age, anyway, on a night like tonight?"

"The difference between jail time and a good tip. Now, either get me a valid ID or pick a new drink. I'm shutting down in ten minutes."

My smile dies. "A Sprite, then." Geez. Who sneezed in his Cheerios this morning?

He grabs a tumbler, throws in some ice and squeezes the button on his soda dispenser.

"Your customer service skills are stellar," I deadpan, annoyed that talking to him has made me feel worse, not better.

He eyes my ridiculous costume. Slams the soda on a napkin and slides it to me. "So is your taste."

Gloves just came off. I've had a crappy spring, crappy June, and, in no way, was I letting him make my already crappy vacation even worse. "You didn't seem to mind so much last night when you begged my drunk mother for an introduction."

"Yes, well that poor lapse of judgment was my brother, who as you can see, was too sloshed to show up for work today. And since I really don't want him losing the fourth job he's attempted this summer, I'm pinch-hitting." He turns, wipes the other side of the bar and mutters something about lack of direction.

I wrap my fingers around the glass and seriously consider throwing it right into his pompous, smug, judgmental face. Hot or not, the last thing I need is another controlling man in my life.

Direction. Direction. Direction. Well, maybe some of us didn't want a direction. Maybe some of us want the freedom to go absolutely nowhere.

"Did you ever think that your brother is happy doing what you find so unimpressive?"

He turns, furrows his brow even more. "What do you mean?"

"Let me guess, 'Mr. line up glasses by height, weight, and color,' you have it all figured out. Probably have your entire life mapped out on some three-page spreadsheet."

The clench of his jaw says I hit a nerve. Good. I want to hit a whole arsenal of them.

"So what?"

"So maybe your brother isn't interested in following the same path as you. Maybe he wants the freedom to try something new. Fail at something, even. Who made you the decider of his fate?" My heart races, and I know it's because I just said all the things I wish I had the courage to say to my father.

"Oh, my brother has failure down to a science. And the only path he's on is the one leading to unlimited Budweiser and twenty-four hour cable."

I down the un-alcoholic Sprite in one gulp. "No thanks to you."

His hands clench on the top of the bar. "You don't even know me."

Oh, I know. I was almost engaged to someone just like him. "Let me give you some free advice from a girl who's been there. Your brother disappoints you because, somewhere down the line, you stopped seeing him as a person and started seeing only what you wanted him to be."

I shove the empty glass toward him and stand like I'm Cleopatra and not the bartender's reject for the evening. "Thanks for the drink."

With that, I shimmy forward, with my too-tight dress and my beaded belt clinking all the way to the house. I must be a masochist. An entire party of guests, and I choose to talk to the one person who reminds me of everything I want to leave behind.

Chapter Two

TO MY SHOCK and awe, creepy Richard actually did a good thing. Housekeepers, four of them to be exact, showed up at my door this morning. The manager of the crew even handed me a gift card for an hour massage while they cleaned.

My limbs freshly mashed and oiled, I grab my beach bag and head toward the waves. The area is somewhat empty for early July, but only because Richard's summer home sits a good distance from any public access point. Of course, the beach town being twenty miles south of Myrtle also helps. Garden City is for the locals, and a blessed escape from the drunken rowdiness that is college life.

I spread out a towel and turn on my beloved Kindle. The massage may have released the tension in my back, but the pressure in my head still throbs. I'll be a junior in the fall, yet I have no better idea of my life path than I did my freshman year. Of course, if you ask my dad or my ex-boyfriend, they'd tell you I'm two years shy of law school. The thought makes my eardrums itch.

I drop my Kindle and close my eyes. The main couple in the novel I'm reading is about to break up in a dramatic, angsty way. I know it's coming because it always does. In all the romance books I've spent hundreds of dollars downloading, they break up and then get back together. It's the formula that keeps me hooked, keeps me reading till all hours of the night. But right now, I can't handle any more drama.

My life is one big, fat mess of drama.

As if on cue, Nathan's face shows up on my phone along with the shrill of "Endless Love." I hate that ring tone, but Nathan insisted, so of course it's there, haunting me. Reminding me he's still in control. Tomorrow I'm changing it to "Freefalling." Maybe doing so will give me the courage to tell my mom I broke up with the man of her dreams.

"Hey." My answer comes as a surprise to both of us. We haven't spoken since the night he proposed and didn't get the answer he expected.

"Wow. You actually answered. Does that mean you've come to your senses?" The irritation in his voice makes me wish I'd pressed ignore.

A familiar heat stretches through my stomach. "As in what?"

"Syd." His chastising tone reminds me why I left. I hate that tone.

A long stretch of silence. It's a standoff. One I usually lose, but not today.

"I spoke to your father," Nathan says.

The blow hits me in the chest. "What? Why?"

"Because this behavior is not rational. We had a life together. Plans. Then your mom calls with this crazy new wedding, and you freak out and change everything."

My head pounds. "It wasn't the wedding. It's us. We aren't right anymore. You and I don't want the same things."

He takes a deep breath. "Then what do you want?"

"I don't know."

"That's a cop-out. You just want an excuse to be afraid. Our breakup is your way of running away from commitment. But you're not your mom."

No, no, no. He isn't listening. He never listens. "Nathan, I need space. Time away from you and my parents. I need to breathe again."

"Time is not what you need. You're scared. I get it. I am too. I'm asking you to follow me to a new school. To be my wife. Those are all monumental things, but I'm ready. We're ready."

"Nathan, please. Just stop. Stop calling. Stop pushing. I need you to just stop." I had no more words to say that I hadn't already said.

"I'll never stop fighting for us. We belong together. I won't let you ruin our future."

His future. Not mine. It has never been mine. "I have to go."

"Syd."

I ignore his plea and end the call. Waves crash against the shore, but they are nothing compared to the chaos slamming around in my mind.

"Endless Love" sings from my phone again. I close my eyes and count until the infuriating music stops.

                              ⚬

A SHADOW COVERS my sun and I scowl. Peeking through one eye, I see a halo surrounding dark hair. Hair that looks suspiciously like the Sprite-pushing bartender's. It's hard to tell, though, since his face is sideways and shadowed.

"Who are you and why are you blocking my light?"

The shadow moves, and I hear a thump beside me. "I want to talk about what you said last night."

Great. Now he wants conversation. I toss out my palm, not bothering to move any other part of my body. "ID?"

"What?"

"I'm sorry, I don't do conversations with rude, wanna-be bartenders over the age of twenty-one." I flick my wrist to let him know I'm dismissing him and bite back a smile. Dang that sounded even better in person than it did in the mirror last night.

"Okay, I guess I had that coming. I was ticked. And tired." His low, calm voice seems slightly less cool than last night.

"What's changed?"

He studies the water and his face is a web of emotion. "Now I'm just tired. I was up all night thinking about what you said about me and my brother."

"Really?" I lift myself on my elbows and take a good look at him through my sunglasses. Crap. He's still beautiful. "And here I thought you couldn't stand me. Why would my opinion matter so much?" My opinion never matters. It's lost in the wake of a million people making decisions for me.

"It was the way you looked when you said it. You reminded me of Aaron, my brother. You had that same hostility. That same resentment." He pulls at his collar, like he's said more than he intended.

Resentful? I think of Nathan. Yeah, probably.

My gaze follows his hand as it falls back to his lap. His clothing is much more "him." Starched, white linen shirt and khakis. Even his flip-flops are lined up exactly a half-inch from the edge of my towel. My own have been moved to match his.

Weirdo. OCD weirdo, nonetheless.

"Not everyone likes his or her life to line up in a perfect row." I sit up, grab my shoes and toss them in the sand. They land in a beautiful crisscross pattern. "Your brother may like being 'unstable.'" I mock the word because it's the same one Nathan used when we broke up.

Sexy bartender turns his gaze to me, focused and intense. His eyes are brighter than I remember. A sapphire blue that contradicts his dark hair and summer tan. They're eyes that should be alive with humor and fun, not dimmed by sadness.

"You said I stopped seeing him. What did you mean by that?" He pulls up his knees and wraps his arms around them. Arms that say sexy bartender must have a gym membership. I follow the line of muscle. *No Sydney. Your sick attraction to type A, controlling men must stop!*

I pull my eyes away. "Don't put too much stock into my words. I've never actually met your brother, and I was also irritable last night." I lie back down, inhale the wonderful salty air and try not to the think about the buckets of sand I'll be scraping from my unmentionables later.

He blows out a breath that's loud enough to be heard over the surf. "I've spent a year trying to understand my brother. Make sense of his mind. Yet, in one statement, you summed up everything he's probably feeling, and I don't know how to fix it."

"Maybe that's your problem. You are trying to *fix* the relationship. Or better put, *fix* your brother."

"I'm not—"

"Really? You sure about that? I distinctly remember phases like 'poor lapse in judgment' and 'can't hold down a job.'"

"You've never met my brother. He's the epitome of beach bum." The disdain in his voice is easy to pick up on, even by a stranger. Ten bucks says brother probably has that tone memorized.

"And that bothers you, why?" I really want to understand. Why should he get a voice in his brother's life? Why does everyone insist on having a voice in mine?

"Because he could be so much more. *Was* so much more. I can't get past it."

I try to make the swirling in my gut stop. "But it's not your story." The words are more for my sake than his.

"It's not Aaron's either," he says with absolutely no hesitation. "He's hiding from something."

I need to move. Need to get away. I pop up, and hop around until the first round of sand is knocked off.

He jumps up and out of my sand-flinging path and brushes three precise strokes against his shirt.

"Sorry," I mutter. "I was getting hot."

"No, it's fine. You seem agitated." He's studying me. I don't like it. His gaze is the kind that can see through sheets of armor. "I didn't mean to dump all this on you. I don't know. I just thought maybe you could help. And here I didn't even ask you your name."

"Sydney Andrews."

His brow furrows. "Why does that sound familiar?"

"Because my mom spent my nine-month gestation period watching Melrose Place."

His smile grows, and his sober face becomes an adorable canvas. "My mom used to watch that too. She was the redhead, right?"

I pull up my beach towel to shake it out. "Yeah."

"I'm Jacob Massey. Stand-in bartender, beach crasher, and brother fixer."

This time I get a chuckle and darn if my neck doesn't break out in a fever. I like his laugh. Like this side of him that's not so burdened and calculated. Like it more than I should.

I pull on a white cover dress and tighten my ponytail. "You know, maybe if you left him alone for awhile. Gave him some space without bugging him to do more. Maybe it would open communication." I think of the "space" I asked for. The space Nathan seems unwilling to give me.

He nods like he's dissecting each word I said. "Okay. I can do that. Thanks, I think."

"Sure." I grab my bag and hike it on my shoulders. "I guess I'll see you around then. Maybe the next time you need some brotherly advice."

"Yeah. Maybe. Nice to meet you, Sydney."

"You too."

He stuffs his hands in his pockets and strolls down the beach. Part of me envies people like him. People who can map out their future and trust each step. I trust nothing. Well, except my three best friends. But even they seem a million years away.

Chapter Three

MY BUZZING PHONE wakes me at nine in the morning.

It irritates me that Nathan is calling ... again. And before nine, which means he's doing it to bug me. He knows I hate mornings. Missed call (10) flashes on my screen, followed by a text.

Nathan: *You need to stop running.*

I'm half-tempted to text back, *You need to stop calling*, but that will only confirm I'm listening, which I'm not. Any compassion I had for him ended when he told my dad I turned down his proposal. Now my dad will ask a million questions, and I'll have them both ganging up on me. Thank goodness my mother still thinks Nathan did the leaving. She'd make three.

I pull the covers over my head and try to return to the delicious dream I was having. But my mind is too full of all the expectations hanging over me. The decisions I've yet to make and can't even process. It's like my future is a maze and every time I think I know the solution, a dead end appears. I don't want to live a dead-end life.

Kicking at the comforter suddenly smothering me, I give up on sleep.

I have exactly a month and a half left of my summer hiatus, and I plan on exploring every island secret. Today's agenda, fishing.

Taking my time, I enjoy two cups of coffee, shower, blow out my hair, and throw on some cutoffs and a tank top.

I smile as I pour out the remnants in the coffee pot. Joss would call me sacrilegious for wasting good brew. If coffee addiction had a name, it would be hers. My smile turns sad. She went on to the cabin without us. Brave and steady, that girl. If only I could possess half of her determination. Then maybe walking the path to my future wouldn't seem so debilitating.

A knock pulls me out of my head, and I shake off the depression. Summer. Fun. No drama. I wipe my hands on the leopard print kitchen towel my mother just "had to have" and open the door.

"Jacob?" He looks down at his flip-flops when I say his name. "What are you doing here?"

Finally glancing up, his breath hitches. "Um…wow, you look…"

I peak an eyebrow. "Gorgeous? Stunning? The most beautiful woman you've ever seen?"

"Different."

I start to shut the door again. Introspective beach Jacob was obviously eaten by his haughty bartending alter ego. Probably better. I liked beach Jacob a little too much.

He reaches out, stops the door. "Sorry, I didn't mean it in a bad way. It's just that the other day, you had the poof and the blue shadow. And then yesterday it was the ponytail and big sunglasses. I just didn't know you were so…so…"

I wait for the punch line.

"Naturally pretty." His neck and ears turn shades of red.

I bite back the smile that started lower than my mouth and decide to give him a break. I open the door wider, look over his pressed khakis and blue striped polo. "Don't you have a life? Or at least a job?"

He grins, and, good night, my stomach dips. "My dad makes me take off a couple months each summer. Sends me here to bond with my brother, Aaron."

"Ah, the irresponsible sibling."

"Yeah. Anyway, you said to give him some space, so I'm here."

"Bugging me instead?"

His shoulders relax as his hands find his pockets. "Well, I hope not, but yeah, if that's what it takes."

I step back, allowing him access into the pink nightmare that is my mother's "diva-beach" living room. I feign annoyance, but secretly I'm flattered. He actually listened to my advice. Actually considered my opinion worthy of action. Confidence swells in my chest. It's a strange feeling, but I like it. "I'm going fishing. You know slimy worms, vicious hooks, possibility of messing up your pristine Dockers."

"I fish." He looks around, but his grin doesn't widen or diminish. "And they're Tommy Bahama."

"Good to know."

He ignores my sarcasm, and I feel a strange desire to get inside that head of his. I have a sinking suspicion he only verbalizes about ten percent of what he thinks. While I, on the other hand, think about only ten percent of what I say. The Andrews curse, my mother calls it. She's referring to my elitist grandma who called her trailer trash the entire seven years my parents were married.

"Poles? Bait? Fishing line?" He looks around the foyer for my non-existent gear.

"Um, yeah. I haven't gotten that far."

"How were you planning to go fishing?"

The confusion on his face has me giggling. "I don't know. I don't map out every step I take in the morning. It's the beach. There's a pier. I saw a brochure on it. No doubt that somewhere between here and the water, I can find a stupid fishing pole."

"Do you even have a fishing license? An ice chest or fileting knife? How were you going to clean them?"

"I don't know! Geez, Jacob, I feel like I just flunked my SATs."

He grimaces, does that weird head-scratch thing men do when backed in a corner. "Sorry. I'm doing it again. I didn't get the sponta-neity gene."

I'm starting to understand his rift with his brother. "How about this? I won't fault you for being an overzealous planner if you don't fault me for not having a clue. Agree?"

His hands find his pockets again, and that adorable grin finds his mouth. "Agree."

Chapter Four

WE'VE BEEN STANDING on the Garden City pier for hours and even the wood is starting to vaporize under the scorching heat. It turns out spontaneous fishing is easy and relatively inexpensive. Only problem is, I absolutely hate it. I'm secretly grossed out and ready to get Jacob to do something else.

I mentally add fishing to my list of dislikes. One, law. Two, school in general. Three, Nathan's pushiness. Four, standing for hours watching a bobber not move. Maybe I'll send the list to my dad as a way to break the news. I picture his disappointed frown. Maybe not.

"I think I'm done," I say.

"What? We just got out here."

"Like two hours ago." Enough time to be sweaty, sticky, and getting a tan line around my tank top.

Jacob looks down as his watch. "More like an hour and a half. And you spent the first fifteen minutes freaking out over the worms."

"They were slimy and squirmy." I pinch my nose and shiver remembering the way they slithered through my fingers.

"Fishing requires patience."

The sun is blinding as it reflects off the ocean and even with shades, I squint to see his face. "I don't possess patience." Jacob has been doing his silent reflection thing all morning. His thinking makes me think, and I'm not here to think. I'm here to breathe. "If you want to stay, you're going to have to at least entertain me."

"Entertain you?" He stands from his slouched position over the pier and rests a hip on the rail. "How?"

"I don't know. Dialogue. Ask questions. Tell stories. You know, social interaction." Why am I surprised I have to spell this out for him?

"Okay, where are you from?"

Crap. I should have known he'd start with that. "Too easy. Pick a different question." Truth is, that question isn't easy or fun to answer. Following my mother to two different homes just to watch her marriages crumble puts a kink in the childhood memories.

"So, you want me to talk, but I can't ask certain questions? Now who's being the obsessive control freak?"

"I just think you need to dig deeper. Ask a question that matters." I tilt my head and try to read his expression. I can't tell if he is intrigued or annoyed. I seem to do both to him. It's nice, though, to be around someone who's trying to understand me instead of trying to change me.

He finally grins. "So why a villain? There were lots of characters on Melrose that were a better choice than Sydney. Was it the last name thing?"

I'm impressed, although I'm sure he Googled the name. "No. It was a Vivian Andrews/ Cunningham/ Holister and now Worchester thing," I say as I simultaneously count down my mother's many surnames on my left hand. "My mom likes women who can get their man no matter the cost or collateral damage."

He moves closer, his grin turning pensive, concerned even. "Were you the collateral damage?"

My heart is beating fast, too fast. It's a question Nathan never dared to ask. I don't know if it is because it would ruin our "perfect" image or because it would require him to admit I'm slightly screwed up. Either way, my mother's lifestyle was a joke between us, a punch line.

Jacob should have tossed in a one-liner, not seen my pain. Not after knowing me two days.

I watch the ocean, look out into the vast blue against the bright sky, and pray a breeze will cool my flushed skin. "Did you know that a Gray Man ghost warns the natives of hurricanes?"

"I don't believe in ghosts."

I take in his serious expression and roll my eyes. "Just go with it."

He motions for me to continue.

"The story says that a soldier was returning home to marry his sweetheart and was killed in a horseback accident. His spirit, however, lives on, and he is able to warn his lover of an approaching hurricane and save her life. On certain nights, when the sky is clear, you can see him."

"I'm sure you can, right after downing a quart of cheap booze from the local bar." He squats and adjusts our rods. The water is so calm, I wonder if the Atlantic is even alive this morning.

"Hey, you want to hear something crazy?" I ask, remembering the other ghost story Richard's batty Aunt Betty told me at the bachelorette party.

"Because everything up to this point has been so normal?" His voice holds absolutely no inflection.

I ignore his comment. "I'm going to snorkel for a long lost ring."

He stands and his brow crinkles. "What? Where?"

"Murrells Inlet. According to legend, in the 1800s, Alice Flagg received a ring from a young man her family didn't approve of. Her crazy brother saw it around her neck, got furious and flung it into the inlet. She died soon after and continues to search for her lost treasure today."

His eyes say I'm gullible. "Even if I did believe the story, which I don't, why do you care about a two-hundred-year-old ghost?"

Because she wants peace. She wants to be free from a controlling family. Because maybe if I find what she's lost, then I'll find what I'm missing as well. "I don't know. I just do."

"But why? It's tragic."

I shrug. "Tragic love is romantic sometimes." Or maybe it's the fact that I'd never seen healthy love, so the idea of losing it before it falls apart feels so much better than realizing you've made a mistake.

I suddenly feel lost all over again. Two years wasted in an empty relationship. That's supposed to be my mother. Not me. I turn around, lean my back against the rail, and begin to people watch. "Where did you learn to fish?"

"You are the queen of subject changes."

I smile. "It's an art I mastered when I turned sixteen." Not that I'd ever been much for rebellion. I'm more like a divided section of clay being molded by two overbearing parents. Nathan is the one thing they both agree on.

Jacob spins the reel and sets the pole against the rail. "My father taught me to fish when I was a kid. We used to come out here all the time." There's an edge to his tone that implies those days are long gone.

"Do you like your dad?" I ask. He freezes. A heartbeat passes, and then he goes about setting up our second rod. "I mean, you said he gave you time off for your brother, so I assume you work for him. Right?"

"Yeah, I work for him." He pauses and I can't tell if that's good or bad thing. "My father tries, but father-son relationships are complicated."

So are father-daughter relationships.

"What about your dad and brother? Do they get along? Or is his 'lack of direction' a problem for your dad as well?"

He doesn't answer. His mouth is tight, his shoulders rock hard as he sets the second pole in place.

I should take the hint, but something in me wants to intrude. His strained relationship with his father and brother, I get. I understand him more than he knows.

"Let me meet Aaron. Today. Right now."

Our eyes lock. "Why?"

"Because I want to." Because if I can understand how his brother escaped family expectations, then maybe I can learn how to break free from mine.

Jacob hesitates.

The red pole bobs behind his back. "Tell you what," I say. "If the blue pole catches the first fish, we'll go do something else and avoid family talk. If the red pole does, I get to meet your brother."

"I don't bet."

Ugh. He is exasperatingly stubborn. I grab his arms and shake him. "Can you just once do something without thinking?"

Jacob's eyes go soft and suddenly he looks different. Taller, stronger, sexier. His mouth curves slightly and I'm too aware of how full they are.

I drop my hands. "I get it. You're scared."

He flinches. "I am not scared."

The red pole moves again. "Then let me have my fun. One bet. It won't kill you." I top off my plea with sad puppy eyes.

He caves. "Fine. Red, my brother; blue, my choice."

I smile like a woman holding a twenty-one hand in blackjack. "Yay!"

He shakes his head, but I see that he's fighting a grin. Whether he admits it or not, Jacob likes when I push him.

"Um, Jacob?"

"Yeah?"

I point behind him. "We caught a fish."

He spins around and stares at the rod sliding against the rail.

My hand grazes his back, partly in victory and partly because I just want to touch him again. "I can't wait to meet your brother."

Chapter Five

*I*T ONLY TAKES us six minutes to walk to Jacob's house from mine. I insisted on a shower before our little meet and greet. His place is two blocks off the beach, but practically cattycornered to Richard's.

"This is yours?" I ask when he stops at the two story blue house with sea green shutters.

"My dad's."

He doesn't give me more, nor have I been able to pull another smile from his troubled face. It seems the closer we get to his house, the more withdrawn and burdened he becomes.

"Aaron has an apartment over the garage. He's the only one who stays here year-round." He takes the stairs two at a time and bangs on the door. I feel intrusive following him, so I wait. "You coming? This was your brilliant idea."

Obviously waiting is the wrong decision. I slam my foot on each step. "You don't have to be such a sore loser."

"You cheated."

"No, I was simply more aware of my surroundings than you were."

He shoots me a "you're-full-of-it" glare and hammers on the door again. It cracks open right as I hit the top step.

Aaron shields his eyes from the late afternoon sun and stares at his brother. He runs a hand through sandy blond hair that falls like a mane to his shoulders. "What'd I do now?"

It's then I realize that my mother was hallucinating. Apart from having the same straight nose and wide, sharp jawline, the two brothers don't look anything alike. Jacob's hair is practically black and cut close on the sides and in the back. He's also shorter than his brother, but carries himself like a Fortune 500 CEO.

Jacob studies Aaron's bed head and wrinkled clothes. He's planning to say something rude, I'm sure, but I pinch him. I don't want them arguing while I'm here.

"Ouch." Jacob rubs his arm.

Aaron whips his gaze to me. A smile moves in across his face and lines crinkle. His arm lifts, and he shifts so his forearm is leaning on my side of the door frame. "Wedding girl." He says the name as if I'm a birthday present.

"Sydney."

His gaze dips to the front of my sundress. Then it seems to dawn on him that I'm standing next to his brother. "Wait, why are you with him?"

"I really don't know." I duck under the space Aaron leaves in the doorway, which isn't difficult considering he's a giant, and step into a living room that hasn't seen a vacuum in easily two years.

"Whoa." Aaron stumbles, looks around. "It's not exactly company ready."

"It's not exactly human ready," Jacob mumbles under his breath.

We both ignore him.

Shirts line the couch, each bursting with color and flowers, while shoes, video games and a few towels litter the carpet. A cut out in the wall reveals a small kitchen, which is surprisingly spotless. Not a dish. Either Aaron doesn't eat or Jacob snuck in there and cleaned. I'm guessing the latter.

I spin back to the two men, ignoring the mess and pull out the smile I use on kids. "Jacob says you can show me all the local secrets. Best food, best dancing, greatest beaches."

A hint of pride lights Aaron's face while Jacob stares at me like I've betrayed him somehow. Maybe he thought I'd take one look at Aaron's life and hop over to team Better Judgment. If so, the guy hasn't got a clue.

"I know exactly the place. Two seconds," Aaron says, clapping his hands then rubbing them together. He grabs a shirt with splashes of blue, green and yellow off the recliner and darts to the back of the apartment.

Jacob rubs his hands over his face. "Why are we here, again?"

I spot a Nerf gun on the ground and squat to pick it up. The chamber is loaded with at least twenty neon disks, and I pop him twice. Once in the chest, the other on the side of his neck.

He jumps, rubs at the red streak I left. "What was that for?"

"Stop huffing and puffing, and looking at your brother like he's the red-headed step child."

Jacob clenches his jaw, sweeps his arm out. "Do you not see this place?"

"Do you live here with him?"

"Absolutely not."

"Then get over it. It's his house, not yours."

"But—"

I pop him again, a lower target this time.

"Stop." He crosses his legs, takes a step forward like he's going to grab my weapon.

Not a chance. I run to the front of the couch, tripping over two pairs of shoes and take aim right at his face. "Don't make me do it," I warn.

A door slams and Aaron walks in and blows a piece of hair out of his face. He smells like Irish Spring soap and too much cologne, yet something about his easy gait and his bright blue eyes is captivating. Not in an I-want-to-jump-you way, but in a you're-the-coolest-guy-I-know kind of way.

"So how'd you meet my baby bro?" He grabs his keys, tossing them in the air before catching them again.

My mouth drops, my fist landing at my hip. I stare at Jacob. "You're younger than him?"

Aaron laugh is rich and full. "Two years. Sasquatch just hit twenty-one a few months ago. Not that it made a bit of difference."

Three disks fly from my gun and hit Jacob on the side of his head.

He tries to slap at the disks while Aaron howls.

"Seriously, what's your deal? I didn't even say a word this time!" Jacob demands.

"My deal? The other night you made me feel like a teeny-bopper while you smugly sat there barely legal yourself."

"You were dressed like a reject from Solomon's harem. What was I supposed to think?"

I crack a smile. "That was actually funny." I blow on the tip of my gun and start to lower it when I notice Aaron gawking at my chest again. I pop him next, and he blanches. "That's for staring at my breasts. Twice."

He scrunches his face, rubs at the spot on his head. "Dang, just paying you a compliment."

"Get a clue, Fabio. Girls like more creative *compliments*."

A sound behind me has Aaron staring ahead, disbelief etched on his face.

Jacob is laughing. Doubled over, gasping for air laughing. I'd seen him smile, even heard a little chuckle from him, but the depth of his explosive rumble slams against my chest. It reminds me why I left Nathan and school and the future I didn't want. Why I may never go back. It reminds me that life is meant to be lived, and I decide it's the sweetest sound I've ever heard.

Chapter Six

THE RESTAURANT AARON takes us to is small and under lit, but charming in a seaside meets southern rustic way. Old time country music streams from hidden speakers, but the sound is mostly masked by the chatter filling the crowded dining room. Anchors and ships decorate the walls along with certificates for serving the "best" hush-puppies in 2004 and 2006. I'm thinking a sign that old should worry customers, but hey, to each his own.

Jacob and I slide into a thick hardwood booth etched to resemble driftwood. Aaron hangs by the bar, chatting with people and the bartender. It's obvious he's a regular here. Jacob, on the other hand, wipes off the table with his a napkin and then pulls a small bottle of hand sanitizer from his pocket.

"Don't eat any fish here. You'll be puking for days." He looks around, scrunches his nose.

"You saying that from experience or initial judgment?"

"Unfortunately, experience. Only the local crowd can keep it down." He picks up the greasy menu with two fingers and glances at it for only two seconds. "Finnian's is known for its happy hour and karaoke. Not the food."

I stifle a laugh and seek out Aaron again. A tall blond has joined him at the bar and watches him like rich chocolate at a Weight Watcher's convention. His quick side hug and continuation of his conversation says she's either in the "friend zone," or they've been in a relationship for too long. I hated when Nathan would dismiss me like that.

"That's Trish," Jacob says, watching me watch her. "We've know her since we were kids. Her grandpa is Finnian." He points at the menu, so I realize the connection.

"Are they dating?" I almost hope not. Aaron and my similarities are becoming eerie.

"No."

"Then she has a crush on your brother." I turn away from the couple.

"What?" He shoots a glance back in their direction. "Nah. Trish has a line of guys she refuses to date."

"Ever wonder why?"

"Huh?" He shrugs and makes a show of looking around the saloon-like restaurant. "This place never changes. Dad took us here the first time when I was five. We'd just bought the summer home, and Mom was in whirlwind decorating mode."

It's the second time Jacob mentions his mom, and both times he did so with reverence. They're close. The difference his voice takes when he mentions his dad has me itching to ask questions.

A round of drinks being slammed on the table pulls me from my musing.

"All Jacob-approved choices," Aaron says.

I glance up at his wide, chestier grin and reach for the glass with water. The other two look like tea and some kind of dark soda.

Trish steps up next to Aaron and gives us both a warm, heartfelt smile. "Jacob! It's been ages. When did you get back in town?"

Jacob slides out of the booth and envelopes her in a bear hug. They are close to the same height, but look like yin and yang in their embrace, his dark hair and skin magnifying her paleness.

Aaron watches without a word, but seems oddly satisfied by Jacob's show of affection. I don't know how I feel. Part of me wants to trade places with her. The other part scolds me for even considering it. I'm supposed to be emptying my life right now, not filling it with deep blue eyes that like to reach into my soul.

Jacob releases her and turns. "This is Sydney. She's here for the summer."

Trish reaches out a hand and shakes mine heartily. "So nice to meet ya!" Her southern drawl surprises me. It's thicker than most of the locals I've talked to. "Where're ya from?"

Jacob's eyebrows pitch. He's waiting. It's the same question I refused to answer earlier. Because I hate the answer—I have no home. My mom and I left Washington State when I was in grade school, and for a long time I called it home. But when my friends all left for college, I realized home was them and not a place.

I shrug off the loneliness. "My mom now lives in Charleston, my dad, in Washington. I've been at Virginia Tech the last two years."

Jacob lights up with interest. "Really? That's a great school. What's your major?"

I hate Jacob's eagerness. I don't want to talk about school.

Aaron eyes my reaction and howls with laugher. He scooches me over so he can share the bench and teases Jacob. "No wonder you're still single with pick-up lines like that."

"It wasn't a pick-up line. I'm curious. Some of us care about our future."

I narrow my eyes, sending telepathic darts. "Not me. I'm technically still undecided." A formality if my dad has his say. He's a fourth generation lawyer, and I'm his only kid. The math is easy on that one.

Aaron wraps an arm around my shoulder, pulls me next to his bright, Hawaiian shirt and squeezes. "Will you marry me?" His eyes stare longingly into mine, but the left side of his mouth twitches up.

"Not with that cologne." I push him away.

Laughter erupts around me to include Trish's girly giggle that is surprisingly not annoying.

"Sit with us," I say, pointing toward Jacob's side of the table.

"Really? Okay, great." She sits and grabs one the two unclaimed glasses left on the table.

Aaron makes an exaggerated show of his exhaustion for having to get up and get another drink, but Trish doesn't even flinch. She takes an extra long sip and sighs like it's water in the desert.

"Sydney, what brings you to Garden City?" she asks.

"My mom's wedding was a couple days ago. That's actually where I met this charmer," I eye Jacob, sarcasm lacing my voice.

"Do you really want to rehash that circus?" His expression warns that he will gladly share my humiliating attempt to pick him up that night.

I suck in a deep breath. Jerk. "No."

He winks at me. Actually has the nerve to wink. And worse, it makes tingles dance along the edge of my skin like his stare contains electrical energy. I mentally make a list of his flaws, but the number gets shorter every moment we spend together.

The table shifts and Aaron rejoins us, a frothy beer in hand. He starts in on a long diatribe about some guy who caught an insanely large tarpon. Not that I know the normal size of a tarpon or even what it looks like. Trish, though, seems completely fascinated, hanging on every animated word.

I peek at Jacob. He's watching me. Not even subtly, but a full on, invasive stare that has me wishing my skin was made of steel. His uncanny ability to sense when I'm upset and see past my sarcasm and humor, makes me twitch. My knee bounces and shakes the table. I stop and turn back to Trish, wishing Jacob would find something else to focus on.

"Jacob says you grew up here. That's kind of cool." I pray the sweat on the back of my neck isn't visible.

"Not really. I mean, it's cool to the tourists, but I've never been out of South Carolina. That's just wrong on so many levels." Her smile falters, but mine grows.

It's funny how two people can look at life so differently. I would have loved to grow up in the same small town, sit in a restaurant with friends I'd known since I was five, never have to wonder what to say when people ask about my past or my future. When you grow up floating from place to place, life always kind of feels like an ocean.

"Where would you go?" Aaron's quiet voice makes me wonder if what she said bothered him.

Her eyes dance with excitement, the kind that only comes when someone is about to share their dreams. "Greece and Ireland and Morocco and—"

Jacob's burst of laughter cuts her off. "Sydney knows all about beaded belly dancing outfits," he says between sucks of air. "Show her a picture."

My cheeks burn because I hate that was his first impression of me, and I attempt to kick him under the table. But Finnian's slab of wood is not nearly as stable as it looks. My knee catches the edge and before I can grab the tittering glass, it circles and falls over. Right into my lap.

I bolt to my feet and the other three jerk forward and save their own drinks from the same fate. I'm mortified, seething and ready to dump Aaron's smelly draft beer over Jacob's head.

Trish attempts to look sympathetic, but her eyes are watering with repressed laughter. "Come with me. I'll get you cleaned up."

"You," I say and point to a laughing Jacob.

"What did I do? You kicked the table."

"You made me," I yell.

Aaron moves out so I can pass by but he gives me no help. "Sorry, Sydney," he says with eyes so full of humor I want to poke them. "Party foul is all on you."

I glare between the two men and follow Trish to the bathroom. That's it. The Massey brothers are going down.

Chapter Seven

THE LADIES BATHROOM in Finnian's smells like bleach and lingering perfume.

"Here." Trish offers me a fluffy, dry towel she'd grabbed from the kitchen. "I still can't believe he teased you like that. Jacob's always so solemn and controlled lately."

I stare at the bathroom mirror and wipe at my clothes. "I must bring out the worst in him, then."

"Or maybe the best." She leans her rear against the sink and studies me as I dry off. "It'd be great if Aaron and Jacob could make up. They used to be so close. I mean like super, super close."

I turn from the mirror to face her. "What happened?"

She offers a slow shrug. "No one knows. One day, it's Aaron and Jacob in here. The next, it's just Aaron. And he's not the same." There's sadness and resignation in her tone, like she's given up on Aaron ever going back to who he was.

I take the opportunity to fish. "You like him, huh?"

Her pale cheeks start to match the strawberry shade of highlights in her hair. "Me? No. We're just friends. Always have been." She stands straight and picks at imaginary lint on her t-shirt.

"Ever try being more?"

She leans back against the sink. "A couple years ago, I thought…maybe. He'd hinted, you know. Like would make comments about us being soul mates and get mad when other guys came around. But when Jacob quit showing up, I don't know. Aaron just stopped…everything."

"Ever ask him why?" I set down the towel, satisfied I'd wiped away all the water. Conversations like these, I'm comfortable with. Solving other people's problems gives me time to ignore mine.

"Aaron isn't one to share."

The pained look on her face tells me she wishes he was. But I can't really blame him. Sharing requires trust and some of us have had it broken too many times not to be jaded.

She gives a weak smile. "You ready?"

"Sure. I just have to plot my revenge before we make it back to the table."

She laughs and holds the bathroom door open until I walk through. "Just go easy on him. Jacob's a lot softer than he seems."

My heart pinches because I know she's right. I've seen the way he hurts for Aaron. Brothers should be close. I'd do anything for my "sisters," and here the guys are letting each other slip away.

I TIME MY revenge perfectly. The last two hours have been full of jokes and laughter. A few snide comments here and there from the brothers, but relatively hostility free.

Jacob now sits relaxed, an easy grin filling his face as another local butchers a Mariah Carey song on the Karaoke machine.

I push Aaron over and slide out of the booth.

"Where ya goin'?" Aaron asks.

I point to the small stage in the corner and raise my eyebrows. "Where do you think?"

Jacob sits straight, loses the grin. "Oh, please, say you're not."

"Just wait, Jacob. I have quite a treat in store for you."

The crowd halfheartedly claps as the woman finishes her song and steps off the stage. I take her place, getting cheers and curious glances.

The microphone vibrates with an energy I love. "Hi everyone. I'm Sydney, and I have something special for you tonight."

More cheers and laughter fill the air.

"But I'm going to need your help. You all know the Massey brothers over there." I stretch out my hand and point to where the boys are sitting. Trish covers her mouth with a hand.

The room explodes into applause.

"Does anyone want to hear them sing? Can you help me get them up here?"

The resulting thunderous boom has me laughing. I'd expected a reaction from the crowd, but nothing like the uproar that's occurring.

Aaron stands and bows to the crowd. I see Jacob mouthing "no way," while adamantly shaking his head. It's no use. Trish is tugging his arm, and soon he's standing next to Aaron, creating an even bigger frenzy.

Ignoring his brother's resistance, Aaron pushes him forward. I laugh and cheer too. The energy has soared well past the microphone. It's a life of its own, springing off the walls as the boys walk forward.

Jacob steps on stage and pulls the mic from my hands. Covering it with his other one, he leans in, his voice grim. "You shouldn't have done this."

I pull away, surprised by the anger in his words. It's just a song. A joke among friends. But maybe I went too far. My legs tremble when I step down and return to my seat.

Trish greets me with an eager smile and delight in her eyes. "How did ya know?"

"Know what?"

"That Aaron and Jacob used to sing together all the time."

The guy controlling the machine must have remembered because soon "Fire and Rain" by James Taylor is pumping from the speakers. The crowd goes silent, but my heart pounds like hummingbird wings. It wasn't anger in Jacob's tone. It was fear.

Aaron's rich voice fills the air, the first verse sung with a tone and clarity most musicians would kill for. It's soft and smooth and lays on your skin like a down comforter.

Jacob sings the second verse. Though not as good as Aaron's, his voice has a grit that pulls the heart and soul from a song.

I watch him, mesmerized and find my palms sweating.

Then, they harmonize and the world stops. The melding of their voices is so unique, so perfect, that's it's like they were created just to make that sound.

"Wow," I whisper.

Trish looks at me and then back to the brothers. "You should hear them sing it when Aaron plays the guitar. It's magic."

"Aaron plays?"

Her smile dies. "Not anymore."

They finish the song, and we stand with the rest of the room, whistling and clapping. My chest and throat burn. How could they hide such a beautiful gift?

Aaron pulls his younger brother in for a hug. They hold the embrace, and I see the hint of tears glistening in Jacob's eyes.

Trish is unashamedly crying next to me and clapping. The boys wave and leave the stage and head toward us.

I don't know what to do or say. So I watch. Every step, every muscle, as Jacob comes toward me. I become hyperaware that he's studying me too. People slap his back or speak as he walks, but nothing pulls his gaze from mine. This man is dangerous. This man is intense and determined and making my pulse jump with every breath he exhales.

He stops barely a foot from me. The fine hairs on my arm stand and goose bumps cover every inch of my flesh. My eyes drop to his lips, and I know it's pointless denying the attraction any longer. It's not because I'm running from life or because I need a distraction. It's something about *him*.

His hands go to my waist, but instead of tugging, he comes to me and leans in. "Now I owe you one."

The heat on my neck has my breath hitching, my voice coming out a squeak. "We're even."

He pulls back, but never blinks. "We're not even close."

The promise in his voice lingers far longer than his touch. It lingers through another hour of laugher and jokes. It lingers every time our eyes catch across the table. It lingers when I shut the door of Richard's house and take my first real breath since Jacob sang into the microphone.

Chapter Eight

*J*ACOB DOESN'T COME by the next day or the day after. By day three of silence, I muster enough confidence to knock on his door. When he doesn't answer, I push the doorbell twice figuring it won't take much to rattle him.

Two cars pass while I'm standing there. One has the bass pumping out of open back windows, and the steady rhythm matches the beat of my pulse against my wrist.

The door moves, finally, and Jacob's sour face replaces it. But even with the scowl, I smile because I missed him. It's a strange sensation, especially after months of people forcing themselves into my life and my future. Jacob just kind of appeared and somehow when he's around, things are better. I don't bother with why. For now, I just want to enjoy.

An invitation to come in is apparently not happening, so I slide past him into the house. "You know it's wrong to take a girl to karaoke and never come by again."

The door clicks shut and footsteps behind me land against the wood floors. They get closer until Jacob is in my line of sight, brown eyes on narrowed blue. "I'm still trying to get over how much upheaval you can cause in twenty-four hours." He doesn't move, doesn't smile. He's still mad.

I pull away from his heated gaze and step around him. There's a banister only a foot away, and I reach out to grip the wood, to have something to hold on to as I try to repair what's broken.

I clear my throat. "How's it been? Between you and Aaron?" It's a good place to start since Aaron has been the center of our friendship since the beginning. But I really just want to know how he is. If the sadness from the beach is starting to fade.

He walks away. "It's different than it was."

I follow him into a living room with plush cream couches covered with warm blue and green pillows. It's the kind of room I'd expect to find in Southern Living, where the perfect family smiles and holds a miniature Yorkie. "That's a good thing, right?"

He sinks into the sofa. Fifty pounds of worry weighs on his shoulders. "Not everything is simple. Not every problem can be solved by a night out or even a walk down memory lane. Open wounds fester, Sydney, no matter how many smiles you pour over them."

His words feel like a two-sided spear, targeting not only Aaron, but me as well. But I'm not here to deal with my wounds. I scowl. "So, you're still fighting?" I'd had visions of him and Aaron bonding the last couple days. But it seems I'm not the only one he's freezing out.

"No, just the opposite. We're being polite. Cordial. Friendly. Dinner together, but we talk about nothing important." He says each word like its poison. "Just like we did the first year after Mom died. At least before, when we were arguing, there was some truth in our words. Now it's all just fake." He levels his stare at me again. "We've gone backwards, Sydney, not forward."

I take the space next to him on the couch. "I'm sorry." I didn't know his mom had passed away. "How long ago did she die?"

"Two years." He sets his head in his hands. "I did what you said. I went to him. Tried to understand his world. But that's the thing. It's not his world that bothers me. It's him. It's how he's stalled and doesn't seem to be able to move at all."

My heart stills and part of me wants to shake him. But I don't because how do you explain fear to a person who freely runs toward the future? You can't. Like Nathan. Like my father. Even my mother, in her own way, plans for the next marriage just in case the one she's in fails.

I stare at his agony. I hadn't meant to hurt him. I just wanted to help him see his brother through different eyes. "I didn't realize that you and Aaron singing together would cause such turmoil. It was just a fun joke at the time. A way to push your buttons a little. It's what I do sometimes to lighten a mood."

He stares at a spot on the carpet. "It's fine. You didn't know our history."

"All the same. I'm sorry."

He lifts his head and smile seeps through his darkness. "You're forgiven."

My cheeks suddenly feel warm. Not from his words so much as the way he stares at me. The way his gaze follows a trail from my forehead to my lips and back up again.

I clear my throat. "I think you need some fresh air, and some fun. Come surfing with me. It's beautiful outside, and I have a private lesson for us with the surf shop."

His eyes look amused, unsettled, interested and confused all at once.

"Come on." I push his arm and stand. "If I go alone, I'll be vulnerable to a shirtless surfer dude whose nickname is Junkhead."

"Junkhead? Not Sharkbait or Hammerhead food?"

"I know. Shocking, isn't it?" His shoulders have eased, his tone softer. A chill dances down my spine. "I mean, come on. What else is there to do but sit here and brood?"

He stares up at me like we're playing a game he's losing. "All right, Sydney, you win. Surfing it is."

⌢⌣

WATER RUSHES INTO my mouth, choking me. I've swallowed enough salt to raise my blood pressure at least a hundred points.

"That was better," Jacob yells from the shore. He's standing next to our surf instructor getting another pat on the back for how quickly he could steady his body on an over-waxed board.

They shake hands and "Junkhead" walks away. We already exceed-ed our time by twenty minutes, but the instructor stayed, claiming to never have a student fail. I guess he recognizes a lost cause.

I have yet to conquer the surfboard. But why am I surprised? I can't balance my life. Why in the world did I think I could balance my body on a board in the Atlantic Ocean?

I trudge toward the beach, hauling the rented devil plank behind me. Jacob eases it from my hands before I leave the water, and I collapse on the sand. Arms, legs, abs, muscles that have no names burn and ache. I'll be lucky to walk tomorrow.

"Worst idea ever." I collapse on the sand, and close my eyes.

"Ah, come on. It was fun," he says, dropping next to me.

"For you, maybe." I change my voice to match our instructor's. "'Jacob, dude, you're a natural. Dude, you should like compete or something. Dude, your girl needs some serious mojo, man.'"

Jacob laughs and the heat of his presence warms me even though I can't see him. Our legs are close, almost touching, and it bothers me that I want to shift right a few inches and close the gap. It bothers me even more that I didn't correct Junkhead when he assumed I was Jacob's girlfriend.

"You really weren't that bad," Jacob says, but we both know he's wrong.

"I don't want to think about it any more. I just want to lie here and not move for the next ten years. Maybe I'll turn into a jellyfish and sting him next time he has lessons." The idea wasn't far-fetched. My limbs were the equivalent of Gumby on a blistering hot day.

"Sydney, can I ask you a question?"

"Sure."

"Why are you here?"

"Because I paid good money for this torture." I turn so the sun is at my back and can see Jacob's face without squinting.

His hand settles on my arm. It's light and rough from the sand. I want the warmth of his touch to stay, but I also want it to go far, far away. "No, I mean, why are you still here? In Garden City. Why aren't you with friends or family?"

I stare at the man who's trying to pry into my life. His hardened features are softer with the setting sun on them. The look in his eyes is equally soft as if he knows I'm hiding and doesn't want to spook me. For a fraction of second, I consider telling him why I'm here. That I'm running from a future I don't want, and I'm too afraid to tell my parents. But the idea washes away with the latest wave back to the ocean. He'd never understand.

"My friends are all scattered this summer. Washington, Arkansas, L.A. My family, well, enough said there. You've met my mom."

"Do your friends go to Virginia Tech too?"

"No. They're childhood friends. Back when I lived out West." I stand, ready to be done with this conversation. We're heading down a path that will lead straight to Nathan, and he's the last person I want to talk about, especially with Jacob.

"You don't like to talk about your friends?" Jacob watches me with interest.

"No, it's just that talking about them makes me sad. It's the first summer we've spent apart."

"How come?"

I wrinkle my forehead. "Not really in the mood to be sad right now. Especially after my epic fail on the surfboard."

He stands and brushes off the sand sticking to his orange swim trunks. "Okay, fine. How about ice cream? Can we talk about ice cream?"

"I like ice cream," I say immediately. He's catching on. Learning when tension is too high and when to back down. I wonder if he's doing the same with Aaron and if their new politeness might just morph to friendship after all.

I turn to walk toward my car, but he takes my hand and pulls. His palm feels warm, strong and terrifyingly wonderful.

We're facing one another and the tension coils tighter than it was. How is it he can ask a million questions with just one look?

Who are you? I don't know. *Why are you here?* I don't know. *What is happening between us?* I don't know.

"I'm not good at this," he whispers.

"At what?" The words come out a choke because he reads me better than he realizes. And if he says what I've been thinking and feeling for the last few days, then all we have is lost. He'll become one more decision I have to make. One more path that scares the hell out of me.

"This idea of friendship without depth. You and Aaron. You're the same. You want me to be okay with shallow words and a few good laughs. I want more."

"I'm giving you all I'm capable of right now." I let go of his hand, missing it immediately. This shift from friendship to more is too dangerous to continue.

Jacob shoulders fall, and the smile he forces does more to crack my walls than his caring questions. "So, tell me, Sydney, what kind of ice cream does a girl like you eat?"

I walk backward and he follows, listening to me spout ice cream flavors. Each step away from the word, "more" is a pressure release on my chest. Meeting Jacob was a surprise. Spending time with him, a nice distraction. But giving one more person a say in my life?

An absolute deal breaker.

Chapter Nine

THE SUN RISING over the ocean is almost enough to push away my restlessness. It had been two weeks of snorkeling, karaoke, water skiing, sand castle building and bar hopping. All with Jacob and all more fun than I've had in months. He'd stopped pushing. But my dad and Nathan are relentless with the calls and texts. Nathan's are easy to ignore, but freezing out my dad is harder. We've always been close. Bonded by the very thing I want to walk away from—Law.

I stare at my dad's text and wish it away. The fall deadline for late admission to UConn is only ten days away.

> **Dad:** *I expect an answer by Friday or I'm telling your mother about the proposal.*

My father and mother only talk when there's a crisis in my life. I guess he considers this a crisis. My mom will consider it a catastrophe. Turning down a wedding proposal from a wealthy, handsome, ambitious man is up there with world wars and widespread famine.

At least her cell phone service sucks in Bora Bora, so I know I'm safe from her shrilling lecture for a little while longer.

When Mom first told me about her last-minute wedding, I'd been furious. Resented almost every moment of bridal planning. But now, this time alone has been…dare I say, good? Nathan thinks I'm running. My dad thinks I'm rebelling. My friends think I'm brooding. But really, I'm just listening to the silence. Everyone's been so loud, I've forgotten what my own voice sounds like. I'm not willing to turn up the volume again.

The phone is in my hand, heavy, ready, but I don't press the keys. Instead I think of Nathan. Try to remember a time when I loved him. Only no time comes to mind. Because it was never about love. My stomach churns like the crashing waves. I'm just like the mother I swore I'd never be.

Nathan is easy, convenient, and keeps my parents off my back. He has the right pedigree, a bright future, and he loves me...for now, anyway.

I stare at my phone again and wonder how different things would be if I'd just said no the first time my father introduced me to his handsome summer intern who also happened to be going to school out east. But I didn't say no. I said yes. To one, then two, then twenty dates. Now, two years later, they all expect me to say yes again.

The phone vibrates in my hand. I look down, fully expecting to see my father's name. But instead it's a mug shot of Aaron with his tongue sticking out. The Jerk must have taken my phone at dinner the other night.

A shiver runs down my legs. Did he see Nathan's texts? Did Jacob?

The phone buzzes again, and this time I answer, but can't take the shakiness out of my voice. "Aaron?"

"Wedding girl! I'm still waiting on you to marry me!"

The man's insane and sounds slightly intoxicated. "It's six in the morning. Wedding proposals are only allowed after noon."

"But I'm still on yesterday time, so does that count?"

"You've been up all night? What've you been doing?" I prop up my feet, knowing a great story is coming. Bonding with Aaron was easy. Fun. Teasing. No depth. Easy. I like easy.

"Hangin' with my baby bro!"

Heat fills my cheeks at the mention of his name. "Jacob went out with you all night? Did the universe spin completely out of control?"

"Not the universe, but Jacob needs some serious dance lessons." Another laugh fills the phone, and then I hear him try to rouse an apparently passed out Jacob. "Ah man, his stamina is lacking though." His teasing voice is slightly slurred and sleepy, letting me know that Aaron's stamina is fading, too.

"Aaron?"

"Yeah?"

"Why are you calling me?"

He whispers like he's got the juiciest gossip on the coast. "Beach party. Eight o'clock. Bikinis optional."

"Sounds like fun. Is Jacob going?"

"Why do you want to know?"

Because I can't stop thinking about him. "Just wondering. He's cooler than you."

Aaron gasps. "Like you know what cool is. You're practically a Yankee. And you eat peanut butter and bologna sandwiches."

"And you haven't seen your bathroom floor in over two years."

We continue to banter, each insulting the other's bad habits. But soon the casual fades and something in Aaron's voice changes, grows serious.

"Go easy on him. Jacob seems tough, but his heart is soft."

I bite my lip and try to ignore the flutter those words cause in my stomach. "I'm just here for one summer." And I have no idea what my future looks like.

His voice turns solemn, reflective. "One summer can change everything, even the truth of who you are." His breath is steady and then deeper, fuller. The line goes dead.

The waves slam on the beach like they understand my sadness or maybe even my fear. Aaron's words, "The truth of who you are," pierce my heart.

Sweat prickles on my forehead, and I grip the patio table trying to regain my bearing. I'm supposed to be an adult now, but still can't answer that question. I've been whatever I need to be. Whatever suits the environment best. Whatever causes the least amount of pain.

I close my eyes, let the silence push back the panic, hoping with each heartbeat that it will help me find Sydney once again.

GETTING READY FOR a beach party is harder than it seems. You have to find that perfect balance of looking like you don't care and totally hot at the same time. It's a talent my girlfriends have mastered, but a sundress and lip-gloss are the extent of my prepping.

I'm supposed to meet Jacob and Aaron on the beach in five minutes, but I'm nervous. Nervous and excited. And frustrated that I feel both. It seems I want to run away from everyone in my life except the Massey brothers. Go figure.

My phone buzzes. I walk toward it until I can see the words that punch through my skin and scrape along the bone.

Nathan: *I sent in the application.*

He was already forging my future, why am I surprised he's moved on to forging my signature? I grip the device and resist every urge to text him back. He's baiting me. And I'm done being blindly pushed into a rabbit hole. I told him it was over. It's not my fault if he won't listen.

The screen door slams behind me, and I can see the smoke from the party's bonfire several houses down. The music is barely a whisper over the ocean waves, but the mass of human dots lining the beach promises a perfect escape.

The brothers stand side by side with their backs turned. They're watching the ocean together, but don't seem to be talking. I move closer. Jacob's back is rigid through his t-shirt, his neck straining even though it hasn't moved. He's wearing trunks with blue and white fire lapping around his legs, and the same fire wraps around me when I see him. Not good. Not good at all.

Aaron turns and sees me first, a huge smile lighting his habitually jolly face. "There she is!" He picks me up and spins me, sending my dress high enough to showcase my bright yellow swimsuit bottoms.

I struggle out of his grasp, look around, and avoid Jacob's stare. "Where's Trish? I thought she was coming."

"She'll meet us there," Aaron says, draping an arm around my bare shoulder and guiding me back to his brother.

I smile at Jacob, trying for easy, even though his gaze is laser-focused on Aaron's arm. "Hey! So I heard you had quite the night last night. I'm surprised you're awake."

"Yes, I learned two important lessons. Never trust my brother when he says it will just be an hour, and never hand my keys to a woman with a vendetta against her ex." He sends an accusing glare to Aaron, who is obviously "her ex."

I slip my hand over my mouth, forcing Aaron's arm to fall away. "Oh no. Where's your car?"

Jacob's voice is still laced with sarcasm. "Let's see. It wasn't at Revolutions or Froggy Bottomz. It wasn't at the docks or at Ocean Annie's."

"Jacob has terrible perspective. He sees a vengeful scavenger hunt. I see a perfect night of mystery, music and spontaneity."

"Yes, the two-mile walk at 4 A.M. to her cousin's garage was the epitome of a good time. You should call her. Bring her to Thanksgiving. I'm sure Dad would love her."

The air suddenly turns heavy, and now Aaron is as stiff as Jacob.

"Maybe I'll call her," I say. "You knocked off four places I wanted to visit in Myrtle Beach. She sounds like a blast."

"A psychotic blast!" Aaron blurts out. "One lousy date—and it was lousy, six months ago—and she still stakes me out with drive-bys."

I squeeze his cheek. "That's just because you're irresistible."

He wags his eyebrows. "Yes, yes, I am."

I sense Jacob watching us. I feel awkward being next to him today. My palms feel sweaty and my neck, flushed. I blame it on the setting sun. It bounces off Jacob's jaw and makes it look like polished stone. Stone I want to touch.

Aaron takes off running down the beach to tackle two guys in bright green t-shirts with, "That's what she said," on the back. I'm afraid to see what's written on the front.

"What's wrong with you?"

Jacob's question takes me by surprise, but it's his touch that has me frozen to the hot sand. His fingers are grazing mine. Not to hold, just a brief second of contact that shouldn't come with electricity, but does.

"Nothing, why?"

"You won't look at me."

I tilt my head up, ready to show him he's wrong. That I'm easy-going. Carefree. Not at all confused. But his blue eyes are too demanding, his fingertips too searching.

His hand moves to my flushed cheek. "You make it look so easy."

"What?"

He moves closer. "Pretending."

The six inches between us become a zapping circuit of frustration. I step away from his touch. "I'm not pretending anything." Yes, I am. But he's not supposed to know that.

He crosses his arms, his jaw tight. "Yeah? Then who's Nathan?"

I gasp, my heart slamming against my chest as if a bomb just exploded. "He's my…" I have no words because I'm still trying to figure out how Jacob knows. Then it hits me. My phone. My stupid, stupid phone. "He's…none of your business."

"Are you kidding me?" He runs both hands through his hair and then drops his arms. "So you're saying I've misread everything between us? That's there's nothing going on here?"

No, no, no. The voices swarm from all directions. *Your youth won't last forever. Law school is the only future that matters. Marry me.* But Jacob's is the loudest of all. *I want more.*

"Sydney…"

Darn, those eyes. Why do they have to demand so much? "This is what I warned you about, Jacob. You push too hard!"

He stares like I've cut out his heart.

I feel like I'm drowning, and Jacob is holding me under.

I storm away, getting lost in the center of bodies dancing and drinking. I spin around, hoping to find any direction.

But as always, I have no idea where I'm going.

Chapter Ten

THE PARTY IS lame. Too many half-dressed men trying to pick up half-dressed women and neither of them are using enough brain cells to even be picky about it.

Trish never showed up, and when I asked Aaron where she was, I got a brush off answer like, "I'm not her keeper." Whatever. They obviously have issues.

I scan the beach. Jacob sits near the surf. Alone. He's been there an hour, ever since I bolted. My throat tightens. I don't want there to be conflict between us. I'm already in conflict with too many people to add his name to the list.

I drag my feet in his direction and plop down, resigned to fix whatever it was our earlier conversation had broken.

He briefly glances my way and then back to the water that stretches on to infinity.

"I'm sorry," I say.

"No. You were right. Your relationship is none of my business."

I reach out and squeeze his hand. "Still friends?"

He shrugs, but I'll take it.

Jacob's leans back on his elbows and stretches long, muscular legs out in front of himself. "For the record, Aaron was the one nosing around in your phone. Not me."

I mimic his position, kicking off my flip flops in the process. "I figured as much when I saw his contact information suddenly appear." Stupid Aaron. For a man harboring his own demons, he sure was eager to set mine free.

"I guess I didn't figure you for the boyfriend type. You know, living for the moment and all."

"Who says Nathan is my boyfriend?"

Jacob pushes sand with his heel. "Fifty texts and words like 'I love you' tend to give it away."

I sit straight. "He read my texts!" That jerk. Looking at a contact is one thing, but actually reading the message is a serious invasion of privacy. I swivel my head, searching the darkened beach for Aaron. "I'm going to kill him."

Jacob laughs and lies down, arms folded under his head. "One thing to know about my brother. He's obsessive about finding out who people really are. He doesn't trust anyone anymore."

I crisscross my legs, turn so I can watch Jacob instead of the beach. His eyes are closed, his chest rising and falling in slow, easy rhythm. I glance at his lips, full and pressed together, and wonder…

"Wedding girl!" Aaron calls from his sprint toward us. "We're taking the party to my place. Grab your stick in the sand and come on."

I walk toward him, leaving Jacob behind, and glare until he comes to a stop in front of me.

He notices my scowl and glances at his brother. "What did he do?"

Unable to rein in my anger, I smack his arm. Twice. "You hijacked my phone, you stalker."

"Sweetheart, if you leave the thing on the table with the password disabled, it's fair game. You should know better."

I blow air through my nose, understanding for the first time why Jacob wants to kill his brother. "And you should know better than to read people's personal conversations. It's rude."

"So is hanging out with another guy when you have a boyfriend." Aaron's words are harsh, and I step back from him, shocked at his abrupt change in tone.

"I… I don't have a boyfriend. Not anymore." It's the first time I've said the words out loud. First time I've admitted Nathan and I are really over. That I walked away from the future my parents expected.

A slow, calculated smile slides over Aaron's face. "Well, now. That is good to know." He doesn't wait for a response and heads straight to Jacob who's ten feet away from us. He lightly kicks him in the side, and Jacob slaps his leg. They repeat the motion until the boys are wrestling around with sand flying up in all directions.

Aaron gets Jacob into a headlock. "That fancy gym membership can't beat good, ole fashioned hard work. I own you, sucker." His baiting words are strained and just the motivation Jacob needs to break free and knock Aaron to his back.

"You haven't owned me since I hit puberty," Jacob retorts as Aaron scrambles to get up.

I hear laughter and grunting between their bodies smacking against each other, and feel a slight prick of tears behind my eyes.

I watch the two brothers and realize how I've missed being part of a real family. Nathan offered me one on a silver platter. Marry him. Move to Connecticut. Practice law together and have two point four kids and a Golden Retriever. But when I stared at him on one knee, I couldn't say yes to the future he envisioned. And if I loved him, truly loved him, shouldn't "yes" be easy?

❧

JACOB'S HOUSE IS a mass of sweaty bodies, loud music and Margaritas. Aaron convinced Jacob to not only move the party to their place, but to open up the main house. And, to my shock, Jacob is having fun. Genuine fun. The kind that comes with smiles and laughter and good-natured razzing.

I grab a drink from the counter and stand next to Trish. She looks especially pretty tonight, and I wonder if the added make-up and curly hair have something to do with Aaron.

"Hey," I say.

She quickly flicks her eyes away from Aaron, but not fast enough that I don't see. "Hey! Can you believe this? A party in the Massey house. Hasn't happened since their mom passed away."

Wistfulness crosses her face, but she covers it with a smile. "You hear about the scavenger hunt last night?"

I let her change the subject even though I'm dying to ask for more details. I scolded Jacob earlier for nosing in my past. I'm not going to do the same to him.

"I got bits and pieces."

She rolls her eyes. "I told him that girl was crazy. I'd seen her stalk at least two other regulars, but nope. He has to do things his way."

"Seems to be a Massey trait."

She nods vehemently. "Yes, it is."

I hear the door open a few feet from us and look to see who else has come to join the party. A man who could be Jacob's future double steps into the foyer and drops his duffle bag on the floor. He has Jacob's hair color, build and his full mouth. One that is frowning as he takes in the scene.

"Um, Trish. I think we may have a problem." I jerk my head toward door.

Her gasp is the first indication she's seen the man too. "Oh no," she says before he hits the power button on the stereo, and the room goes silent.

Chapter Eleven

I STAND IN front of Jacob's house and listen to the angry voices that carry well past the porch. I didn't want to leave, but Trish pushed me out the door even before Jacob's father started throwing out their guests.

Trish is pacing, chewing nails that hardly exist and shaking her head. "We should have known better. Mr. Massey has only one rule. No people in the main house."

"Why?"

"I think he's afraid to lose what's left of her, you know? She picked out everything. A spilled drink is more than a stain. It's death all over again."

Richard's house is within walking distance, but I haven't made one step in that direction. Something compels me to stay. Maybe it's the same something that keeps Trish pacing.

I think of Jacob's words about fathers and sons and wonder if the relationship is worse than he indicated. "Is Mr. Massey violent?"

Trish shakes her head. "No. He never has been, at least. But everything changed when his wife died. It's like all the cords that held them together just snapped."

A door slams and Aaron is barreling to the stairs of his garage apartment. Trish rushes to him, but he brushes her off. She follows anyway until the two of them disappear behind his apartment door.

My stomach twists and dips, the pressure to run away is stifling. I turn to leave, take three steps and then turn back again. Jacob and his father are still shouting in the main house. I can see the silhouette of Aaron and Trish fighting in front of his small apartment window. They're in chaos, all of them, and I'm standing here like a Peeping Tom.

The front door rattles again and Jacob is now the one to take the stairs two at a time to Aaron's apartment. He bangs on the door.

Aaron flings it open and the two brothers stare at each other like rams ready to attack.

"How could you have turned it down?" Jacob demands.

"Back off. It's none of your business."

"It's the opportunity of a lifetime!"

"It's a tactic, Jacob. Can't you see that? Can't you see what a manipulative liar he is?"

Jacob's voice gets higher. "Dad just wants to help you."

"He wants to own me. Control the kid who constantly embarrasses him. The kid he's forced to claim, but doesn't want to."

"What are you talking about?"

Aaron's trembling, but I can tell he's trying to find some calm. "You and Dad are the same. You want to mold me into some carbon copy of the two of you. But I'm different. And I won't be bought with a job or any other means he tries to use."

Jacob stumbles as if the words rocked him backward. "Yeah? And whose house to do you live in, huh?" His voice is a verbal punch. "You're the worst kind of freeloader. One who's convinced he has some superior life because he's deluded himself into thinking he's independent. You're not." Jacob spins around and rushes down the stairs.

Aaron leans over the rail. "I pay rent, you son-of-a—" Then he's gone, lost behind a slam that could wake the dead.

I'm once again rocked with the need to flee, but I can't pull my eyes from Jacob, who's shaking as he grips the railing. I take a tentative step forward, then two until I'm only a foot away.

"Please leave me alone," he says in a pained whisper. His face is iron hard and his shoulders are tight enough to break a concrete barrier.

When I make no attempt to move, he stalks past me toward a sleek, black sedan.

"It's dark. I need a ride home." The words aren't true, but I'm hoping Jacob's gentlemanly enough to consider it.

He turns, stares at me so long that I break eye contact and look down. There's too much anguish in his gaze, too much repressed anger in the set of his jaw.

"Get in."

When I glance back up, he's already behind the wheel and pulling the driver side door shut. Two breaths later, I pull the handle and lower myself into the leather bucket seat.

He reaches out, turns the XM radio up until I think the electric guitar is actually sitting inside my eardrum and presses the accelerator.

I don't say a word when he shifts down to third and drives right past Richard's street.

IT'S BEEN THIRTY minutes without a word, and I've long since lost any clue as to where we are. Jacob slows the car and turns the wheel. He's turned right five times, and part of me wonders if we've just been driving in one enormous circle.

Another right, but this time it's into a small parking lot next to a ten-story hotel. A pathway and sign that says public beach access #5 catches my attention. I'm quickly diverted from sign reading by two teenagers making out as they lean against a blue SUV.

Jacob doesn't look at me, just keeps gripping his steering wheel. "I need some fresh air. You can stay here if you want."

Since he practically kidnapped me and forced me on this odd quest for self-reflection, I have a suspicion he'd rather I get some fresh air with him. Even if his pride won't allow him to say so.

"I wouldn't mind some air. Where are we, by the way?"

"About a half-mile from your house. We could probably walk the beach and get there." The anger has disappeared from his voice, but the empty heartache is worse.

The path takes us past the sea grass and onto the beach. I slip off my flip flops and hold them in one hand while Jacob waits, watching the water like it can offer him an escape. We start walking, and the waves inch toward our feet. It's high tide and the beach looks lost in darkness.

Jacob's steps are quick and deliberate, and I'm practically jogging to keep up.

"Are we timing this?" I ask between puffs of air. "Because I'm pretty sure you said fresh air, not collapse a lung."

He stops, and I lean over to catch my breath. "I really need to rethink my pizza and chips diet."

I hear something that sounds like a chuckle and look up to see if it's possible Jacob is calming down. He's watching me and there's no smile. But he's not scowling either.

I stand straight, begin a more normal stroll that Jacob mimics.

"Has it always been like that between Aaron and your dad?"

Jacob shoves his hands into his pockets. "They are very different, so it's always been strained, but Aaron's grown hostile ever since my mom died. My father has tried, but all they do now is fight, and I'm constantly trying to make peace." Jacob stops and looks up at the sky. "And failing."

I follow his gaze and see the Big Dipper through a dusting of clouds.

"Have you ever felt like every one around you is keeping something from you? Something you know is monumental, yet you have no idea what it could be?" he asks.

We both look forward at the same time.

"No, not really." With the string of bad marriages, Mom always told me more than I wanted to know.

He rolls his eyes. "That's because you're as bad as they are." He suddenly wraps his hands around my biceps. "I need you to talk to me. I need you to tell me what you're feeling because the way you look at me doesn't match the things you say. I need to feel like at least one of the relationships in my life is real or I'm going to explode."

I stare at his pleading eyes, and the words tumble out. "Nathan asked me to marry him."

Jacob is as surprised by my confession as I am. He drops his hands. "What did you say?"

"I said 'no.' " I press my fingers to my forehead and run my hands down the side of my face. "Fast forward a month, and I'm here playing dutiful maid of honor for the third time. Meeting you and Aaron. Caring about the two of you. They're feelings I never anticipated having."

Jacob's hands are back in his pockets, and we're walking again. For as much as he wanted to know my secret, it only seems to create a deeper chasm between us.

The question I feel pulsing through his body comes two minutes after I'm sure Jacob has analyzed it ten different ways. "Do you love him?"

"Not enough to marry him. After two years, that should tell me something." I play with a lock of hair, embarrassed to say the next words out loud. "I promised myself I'd never be with a guy for convenience. That I'd be single before I settled for less than someone I could be with forever. Look at me now. The only difference between my mother and me is a divorce lawyer."

"And a few shots of Botox."

I laugh even though I should feel some inkling to defend my mother. But the laughter is nice and so is Jacob's smile.

"This is you," he says, and I realize we're behind Richard's house.

I want to say more to Jacob, but nothing sounds right in my head. He's looking at me, and his gaze feels deeper than my skin. It glides down my face as if caressing each square inch. Sweat forms on my palms and I rub them against my thighs, trying to convince myself I'm not nervous.

His fingers graze my shoulders and then slide to my back, pulling me closer. The pressure is the right mixture of strength and gentleness. I don't resist and let both his arms encircle me in a hug that feels more intimate than friendly.

My nose presses against the space between his neck and chest. I turn my head to the side, afraid I'll kiss the bump of his collar bone. Focusing on my hands is no better. His back is a layer of heat and muscle. Shivers slide though my body. We've been touching for five seconds, and I feel certain Jacob's grip keeps getting tighter.

"Thank you," he whispers into the folds of my hair. "For trusting me. For making this summer not a complete disaster."

I pull back enough to break his hold and catch my breath. Jacob gives me that glorious smile. The sexy one where one side of his mouth lifts higher than the other.

His hands slide away, but one finds mine. His thumb makes a circle across the top. "I guess you're not nearly as tough to crack as I thought."

With my free arm I lightly punch his shoulder, unwilling to lose his touch. The action seems to pull me closer. "That's just because I felt sorry for you."

For a second, I wonder how it would feel if he pulled me in again. If instead of a hug, his lips could caress as carefully as his thumb.

He must read my thoughts because his smile widens. "Good to know. I'll have to use that next time."

I let go and study my hands, feeling lost by how much I want there to be a next time with Jacob. I'm supposed to find my voice this summer. Not get caught up in another romance with spreadsheets and schools I don't want to go to.

His brow furrows like I'm confusing him. "Sydney, what is going on with you? We've been hanging out for weeks and something's there. I feel it. I know you do, too."

I point to the house. It's empty and holds nothing I want to return to. "I have to go."

Jacob shoves his hand through his hair, and I know I've upset him. "Yeah, I guess you do." And with that, he starts back down the beach with his head lowered.

Chapter Twelve

THAT NIGHT I can't sleep. I blame the voices in my head that are an octave higher than usual. The space and time were supposed to make them go away, but lately they're getting louder, demanding decisions I'm too afraid to make.

Even the morning sun shimmering off the ocean doesn't calm me. I glance at the phone. It's 4:30 on the West Coast, but part of me doesn't care. Dad has no problem waking me up when he wants to talk.

The phone rings twice before his sleepy voice answers. "Sydney? You okay?"

"Yeah, Dad. I'm fine. Just finally returning your call."

I hear the rustling of sheets and his morning yawn. "You mean my twenty calls?"

"Yeah. Sorry about that. I've been thinking." I slide into my favorite chair—the wicker one with two fluffy cushions—and pull my knees to my chest.

"About school or about Nathan?"

"About everything." I groan, wishing I could just say, "Dad, I don't want to be a lawyer," instead I ask him, "Why didn't you ever remarry? I mean, you and Mom have been divorced for thirteen years now."

There's a long pause followed by a sigh. "Sweetie, your mom and I got divorced for very specific reasons. One of them being that I work too much. And since that's not going to change, I figure it's best to keep my life simple."

"But aren't you lonely?"

He laughs lightly. "I have girlfriends, Syd. And there's you. That's always been enough."

My chest constricts. From the time I could speak, we had a plan. Law school. Even in junior high, I'd go to his office with him and pretend my chapter books were depositions. He'd play like I was his clerk and let me file and organize old papers. "But what if I'm not there like we planned?"

"Oh, hon, don't let the distance worry you. UConn is a great school, and you'll only be there for a few years. Before you know it, you and Nathan will move back here and join the practice. Then I'll retire and spend all my time spoiling my grandkids." His voice is nostalgic like he's picturing little boys with lollipop faces and bright smiles.

"That's a pretty great dream, Dad." I just wish it were mine, too.

"You sure you're okay? You sound upset."

"I'm good. Sorry I woke you up."

"Nah. I needed to workout this morning anyway. Keep all those girlfriends happy."

I gag. "TMI."

He laughs and tells me he loves me. I say goodbye, having chickened out again. I lower my head to my hands and wish for the fiftieth time that I was braver.

A pounding on my front door startles me. "Sydney, open up." The voice is muffled, but I have my suspicions. "Sydney!"

"I'm coming. Quiet down." One deadbolt, two, and I swing the door open. "What's the emergency?"

Jacob doesn't hesitate. He lifts the large cardboard box he has balancing on his leg and pushes past me. "Aaron finally told me."

"Told you what?" I shut the door and examine my uninvited guest. His hair is sticking up in two places, and he's jittery like he's on his fourth cup of espresso. He's also in gym shorts and a t-shirt, which I've never seen on him before.

His arms flex under the snug shirt, and he drops the box in the center of Richard's living room, right on my mother's furry, heart-shaped rug. "Aaron's not my dad's kid. That's why he's been so distant since my mom died."

My mouth drops open, and it takes me a second to process his words. "When did he tell you this?"

"After Dad left, we got into another fight. I just kept pushing and pushing, until he finally told me to the truth. Mom had an affair a year after my parents were married. The night she died, she asked to speak to Aaron alone. That's when she told him."

"Did your dad know?"

"Yeah. They had a paternity test done after Aaron was born."

Grief curls in my stomach. I know all too well what it feels like to have a piece of paper unravel a family. Mine came with two signatures and a division of assets, but the rip is still deep and painful.

"Did she tell him who his father is?"

Jacob laces his hands on his head and looks at the ceiling. "She tried the night she died, but he wouldn't let her. He doesn't want to know."

I step closer to Jacob. "Why?"

"Because he's a stubborn idiot. He refuses to listen to reason. Refuses to move forward and deal with the situation. He'd rather just forget all he knows and act like everything is just fine. He hasn't even told my dad he knows."

His frustrated growl sets my muscles on edge. His words hit too close to my own struggles, and I find myself feeling defensive. "And you wonder why he didn't want to tell you."

Jacob meets my stare and doesn't blink. "He's being a coward."

I turn away because the words seem directed at me, even though I know he's talking about Aaron. "And you're being pushy. It's *his* business, not yours." I say it with more anger than I intend.

Jacob throws up his arms and lets them land again. "You know, I am so sick of that excuse. It *is* my business because *I'm* being affected."

He steps into my line of sight, so I have to look at him. "You and Aaron don't live in a bubble. Yes, you make your own decisions, but they matter to people. They affect lives and you can't just act like we all need to sit around and let you destroy relationships because you're too afraid to act."

I want to disappear. "This isn't about me," I finally force out, even while images of my parents bombard my mind. I'm not a coward. I'll tell them. I will. I'm just not ready yet.

Jacob exhales and rubs the top of his head. "I wish I could believe you. But you say the same words he does, and it makes me crazy."

I open my mouth to respond, but his lifted hand shuts me up. He's not here to argue. Jacob walks back to his box and pulls open the flaps. "I ransacked the beach house and found everything Mom had ever written or saved. Letters, cards, pictures."

I wrap my arms around my torso, still trying to fend off the word *coward*. "Why?"

He drops to his knees and starts pulling out stacks of paper. They topple over and slide across the rug. "I think there may be a clue about Aaron's father in here."

I suck in a breath. "Jacob, you can't. He told you he didn't want to know."

He doesn't stop pulling pages from the box. "My mom cheated on my father. She pretended my whole life. I have to know why." He stops and looks at me. "Don't you get that?"

Oh, I get it. I also know the answers won't make him feel any better. Just because you understand someone's reasons, it doesn't make the pain go away. Sometimes it just creates new pains, new reasons to explore until your heart is empty with all the broken promises.

But all the same, I can't dismiss the pleading in Jacob's eyes. "I need a shower. Make coffee and don't think I'm sorting all these into stacks by date, time or whatever crazy OCD thing you dream up. If I'm helping, we do it my way."

He smiles at my don't-mess-with-me-stare and jumps up. He's already filling the coffee pot when I shut the door to my bedroom. My phone dings and, with hesitant steps, I move its direction.

> **Dad:** *School emailed to confirm finances for your application. You should have told me when we talked. Proud of you.*

The heaviness on my chest feels like a vice now, squeezing the little air I have. I scroll through the rest of the messages I ignored earlier.

> **Mom:** *Nathan called. Seems we have a lot to discuss. Not happy.*
>
> **Nathan:** *All packed. Heading to my parents for the week. Movers are coming a week from Saturday. I still have your key, so say the word, and I'll get you packed up too.*
>
> **Nathan:** *You have got to stop this! A two-year relationship doesn't end this way. It's unfair and cruel. CALL ME BACK!!!*
>
> **Nathan:** *I love you. I know you love me. Don't do this. I won't push so hard next time.*

There're two more, but I can't look any longer. Jacob's right. I am a coward.

Chapter Thirteen

I SLIDE ANOTHER letter back into an envelope. We've been at it for two hours with barely any headway.

We did end up making piles, but only two of them. One for anything suspicious and the other for the rest. Our "suspicious" pile held only two things. A picture Jacob didn't recognize of his mom, dad and an older gentleman. The other was a receipt for five marriage counseling sessions. The "rest" included bills, letters from a myriad of businesses, old pictures, school reports from Jacob's childhood and fourteen love letters from his father.

"I think I'm getting carpal tunnel syndrome," I say.

Jacob looks up from reading a journal his mom kept from high school. "You don't get carpal tunnel from opening envelopes." He shuts the book. "I, however, want to poke my eyes out. My parents were disgusting. This whole journal was about them sneaking off together when my grandpa was at work. Shameful."

Through his distaste, I see a smile. "It's nice to know your parents loved each other, even if the thought does make you want to puke."

His lifts his shoulder in a half-hearted shrug. I want to pull him close and chase away the demons in his eyes. But I don't.

"So, no clue? No sneaky love triangle in there?" I ask.

"Nope. My mom was 100 percent obsessed with my dad and vice versa."

I drop my stack and sprawl out on the floor, my head near Jacob's thigh. "Can we quit? Please? Pretty please?" I flutter my eyelashes at him, hoping.

"No." He glances around at our mess. "I just don't get it. They were so in love. How did this happen?"

I roll over and prop myself up on my elbow. "Your mom made a mistake, obviously. But your parents stuck it out. They took the vow 'for better or worse' to heart and fought for their marriage." I think of how many times my mom walked away when things got tough and feel a new surge of respect for Jacob's father. "I'm sure your dad wasn't perfect with Aaron, but he did raise him as his own. Maybe you need to stop worrying about his new father and help him fix things with the old one."

"Yeah. Maybe." Jacob stands and walks toward the glass doors at the back of the living room. He slides one open and disappears onto the deck.

The defeated set of his shoulders makes me sit up. We're halfway through the box, and most of what's left are pictures and old newspaper clippings. I reach in for another chunk. Half of what I grab is pictures of Aaron and Jacob as little boys. She liked to dress them the same and, in every one, the boys have big, goofy grins on their faces. Faces usually smudged with some kind of dirt or food. I set them aside and focus on the paper clippings.

They cover a span of two years, but each one is either a review or event about art exhibits. I read through three of them and find the same name mentioned: Sebastian Remy.

I quickly scan the rest for his name. He's in every one of them.

"Jacob," I call, my heart palpitating. "I think I found something."

He comes back through the door, his shoulders a little less fallen than they were a few minutes ago. "What?"

I gather the clippings and stand. "Did your parents ever mention a Sebastian Remy?"

He takes the fragile papers. "I don't know. The name doesn't stand out."

I read over Jacob's shoulder while he shuffles through the articles.

His hand suddenly stills on a picture of Sebastian. It's fuzzy and aged, but it only takes me a second to see what Jacob sees. The smile. It's Aaron's.

Jacob is suddenly in a frenzy, ripping through the rest of the items in the box until he pulls out an old picture from his parents' wedding. He stares and I come up behind him to see what has his back rigid straight.

"He was my father's best man." Jacob's words are etched in pain. The picture is his dad and Sebastian in tuxes with their arms locked around each other's shoulders.

I gasp. The picture could be of Jacob and Aaron.

Jacob stares at the picture so long I think it might burst into flames, and part of me wonders if he wants it to do just that.

I don't know what to do with myself, so I start putting our "rest" pile back into the box. Without looking at Jacob, I ask, "Are you going to tell Aaron?"

"Yes. He should know the truth."

I finish with my clean up and close the box. I'm glad it's shut. Sorting through their life and their love story only reminds me that I am running from mine. I stare out at the ocean, stretch and pull my hair up into a ponytail. "We can take a walk. Let the salty air push away cobwebs and chase away demons." When Jacob doesn't respond, I turn in his direction to see if he's still obsessing over the picture.

He's not. He's looking at me. The way he did the night of karaoke and the night we hugged on the beach. I'm suddenly flustered, and the breeze through the open door is the only relief I have from how stuffy the room feels. I turn away, focus on the wooden folded chair that sits on the patio. "Or…or we could go parasailing. I still haven't finished all my summer adventures."

My eyes refuse to meet his, but I can sense his body moving closer and closer until he's standing right next to me. I flinch slightly when his fingers graze my temple and tuck a stray hair behind my ear.

"I didn't just come here for your amazing letter-sorting ability." He rubs his thumb across my cheek.

I can't help but react to the softness in his voice and his touch. I turn my head. "You didn't?"

His hand lingers on my neck. "I shouldn't have walked away last night. Not until I said what I needed to." He pauses, the look in his eyes telling me what's coming. It's been building for days, weeks, since that first night we argued. "I know you prefer easy and uncomplicated, but…"

I blurt out, "There's a club in Myrtle Beach that's on my list. Will you take me there? Tomorrow night? We can see if Trish and Aaron want to go."

Jacob stills. He's only a breath away from contact, and I sense the shift as he pulls back. "You know this is like the tenth date you've asked me on that includes some kind of personal mission. I'm beginning to feel a little used." Jacob picks up his box, and I'm relieved to see his face relax into a smile.

Jacob's teasing, but there's truth in his words. I've been running, avoiding, unwilling to decide who and what I want. It's not fair to him. "I'm not using you."

I watch him and wonder what he's thinking. Wonder if he has any idea how much his journey with Aaron has changed my perspective. I've seen myself through a different lens and somehow it makes it easier to accept who I want to be.

"Then what are we doing?" His gaze meets mine, and I know my time is up. He's been patient and honest while I've sorted through the baggage I brought to the beach.

I bite my lip, but feel strangely empowered by the choice he's giving me. "Going out tomorrow…as more than friends."

His smile widens. "I'll pick you up at seven, then."

The door shuts behind him, and I can suddenly breathe fully for the first time in months. I know the hard decisions I'm going to make. Decisions for me. Decisions I should have made months ago. My voice, the one that has been dormant for so long, is roaring, and it feels victorious.

Chapter Fourteen

I HAVE ONLY two hours before Jacob shows up for our date, and my mind is somewhere between freaking out and complete, total meltdown.

I call Darby. "Help."

"Okaaay. Give me some kind of reference point."

I hear a buzz in the background. "Where are you?"

"Where do you think? Work. It's all I ever do anymore."

"I still can't believe you work in a tattoo parlor. In Los Angeles of all places." I toss away another rejected shirt.

"I know. Life is strange."

More like freakishly bizarre. The girl is terrified of blood. There has to be a guy. "Who is he?"

"No comment."

"Darby!"

"Fine. I'll tell you everything later. Right now I'm answering your S.O.S., remember?"

Oh, yeah. Jacob. Date. I spend the next hour detailing my drama filled phone call with Nathan last night.

"So, did he finally hear you this time?"

I drop down on the bed and sigh. "I think so. He cried. I cried. It was all very Dawson's Creek. I swear, Darby, it's like the break up that never ends."

"That's what happens when you let a man control you for two years."

"Ouch."

"You know I love you. What about your parents?"

I hear the hesitation in Darby's voice. She knows all about overbearing parents. "Baby steps. Those calls are going to require a little more preparation and maybe a few shots."

Darby laughs because that's what she does when things get intense. I love that about her. She's steady, yet hilariously sarcastic and truly loyal. "So, tonight. First date with the new man, huh?"

I groan and look around at the piles I've made on my bedroom floor. "It was so much easier when we were just friends."

"It doesn't sound like you were ever just friends. It sounds like you finally admitted you like him."

I hate that she knows me so well. "That still doesn't help me find the perfect used-to-be-friends-now-dating outfit."

"You do have a mom who is clothing obsessed. Have you checked her closet?"

"I'll be swallowed by sequins and rhinestones. I can't go in there."

"Sydney, you just complained not thirty minutes ago that all you own is boring and beach bum. The woman has a closet the size of most bedrooms. Go in there."

"Fine, but I'm holding you responsible if I don't come out."

Darby laughs. "Text me how it goes."

"I will. Bye."

I toss my cell phone on the bed and glance around my room one more time. It looks like Aaron's apartment, and I want to smile. I think of the Nerf gun battle and the water that spilled in my lap. I think of almost drowning at our surf lessons and how he shows up half the time before I even shower.

My nerves fade and suddenly the choice on what to wear doesn't feel so dramatic. With Jacob, I'm me. I don't have to pretend my faults away or dress in sparkles. He's never been interested in the façade, only the truth of who I am.

JACOB ARRIVES RIGHT on time. Not a minute early or late. I tease him about it when I open the door, but he doesn't say a word. Just stares.

I'm in a light blue sundress I bought with Avery last summer. It's simple and sexy and very *me*. I can tell he loves it. And I love that he loves it.

"I think you get prettier every time I see you."

"Thank you."

He's not looking too shabby himself, not that he looks any different. His shorts are still pressed and so is his buttoned-up shirt. But I notice an extra button is undone and he's rolled up the sleeves casually, not his usual rule-accurate cuffs.

He backs away so I can shut and lock the door. There's a strange awkwardness between us, but I like it. It's full of energy and the unknown. The idea of taking a great friendship and making it more. It's terrifying, yet exhilarating at the same time.

"Are Aaron and Trish coming?"

Jacob opens the passenger door and waits until I'm settled. "We'll meet up with them later. I thought I'd be a little selfish for a while and not share. Is that okay?"

I smile because that's what Jacob makes me want to do. Smile all the time. "I think it's a great idea."

"Good."

I watch him walk around but hit the lock right as he goes to open it.

He tugs, but nothing happens. "Sydney."

"What's the magic word?" I yell though the closed window.

He tugs again. "Please?"

"No way! Come on, that's much too boring for me." My hand hovers over the lock, loving this game. Loving how it's taking us back to the bantering I've come to cherish.

"Fine. Broken glass. Which is exactly what's going to happen if you don't unlock the door in two seconds."

I hit the lock and belt out a laugh when Jacob slams the door behind him. "You are seriously a toddler." He presses the button to start the car, but before we've even left the driveway, he's laughing with me.

I reach over and take his free hand. It surprises him. I can tell by the way he takes his eyes from the road and glances at our fingers entwined. It's the first time I've initiated affection, but it's also the first time I'm with him and not denying my feelings.

He squeezes and looks back at the road. "I showed Aaron the picture and the clippings."

"What did he say?"

"Not much at first, but I think it helped." He flexes his fingers and regrips the steering wheel with his free hand. The other stays locked in mine like it's his lifeline. "Knowing his father isn't some random man makes it better. My guess is Aaron's father stayed away out of respect for my dad, not because he didn't care."

"Will Aaron look for him?"

Jacob shrugs and slows the car to take a turn. "Who knows. It's Aaron. Trying to predict him is like trying to predict an avalanche."

I scoot as close as the car allows. "This doesn't sound like the same man who furiously wiped down counters in the Traveling Rum Hut."

Jacob pulls my hand until his lips graze my knuckles so softly that I shiver. "I'm not the same man, thanks to you." Our hands drop to this thigh, and he chuckles. "Who would have thought? Me and the belly dancer."

"Ha ha." A realization hits me and I pull back to my seat hitting the passenger door so hard my side is dented from the door handle. "Oh my gosh. My mom is totally going to take credit for setting us up. Do you know what this means?" I raise my fingers to my head, already picturing the embarrassment.

Jacob looks at me like I've lost my mind. "No?"

"She'll have our wedding planned before the end of the summer. It will be awful and sparkly, and I'll probably have a dress made of feathers. And you won't show because you hate feathers and my mom."

Jacob pulls into the restaurant parking lot, but he's laughing so hard it takes him two attempts before he can get the car in park.

I push his arm. "Jacob, this is serious. You don't know how crazy she can be."

The plea in my voice makes his laughter stop, but his face is still bright and happy when he looks at me. "Sydney, I'm pretty sure I have an idea."

I narrow my eyes and go in for a punch, but he pulls me close instead. His lips brush mine and I freeze.

"I'm tired of waiting to do this."

Hot breath is replaced by contact. Warm and soft at first, and then eager like two people who've waited much too long. We each feed off the moment, trying to get closer while the car's natural design does everything to keep us apart. My left arm is trapped, but my right hand finds his hair, his neck, the bulge of his bicep through his thin shirt. I pull closer, wanting more.

Jacob's hand cradles my face, and it's so gentle that his touch slows our frenzy. He pulls back and cool air seeps between us, but only for a moment because his forehead is resting against mine. "I've never felt like this," he whispers.

This is usually where I run. Where the idea of loving someone brings fear and the assurance of pain. But I don't want to run from Jacob and his starched shirts or spreadsheet planned future. I want to stay and kiss him more.

For the first time in my life, I want to make a decision. And it's easy.

It's him.

Chapter Fifteen

I CAN'T STOP laughing.

First, through dinner and now watching Aaron belt out *Dancing Queen* on stage. Trish is working the bar, but I've seen her stop and stare at Aaron several times. But I get it, because I haven't stopped staring at or touching Jacob since we kissed in the car.

The Massey brothers have that effect. They get in your life, under your skin, and you know your heart is forever changed.

Jacob tickles my neck with his nose and kisses the soft skin behind my ear. I close my eyes, enjoy the rush of heat down my neck, and snuggle into him.

"This is so much better than pretending I'm not crazy about you." His hands snake around my waist. Soft lips move down, roll along the tender skin until he's kissing my shoulder just above the thin strap of my dress.

Goose bumps prick my arms. He's teasing me, like he's done all night, and I want to turn around and put an end to my glorious suffering. He hasn't fully kissed me since we got to the restaurant and now my anticipation for the second one is higher than the first.

Aaron's song finishes and we scoot apart, cheering like the rest of the crowd. An exaggerated bow and leap off the stage later, and Aaron is back at our table.

"You're an animal," Jacob says. We've put several inches between us, but his fingers are still on my neck, rubbing slow circles.

"That I am, young one." Aaron's voice sounds playful, but he's distracted. He takes a drink and looks over at the bar for the third time since he got to the table.

I see why. Trish is talking and laughing with the same guy who walked up while Aaron was singing. They hugged like friends, but now they're both leaning on the bar, their faces only inches apart.

Jacob's hand stills. "Hey, isn't that Paul? I thought he moved away last year."

I shift, ignoring the fact that Aaron's only answer is a grunt. "Who's Paul?"

"Trish's ex-boyfriend."

"They dated years ago in high school. I'd hardly call him her ex-boyfriend." Aaron's tone is so condescending, I smirk. He glances at the bar again, and his hand tightens around his glass.

"Well, she hasn't dated anyone since, so he must have meant something to her. I'm glad he's back. Trish deserves a good man." Jacob is either completely oblivious or he's trying to provoke his brother. Which, I'm not sure.

Aaron's ears turn red, and I mouth "stop" to Jacob.

"I've got this," he whispers.

Aaron is practically dancing in his seat. His foot taps the ground. His fingers drum on the table. He turns to look at Trish again right as Paul pushes a piece of hair away from her face.

"Yeah, that's not happening." Aaron slams down his glass and stands. In three quick strides he's behind the bar. He grabs Trish by the waist and spins her around, giving her only a second to react before he kisses her.

Jacob laughs and whistles at the couple while the bar cheers. The kiss is movie worthy. Hands in her hair and around her waist, he dips her back and pulls her up without losing contact.

"Now, that's a kiss," I say, watching them with a smile so wide it hurts.

"Ours was better." Jacob's breath is back in my ear, and my pulse skips in response.

I turn my back to Trish and Aaron so I can face Jacob. "I don't know. I think I've forgotten." My words are barely audible partly because his touch is sucking the air from my lungs.

His smile is daring, but his fingers caress my face like I'm precious and special and more valuable than fine china. "My brother is the king of grand gestures and always will be. I'm the guy who's steady. Who loves once and doesn't need some other guy showing up to know he's got a perfect girl."

Jacob leans in and lightly brushes his lips to mine for only a moment. It's not grand or dramatic. No one cheered our display, but when I look back on that kiss, I know perfection will always be the word I use.

∽

IT'S AFTER ONE when we finally make it back to Richard's beach house. I'm tired, but so deliriously happy I wish the night would never end.

Jacob takes my hand and kisses my knuckles. "Come on, I'll walk you to the door."

I breathe in the salty air. The moon is full and shining like a lamp over Richard's house. I have a little less than a month left of my summer vacation. Those days had started like a prison sentence, but now they're a promise. Aaron was right. One summer is sometimes all it takes to change who you are.

Jacob wraps his arm around my shoulders, and I hug his waist. We walk like that to my door, and he kisses me every few steps.

I freeze. Jacob is looking at me, so he doesn't see what I do. Nathan, sitting on the front porch swing, waiting for me.

He stands and I can't take my eyes off him. I know Jacob realizes what's going on because his arm tightens around me.

Nathan steps forward. "I guess one of my questions is answered."

I drop my arm from Jacob right as Nathan offers him a hand. "Nathan."

Jacob releases me and shakes Nathan's hand. "Yes. Sydney told me about you." His grip is firm, but not threatening. I release the breath I'm holding.

Nathan's eyebrows raise. He's surprised by that, and I see a hint of hurt. "Well, she didn't have the courtesy to do the same here." He stares at me. It's the same one he uses when we fight, something we've been doing more and more these last couple of months. "I deserve a face to face conversation."

I nod because I know he does and hand him my house keys. He turns and without another look disappears inside the house.

"That wasn't exactly how I expected our night to end." I try to add humor in my voice, but nothing about Jacob's stance is amused.

"I'm gonna go," he says, his eyes still locked on the front door.

I reach up and rest a hand on his arm. "Jacob."

He lightly kisses my forehead and walks back to his car. I watch him leave until the taillights have disappeared. Not once since Nathan stood did Jacob look me in the eyes.

Chapter Sixteen

I SHUT THE front door and turn the bolt.

"This place definitely has your mom stamped on it." Nathan's back is to me. He's by the fireplace, staring at the multiple frames that cover the mantle. He picks one up. It's of me at graduation. My head is thrown back, and I'm laughing.

"This has always been my favorite picture of you," he says and sets it back down.

I drop my purse on the floor and step into the living room.

Nathan moves to the couch and sits. Puts his head in his hands. "I feel kind of sick right now." He blows out a breath and sucks in more air.

"I met Jacob this summer. My saying no had nothing to do with him." I sit next to Nathan on the couch and his hand immediately finds my knee. The touch is so familiar, it makes me sorry. I never wanted to hurt him.

"I did everything wrong. I know that now." He comes alive with new conviction and takes both my hands. "I won't push. You can set the terms. We can try the long distance thing. I just don't want to lose us."

I stand because I need space from him. Coming here, after I made my choice clear, is so classic Nathan, I wonder why I'm surprised. "You are going to law school. You'll be lucky if you have time to sleep let alone be in a relationship. I don't even know what next year will look like for me. We been grasping at pieces for months now. It's time to just let go."

"Syd. Don't do this because you're afraid." The frustrating thing is Nathan truly believes he knows me.

"I'm not afraid. This is the most clarity I've had in months."

"So that's it. You get to say the word, and we're through. I get no voice."

I close my eyes for the count of five. He's had the voice for two years. It's my turn. "I'm sorry. But coming here doesn't change anything. I know you thought it would, but it doesn't."

Nathan's shoulders slump and I hear a resigned sigh. He stands and within seconds his arms are wrapped around me. I breathe in his scent, one I held on to for much too long. "One more chance."

"Nathan."

He releases me and wipes away a stray tear. "Okay. Okay. Sorry."

I inhale deeply, hating the pain in his eyes and knowing I put it there. He picks up his keys and heads to the door.

"Nathan, it's late. You can stay here tonight." It's not much, but it's the least I can offer him.

He reaches for the knob. "I can't stay and not be with you." And with his head lowered, he leaves.

I open the sliding glass door and step out onto the deck. The moon flickers like it's proud of me. The water rolls its approval too, right up to the feet of a man sitting on the beach, watching the waves come and go.

The breeze lifts my hair, and I hear it whisper its support. *Go to him.*

Without a second thought, I'm sliding the door shut, running down the wood bridge over the sea grass and stepping my bare feet on the sand.

He doesn't move when I drop next to him. "I'm sorry."

Jacob shrugs and continues to watch the water. "It's not your fault. If I were Nathan, I'd fight for you too." He waits a beat and turns to meet my gaze. "Did he win?"

I lean forward, rest a palm on his cheek and kiss the question away. His arms tighten around me, pull me close in a way that possesses, but doesn't scare me. I know he left tonight for me. I know he didn't force a confrontation because he knew I'd hate it. My heart bursts. This guy who needs to control everything made it clear he doesn't want to control me.

He pulls back and shifts us until I'm in between his legs and tucked tight against his chest. We sit in comfortable silence, our lungs rising and falling in unison.

"Can I tell you something?" I ask.

His nose tickles my neck. "Anything."

"I'm not going back to school." He stills and I pray he doesn't think I'm wasting my life. "I talked to my counselor before I left, and I have enough credits for an associate's degree."

"What will you do?"

Relief stretches through me. There's no judgment in his voice. "I think I'll stay here. Maybe work out something with my mom and Richard. I'll get a job and if I hate it, get another one. I just want a year to find some passion for my life. All this time, I've been so afraid of making a decision that traps me, that I've let everyone else make decisions for me."

I unclasp his arms and spin around. I want to see his face. Want him to know what a risk I'm taking. "My parents picked my college, and my mom practically gave Nathan a dowry when she met him. Nathan chose my apartment. The only thing I've ever done on my own was meet up with my best friends every summer. And I even let that get sucked away this year by someone else's demands."

"And this is definitely for you?"

"Yes." I could sing with the absolute truth of those words.

Jacob falls silent and for a moment I'm nervous wondering what he's thinking. Too much happens in the recesses of his mind.

He suddenly jumps up and pulls me with him. "Time to celebrate."

"What? It's almost two in the morning and I just told you I'm dropping out of college."

Jacob's pulling me toward the surf, his bare feet leaving prints in the wet sand. "You just told me you took control of your life. That's something to celebrate." He's shin deep in the water now, but I'm hesitating. "Come on, Sydney, or else someone might think I'm the spontaneous one in this relationship."

There's a challenge in his voice that I gladly accept. I rush toward him, leap up and wrap my legs around his waist. He catches me but doesn't fall back like I expect.

Two steps later, the waves are lapping my thighs and I'm lost in the depths of Jacob's blue eyes. My arms tighten around his neck, pulling him in.

The kiss is faster and more heated than before. There's a rhythm, a dance that only comes from two people who have broken all barriers with each other. He grips my wet dress at the waist and takes us deeper into the ocean. The water is too warm to stop the inferno rushing though my core and down my arms.

It's not until water touches my chest that I feel him pull away.

"I love kissing you, but that wasn't the celebrating I had in mind."

I tilt my head and raise an amused eyebrow. "Really? What did you have in mind?" My voice is seductive, but it wavers when I see a hint on mischief in his eyes.

"I believe I still owe you one." And with that, I go sailing in the air.

I hit the water and sink under, barely getting my nose pinched before water submerges around my face. Strong hands lift me back on my feet.

Jacob's laughing while I stand there like a drowned rat in a rainstorm.

I push a tangle of wet hair from my face. "That's it, College Boy, you're going down!" And with that, the battle begins.

Chapter Seventeen

THERE'S A BUZZ in the air. An excitement that sizzles and pops through Finnian's bar. Aaron and Jacob are both on stage.

"How y'all doin' tonight?" Aaron's voice is as smooth as the confident smile on his face.

The crowd cheers and Aaron rewards them with more finger picks on his guitar. He leads back to the microphone. "I've got a little James Taylor song for you that hits pretty close to home. Hope you enjoy."

The room silences as Aaron starts the rhythm and lyrics of "You've Got a Friend." He's singing to the crowd, but I know he picked the song for Jacob. They've been through so much and are finally healing and learning to trust each other again.

On the chorus, Jacob joins his brother and the perfection of the harmony makes me want to close my eyes and completely drown in the melody. Jacob catches my eye and winks. Flurries fill my stomach and tickle the hair on the back of my neck. He's beautiful and he's all mine.

Trish slides next to me in the booth and watches the brothers with dreamy eyes. She and Aaron officially started dating, and she hasn't stopped smiling since.

"So, Aaron told me you're going to stick around after the summer," Trish says.

"That's the plan. My parents weren't happy, but they're getting used to the idea. At least Richard convinced my mom to let me stay in the beach house." I recall the phone conversation and sigh. Richard has turned out to be a much better guy than I gave him credit for in the beginning.

"Well, if you're looking for a job, my uncle owns the Traveling Rum Hut. He wants to retire and is looking for someone who can manage the bookings and paperwork."

Laughter slides from my mouth when I realize that Trish is serious. I glance at Jacob. "I think the Traveling Rum Hut has brought me all the luck it's going to this summer. But thank you." I pat her hand so she's knows I'm not being condescending. "I actually have an interview on Monday."

"Really? Where?"

"My father knows a family practice lawyer in Myrtle and put in a word for me."

Trish's eyebrows scrunch. "But I thought you didn't want to be a lawyer."

A shiver snakes through my spine at how close I came following Nathan right down that path. "I don't. Believe me, that's the one thing I'm sure of. No, this practice has a therapy division where it offers divorce counseling for children." I've never been so anxious, but so excited about a job prospect.

"Sydney, that's wonderful! You can make such a difference with those kids."

I blush at her belief in me. "Well, it will be mostly secretarial stuff. I mean, that's the job. But I'm hoping I can maybe learn something while I'm there."

I lean back, take a sip of my Coke, and watch Jacob finish his set. The patrons clap and cheer the duo while Aaron slides his guitar into a stand.

"We'll be back in ten," he says into the mic.

They hop off the stage and Aaron wraps his long arm around his brother and squeezes. "Well, there's no question who got the talent in the family. You're practically tone deaf."

Jacob pushes him off, but his smile is warm and amused. "You missed at least three cords in that last song."

"Whatever." Aaron dismisses his brother and pulls Trish from the bench, planting a huge smack on her mouth. "My baby still thinks I rock."

Trish giggles. "Yes, I do."

I feel the warmth of Jacob sliding next to me. His hand laces mine. A sheen of sweat coats his hairline as he leans in and sneaks a kiss that's as tender as it is sexy. "What did you think?"

I glance around the bar and then back to Trish and Aaron. Finally, my gaze lands on the man who dared me to be real. I touch his cheek and smile. "I think this has been one extremely fabulous summer."

The End

About the Author

Tammy L. Gray is the kindle best selling author of the Winsor series and Mercy's Fight. She writes modern Christian romance and clean YA/NA romance. She believes hope and healing can be found through high quality fiction that inspires and provokes change.

Other books by Tammy L. Gray

<u>Winsor Series:</u>

Shattered Rose

Shackled Lily

Splintered Oak

Mercy's Fight

When the Circle Fades: A Kindle Serial (Coming Aug 2015)

<u>Fight for Truth Series:</u>

Sell out (Coming Sept 2015)

Sign up at tlgray.com for Tammy's Occasional Newsletter along with:

* Bonus Scenes

* New releases

* Book news

* Cover reveals and sneak peeks

* and even some exclusive giveaways

You can also connect with Tammy at:

Website: tlgray.com

Facebook: facebook.com/tlgraybooks

Twitter: @tlgraybooks

Instagram: tlgraybooks

email: tlgraybooks@gmail.com

Keep reading for Darby's summer adventure in Los Angeles!!

A Painted Summer

By

Amy Matayo

Chapter One

I AM DARBY Sparks, and I'm afraid of almost everything. Being
alone. Darkness. Heights. And any other thing that doesn't involve
me tucked safely inside the confines of my own home. It's a learned
trait…not something I intended when I was a child who looked at the
world through the blue irises of wide-eyed wonder. No one plans their
fear. No one wakes up one day and thinks: this is going to get me. This
is going to flatten me. This is going to take control over the rest of my
life with such a paralyzing force that the courage to move ceases at a
single word or mention.

At least I didn't.

It's the reason I left home six weeks ago, intent on running from
my fears and chasing my dreams. I figured fear wouldn't catch me if I
moved fast enough, so move I did.

But fear got me anyway.

In the most obnoxious, unbelievable way.

A sharp rap on the door knocks the pen I'm holding out of my
hand, and it falls to the floor.

With a gasp, I realize what I've done and look at the incriminating
evidence in front of me. One line of poetry. Another. And finishing it
off, the words *pierce me with your cold-blooded words* written in the best
calligraphy I can manage considering the sad, nearly dried-up ballpoint
pen I had to work with. It's cheesy. Embarrassing. Exposing in a way I
never intended. And now everyone will see it.

Because I've just scribbled all over the bathroom wall.

For the third time this week.

It's a bad habit I've had since childhood; I start daydreaming and my imagination morphs into something only a gel pen and a continuous stream of words can rectify. It wasn't until my parents sold our home last year that they discovered the mess I'd made all over my closet wall.

By then, I was too old to punish.

I blink. Blink again. And look around for something, anything, to cover the evidence. I reach for a paper towel, wet it, and hold my breath as I try to erase the words—scrubbing back and forth as if getting rid of the evidence is the key to living a long life without the inconvenience of pain or suffering.

Because if Lennon sees it, he will kill me.

Strike me dead with the jab of a poisonous needle plunged into my skin by his graffiti-covered wrist. My worst nightmare come to life.

I had nightmares of needles as a kid. Still have them as an adult. Despite three best friends who all have their ears pierced and have bugged me to get mine done for years, I've never been stuck with one in my life. I don't plan on it now.

Lennon bangs on the door again, and I jump.

"What do you need?" The words still stain the wall like drippy chocolate ice cream on a white summer dress, but I'm almost out of time. Plus my wrist hurts from all the cleaning.

"Sparky, there's a customer waiting at the counter. If you're not too busy, do you think you could come out for a second and help her?"

Nicknames. Sarcasm. The worst combination, especially when they are coming from him and directed at me. I look around for something…anything…then decide on two packages of unopened toilet paper and position them just so in front of the picture. Not the best disguise, but it will have to do for now.

With sweaty palms and ragged breaths, I scramble for an excuse and fling open the door only to jolt to a stop. Just like that, my excuse dies on my lips.

Lennon stands in front of me, his arms propped against the doorway with muscles in full view. Guys know better than to do this. It puts girls like me at a definite disadvantage—the kind of disadvantage that turns a fully-functioning female mind into nothing more than a pitiful state of wishful thinking. The sight alone makes my heart pound and my insides ache. He's the oddest combination of intimidation, grace, chin-length brown hair, and black ink that defines both biceps. And it's the ink that leaves me transfixed, every single time.

He leans a little closer. Too close, if you ask me. "What were you doing in there so long?" His words slide over me like soft butter.

Slowly my eyes travel from his arms—*those tattoos…they're just so pretty*—to his face. The fog lifts, and I clear my throat. "Um…that's a little personal, don't you think?"

When he looks at me and winks, I suck in a breath and keep talking.

"Can't a girl get a little privacy around here?" Without looking him in the eyes, I walk around him and toss what I hope is a threatening glare over my shoulder. My heart hammers in my chest, but I need to look tough even if I don't feel it. "And for the last time, stop calling me Sparky."

He comes up behind me and gives my hair a little tug. "With hair that red, it's the only thing that fits."

I keep walking and try to ignore the way my mind screams *he just touched your hair!* Besides, he's right. My hair is awful. A ridiculous combination of Emma Stone after rolling out of bed and Little Orphan Annie after three days without bathing. All my life, people have told me it's pretty.

All my life, I've wanted to set those compliments on fire.

So, maybe Sparky fits, after all.

But still.

"Keep calling me Sparky, and I'll start calling you Lenny." My voice sings with amusement, but my nerves hum a line that goes something like *please don't hurt me and please stop being so good-looking.*

Lennon is as handsome as he is slightly scary. It's the tattoos. And the longish hair. And the devilish grin. As a homeschooled girl who grew up in the tiniest town Washington has to offer, I've never been around anything remotely close to all that is Lennon Dixon.

"Do it and I'll fire you," he sings right back.

Touché and totally not fair.

I suppress a sigh and round the corner into the waiting area, quickly pasting on a smile. It falters for a moment when I see the girl standing in front of me with one hand resting on the glass counter and the other in a tight fist. She's young. And nervous. And has no business being in this place because fourteen or fifteen isn't old enough to make a decision as painful and permanent as this one. But, like a handful of teenage girls her age, she's clutching a note from home.

She has permission. Probably scratched out in a hurry from dad because he was too busy to pay attention and think about the decision he was allowing her to make.

But I'm paying attention. And you can darn well be sure she won't walk out of here with a colorful butterfly on her lower back. Not if I can help it.

I smile the most reassuring smile I can muster.

"Welcome to Brainstorm. Can I help you?"

Her lower lip ducks for cover between her teeth. "I just wanted to look around for a minute. My mom said I could get a tattoo, but I'm not sure what I want…"

In most cases, no one ever is.

"Well, do you have any ideas?" I ask. "If not, I can let you flip through a few design books to see if anything catches your eye. But first, can I see your note? Because, honestly sweetie, you don't look old enough to be here."

It's the wrong thing to say, I realize a second too late. Her chin comes up and she ages three years in the process. She hands over the note with a slight flick of her wrist. The paper is legitimate, legal, a California birth certificate. Today is her eighteenth birthday. I reach for the books.

"So, I guess everything is in order." I take a deep breath and give it one more try. Someone needs to save this girl, and I'm the only one around. "But are you sure you want to get a tattoo? It's gonna hurt. *A lot.*"

"It is?" She swallows and looks at me with wide eyes.

I start to nod and say something else, but—

"Sparky," Lennon warns from across the room.

I flick a glance at him and give a pitiful laugh. "Just kidding. You'll barely feel a thing." Except pain and torture and tears for days. But I don't say this because Lennon is still looking at me. I press my lips together and hand her the books. "Here you go. Why don't you take a minute to look through these, and when you find something you like we'll get started?"

Another nod. Another bitten lip.

There's a framed picture on the wall across from me, a black and gray pencil sketch drawn in painstakingly accurate detail. It's of a woman who appears to be in her early thirties. She's beautiful. Striking. With haunting, hollow eyes. She stares through me as I work, following me as I go. Sometimes I look at her, wondering if she can see my fears, curious if we share any of the same private ones.

It's a stupid thing to think. Ridiculous, really.

I glance over at the birthday girl as she flips through books, simultaneously feeling bad for her and fighting against the desire to yell, "Fire!" and tell her to run for her life. Why people would willingly subject themselves to this kind of pain and suffering just for a stupid picture leaves me wondering about the state of humanity's saneness.

Then again, no one forced her into this place. No one forced me here either. I glance at the drawing again. The only thing I can hope is that this girl doesn't share my fear.

⁓

ONE HOUR AND three starts and stops later, the girl walks out of here with an infinity sign on her right ankle and a smile on her face. I, on the other hand, plop on the sofa, toss aside the notebook I've been writing in, and fight back tears. The needles. The sight of them dotting her skin in a figure eight and leaving that painful series of red and black marks. I'm still not used to them. Sometimes the visions alone leave me balancing on the ledge of sanity and hysterics with no clue on which side I'll fall. But with my limited experience at life in general, this is the only job I could find, especially because I had only a few hours to find it. After being turned down by one fast-food place after another—how hard is it to find a job in fast food anyway?—Lennon hired me on the spot. His receptionist had quit the hour before—walked off the job, leaving him here to fend for himself. Lucky or unlucky me.

Either way, it's poetic justice at its finest.

"Sparky, why the long face? Is it because of the girl who just left or because of the awful line of prose you wrote on the bathroom wall? Cold-blooded words, really?"

I blink up at a frowning Lennon as he dries his hands on a questionably clean towel. Darn him and his apparently small bladder.

"What are you talking about?"

He rolls up the towel and tries to flick me with it, but misses. "Nice try, liar. The toilet paper tower you used to hide it made things pretty obvious."

I press my lips together and pick at a fingernail. "First Sparky and now liar. What is it with you and nicknames?" I sigh. "I'm sorry. I won't let it happen again, I promise."

He tosses the towel on a nearby chair and shoots me a wink. "It's the fifth picture I've found in half as many weeks, Sparky. It will most definitely happen again." He reaches for my notebook and opens it before I have the chance to snatch it out of his hands.

"What are you working on here?"

Mortified, I lunge, ripping a sheet of paper in an effort to get it back in my possession. No one can read my words. They're too private.

Too intimate. And probably not any good.

"Nothing, just something I thought of when that girl was here." I was writing a short story about a girl who gets an infection from a tattoo needle, but not in the way one might think. No medicine or hospital visits are involved. Just superpowers. Like the ability to mind-read and time travel and blink one's way from planet to planet while hopping on one foot.

Seriously, not any good.

Lennon grins. "Maybe one day you'll let me read it."

Not a chance. When hell freezes over. After I'm dead and not a moment before.

"Maybe," I say instead, managing a small smile, thankful he isn't mad. And then I change the subject. "Do you think you will ever, *ever* call me Darby? Or will the string of dumb nicknames just keep piling up?"

He sits down and leans back, resting his feet on the table in front of us. His thigh touches mine, and while the contact is all I can think about, I'm not sure he even notices.

"Why would I call you Darby when Sparky fits you better?" It's the answer he always gives.

I can't help the smile that slides up my lips. Lennon is four years older than I am in age and about two decades older in soul. With his piercing blue eyes and the detailed collage of tattoos on his arms, all of it combined makes the most interesting combination.

A little too interesting.

A little bit frightening.

My parents would be mortified.

I shift position on the sofa to get a better look at him. "The girl who was here earlier? She turned eighteen today and looked scared to death. I wish people would give it some time before making decisions like this. Especially ones that are so permanent."

He breathes a laugh and eyes me up and down. I decided weeks ago that he means nothing by it. It's his way of sizing me up before delivering a statement that simultaneously makes me think and puts me in my place. It's the one thing about him that has me perpetually confused. His exterior shouts dangerous tough guy. His interior whispers reflective, thoughtful poet. Two appealing contradictions that slam together and smash apart everything my parents taught me.

One thing is for sure: Lennon is proof the world is much more colorful than the black and white way I was raised.

"You're right, maybe people should give things a little more thought," he says. "Then again, sometimes in life it's better to jump in with both feet instead of overthinking things to death. Besides, what's the worst thing that can happen to that girl?"

"She could wake up in a lot of pain or, at the very least, with a lot of regret tomorrow, that's what."

"Over a tattoo?" He sighs and rubs an eyebrow. "In my opinion, regret is better saved for wrong relationships and dreams you didn't accomplish. If more people would think about the big things in life instead of the superficial like piercings and body art, we all might get along a little better and save ourselves a lot of unnecessary heartache." He pats me on the knee and stands up. "Sparky, cut your hair if you hate it. Wear orange lipstick if you like it. Get a freaking tattoo if you want one. None of those things matter; you can undo them tomorrow if you want to. But dreams? Go find yours and follow it. That's what lasts."

And with those words, Lennon tweaks my chin with his thumb and walks into the back room, leaving me to stare after him like an abandoned puppy left in a gated laundry room by its oblivious owner. All I want is to be noticed. To be special. To hear Lennon call me his girlfriend in front of everyone within a ten-block radius. Ridiculous, because he isn't my type.

Lennon is twenty-five.

Slightly eccentric.

Looks a little rough.

Owns a tattoo parlor named Brainstorm.

Is covered in a fair share of ink.

Refuses to call me by my real name.

Never sees things my way.

But no matter how much I try to convince myself otherwise, all these things add up to Lennon being one of the kindest souls I've ever met.

Chapter Two

"*Y*OUR PHONE IS ringing again."

My phone has been ringing all morning, but I haven't answered it. I won't answer it until I'm home tonight and in the privacy of my own apartment. I have a lot of explaining to do, and I don't want to start it in front of Lennon. If history has any bearing on what lies ahead, I'll be stuck in the throes of a three-hour conversation. And call me crazy, but something tells me my boss might frown on my being away from the front desk that long.

"Ignore it. I'll call them back tonight."

Lennon stops flipping through design books and looks up at me with deep brown eyes I could swim in. "That's what you've said every day for the last two weeks. Call your parents, Sparky. They obviously want to talk to you."

I ignore his melted chocolate gaze and the way it reduces my insides to a puddle of nothingness. "How do you know it's my parents calling?"

"Because believe it or not, I have a couple of them too. And they still call almost every day, especially my mother, despite my old age and obvious financial success."

He spreads his arms wide in an attempt to belittle his situation, but I've seen his car. He's more successful than he lets on, though I'm still not sure how he's managed to do so well owning just one tattoo parlor in downtown Los Angeles. Sure, we're busy all the time, but not *that* overrun with customers.

"You drive a Land Rover."

He grins and scratches his forearm. "It's old."

"You said you bought it brand new last year."

"See? Old." He cocks his head to the side, waiting. Lennon isn't one to fall for an attempt in subject change. I've learned quickly that it's one of his worst traits. That, and drinking a kale and spinach smoothie every morning for breakfast.

"My parents always want to talk to me," I complain.

"And you never want to talk to them."

It's not that I don't want to talk to them. I love my parents, I really do. But if I talk to them, they'll try to convince me to come home. Considering my current life state and the fact that the only fear I've managed to conquer so far is fear of driving by myself—turns out the possibility of a fake police officer pulling me over on a deserted road late at night is a very slim one—I doubt it will take much.

My parents have very high expectations. Expectations that include me living at home in Washington, married to a college sweetheart who never existed, and making a start on an ever-expanding family. Three kids. Maybe five by now. Those exact expectations forced me to shoulder my fear, flee home, and set out to prove I can make it on my own. No parents or husband or anyone telling me what to do. At first I had no plan, just money in my pocket, gas in my tank, and an idea swirling in my mind.

All I ever wanted to do was have a career in the arts, and acting seemed like as good a place as any to start. Small roles, large roles, television, movies. Anything that would feed the creative streak that has been locked inside me forever.

So, I came to Los Angeles six weeks ago, one day after celebrating my twenty-first birthday and two days after wrapping up my sophomore year in college. I've been taking classes online.

I still haven't told my parents I'm quitting.

I've auditioned seventeen times for various parts, and somehow garnered eighteen rejections when an agency accidently delivered someone else's bad news to me by mistake. A sharp knife cutting further into my already bruised and sliced ego.

I ran out of money just before my last audition.

None for food. None for gas. None for anything.

Which led me to this job. Lennon says he saw something in me— ambition and eagerness and a desire to better myself. I'm more certain it was desperation for a job mixed with tear stains from crying about not being able to find one, though he never admitted as much.

And since he's a guy whose grace matches his vibrant ink in amount, style, and color, I know he never will.

"I'll call my parents tonight. I swear."

"Okay, but tomorrow morning I'm going to question you about—"

On cue, my phone starts ringing again. And being the fine and up-standing and caring guy he is, Lennon picks it up and hands it to me.

"Never mind tomorrow. Answer it now and put them out of their misery."

Being the mature girl I am, I stick out my tongue and answer.

"Hello?"

"Darby, I've been calling you all morning. Answer your dang phone."

The sound of Lennon's soft chuckle fills the background as waves of relief and curiosity wash over me. The guilt from supposedly ignoring my parent's calls lifts, but Avery sounds anxious. In all the years she's been my best friend, anxiety always means bad news.

She is never in a foul mood just for the sake of being temperamental.

"What's wrong?"

"My internship got cancelled, and now I'm stuck spending the summer in Arkansas."

I try to stifle a laugh but instead wind up coughing into the phone. Of all the things she could have said to me, this wasn't on the list of possibilities. Not even in the same area code as the list of possibilities. As a chef-in-training, Avery was supposed to intern at some big-time restaurant in Chicago all summer. And unless Arkansas has something besides farms and fast-food, this a major let down.

"You might want to re-think that," I say. "Something tells me flipping burgers at McDonald's won't look that great on your resume."

She huffs into the phone. "Arkansas has more than fast-food chains, Darby."

"Like?"

Silence. Silence that speaks volumes on the other end of the line. "Like my grandfather's dude ranch."

This time I can't hold it in. "You? Miss big-time, big-city? Are going to work on a dude ranch?"

"Shut up, Darby. It's only for the summer, and it's not like I have another choice. I have to intern somewhere, and he has all these campers who come in and expect to eat three times a day…"

Something about her tone kills the laughter inside me. Avery sounds desperate. A little panicked. We've been friends since fourth grade, and only because Avery took pity on me—the only home-schooled kid at the Sunday School Easter Egg Hunt—and invited me to play with her group of friends. Despite our differences, we clicked that day. We've stayed locked together all these years, and I don't see the friendship fading any time soon.

I paste on a smile she can't see and force some cheer into my voice.

"Who needs Chicago anyway? You'll do great, and who knows? Maybe you'll fall for some hot cowboy and go riding off into the sunset. Happens all the time in movies."

She laughs, and I breathe a sigh of relief. "My life is not a Hallmark movie, Darby. It's more like a blooper reel on repeat." She sighs into the phone. "So you don't think I'm crazy for doing this?"

"You remember where I'm working, right? I, of all people, don't think you're crazy."

"True, you have no room to judge me. How's Lennon the hot tattoo artist? Has he stuck you with anything yet?"

I blush at her double entendre and turn toward the wall. I've told her all about Lennon. I've also promised to pluck out her fingernails one by one if she tells anybody. "As hot as ever, and completely oblivious to the pathetic girl who works for him."

"I don't know about that. Besides, if he doesn't notice you eventually, then he's out of his mind and who wants him anyway?"

She's right. Who wants him anyway?

I look across the parlor and sigh at the sight of Lennon working over a customer. My shoulders fall in defeat.

Me, that's who. I want him anyway.

"Not me. That's for sure."

After a relieved *Thatta girl* and a quick goodbye, Avery hangs up.

As for me, I stand there holding the phone to my ear, a sad feeling rolling through my heart, my soul, and my mind.

For the first time ever, I lied to my friend.

Chapter Three

*I*T'S BEEN AN hour since I arrived at the audition, but there are at least three people ahead of me, if not four. Hard to tell since I've spent the majority of my time filling my notebooks with random sentences. I'm not sure where the sentences are leading. A short story maybe? Or rhymes that may eventually make up an entire poem? But they're growing in length and structure. Who knows, before the wait is over I might have something on paper that actually makes sense.

A few seconds later I hear my name called. Looking up from my notebook, I blink at a woman who can't be much older than I am, though she looks a lot more jaded. With her bleached blonde hair pulled into a severe ponytail and her face decorated with enough make-up to cover the blemishes of half the girls in my old Sunday school class, she's rough around the edges. Like she's seen too much of the world already and can't wait for the travel to end and the suitcases to get unpacked.

"I'm Darby Sparks," I say, quickly stuffing my notebook inside a faux leather bag I bought on sale at Target before I left Washington. I'll get back to my story as soon as this thing is over. I stand, brush my hands on my black skirt, and shake the woman's outstretched hand.

"Well, Ms. Sparks," she says and eyes me up and down with obvious displeasure. "I'll lead the way back. I hope you're prepared, unlike everyone else today. Mr. Hastings doesn't like it when people aren't ready to audition. It's definitely not the best way to get the job." She glances my way with a smirk. "You do realize this isn't an audition for

Annie, don't you? Not that you're young enough to land the role."

I run my hand through my long red hair and almost trip over my own feet at her directness, but I concentrate on putting one foot in front of the other and at least manage to pull myself together. Besides, my hair isn't *that* curly, and I did brush it today.

"I realize that, yes."

I clutch the script my chest because it's the only way I can keep my hands from shooting out to karate chop her throat and tell her I am prepared. Although I'm not sure one can ever be truly ready to be on display and judged like a pie at a county fair baking contest.

Too sour.

Too sweet.

Too bitter.

Not worth the extra bite or calories.

Definitely not worth the money.

She ushers me into a cold room where three men and one woman wait behind a long white table. The rooms are always cold. The people are even chillier. Finally, the man on the right manages a small smile and instructs me to read a few lines from scene three. It's a short scene. One I have memorized.

Just like the looks of displeasure from the judges that I also have memorized.

Ten minutes later I walk out of the building with knowledge I didn't have before.

One, I won't get the job.

Two, I'm as disappointed as I should be.

And three, my move to California was as pointless as that audition.

⌒

"SO, ARE YOU famous yet?"

My mother, forever skilled in the ways of creative sarcasm. At least one of us is good at what she does. I take a sip of Diet Coke and reach for a rag. My bathroom is a mess, and I finally have five minutes to clean it.

"Not yet. I had another audition earlier this morning, but I'm still waiting to hear back from them."

Because I need a call to *officially* inform me that they hated my outfit, my hair, my ability to act, and my accent. Of course, they didn't delve into that last one, but they may as well have with the negative way my entire performance was received. With tongue clicks. Sighs. A pencil slap followed by a, "Can this day get worse?" from the bald guy sitting left of center. And after? A polite, "We'll call you," from all four just before the door slammed shut behind me.

"I still don't understand why you left, but I have faith in you," my mother says. "If they don't hire you, they'll be missing out on the best actress Washington State has to offer."

She may be sarcastic, but she loves me. Though her compliment doesn't quite hit its mark. How many actresses could possibly come from my home state, anyway? Plus, I'm clearly not that good.

"Thank you, Mom. I'll be sure to let them know you said so."

"You do that. And remember not to take off your clothes or drink alcohol or say any bad words in those auditions of yours. You know how Hollywood can be. I don't want my little girl going out there and getting corrupted. I've heard women even sleep with producers to get roles, can you imagine?"

My head dips to my chest at the same time my eyes roll toward my brain. I've heard this line a hundred times, but why my mother thinks I need the constant reminder is lost on me. As if I would sleep with some random stranger just to get a part. Kiss, maybe. Possibly a foot rub. But sleep?

No, thank you. Besides, I've been told I snore, and that would be so embarrassing.

I keep this thought to myself. My mother doesn't often appreciate my sarcasm as much as she does her own.

"I remember. And I promise not to sleep with strangers." I deliver the line like a Girl Scout pledge—bored, bland, and ready to get on with cookie details.

My mother sighs like I knew she would. Her mockery radar is honed in on me with striking precision, even over the phone.

"I hear your tone, young lady. Just keep my advice in mind. And speaking of keeping something in mind, I wanted to let you know that your father and I are thinking about coming for a visit."

Diet soda bubbles up from my throat and spews all over my newly clean bathroom mirror. It burns, but not as much as the words she just spoke into my horrified, flaming hot ears. I miss my family desperately, but that doesn't mean I'm ready to see them.

"You're coming here? So soon?" There's terror in my voice. It's well-deserved, because one, I live in a tiny and unimpressive apartment the size of a large closet. Two, I work in a tattoo parlor—not exactly considered a moral and upstanding place of business back where I come from. And three, there's Lennon. One look at him, and I'll be hustled back home so fast there won't even be time to pack underwear.

"We're considering it," she says.

I try to tone down the coughing. "Why? I mean, it's a long drive and—"

"They have airplanes, and we haven't seen you in four weeks, Darby."

She says this in a way only my mother can, and I stifle a sigh. It's the kind of tone a pastor might use on a congregation that fell asleep mid-prayer...a science teacher might use on a student who blew up the chemistry lab...a husband might use on a wife he caught cheating in their own bed.

Four. Weeks.

You would think I missed Christmas, birthdays, anniversaries, and an entire calendar year of personal events.

"I guess that is a long time," I hear myself say. "But can you let me know beforehand? That way I can make sure the apartment is ready and the sheets on the extra bed are clean." I leave out the part about not having an extra bed. And the part about it taking me exactly five minutes to clean this place, and that's if I really take my time. I grew up in a fairly large house in Washington. The fact that this apartment is the size of my parent's closet will automatically land it into the This Place Isn't Good Enough For Our Only Child category.

"I'll let you know. But I can promise you it won't be long before we do."

"Okay, great," I say. "Can't wait."

She agrees.

Minutes later I hang up the phone and chew all my fingernails down to the skin.

Chapter Four

I PUSH THE off button, toss the phone away from me, then sit back in my chair with a huff.

Nineteen.

I'm now up to nineteen audition rejections and counting because apparently I tried out for parts I no longer remember. The phone could keep chiming with bad news indefinitely, and I'll get the joy of rejection piling on me like a mass of unpaid parking tickets.

Of which I have two.

Of which I have no way to pay unless Lennon decides to give me a raise. Unlikely since he caught me carving my initials into the break room door this morning right before I nearly passed out at the sight of a drop of blood oozing from a customer's arm. I caught myself against the counter just before Lennon ran over and lowered me to the sofa and shoved my head between my knees.

My dignity fell as low as my gracefulness in that moment. But when I subsequently grabbed a nearby trash can and lost what remained of the toast I ate for breakfast, both disappeared altogether.

I may not show up for work tomorrow at all.

In fact, I may just quit the rest of my life forever and ever.

The email I'm seeing on my computer screen might make the decision an easy one. My electric bill is three days late. I have a week to pay it or everything gets shut off, which means my blissful honeymoon period with Los Angeles is officially over.

Funny how fast I find myself wishing for a quickie divorce.

I can't tell my parents or ask them for money. Not because I'm worried they will hit me with a big fat, "I told you so," but because leaving for Los Angeles was the first openly rebellious decision I've made in my twenty-one years of living. And I did it with more confidence than I've felt in years—with my hand on my hip, money in my pocket, and the phrase, "I'll show you" offered as parting words to the worried twosome watching me go.

To head back now would be to admit defeat.

To admit failure.

To admit I'm too naïve and stupid to be on my own.

But more than anything, to head home would be to admit I'm talentless. That my dream is just that—a dream without merit, a childhood fantasy that never panned out. Time to grow up, suck it up, and hang up any thought of being more than a factory-working mother of twelve in a small town that no one ever leaves or always finds their way back to if they were once brave enough to venture off.

Not that there's anything wrong with being a mother.

Or a factory worker.

I'm working as a receptionist in a tattoo parlor, after all.

But I want more. And the sad fact is, more just might not want me.

To distract myself, I open up a travel website and scan the home page. Just as I start to dream about escaping my problems and heading for Hawaii with money I don't have, a knock sounds on the door. Looking at the blue penguin pajama bottoms, old Def Leppard tee, and Darth Vader slippers I'm wearing, I debate answering. It's a serious dilemma, especially when my hand drifts to my messy ponytail and my mind remembers the make-up I removed and washed down the drain an hour ago.

The knock sounds again. With an irritated growl, I stand to answer it and fling the front door open without checking the identity of the visitor. It's a decision I regret immediately. Especially when his eyes travel slowly up and down the length of me and pause entirely too long on my midsection.

"Nice outfit."

I cross my arms and give him a second.

Okay, time's up.

"Hey, Lenny, stop staring at my chest. It isn't that great." Trying to force my erratic nerves down to a low buzz, I wait until he connects with my green irises. It's hard not to smile when he hits me with a smirk.

"I'll fire you right now for calling me that, Sparky. Don't think I won't. But as for your chest, that's a matter of opinion."

I swallow and focus on the first part of his sentence. "You threaten to fire me so often, I'm starting to think you don't mean a word of it. What are you doing here?"

"I came to check on you, and I brought food."

Without waiting for an invitation, he moves past me and walks inside, then deposits two brown bags on my make-shift kitchen table. My gaze darts around the room, and I wince. Clutter is everywhere—a blanket on the floor, a pile of books on the edge of the sofa, a paper plate on the table from last night's Chinese takeout, writing notebooks stacked on my tiny countertop. My mother believed in a spotless house, no exceptions. I moved out, got my own place, and lack of organization became my rebellious streak. Plus Lennon has never been to my apartment before. Looking at it through his eyes, it hits hard how tiny and disorganized and gross the place is.

Plus I'm still not sure how he found my address.

"How did you know where I live?"

He glances back at me with an amused grin. "You wrote down your apartment number on your application form."

I take a sudden interest in the ceiling, hating myself when I feel my neck begin to burn. "Oh. I forgot about that."

Most people would probably be used to the basics of application forms already, but the world of jobs is new to me. Other than a short stint babysitting second-grade twins the summer after high school graduation, working at the tattoo parlor is the first official grown-up thing I've done. Unless you count college; then again, I'm quitting.

Except for driving to a new state to pursue a career in acting, though some might argue the move was extremely immature. To that, I say whatever. I've got to do something with my life. That seemed a good enough place to start.

While I've been doing all this thinking, Lennon has pulled out plates and napkins and now sits at my kitchen table. His elbows rest on it—a move my mother would reward with a smack on top of the head—and he's looking up at me as though he's waiting. For what, I still don't understand.

"Okay, we've covered why you came. But I don't know what made you think to bring food. It's not like I'm sick or anything." I hug myself tighter and resist the urge to sit across from him. The contents of the two bags smell like pickles and salt and grease, and the last thing I remember eating was a piece of dry toast this morning in a rush to get out the door. My mouth is already watering. "I mean, I'm glad you brought it because I haven't eaten dinner yet and—"

"I'm here because of your fainting spell earlier this afternoon. I just wanted to make sure you're okay." Lennon opens the bag and pulls out a napkin. It's all I can do not to stand on tiptoe to see what else might be inside.

"I didn't faint." I sound distracted.

"Only because I rescued you." That gets my attention, and my eyes snap to his.

"You didn't rescue me. I sat on the sofa."

"Only after I lead you there and shoved your head between your knees."

As if I needed the reminder.

He pulls out a carton of French fries, and now I can't think of a single comeback. One that doesn't sound lame and meaningless and laced with a longing for ketchup.

"What else is in there?" I say, my stupid voice betraying the nonchalance I'm clinging to. Then my stomach growls loudly and sends me straight to the Land of the Curious and the Hungry.

Lennon doesn't miss the sound. Of course he doesn't miss it.

"Why don't you sit down and find out?" He pulls out a napkin and salt packets. I stifle a growl and plop down in front of him.

"Fine. Hand me a bag."

He does, and before he can open his own burger I've wrapped my mouth around two beef patties and glorious layers of tomatoes and lettuce. I've never tasted anything so good in my life. Grease slides toward my chin. I catch it with the back of my hand and reach for a French fry.

"Wow," Lennon says with an eyebrow raised. "Manners much?"

I lick my fingers one at a time, taking extra care to smack loudly. "If you wanted me to eat properly, you should have brought sushi. I'm pretty cultured with chopsticks. Right up there with the Chinese, if I do say so myself."

He doesn't laugh, just stares at my fingers, his chest rising up and down in slow series of curious breaths. Finally, he flexes his neck and brings his attention to me. "Sushi is Japanese, but something tells me you already knew that."

I bite the inside of my cheek and reach for another fry. "I did."

We eat in an awkward silence for a few moments, but it isn't unpleasant. Not with Lennon sitting across from me in a black t-shirt and shorts as though he's just come from the gym. The guy has style, lots of it, even in casual clothes.

I'm so busy appreciating him that I don't hear his question. At first.

"What did you say?"

But I process it, the original question. A question that lets me know that despite early indication, this isn't just a casual dinner.

Panic rises in my chest as he delivers it a second time.

"I said, tell me something Sparky. Why in the world are you so afraid of needles?"

Chapter Five

FEAR IS A powerful thing, possibly the rawest of all emotions. While sadness drives us into false episodes of highs and lows—those moments we convince ourselves we can overcome every obstacle in our way followed by the more common moments when we easily persuade ourselves that all is lost—fear doesn't require convincing.

Fear doesn't ask for an invitation but shows up anyway. Fear doesn't cower from a little green pill or a psychiatrist's overstuffed sofa. Fear doesn't listen to screams or cries of desperation.

But the thing about fear is that it's almost always ushered in by previous experience. A child is afraid of a swing because she once fell from one. A man is afraid of wasps because he was once stung by one. A woman is afraid of strangers because she was once attacked by one. A veteran is afraid of war because he once fought in one.

And then there's me.

I'm afraid of needles because they stick you.

And they hurt.

And they're sharp and pointy and painful.

So I've been told.

And that's the extent of my rationale, though the word rationale seems so ridiculous because there's nothing *rational* about it.

But to say as much to Lennon is to admit my very raw—but extremely immature—cowardice. I've been afraid of needles since before elementary school. And when I say afraid, I mean deathly.

Tears for days.

Kicks that had grown adults running for cover.

Screams that reverberated off the walls of the doctor's office.

Parents who covered their children's ears in a desperate attempt to shelter them from my bad example.

I've never had a shot that I remember. Never been vaccinated past my second birthday. Never even gotten my ears pierced, the dumbest aspect of my sometimes debilitating fear.

And not because I was raised by Earth-loving, homeschooling, parents.

But because when I grew to a certain age—the age of vivid memory, it seems—I was the world's biggest brat about it. Some kids are afraid of monsters or clowns or Barney the horrid purple dinosaur. I was afraid of needles.

But again, to tell this to Lennon would be foolish and immature.

But I tell him anyway.

The whole stupid story.

He listens without laughing. His ability to focus without making fun of me is an attribute I admire…all the way up to the very end.

The reaction I get is a loud burst of laughter followed by, "You've got to be kidding me."

I sit back in my chair and glare, waiting for him to say something nicer. Something encouraging. Something freaking supportive. He doesn't.

"I'm not kidding."

He balls up his hamburger wrapper and laughs harder; it makes me angrier.

"What's so funny?" I snatch a French fry and throw it at him. In typical fashion, my aim sucks, and it sails over his shoulder. Just what I needed; more crap to clean up later.

"You're what's funny." He's still laughing, and the charm I used to find behind that smile is now obnoxious. "I can't believe you're that afraid of something you've never even experienced. What if you find out it's not that big a deal? That all this fuss was for nothing?"

I roll my eyes. "Nothing? Blood isn't nothing. Pain isn't nothing, Lennon." I huff at the end for extra emphasis.

For some dumb reason, he fails to see things from my perspective. His eyes—all shiny and blue and pretty—don't grow concerned like I want them to. Instead, they begin to twinkle with the most annoying light.

"Tell me something, Sparky. Have you ever broken a bone?"

"I don't see what that has to do with—"

"Have you ever been cut with a knife?"

"Do you have a point here or—"

"So you have, to both." He wipes his mouth with a mustard-stained napkin. "Which bone?"

"My left arm in an unfortunate trampoline accident when I was nine. But I still don't see—"

"How deep was the cut?"

I roll my eyes. He won't even let me finish a sentence. "My dad put a Band-Aid on it to stop the bleeding. So?"

He stands up and pushes his chair back, effectively cutting me off again. "That's real pain, Sparky. Broken flesh, a broken bone, a broken heart. A needle is nothing compared to that. Unless you're using it to inject drugs, I mean."

My mouth falls open. "I've never used drugs in my life."

He smiles and shakes his head. "Big surprise."

And with that he walks around me, tosses his trash in the basket, pats me on the head, and gives me a lighthearted, "See you tomorrow."

He leaves.

Just walks out.

I stare after him, dumbfounded.

Wondering how the heck I just got insulted for *not* being a drug user.

Chapter Six

*T*WO DAYS LATER, I look up from the sketch book I've been thumbing through and stare at Lennon. He's across the room, pressing a stencil onto some guy's arm and dabbing at it with a damp towel. I'm used to this now, but on my first day I foolishly hoped this was the extent of tattoo-getting. Not much different than buying one from the quarter machine at a pizza parlor and slapping it on in the bathroom with a crumbling paper towel before your parents found out.

But then out came the needle, and up went my panic level. Now, I just take a step back when I see him begin.

I don't care what he said the other night at my apartment—needles *do* hurt, but they can't hurt me from thirty feet away. Exactly the distance I am from him now. Still, I'm close enough to know I've missed the obvious the entire time I've worked here.

I look up at him in disbelief.

"Hey, why is the name Dixon signed under every sketch in this book?" I ask.

He glances over at me. He looks guilty. But there's something in his expression that looks like resignation as well. Like I've just stumbled on a secret he's been keeping for years and he's not sure where to go from here.

With a frown, I tap the open leather-bound album open on my lap. "Like this sketch here. And this one." I point to the most popular design—the one added to almost every sleeve on the arm of every customer who walks into this place. It's a cross and key design with barbed wire coiled around them, droplets of blood running along the outside. The significance is lost on me, though I have a few ideas. Lennon himself has a small one just above his left wrist. The key turns to unlock something every time he moves his hand. I've stared at it often. Come to think of it, I'm always staring at Lennon.

Like now. He shrugs. "Good question."

The guy sitting in the chair beneath him laughs, and I sit up a little straighter to study both of them. It's obvious neither of them are going to let me in on the joke, so I dismiss them both and reach for another book. And then another. And another. Within seconds, I'm beginning to figure some things out. Like, the name Dixon is scratched underneath each photo in every book.

"Lennon, your last name is Dixon."

He looks taken aback. "It is?"

More laughter. From everyone but me. "Did you draw all of these?"

Even from here, I can see the faint red stain begin to travel up his neck. "I don't remember."

"Dude, you're blushing," the guy says with a breathy laugh.

He's right. And I find it…interesting. "Why didn't you tell me you were an artist? I thought you just worked with needles."

He pauses to look over at me with a raised eyebrow. "So, basically your opinion of me is on par with that of a drug user."

I give him a look. "Funny how we both keep using that example to describe each other."

He winks. "Just giving you a hard time, Sparky."

I swallow a smile, secretly thrilled at another wink. Each time he does it, I like it a little more.

He turns away, once again focusing on the arm in front of him. I use the moment to clear my head and grab another book. Opening it, I discover kaleidoscopes, holograms, skulls, spider webs, crosses, faces of men and women and children; the drawings are intricate, precise. Painstaking in detail, every corner and curve uniform in size and shape—even the misshapen ones. It's art like I've never seen in person before. Not unlike something Michelangelo might have drawn if his canvas had been the human body instead of the Sistine Chapel.

Lennon all but admitted these were his designs, but I still can't believe what I'm seeing.

"Why didn't you tell me you could draw like this?" I ask. "I assumed all these books were ordered from…I don't know, Amazon or something."

I realize how dumb that statement is the moment a chorus of male laughter rings across the room. Even the UPS guy—who just walked in with his afternoon delivery—smiles at me.

He hands me a clipboard. I reach for the pen and duck my head, grateful for the chance to ignore the two still-cackling men—though I'd like to throw something at both of them. Who laughs while someone is sticking them with a needle, anyway?

It's a bit harder to ignore the guy in uniform still grinning at me.

"What?" I say, giving him a hard glance. "It was an honest mistake."

He stops smiling, and of course I immediately apologize for my bad mood because it's what I do. I try to be tough, I try to appear street smart because I'm working in downtown Los Angeles, and the natives know better than to be too friendly. But where I'm from, neighbors pot-luck on weekends and take care of each other's pets during family vacations.

Friendliness and frequent apologies are my natural way of life.

The door closes, and I pick up another book. Lennon is busy, and there's currently nothing for me to do. Before I know it thirty minutes have passed, and there's a stack of photo albums in various shades of leather piled in front of my feet. I've thumbed through all of them, and one thought makes my mind numb.

Lennon is a genius.

In the world of art, he is a master.

In the way I've dreamed of acting my whole life…of making it big on the stage or screen…he's already arrived. Though why his life's work is confined to a tattoo parlor is something I don't understand.

The thought is enough to jolt my head up.

"Lennon, you could sell these and make a ton of money. Maybe even have your own gallery."

The guy looks over at me and grins. "Honey, don't you know Lennon here is—"

"I'm happy here," Lennon says, cutting him off. "This is what I like to do."

And with that, he continues to etch the pattern currently filling up the customer's forearm. Discussion over. End of explanation.

Something tells me there's more to know.

Something tells me I'm going to figure it out.

But first I grab a pen and my own sheet of paper.

There's a story behind this spider web design in front of me, and I begin to write it.

Chapter Seven

"**M**OM, I DON'T need anything. Seriously."

It's the third time she's called this morning, but this is the first time I've answered. A few days ago, I decided the less I actually talk to her, the less chance I have of lying, so now I'm limiting myself to talking to her once a week on Sundays. Which makes me feel awful because Sundays are for church, and lying should be avoided at all costs on that day. But since I slept in and skipped church today, I figure it's not as bad as it could be.

I also figure my logic might be a little skewed.

Still, so far this is the only lie I've told today.

Score one for me.

"Not money or clothes or a reference letter for a job?" she asks. I'm pretty sure she's been talking for a while, but I managed to tune her out for most of it. "You've got to find a job soon, Darby. The money you left with won't last forever, not in Los Angeles."

I'm a few blocks away from work, driving through Taco Bell in plaid flannel pants and a lint-covered navy tee because it's my day off and hey, who's going to see me? Plus I'm starving and there's nothing but dill pickles and a container of outdated yogurt in my refrigerator.

But my mother.

I don't tell my mother the money I left home with ran out five weeks ago. Or that I spent my last dollar on a roll of Wintergreen Life Savers because I was headed to an audition for a part I desperately hoped to land and didn't want bad breath to be the reason my dreams collapsed around me.

It wasn't the reason. A gorgeous Disney Channel chick auditioned ahead of me.

That was the reason.

I also don't tell her about my job. My parents still don't know where I work or with whom. And if luck lands on my side, they never, ever will.

"I'll find a job," I say, praying it isn't technically lying to leave out a detail or two. "And if I need anything, I'll be sure to let you know."

"Okay Darby, but I'll have you know that—"

A loud pop blasts through the car, and almost immediately an odd *thump thump* begins with what feels like my back right tire. A flat. Probably caused by a nail from California's endless stretches of road construction. Though my tires have been bald for weeks, much like my threadbare bank account.

With traffic buzzing by me and my mother still talking in my ear, I don't have time to analyze it.

"Mom, I gotta go. I'll call you next week." I hang up, trying not to cringe at the indignant sigh that reverberates through my ear. I'll pay for that later; Natalie Sparks always gets what she wants. One way or another, we'll be talking again in an hour.

I pull my car over to the side of the road and slam the gear in park. All I wanted was a bean burrito and to remain incognito, but I'm stuck on Western and Beverly Streets during the Sunday church rush wearing dirty pajama pants and—I squeeze my eyes shut, bang my head against the back of the seat, and exhale a strained breath because for the love of all things holy what was I thinking?—no shoes.

Why am I not wearing shoes?

I take mental stock of what to do, whom to call, whether or not I can climb out of my car without anyone noticing me, and wonder if I should just camp out inside this car until the sun goes down. I have a Snickers bar in my console and yesterday's leftover coffee in my cup holder, after all. Who needs Taco Bell?

Not me. Certainly not me.

I repeat these two lines inside my head longer than I should. Too long to notice the car as it pulls up behind me. Or the figure that climbs out the driver's side and approaches my door. Or the hand that comes up to rap on my window.

When it knocks and I jump…that's when I notice.

I look up and around. There's a man. And a car parked behind me. And other cars driving by.

And I'm an idiot with no shoes.

All of this adds up to a very bad day.

Until I blink up at the man still standing by my window. Something doesn't feel right, like I'm sitting in a sauna and someone has locked the doors. Like I'm in a wind tunnel of recurring nightmares that keep sucking me back to the center before spinning me back out to the edge again. Like everything is strange and familiar in a weird rush of déjà vu.

I shade my eyes.

The guy bends down.

And all at once, this very bad day twirls me one more time and then spits me to the ground, and I land with an embarrassing thud.

Chapter Eight

*N*O WAY IS this happening.

I reach for my purse and pretend to be searching for something. Anything. Shoes? Pixie dust to help me disappear? More than the five dollars and twenty-three cents currently in my wallet? When he raps on my door again, I slowly roll my window down and paste on a look of surprise.

"What are you doing here?" I ask.

Lennon leans lower so we're eye to eye. His eyes are blue. So so blue and they lock on mine and I hate them because they're also shining with knowledge of an inside joke.

"I think the better question is what are you doing here? Don't you know the highway isn't a safe place for a girl wearing pajamas?" He scratches the side of his cheek. "And that brings me to another question. Do you own any other clothes?"

I huff and glare up at him. "These are practically sweatpants, and you see me every day. You know I own other clothes."

"None as interesting as this." He looks me up and down, taking way too much time if you ask my opinion.

"It's Sunday," I say with more confidence than I feel, as if those two words explain my style, my empty refrigerator, the California interstate system, and the sun shining high above us.

"True. It's God's day and all. Seems like you would respect him a little more than to look this bad."

I glare up at him. "God doesn't care how I look, and I don't look bad!"

Truthfully, I look terrible. My hair is pulled into a knot I'm not entirely sure I'll be able to untangle later, I haven't showered—I thought about it but decided to wait until tonight, of course—and my shirt was too tight in high school. Now it's nearly obscene.

All three make me want to bury myself alive.

I clamp my lips together and try not to squirm under his scrutiny.

"Are you going to stand there and judge my weekend fashion sense or are you going to help me?"

Lennon smiles and chucks me under the chin. "I'll definitely help. Any chance you have a tire iron or a can of Fix-A-Flat?"

My pulse skids in my throat, and I swallow. "No?"

"Sparky, you might want to invest in one of those. You have a flat tire—looks like a nail is stuck in it—and unless you'd like to blow air into it with that cute little mouth of yours in the future…"

My face flames at the same time I dive-bomb toward the back seat, cursing everyone from my father and mother and great-grandmother for not teaching me the basics of car ownership. To buy myself time, I search for something…anything…on the floor. Composure would be good, but it looks like I'm fresh out. I do find a can of Armor All wipes and hold them up behind me. My butt is in the air and my dignity is a thing of the past, but I'm trying here.

"I found these," I say, my voice muffled. I settle myself back into the driver's seat and pick at a piece of non-existent lint on my pants.

Lennon's silence stretches like a pulled piece of bubble gum over my head. Long, sticky, and hovering. Finally, I glance up.

"What?"

Not surprising that he looks amused. Seems to be a permanent expression directed solely at me.

"Armor-All wipes? No sense in making a tire look shiny if you can't drive on it." He speaks to me like I'm a toddler, and since the flannel pants fit…

"Good point." I lean back and look up at the ceiling, feeling the fire in my face begin to wane. "I don't have anything else. What am I going to do?"

When he plants both hands on the door, I can't help but glance his way. Darn him and his ability to throw me off my game with his ridiculous biceps. Has he ever considered *not* working out?

"Well, you have one of two options," he says, and I have force myself to listen. "You can either sit here until the sun goes down and then walk home to save yourself the embarrassment of letting the world see how you look…"

I don't tell him that was my plan all along.

"Or you can swallow your obvious lack of pride, run to my car real quick, and we'll get something to fix your tire. A few people might spot you, but they'll likely forget the horror by dinnertime."

I look him square in the face, lie to myself by deciding he's not that good-looking after all, raise an eyebrow, and open the door, not caring one bit about giving him time to jump out of the way. The door hits him in the stomach. I give myself a mental high five until my shoeless foot finds a rock at the same time some jerk drives by and whistles at me.

I hop on one foot, fighting the desire to cry out. I think it's been cut. Both my foot and my pride.

I limp to the car, trying to hold my head up despite a deep longing to hurl myself into oncoming traffic.

But then I remember I've never ridden in a Land Rover before.

They have leather seats.

It's the only upside I can find.

Chapter Nine

"WERE YOU AT work? Is that why you happened to find me?" I ask a few minutes later.

It's none of my business, but I'm awkward and still embarrassed and fully aware that I am wearing clothes even a bum wouldn't wear on his most down-and-out day. Worst of all, Lennon looks better than he's ever looked before. The man wears a black button-up like second skin—so well I can see the ripples of his biceps under the soft cotton fabric. The edge of a tattoo peeks out from the rolled sleeve on his right arm. To the casual observer, it might go unnoticed. But I'm not casual, and where Lennon is concerned, I've done a lot more than observe.

The visible black tip of the tattoo is the end of an intricate design made up of diamond and rectangle shapes that fan out into a sunburst. It's a large design that takes up most of his arm; when he wears a sleeveless shirt, I spend the better part of my day staring at it. The gorgeous kaleidoscope draws me in with its ability to hypnotize.

Lennon looks good in sleeveless.

I steal a glance at him and swallow a groan.

He doesn't scare me at all anymore. That's bad. Very, very bad.

Even worse, the man has the best head of hair I've ever seen. I have a thing with men's hair—like it more than muscles and blue eyes and jeans that hug the hips like an invitation to stare. Of course I like those things too.

But Lennon's hair.

It's just.

The ends, thick and long and still slightly damp from an earlier shower, curl around his collar like ribbon against a shiny birthday package. My hands itch from wanting to play with the dark swirls, so I shove my fingers under my lap to make them behave. I wish I could tuck my eyes away too, but they keep betraying me over and over.

I keep stealing glances at him under the guise of looking toward passing cars or searching inside my purse for gum or holding my phone up for a better signal. So far, I don't think he's caught on.

"I was meeting with a client."

"What?" I blink over at him, vaguely recalling that I asked him a question, but not remembering exactly what it was.

"You asked what I was doing in this part of town." He sends me a questioning gaze, one that locks on my lips a little longer than usual. He clears his throat and focuses on the road while I do my best not to beam like an idiot. "I met with a client. We had breakfast at a little pancake place just up the street. I was thinking about heading to church when I saw you on the road." He reaches over to pat my knee, giving it a little squeeze before his hands settles on the steering wheel again. "So, it's your fault if I sin more than normal this week."

I stare at my leg—at the spot he just touched—even though so many things are going through my mind right now, all of which jumble together like string that has been played with for weeks by a kitten.

Client. Doesn't he mean customer?

Church. As in, Lennon goes to church? Even I barely go, and I was raised in the pews twice a week.

Fairies. About a thousand of them just took off flying in my stomach, their wings tickling my insides as they buzz with the memory of Lennon's touch.

I'm not sure which one to tackle first. A hand to my stomach settles the flying creatures. At least that one is taken care of for now.

"So…you have clients? Not just people who walk into your store and ask you to ink them up?"

I don't mean it as a joke, but Lennon laughs. "Ink them up? Is that what you think I do all day? You make me sound like a fourth grader who likes scribbling all over his desk with a pen. And speaking of—"

"A drug dealing fourth grader, don't forget that," I hurry to say. He caught me drawing on a few pieces of letterhead yesterday. It's a conversation I don't want to revisit while wearing sweatpants and ugly hair. Not when my defenses are down. Not when there's no way to distract him with my winning charm and attractive looks.

I can't believe the man hasn't fired me already.

He pulls into a parking space in front of a Goodyear Auto Service Center and shifts in his seat to look at me.

"Yes, I have clients. And no, I don't only deal with walk-ins."

"Then...what? I thought owning a tattoo parlor was pretty straightforward. You learn how to use an instrument, and then viola— some guy's skin goes from plain to all designed up."

He laughs and looks out the windshield, circling the steering wheel with his thumb as he weighs something in his mind. He must decide it isn't worth the effort. After a moment of licking his lip in thought, he takes a breath and looks at me.

"Inked up and designed up. I like the way you describe things, Sparky." Again, his gaze roams over me. Again, it connects with my mouth before he seems to realize what he's doing and looks away. "Now, do you want to go inside with me or hide in the car? And just so you know, I'm good either way. Just...if you come inside, stay about ten feet behind me at all times so no one knows we're together."

He says it with a teasing that falls flat. When he gives me a hopeful grin instead of the grimace I think he intends to, I shove his arm.

"Get out of the car. I'll stay here and hide. Wouldn't want to ruin your respectable reputation or anything."

Lennon opens the door. "Thanks for that. But I was kidding. If anyone can rock a pair of plaid flannel pants, it's definitely you." He winks and takes off inside.

I try not to watch him walk.

I really do.

But pretending not to notice Lennon is about as fruitless as attempting to ignore an approaching funnel cloud. I give up and stare as the sliding glass doors close behind him. Even then I can see his figure browsing the shelves just inside the store. My gaze lingers until he finally disappears around the corner.

I look at the sky.

Something tells me I'm headed for a storm.

∽

"SO, ALL YOU do is spray it in this hole, and it fills up your tire. Should be good for a few days, but you're going to need to get the tire looked at. Your tread is gone, and it probably isn't safe to drive too much longer."

Lennon stands and wipes his palms on the back of his jeans. He walks back to his car and tosses the empty can of Fix-A-Flat—otherwise known as "God's miracle" for a car repair virgin like me—into the back seat. I shift in place, trying to find somewhere to stand void of roadside gravel. Three rocks have broken through the skin on my feet while we've stood here; the shooting pain has dulled but hasn't completely let up. Still, Lennon is a bit of a savior. A small thing like pain won't lessen my appreciation for him.

"Are you sure I can't pay you for that?" I ask, secretly hoping it doesn't cost more than five dollars.

He shoves both hands in his pockets and approaches me again. "I'll deduct it from your paycheck."

I feel my face fall before I can stop it. What if it *is* more than five dollars?

"I'm kidding, Sparky. Every penny was worth it to see you in your pajamas once again." He eyes a handful of cars as they pass by, then tilts his head toward me. "Any big plans for the rest of the day?"

I look down at my attire and tug my shirt in front of me. It snaps back in place and feels somehow tighter than before.

"Clearly, I have a hot date in an hour." I look up. My skin begins to burn at the way he is still staring at my shirt. "I have nothing but a couple of tacos and about a hundred Seinfeld reruns in my future." I try a laugh, but my voice shakes.

He's quiet for longer than normal as he studies me with that same thoughtful expression in his eyes. Like he's weighing something. Something big. Something important. Something that obviously has him worried and a little lost for words. I expect him to shrug and tell me he'll see me tomorrow.

He doesn't.

"Do you want to change those plans and spend the day with me?" he asks. "It's been a long day so far, and I'd rather not spend the rest of it alone."

In that moment my heart lurches. Up or down, I can't be sure. Both directions wind up with me swallowing hard and questioning my sudden dry throat. Still, I take a moment to savor his question before delivering my answer.

Lennon asked me to spend the day with him.

Maybe only because he's bored and apparently I'm the only available distraction.

Still, I jump at the chance because regret doesn't sit well in the bottom of your stomach—not when nervousness has already taken up residence and you don't want to be alone in a big city either and you know exactly two people in this foreign town. All of it leaves very little room for hesitation.

I clear my throat and work to not look too excited. "Sure. But I'm not going anywhere like this. Give me an hour and I'll meet you at work?"

"Deal." Lennon smiles and walks backward toward his car. He studies me, and he looks...happy. "But just so you know, that's not a bad look for you."

His statement makes my pulse race, and I smile. "Sure it isn't."

And with our pledge to meet later, we go our separate directions. I drive a little faster than I should because I don't care what he says…

I've got exactly one hour to transform myself.

It'll take a miracle to be ready on time.

Chapter Ten

"WHY DIDN'T I say 'I'll meet you on Hollywood Boulevard or I'll meet you at the movie'?" I say for the twelfth time. "This might be the worst mistake I've ever made."

"Stop whining and be still. It will all be over in a couple minutes."

"If you stick me with anything, I'll kill you."

"If you kill me, you'll be out of a job. And walking down Hollywood Boulevard could take on a whole new meaning."

I shoot Lennon a look that I hope communicates death and pain and all kinds of offense for insinuating I could ever do *that*. It's a mistake to look at him at all. He's so close that my breath hitches in my throat. I could tilt my head and kiss him in an alternate situation— one where we're dating, and he thinks I'm beautiful and not merely a pliable, easily coerced employee. I try to remember to be annoyed, then work to conjure up some of the residual fear I once felt towards him.

It's pointless.

"I'm not hooker material."

His fingertips brush my bare shoulder in that exact moment. He looks up at me with an unreadable expression that has my heart tightening into a fist.

"That's what they all say right before they kill their bosses and find themselves with no other options." It's an empty threat, one meant to sound teasing. But his voice is thick, his throat raspy.

He looks away and continues to work, his fingers dancing across my skin. I pray he can't feel the hammer of my pulse, and I take a deep breath. It's hard to force annoyance into my voice, but I somehow manage.

"Are you almost done? This is taking forever. And between all the drug and prostitute comments, I'm starting to think you have a bad opinion of me. Stop that." I slap at his hand.

He nudges me with his wrist. "This will only take a few more seconds. You're being a baby."

"You're making me get a tattoo. Of course I'm being a baby."

"For the third time, it's a henna tattoo. There are no needles involved. Sit still. We're almost done."

We continue to trade barbs for a few more minutes until I can't take it anymore and twist my neck to see his progress. My eyes go wide. "It's huge!"

"And temporary. It will only last a month, tops.

"But what if my mom sees it!" The words are out of my mouth before I can close my lips around them and chew them back down. Turns out Lennon's right. I am a baby—all pacifiers and diapers and bracing for a swat on my toddler-sized hand from a woman who isn't even here.

His lips scream *I told you so* without even opening.

"Is your mom flying in this afternoon?"

I roll my eyes. "No."

"Then you have nothing to worry about. But if she shows up, put on a sweater." He uses a fingernail to flick dried paint off my arm. My skin pebbles under his touch. "There, all done. Now tell me you don't love the way that looks." He swivels my chair so that my right side is facing the mirror, and I gasp.

It's beautiful. A sunflower opening across my shoulder with stems and leaves trailing along my upper arm in swirls and points. And, at the very tip, a flame beginning its climb, brushing the stem with hot licks that promise impending destruction. A tiny flame. Barely noticeable. Really, nothing but a spark.

I feel myself smile.

"I love it."

"Glad you like it, Sparky." He turns my chair until I'm facing him. "Now, if you're finished whining, are you ready for the rest of our day?"

I allow myself a single nod. Anything more would end with me bobbing my head like an idiot.

"No more whining, I promise. I'm ready."

"WHERE IS MICHAEL Jackson? I really want to see Michael Jackson," I say again. So far we've seen Patsy Cline, Daniel Radcliff, Clark Gable—who happens to be the greatest actor of all time in my opinion—and countless others I can't begin to remember, but there's still no sign of the King of Pop. Not for my lack of asking. Apparently begging in a long succession of whines and threats does nothing to speed up Lennon's progress. When the man wants to take his time, not even the downward tick of a bomb can't make him move faster.

"We'll get there in a minute, and you're still whining. Because of that, you're missing the entire point of this walk."

"Which is?"

"To respect the talent and effort it took these people to get here."

He bends down and touches the edge of Jim Morrison, leaving his hand there in what looks like a moment of paying homage. I stand back and watch, trying to remember if the guy was a singer or an actor. All I know is that he died in a car wreck. Or maybe from drugs. The knowledge is lost in a blur of Beethoven and other forms of high classical music—the only thing I was allowed to listen to as a child.

I wave my hand in front of me. "I respect all of them, whatever. Now where is Michael Jackson?"

Lennon stands with a labored sigh and takes my hand. I might find it romantic if he wasn't suddenly walking fast and dragging me behind him like I'm a Labrador that needs to get on with things and finish its business. He stops, and I nearly crash into his back.

"There. Now maybe you'll stop complaining." He points and I look down, my throat a clogged drain of emotion.

To everyone else it might be just another star on the Hollywood Walk of Fame, but to me the name Michael Jackson represents everything I missed as a kid. This is the man who hid underneath my bed inside the confines of an old, pre-loaded iPod a friend gave me when I was fifteen. I listened to his songs over and over on walks I pretended to take for exercise, and drives I volunteered to make to help ease my mother's errand load. All I wanted was to escape for a few moments of teenage independence. All I wanted was to learn something besides classical music so that I could feel more like a normal girl and less like an outcast.

I didn't know until later that his relevancy pre-dated my age group by a couple of decades, but by then I didn't care. He was a favorite. My cornerstone as I balanced on the ledge of insecure and self-assured. The former almost always won, at least in my mind. But that's the thing about the mind, it can convince you of nearly anything without needing much reasoning.

"Wow." It's the only word I risk, but my breathy whisper reveals enough to make Lennon glance my way.

"You're a fan?"

I nod. "Always will be." For a moment we just stare, me lost in my own memories and Lennon undoubtedly wondering if I'm as weird as I seem. Depending on the day, the answer is yes.

I whip out my phone to send a text.

> **Me:** You'll never guess where I am.
>
> **Avery:** At the doctor. You saw a drop of blood, hit your head on something hard when you fainted, and now you have amnesia.
>
> **Me:** If I had amnesia, do you really think I'd be texting you? I'm on Hollywood Boulevard staring at Michael Jackson's star.
>
> **Avery:** You're kidding! Make sure you do the Moonwalk over it. Guess where I am?
>
> **Me:** Wiping cow crap off your cowboy boots?

Avery: *Close. I just pulled up to the ranch. God help me. I'll text you later.*

I put my phone away and glance over to see Lennon smiling at me. "Your friend?"

I grin and focus on the star. "Yeah. We've talked about coming here together since we were little kids. Seemed kind of wrong not to share the moment with her."

Lennon gives me another moment. "Do you want to see who I really love? Who I would give my left arm to meet, and maybe even one of my future children?"

I scan the series of stars next to us trying to guess, but see nothing but B-list actors and other entertainers I've never heard of. Giving up, I give him a little shove.

"Lead the way. I'm right behind you."

After two turns and one street crossing, Lennon stops at a star set apart from the others. At first I think maybe there's a problem—a rock he needs to remove from his shoe, maybe he stepped in gum, possibly dropped a quarter and is trying to locate it—but no. We're here. This is the star he dragged me to. This is the superstar he would sell a kid to meet.

I make a mental note to never have children with Lennon.

I make another note as well, and feel a smile coming on as the hilarity of it hits me.

He might think I'm weird, but even to the cool kids who once upon a time thought I was a nerd in every way that counted back then...

Lennon would have been considered so much weirder than me.

Chapter Eleven

*T*WO HOURS LATER we're walking the halls of the Museum of Contemporary Art, and I'm still giggling.

"For the love of God stop laughing. It isn't funny."

"It's hysterical. You have no idea how much."

"Everyone loves her music. It's not like I'm abnormal or something."

"Everyone loved her in 1987." I take a couple of steps to catch up to a retreating Lennon. He keeps trying to lose me among the marble statues. He hasn't yet figured out that I'm like a parasite that regenerates at the first sign of resistance. Especially when the opportunity arises to relentlessly tease someone who doesn't want to be teased. I might have been raised a good, sheltered homeschooled girl, but I do have a bit of a bratty streak.

He looks over his shoulder and shoots me a look. "Says the girl whose idea of a good time is watching the *Thriller* video on repeat."

He has me there, and I frown. But only for a second because Michael Jackson is Michael Jackson, and the person he likes is—

"You like Madonna. You told me you would give up a child for the chance to meet her. What do you expect me to say? It's…Madonna. And you're a guy."

"She's had a brilliant career."

"Built on singing about virginity. And again, you're a guy."

"Stop being sexist. And are you saying you have a problem with virginity?" He knows saying this will fluster me, and he's right. My neck grows hot, and he grins. "Chill. I'm not questioning yours, nor do I care. But I like her. I can't help it. I used to lay in bed at night, wishing she was my mother instead of the absentee one I had. It was one of the many mom issues I dealt with as a kid."

He looks down with a small frown when he says this, and now I'm both jittery and sad. Tchaikovsky's *Symphony No. 6* is playing through the overhead speakers and adds to the sudden somber mood. I know all about parent issues and feel bad for making fun of him. After all, the things that happen in childhood can affect us forever, and if more parents knew that—

Wait.

I remember something Lennon mentioned a few days ago and pause.

That snake. That inked-up, cocky snake.

"You told me your mother hovers. That she still calls you every day."

"Yes, but she's never on time. I have an issue with that," he says.

I slap him on the arm. Soon we're both laughing and getting dirty looks from a smattering of high-class, tie-wearing art lovers around us.

"You need to work on your fighting skills," he says, ignoring the people around us. "Now that you've seen my favorite singer—don't start." He gives me a warning look. "Do you want to see my favorite painting?"

"Only if it isn't girly," I say.

That earns me another look. "It isn't. Follow me and I'll show you."

His favorite painting is past the bathrooms and down two more hallways, but following Lennon isn't something to ever complain about. He walks with a confidence that can't be faked—all male and self-assured like a guy who makes no apologies for who he is. *This is me, take it or leave it.* And in a crowd of well-groomed patrons who give him a double take more than a handful of times—and not in an unpleasant way—I feel proud to be with him in a way I can't explain.

When at least two women send him lingering looks of longing, I resist the urge to stick out my tongue. *I might be wearing jeans and a shirt from Old Navy, but he likes me better than you.*

No one needs to know he's my boss and regularly threatens to fire me.

When he stops and points to what I assume is his favorite piece of art, I turn to look and find myself at a complete loss for words.

It's an original oil on canvas of Salvador Dali's *The Persistence of Memory*—temporarily on loan from the Museum of Modern Art and a classic piece painted in the nineteen thirties that depicts time passing in the literal sense. A clock melting over a tree branch. Another liquefying over a stone ledge. Yet another softening and molding to a blanket lying in the sun. It's a brilliant piece—arguably the artist's most recognizable work.

"This is your favorite painting?" I try to blink the surprise out of my words.

I own a copy. It's hanging over my bed at home.

"It's been my favorite for years," he says. "I have one just like it in my apartment."

I don't tell him that I do, too.

WE'RE ALMOST TO the front door when a man calls out from behind us.

"Mr. Dixon, do you have a minute?"

Lennon halts mid-step and places a hand on my shoulder to stop me. We turn at the same time, facing a man in a designer suit who appears particularly delighted by the sight of Lennon. I wait for him to hurry us the rest of the way out, to tell us we don't belong here in our worn jeans and cheap shirts and fake and not-so-fake tattoos. He doesn't. His smile only grows wider as he takes in the sight of Lennon—silk practically in awe of denim in an odd role-reversal.

The man holds out his hand and Lennon grips it in a firm shake.

"It's been a long time, Mr. Grant."

"Too long, as a matter of fact," the man said. "It's been a while since we've heard from you. Have you given any thought to what we proposed last month?"

Something about the way Lennon glances at me while rubbing the back of his neck lets me know he's uncomfortable, that he would rather have this conversation in private.

"I have, actually," he says. "Could I call you later? Maybe tomorrow?"

The man claps his hands together, clearly not getting the hint. "We would really like to know your decision, if you have a moment."

My eyes volley between them like a birdie in a rapid game of badminton.

Both men go silent and an awkward pause ensues. It dawns on me that I should do the halfway decent thing and excuse myself, but curiosity has me forgetting my manners.

"Where's the restroom?" I blurt the only thing I can think of to provide a reason to leave.

The man gives directions, and I slink down the hallway just as their conversation resumes. Their voices are low, but I manage to make out the words *gallery*, *popular*, and *excited*.

After disappearing into the bathroom and standing against the wall for what I hope is an appropriate amount of time, I make my way back down the hall. Lennon is sitting in a chair waiting for me, his hands clasped in front of him and his mind focused elsewhere. Watching him for a second, I weigh the pros and cons of asking about his conversation before deciding against it.

Finally, I clear my throat. He looks at me with a smile.

It's in that moment that I feel it.

The tightly woven wad of pre-conceived notions I've carried around all my life has loosened. Nearly unraveled completely. Two pulls away from becoming ruined forever. The day I took the job at the tattoo parlor it wound itself tighter—fighting against the unknown in a fierce battle to keep itself intact. Now it's coming undone so fast I can barely hold onto the pieces as they slip through my fingers and float to the ground.

To the naked eye, Lennon doesn't look cultured. He doesn't seem well-versed. He doesn't appear like the sort of man the well-educated and impeccably groomed want to fraternize with.

But apparently he is.

The old me can no longer fit my image of him inside a perfectly square box.

The new me doesn't even want to.

Chapter Twelve

"*I*'M SORRY YOU don't like your design, but what do you want me to do about it? It's not like I can take an eraser to your skin and make it disappear."

I want my mom. I want Lennon to appear. I want someone to come rescue me from this situation because…

Teenagers. They're among the worst of the bunch, always criticizing and complaining and demanding things I don't know how to give. I'm just a girl, not a miracle worker. If I were, I would make this guy disappear with two blinks of my very tired eyes. Last night was short on sleep and long on worry. The gas bill is due, I got another rejection from an audition last week, and on top of it all, I haven't eaten anything since dinner last night. By the time I pay my bills and put gas into my car, there isn't much left in my account. And by much left, I currently have one dollar and sixty-seven cents to my name, and payday isn't until Friday.

It's Tuesday.

This week sucks before it's even gotten a chance to start.

"I want you to fix it now," the guy says. "Find a freaking eraser, do what you've got to do, but fix it." I take a step back, uncomfortable with both the hostile look on his face and the lessening number of inches he has put between us. The guy is skinny, but he looks mean.

I take a deep breath and hope my voice decides to work. "I'm not a tattoo artist. I just work the front desk. But if you'll hold on a second I can—"

"What seems to be the trouble?" Lennon marches out of the back room and heads straight for us, ink still on his hands and anger in his eyes. My heart slows to its normal rhythm when I see him. He glances at me; he looks worried. When he takes my hand and guides me behind him—putting his body between me and this punk kid—all at once I can breathe again.

He doesn't let go. I don't either.

The kid clearly has a death wish because he is still looking at me with blood in his eyes when he starts to answer Lennon's question. "The trouble is, this chick here thinks she can—" He jerks his head toward Lennon and stops, his mouth suspended in an open state of disbelief. "Holy crap, it's you. I'm sorry, man, I didn't know this was your shop. If I had known I wouldn't have—"

"Obviously not. Next time maybe you'll think before you talk to a lady like that. I think you owe Ms. Sparks an apology. And if you want me to take a look at that hot mess some idiot made all over your arm, you'll give her one. Now." His grip tightens on my hand and I squeeze back. I'm not sure why we're still holding hands, but I'm not about to let go.

The guy's eyes go wide as he hesitates for a moment in a battle between pride and humility. Humility wins, although I'm certain it's fake. Still, he clasps his hands together and turns toward me, head down, lip working to fight off embarrassment. I would laugh, except I'm still a little scared and a whole lot mad about his crap attitude.

Plus, I'm confused about his weird nervousness around Lennon.

"I'm sorry, Miss…whatever your name is."

"Sparks," Lennon fills in for him. "Say it to her."

"Sparks," the poor kid stutters, barely making eye contact with me. Lennon isn't making this easy, and I'm actually starting to feel sorry for the kid. "Please accept my apology."

I glance at Lennon. He still looks angry, but he slides me a wink that only I'm supposed to see. I send him a questioning look and it's hard to stifle a smile, but I manage and assure the kid that all is forgiven. Unless he threatens me again. Then I'll punch his scrawny little arm, as long as Lennon is around to witness it and provide security.

"Good job," he tells the kid, letting go of my hand. "Now let's take a look at your arm and see what we can do to fix it up."

"Thank God. I got drunk on spring break and got this awful thing at some parlor in Santa Barbara. Can you make it into something cool? Maybe like a sword or a skull or something like that. I can't believe Lennon Dixon is gonna fix my arm, it's crazy man, and…"

The two wander into the back room to examine the wall of designs while I stand there alone, nursing a mild case of disappointment and a suddenly cold hand.

I glance at the drawing of the woman's face framed on the wall, pick up a receipt pad, and scratch out a couple of lines. There's a story behind her sad expression. Like she's been staring at me this whole time, begging me to solve her issues and write them down. Now's my chance.

As I work, conversation drifts from the back room. The kid is definitely chatty. Definitely enthusiastic. He never stops asking Lennon questions as if he's a celebrity or something. It's funny but confusing.

The story in my mind is beginning to take shape, along with a few questions that tug at my subconscious.

The main one being this: Lennon owns a tattoo parlor. What is so special about that?

∽

A FEW HOURS later, I'm no closer to having an answer than I was the first day I got this job. I am on the brink of passing out from hunger, however, so I flip through today's mail to distract myself. For a Tuesday afternoon when traffic is usually at its lowest in correspondence and customers, Lennon has a stack four inches high. Most of it is junk, but a few pieces catch my eye even though I have no idea what they are. I gather the mail and walk toward Lennon's office in the back.

"Hey, you have mail. A ridiculous amount too, I might add." I unload the pile I've been hugging to my chest to his desk and watch as what has to be fifty envelopes slide toward him. A few fall to the floor. He catches most of them in his lap but has to bend to retrieve a few from underneath his desk—not before tossing me a look.

"What? I didn't mean for them to fall," I say and make a face.

"You're just naturally graceful like that."

Ignoring him, I take the chance to look around the room while he's gathering envelopes off the floor. What I see surprises me a bit.

In all the times I've passed by Lennon's office, including the one time I interviewed for the job while sitting in that brown swivel chair, I've never taken the time to notice just how nice it is. His office looks as though it could be situated inside a law office, not what you would expect from a business like this. A new Macintosh desktop sits on one corner of the desk—I know how outrageously expensive they are—and on the screen is the website of the art museum we visited Sunday. Considering the conversation Lennon had with the owner, I find this both curious and not at all coincidental. I can't ask him about it, though. Something tells me he wouldn't answer anyway.

The desk itself—though not mahogany—isn't garage sale material either. It's solid wood with a gleaming glass top that's been through a recent polishing. The leather chair Lennon's butt currently occupies definitely looks expensive.

Framed certificates line the wall. One looks like a college diploma, another looks like a certificate from tattoo school, maybe. Is there such a thing as tattoo school? I make a mental note to ask him but decide to save the question for later when it doesn't sound as stupid out loud as it does inside my head.

"Why do you have so much mail today?" My stomach chooses this moment to growl. I slap my hand over it to smother the sound.

He glances up at me and continues to flip through envelopes. "Not sure. Most of it is junk though."

"It didn't all look like junk."

"Not everything, but most." He doesn't look at me. I have a feeling Lennon is silently wishing the floor would open up and suck me downward. Except he likes me, which makes it a dilemma tough to reconcile. He swivels his chair so I can't see one particular letter as he opens it.

I stand there and look at him, partly because I'm still curious but mostly because my eyes keep tracing the outline of a particularly large tattoo on his left bicep that I've never seen before. It's a bird with one wing extended, the other bent and broken nearly in half. It's a beautiful depiction, each feather outlined in detail—perfectly smooth and uniform except for that one part. It's so realistic that I feel sorry for it, wonder what might have happened to put the poor creature in so much pain.

"I like your bird."

He flashes me a crooked grin just this side of legal. "Excuse me?"

My face flames red at my stupid choice of words. "Your tattoo. On your arm. The bird with the broken wing. It's pretty. Why is it broken?" I sound like a faucet sputtering water all over a counter, making a mess that some poor fool will need to clean up later. Embarrassed, I run a finger across his desk because I don't know what else to do.

"Thank you." He's back to flipping through letters. "It's broken to remind me that even though it's good thing to take flight in life, you always need to stay grounded. If you don't, something will force you back down to earth, and it won't always be pretty."

I blink. Even while sorting mail, Lennon manages to be profound.

His words take shape in my mind when he gathers the pile of mail toward his body and stacks it into a tall deck. He reaches for a rubber band and binds them all together, then slides the whole thing upright between his computer and the wall. When he's finished, he stands, places a hand on my shoulder, and looks me straight in the eye.

"Sparky, I'm starving. Do you want to grab dinner with me?"

Chapter Thirteen

WE WIND UP at the nicest restaurant I've ever been to, and he insists on paying. I argue against it. Once. But then I remember that I'm penniless, broke, destitute, and all the other adjectives one can think of to describe my current situation. A situation that pride will keep me in for the future since there's no way I can swallow it and call my parents for help.

So I let him buy my dinner. Funny how my pride falls short when food is involved.

I'm scanning the menu and fiddling with the gold bracelet my parents gave me for my sixteenth birthday, sliding it in circles as my mind struggles to decide if this is a date...or a pity dinner. Five minutes in, and I'm no closer to an answer.

"Why are you looking at salads? Please tell me you're getting more than that," he says.

"Everything else costs too much."

This place smells of aged leather and colorless diamonds, and there's a steak on the menu that costs over two hundred dollars. A far cry from the drive-thru hamburger stand I expected, especially considering my attire. I'm in jeans, Converse sneakers, and a Pink Floyd tee. To call me underdressed is like calling Kim Kardashian slightly camera happy. I stand out like a pimple in the middle of a very wide forehead.

Either Lennon doesn't notice or he just doesn't care. Neither option has me feeling any more confident about my situation.

He closes his menu and sets it on the table. "I knew how much everything cost when I brought you here. Order whatever you want. It's on me."

My shoulders slump. "Did you also know about the dress code? I look like I should be washing dishes in the back, not eating out here with the cultured crowd."

He smiles. "You look fine. And if the cultured crowd has a problem with the way you look, they can shove it up their—"

"Okay, I believe you," I rush to say. No one needs to hear Lennon curse. Not before appetizers are served, at least.

Come to think of it, I've never heard him curse at all.

I pause, frowning. This guy keeps defying my assumptions, and I'm not sure how I feel about it.

"You're either very worried or in an awful mood. Want to tell me about it, or should I start guessing?" He rests his elbows on the table.

I blink a few times.

"What? I'm not—"

"You finally talked to your parents, and they wasted no time turning your old bedroom into the jazz exercise studio they've always dreamed of."

I bite back a grin and reach for my water. "Jazz exercise? That's not even a thing anymore."

He blows out a breath and lets his eyes go wide. "There's a studio on South Fuller Avenue. I drive by it every morning on my way to work. Scariest place I've ever seen."

I fight a smile and set the glass down. He's ridiculous.

"Your jeans are too tight, and you're wondering how you're going to inhale that giant salmon you just ordered," he guesses again.

"You told me not to get a salad!"

"Still, you really think you can finish that? It'll add pounds…"

I fake a glare. "I'm not fat."

"I didn't say you were. Let's see…you hate the eye shadow you're wearing."

"You're giving me a complex." I bite my lip to keep from smiling.

"You started your period."

"That's personal!"

"You really want to get a tattoo. And get your ears pierced."

"Not a chance." Stupid man. Now I'm giggling.

"I can keep going if you want me to. Um…you broke a fingernail. You're secretly a vegetarian, but you ordered that salmon so I wouldn't think you're weird. And now that you mention it—"

"You don't cuss," I blurt, lost in a fit of exasperated laughter. "That's what I was thinking about." I take a breath and shrug. "I've never heard you say a bad word."

He looks at me quizzically. "And that's a problem because…?"

"Because you look like you should cuss. Often." I'm pretty sure that's a stereotype, but come on. He's defying all of mine at a break-neck pace, and he needs to stop. Otherwise all the things I've believed my whole life mean nothing, and I've got to hold on to something, even a hoped-for foul word or two to prove that my pre-conceived ideas about scary men with tattoos were valid.

Another fear of mine without merit. It's unfair. It's wrong. It's giving all my others fears a complex, like maybe they aren't valid either.

And this is about me right now.

Not the sweet guy sitting across from me.

"You do realize you sound crazy, right?" he says, moving his napkin out of the way for the server to lower his plate. She smiles at him; he smiles back. I ignore the obnoxious pang of envy that settles in my core. "Most women like a guy with manners, but you're saying you would rather I forgo them and throw f-bombs like a game of darts."

I shake my head and pick up the larger fork. "Not forgo them. Just…"

"Fit into your box?"

I blush. He sprinkles salt on his broccoli. I hope he won't notice my red face.

"I don't have you in a box."

"Sparky, you have me in a two-by-two wooden crate with the lid

Super Glued shut. You think I don't notice the way you study me? The way you look at my ink, my artwork, and spend the better part of the day trying to size me up?" He pops a bite of steak into his mouth and talks around it. It would be disgusting if Lennon wasn't the one doing it. He somehow makes everything look sexy. "That day you had a flat tire? When I mentioned church? You looked at me like I had sprouted horns and a pitchfork just for saying I sometimes go."

I swallow the memory on a forkful of rice. "So you do go?"

He smiles. It isn't bitter; he isn't angry. I practically call him too lowly for God, and he flashes me a genuine grin. "Sometimes, when I feel especially sinful. I like it. Makes me feel better."

I sit back in my chair and look at him. This guy who bought me dinner because he knew I hadn't eaten all day. I sigh and roll my eyes.

"No one could Super Glue a lid over your head, Lennon. Not even me." Feeling a rare rush of boldness, I reach across the table and offer my hand. "My name is Darby—not Sparky as some annoying people sometimes call me. Mind if we start over?"

He wipes his mouth and balls up the napkin, then reaches halfway to meet me. "My name is Lennon. I own a tattoo parlor, have a few on my body, sometimes go to church, and rarely cuss. Got a problem with that?"

"I guess not," I say.

"Mind if I call you Sparky? I like it best." He slides me a wink, and I feel myself blush.

"No. I kind of like it too."

"Good. Then I have a question for you," he says.

I give him a pointed look. "Another one?"

His smile deepens as he reaches into his pocket. "Just one. Maybe two."

I pick up my fork and wait for him to ask. When he does, I find myself wishing I could opt out of this little date we're on. Though I don't know if it is a date. Or just dinner. Or...

He slides a receipt across the table toward me. At first I don't know what it is, but then I remember back to yesterday and the angry kid with the ugly tattoo.

I can't look at him. Not when I know what's coming. Not when I know he read the four lines of prose I wrote on that receipt and knows the meaning behind them.

"I found this under the counter at work. Would you mind telling me what you're up to?"

⌒

"SPARKY, I THINK it's time for a raise."

We left the restaurant ten minutes ago, and this is the first word anyone has spoken. I've spent the majority of the time mulling over the question he asked at the restaurant and the bombshell he dropped shortly afterward. I've also spent a good deal of time wondering if the night is over or if Lennon plans to just keep driving. My hopes hold tightly to that second one.

"You're not giving me a raise."

"Why not? Most people don't turn those down."

I pull my knees to my chest like a ten-year-old-girl and peel my gaze away from oncoming traffic to send him a sidelong look. "I've graffitied your bathroom wall so much it looks like a gang stopped by for a potty break in between gunning each other down. I've fainted more than once, I can't stand the sight of needles and never help you dispose of them, and last week I forgot to charge a customer—"

"Excuse me?"

"I mean, I forgot to thank a customer."

There's a long pause. "Forget the raise."

"Why? You can't take it back already!"

"You said you didn't want one."

"I was lying. It's the polite thing to do."

He laughs. "Fine. But don't forget to charge someone ever again."

I drop my head into my hands. "I won't." My voice is muffled, coming through the cracks between my fingers. "She just kept showing me pictures of her daughter, and we got into a long conversation about college majors because she's studying to be a nurse and one thing led to another…" I sigh. "Why do you even let me work for you?"

He drums a finger on the steering wheel. "Because I like you."

My head snaps around to look at him. "Why? I'm not much help, don't have the greatest personality…and this hair." I run my fingers through it to emphasize its awfulness.

"The hair is the best part. It's the exact opposite of the rest of you."

For a second I don't know what he means. "In what way?"

"Well, you're quiet, a bit subdued, afraid of several things, and not at all hot-tempered. You tell me." He smiles.

"I'm not afraid of anything."

"Let's go get your ears pierced."

"I'm only afraid of one thing." Obnoxious man and his need to be right.

He pulls out onto the highway and merges into traffic. Once at a safe speed, he props a hand on my seat back, the other tracing a crescent moon across the bottom curve of the steering wheel. The action makes my pulse skip…skid…fly…though the reaction is stupid. Lennon is my boss. My superior. I'm beneath him. But his hand is only inches from my shoulder. He's so good-looking. With Lennon, every action and reaction points back to that.

He clears his throat and taps me on the shoulder.

"Tell me something, Sparky. Are you afraid of heights?"

Chapter Fourteen

I SHOULD HAVE known he would do this. It's dark, slightly creepy out here, we're alone, and he's asking me to join him. But there's no way. No way. He's on his own.

"Are you out of your mind? Get down from there! You're going to fall and break your neck, and then there won't be anyone to ink up all the customers!" I feel my chest constrict and pull a few deep breaths to calm myself.

Lennon turns to look at me and laughs. The man stands suspended halfway up what looks like a fifty-foot fire escape on the side of the building that houses the tattoo parlor. He's asking for a broken bone. A crushed corpse. A soul destined for an early entrance into heaven.

I'm all for the pearly gates, but not at twenty-one. I still have things to do. Parents to face. Kids to birth. Phobias to overcome.

"I thought you said you weren't afraid of heights," he calls down to me.

"I'm not in theory," I lie. "Like when it involves iron bars or a sure place to stand. Like a mountain. But ladders and narrow rungs are different. People are superstitious about them for a reason, you know."

"This isn't a ladder, and unless you're planning to walk underneath it instead of climbing up, you have nothing to worry about."

"I'm not climbing up."

"You'll regret it if you don't."

"I'm not climbing. That's my final decision."

"Either start climbing or I'll come back down and shove your butt up ahead of me."

I start climbing. Every few seconds I look over my shoulder for an escape until I'm one rung past what is definitely my safe zone. Then I stare straight ahead and try not t0 think because I'm Darby Sparks. I pass out at the sight of blood. There's no telling what I'll do at the sight of Los Angeles underneath me.

"Where are we going?" I ask, the shake in my voice as rickety as this ladder.

"To the top. I'm almost there."

"Well, that's great for you. I'm not even close."

"Yes, you are. Just keep climbing and try not to think about what you're doing."

Whatever. I hear a moan and the sound of feet shuffling as Lennon heaves himself over the ledge and onto the roof. I'm still a good ten feet away, nothing but rusty rungs and the smell of fear above me.

"Can you at least tell me the point of this? I need to know that risking my life and sanity for your ridiculous whim is worth it." The ladder creaks. I whimper.

"Only two more rungs, Sparky, and you'll find out for yourself."

I brave the last two rungs in silence, then grip the brick ledge of the roof. For a minute I'm paralyzed as my very real fear closes in like a wine press, but Lennon's hands are on my shoulder, my waist, my legs...and I'm up and over. I fall with a less than flattering thud, but at least I'm safe. Standing, I brush bits of gravel from the back of my jeans and get my first real glimpse of the world in front of me.

My breath catches in my throat as I find out for myself.

Stars. City lights. They blend into a million vibrant twinkles until I'm not sure where the sky ends and electricity begins. Miles stretch over miles. Mountains over mountains. The Hollywood sign, Universal Studios, spotlights and halos and slowly moving vehicles that add their own spin to the landscape. It's beautiful, this world that Lennon invited me into. It's my new favorite spot, maybe ever. I've never seen anything like it in my tiny Washington town.

"I can't believe I didn't know this was here."

He smiles in the darkness. Even without looking, I know it's a big one.

"Worth the climb, don't you think?"

I bump his hip with my own. "I wouldn't go that far," I lie. "Do you have any idea what you put me through?" My voice sounds light. It's safe to assume Lennon knows I would climb it again just for this view.

He pulls out two folding chairs leaning against the wall and sets them up, then lowers himself into one, motioning for me to sit next to him.

I look at him through narrowed eyes. "It's almost like you planned this."

He leans back with his hands behind his head. "Don't flatter yourself. These chairs have been here since before I rented the building."

I sit, but not without a tiny pang of disappointment running through me. Maybe I didn't want him to plan it, but it might be nice to be seen as the type of girl worth planning things for.

The view dims a bit as I stay inside my private pity party, but in true Lennon form, he comes along and blows a horn—forcing me to find another way to celebrate.

"Have you given any thought to what I said earlier?"

Lennon asked me a question at the restaurant, and I haven't stopped thinking about it since. A question about my goals and dreams, and I still have no idea how to answer him.

I look up at the sky. "It's been five minutes."

"It's been over an hour, and you didn't speak the whole way here. I'm not an idiot; I know you've thinking about it since I brought it up."

"Don't flatter yourself. You shouldn't assume your words hold that much weight with me."

He laughs. *Laughs.* Stupid man and his ridiculous ego.

I hate him for being right.

"I might have thought about it a little. But it would mean an entirely different mind-set, setting aside a lifetime of goals and dreams that I'm just not sure I can afford to give up."

I can feel his face on me. I refuse to look his way because I know exactly what he's thinking.

"You haven't gotten one call back from any audition since you've been here. Which means you can afford to give up all kinds of things since you haven't made any money at it. Acting might not be your thing."

I turn to glare at him. He either doesn't notice or he just doesn't care. He just keeps talking and talking and talking. "I read that receipt and every piece of prose you have scratched all over my bathroom wall. Writing is your thing." He reaches out to nudge my chin upward. My teeth tap together, and he smirks. "You should be a writer. I would buy any book or article you publish. I would even read the ones you don't publish."

I scoff. "No, you wouldn't. I would probably write silly love stories or something equally disturbing to you. You look like the kind of guy who would be into murder or paranormal." I give him a quick full-body scan—one that I like entirely too much—then look away. "Not romance."

He grows quiet, then locks both hands behind his head and looks at the stars. "There you go, stereotyping again. I actually like a good romance. It's one of my favorite things, in books and in real life."

My heartbeat sputters because I hear them. His words. They're full of unspoken little meanings we're both afraid to say. Teasing him was a big mistake. Now the air is thick with tension, regret, and an uncomfortable longing. At least on my part.

"This might be true," I say, looking for a way to ease it. "You are the guy who has a thing for Madonna."

I hear Lennon smile in the moonlight. "You got me there."

I settle back in my chair. The sounds of Los Angeles play out below us like children tinkering with Matchbox cars—muted, scattered, dotted with the occasional squeal of brakes and murmuring voices. Paired with the image of a million flickering flames dancing across the blackened night sky, it lulls me into a trance-like state. We're blanketed in a comfortable silence for several moments. I don't remember the last time I was this relaxed around anyone. Definitely not a man.

"Do you like it here, Sparky? In Los Angeles, I mean."

For a minute I say nothing, thinking about his question and wanting to give an honest response. Sometimes honesty gets lost in the need to impress, but Lennon has been good to me. It's time to set aside lies and be a bit transparent if only for the sake of fairness.

To him. To me. To a life that hasn't gone exactly the way I planned.

"I think so? It's definitely different than I expected, but I'm not sure that's a bad thing."

"Different how?"

"For one thing, I'd never hung out in a tattoo parlor before moving here. For another..." I lean forward and look out over the edge, careful not to get too close but enthralled by the bustling signs of life below me. "The most people I ever saw in one place back home was probably fifty, and that was only on Sundays at church. And fifty might be a stretch."

"Your town was that small?"

I smile. "You have no idea."

Lennon grows quiet, so quiet that I think our conversation is over. I lean back again and close my eyes, letting the nighttime breeze wash over my face. It's pleasant, even if it's mixed with the faint smell of sewer and motor oil.

"Do you like it enough to stay here?" Lennon says, jolting me back to the present. My eyes open at the same time my mind focuses on his question. There's a hesitancy in his voice, one that swirls a bit of hope through my insides. "I hope so. I kinda like having you around."

With a hand to my middle, I command myself to remain calm. Lennon wants me to stay. And truthfully, so do I.

"I think so. At least for a while." I try to sound nonchalant and even manage to keep my smile low-wattage. I would pat myself on the back, but it might look out-of-the-blue here. Not to mention weird.

"I'm glad." It's a simple statement, but it's the best two-word sentence I've heard in my life.

Lennon squeezes my shoulder and leaves his hand there. A show of solidarity. A nod to understanding. I don't mean to lean into his touch, but I do.

"You know," he says, "if this city gets to be too much for you, you could always move to a suburb and commute. Who knows, someday you could wind up being a suburban housewife and star in your own reality show."

I reach out to punch him, but he catches my hand in his and won't let go. I pull, he pulls, and soon we're in a full battle of wills.

"Let go of my hand!"

"You need to lift weights or something. Your arms are pathetically weak."

The struggle builds at the same time a giggling fit overtakes me. I turn my head to threaten him again, but the laughter dies on my lips when I see his face only inches away. He's breathing heavy and I'm breathing heavy and my breath catches when he scans my eyes, my chin, my mouth. The moment lasts a few seconds and a lifetime and ends when I can't take it anymore and move forward. He follows my lead and for one glorious second our lips touch. The kiss is short—only enough time for my mind to register what's happening, but long enough to taste mint and chocolate and skin so warm I could rest against it forever.

But then he's gone, and we're looking at each other, panic in my eyes and pain in his.

"Darby, I'm your boss." A simple statement. Obvious. But it's cold water over a raging fire.

He called me Darby.

Not Sparky.

Not what I want to hear.

Now or ever.

The worst part is he's right; He's my boss. An angry emoji at the end of a beautiful sentence. A pencil point sharpened only to break at the next use.

The disappointment will not show on my face; I won't let it.

"It was my fault," I say. "I shouldn't have done that. I'm sorry."

I'm sorry. I'm lying all over again.

We don't speak for another hour, but we don't move away, either. At first it's awkward, but the longer his hand stays on my shoulder, the more I lean closer. Maybe we shouldn't have kissed, but that doesn't mean we want the night to end.

Before long, my shoulder is tucked underneath his, and he is playing with the ends of my hair. My heart keeps time with his thumb as it swirls around each strand, my tangled, jumbled insides trying to forget the near kiss that I know will stay with me forever.

My boss. Yet right now…it definitely doesn't feel that way.

The view—dimmed for a moment—brightens again. And that's when I am certain; I can trust Lennon. Could tell him all my worries without fear or judgment. It's nice to know I've found a friend here. A real one.

I ponder this until it's time to leave.

The end of the night comes way too soon.

Chapter Fifteen

"I ACCIDENTLY OPENED this."

Handing off the envelope, I swallow, still in shock and still very aware of the contents inside. Lennon never should have put me in charge of the mail. He knows I still sometimes use my fingers to count and sing the alphabet out loud to remember what letter comes next. The mail is too much responsibility. My expertise stops at the cash register, and we're both aware I'm not very good at that either.

Still, I can't believe I opened his letter.

I can't believe I read it.

I can't believe what I saw.

Though in spite of all this disbelieving, I still have no idea what it means.

He reaches for the envelope and eyes me cautiously. "Did you read it?"

I look to the left. A sure sign I'm thinking up yet another lie. If Lennon has any experience with body language, he knows it too. Forcing myself to look him in the eye, I deliver the truth as I know it.

"Not exactly?"

"That means you did."

"Not entirely." I drag out the word and slide a finger across the counter in a figure eight, buying myself time. To heck with time. I'm out of it. "I just saw the picture and the amount on the check and what it was for."

He sighs. "So, you read the letter."

"I might have a little."

"Sparky."

"Lennon." One word that asks a thousand questions.

He sighs. "Please don't say anything. I'd rather everyone not know what I make on a sale."

I saw the amount. I read the address. But he still manages to stump me with that one explosive statement.

"You made seven-thousand dollars on one drawing? Of a chair? For a *tattoo*?" My forehead hurts from the way I'm scrunching it up, but I can't help it. "You have books and books of artwork over there." My arm swings out like I'm trying to rid my body of it. "Did you sell all those?"

He swallows. "It's not just a chair. It's a prayer bench. With beads and a book. Very personal to a lot of people, and it's not only for a tattoo. People could use it for anything."

"Despite the fact that it's *still a chair*, that's not the point." Although he is right, it's much more than a place to sit—like nothing I've ever seen in detail and style. The picture is so incredibly real that all I wanted to do when I saw it was grab a pair of those beads and kneel down. But we're talking numbers here, not art.

He rubs the space between his eyebrows. "Yes, I made that much off one sale and yes, I sold all the pictures in that book, but—"

"Lennon, you're rich!"

"Sparky, shut up!"

But I see the smile in his eyes, and of course I don't shut up because my mind is spinning like a gumball winding its way to the bottom of a machine. And like that gumball, my thoughts demand a way out.

"So, the guy at the art museum…"

"Can we talk about this later?"

"Sure." He's not getting off that easily. He made me climb on top of a building for heaven's sake. He owes me this. Or maybe he doesn't. Either way, I blink and look him straight in the eye, letting him know

I'm not going anywhere.

He gets the message and flexes his jaw. "They want me to open a gallery."

"A gallery? There?"

He closes his eyes. "Yes, there."

"Holy crap, Lennon! That's huge!"

He laughs and slaps a hand over my mouth. "Would you stop yelling? I don't want anyone else to know, so be quiet."

I giggle into his skin, even consider licking it, but he pulls his hand away before I have the chance. "We're already closed. There's no one here except you and me."

He shakes his head. "Your voice is so loud it could probably carry next door."

"That's insulting, but whatever. So are you going to do it? Open the gallery, I mean?"

He slumps against the wall and crosses one foot over another. "I don't know. That's a lot of exposure, and I'm a big fan of privacy." He looks toward the window, lost in a world of moonlight and escape.

I watch him for a moment, the way his jawline works in contemplation as though an answer will grind its way out of his mouth if he works hard enough. I'm so taken with his mannerisms...so absorbed in his profile...that I don't notice when he turns back to me. As soon as I snap out of it, it's obvious I've been caught. I clear my throat and reach for the ends of my hair, hoping a few pulls will yank away my embarrassment.

"You don't have to give up your privacy," I say. Thankfully my voice sounds strong even though my insides feel pliable and melty. "Just because people enjoy your mind doesn't mean they have to enjoy your body." I frown. "Did that come out right?"

From the gleam in his eye, I think I have my answer. "Not exactly, but thank you."

"I just meant—"

"I know what you meant, and I'll keep it in mind."

With my face burning like I fell asleep in the sun, I turn and busy myself by straightening the counter. That amounts to two wayward receipts and someone's leftover bubblegum wrapper, but I squeeze every extra second out of the cleanup I can manage. Why did I bring up his body? Why can't I ever just say what I mean without getting myself in trouble?

I take a deep breath and resolve to try.

"You're an interesting man, Lennon. Just when I think I have you figured out, you throw me off my game and prove me completely wrong. I like that about you." I refill the register's receipt tape and close the cover with a snap, trying to appear casual. My heartbeat is clanging like a gong inside my head. Casual isn't working.

The clanging lessens a bit with Lennon's non-response. Curious, I turn to see if he's still in the room and come face to face with eyes so intense I have to look away. I focus instead on the picture of the woman, wondering if I said something wrong. She gives me no answer. My words were supposed to be a compliment, but I'm always saying the wrong thing. It's a criticism my mother has made since I was four and yelled a foul word in the middle of their home-church Bible study. She asked where I heard it; I announced in front of everyone that my father said the word all the time. And he did, but never again in front of me.

If memory serves, they also never had that study in our home again. Most people don't think God and the F-word fit in the same room. Crazy, but true.

"That's the thing about stereotypes; they're never right. Take you, for example."

He's baiting me, and I'm swimming straight for the hook. The bite is predictable.

"What about me?" Three words, an invitation to dive in, open up, delve a little deeper. This sudden boldness feels foreign, but not unwelcome. I lean against the counter, facing him. There are ten feet between us, but the electric current stretches the distance. "What was your first impression of me?"

He glances at the ceiling as if a memory reel is playing there: Darby walking into the store. Darby looking frightened and out of her element. Darby interviewing for the job. I remember the highlights. None were worth watching the first time; reruns are bound to be a disaster. He locks eyes with me again.

"I thought you were scared to death of this city, the people, and life in general."

This is true...

"But then I discovered you were a confident girl who knew what she wanted and came in to get it."

What? "I'm not confident. I'm scared to death of everything, even now."

He shakes his head. "No, you're not. You've just believed that lie for so long that you don't know how to let go of it. Scared girls don't drive to a new state by themselves and demand that guys like me give them a job."

"I didn't demand—"

"You demanded." He looks down and grins, lost in the memory.

My mind travels to that day too. I was so afraid that day—of being penniless, of my disintegrating pride, of the customers inside this shop. They weren't my people—these pierced and painted and scary-looking individuals who frequented establishments like this one. Brainstorm was, in many ways, beneath me. Quite possibly sinful. At the very least, a questionable way to make a living. Or so I thought at the time.

Lennon is right. Pre-conceived notions are a wasted way to pass the time. In my case, they nearly kept me from meeting some of the nicest people I've ever had the pleasure of being around. People just like me, but with different shells. But shells are just that—a personalized way of presenting ourselves to the world–a world that's spinning and moving and changing and filled with so much exterior color that often people forget to stop running and take a second to look around. To walk in the grass. To appreciate a flower. To peel back the outer layers of earth and dirt and study what's underneath.

Surprises are found beneath the surface.

Prejudices are destroyed beneath the surface.

I remember that girl from six weeks ago and smile. "I'm glad I didn't let it stop me. If it had, I wouldn't have met you." Another confession. One I didn't plan to make.

We stare at each other. I can see the rise and fall of his chest, the part of his lips, the gaze that clouds itself in questions and longing for one brief second before clearing again. My breathing suspends in my throat, but I don't need air. I need this. I need to revisit the rooftop kiss, only this time make it last.

He is looking at my lips. And then he looks away.

Possibility there. And then gone.

"What I said the other night hasn't changed," he whispers.

I turn to grab the trash can underneath the register. "I know. You're my boss, and I'm your employee. And that's that."

I walk toward the door without looking back.

I hear him say my name as I open it and head outside.

I feel his eyes watching my back until the door slams behind me.

Chapter Sixteen

TWO DAYS LATER it's all sunshine and butterflies. Darn those winged creatures.

Still, for the moment I'm walking a little taller, and Lennon and I are getting along almost as if things are back to normal. As if those five minutes we spent alone in the shop never happened. His whispered *Nothing has changed* was just that...whispered. It's like we can both pretend neither ever happened. Pretend we don't have feelings and we don't have issues and we don't have a whole bunch of unspoken truths stacked up like packs of Marlboros in an ex-smoker's face.

It's perfect, really.

If you're a liar. And now there are two of us.

Still, today we've laughed. We've given each other a hard time. I've made fun of Lennon's lame artwork that apparently sane people line up to pay insane amounts of money for. He draws spiders, for heaven's sake. Ropes and chains. Chairs. How is that even art?

When I voiced that question out loud, he held up a tattoo needle and threatened to jab it into my leg. The good news is I'm a fast runner. I did not die. I came close, but in the end shock paddles and resuscitation drugs were not needed.

I'd call that progress.

I've progressed in other ways too.

The henna tattoo Lennon gave me two weeks ago has begun to fade, and it turns out I liked it. So much, in fact, that I've obsessively checked it every day for extra signs of wear. When I woke up this morning, one half of the sunflower was nearly gone, rubbed off like it was an especially cloudy day and only one side had the strength to bloom. I mentioned having him redo it when I walked in this morning, frowning a bit more than I normally would and adding a little extra whine to my voice.

It worked. I'm now sitting in a chair with my left arm out of my blue shirt sleeve, a towel draped over my shoulder to cover the most important parts. Lennon works beside me, his breath feathering across my shoulder each time he bends to add a little more henna. My skin pebbles from my bare shoulder to my wrist—both from the overhead air conditioning and from his closeness. His fingers dance across my skin like I'm a piano and he's a brilliant composer. I close my eyes, enjoying the music and wanting him to keep playing. The song in my head is beautiful. The hum in his throat is beautiful. The trance that he has me under is beautiful.

So beautiful that I don't hear the front door open.

And because I don't hear it...because Lennon doesn't hear it...I'm unprepared for the nice comfortable world I've made for myself to come crashing at my feet, leaving all those hidden truths peeled back like a scab ripped away from a cut that hasn't had enough time to heal.

"Darby Ellen Sparks, what do you think you're doing?"

I open my eyes and jump out of my chair.

Lennon jerks and drops the brush.

My parents are standing in the doorway, looking at both of us like we're two kindergarteners—me caught with my tongue sticking out and him caught lifting up my dress at the exact moment my flowery pink panties are exposed. There's no way to gracefully slip my arm back inside my shirtsleeve, so I don't. I leave it hanging out, visible and naked, the beautiful sunflower drying up and morphing into an ugly scarlet 'A' the longer we stand there and stare at each other.

My bottom lip trembles. I pull it between my teeth to stop the shaking. "I'm getting a tattoo?" A weak question delivered in an even weaker voice. No sense in explaining the artwork is temporary—it's as permanent as their united disappointment. "What are you doing here? And how did you find me?"

"We have a tracer on your phone. When you stopped answering our calls, we decided to locate you ourselves," my father says.

It's been four days since we talked. I'm twenty-one years old. He says this like it isn't slightly disturbing.

"We came to check on you. Obviously we should have come sooner. Would you mind telling me why my daughter is standing half-naked in a tattoo parlor with your hands all over her?" He says this last part to Lennon, the interrogation is in full swing even though I had no time to prepare notes or line up witnesses.

I'm the one on trial—not him—so even though I'm still stuck on my parents tracing my phone, I'll do the explaining. Lennon's mouth opens, but I start talking before he has time to form a word. "I work here, Daddy. I've worked here for almost six weeks now. And his hands were on my arm, not all over me."

My mother gasps. "Why didn't you tell me this when I asked? You let me think you were jobless and penniless in the middle of Los Angeles!" She skewers me with her gaze. I'm the mushroom in the center of the shish-kabob.

"The penniless part is accurate," I mumble.

"What?"

"What?"

"What?"

This from all three as heads swivel in tandem to look at me.

"You don't have any money?" my mother asks, genuine concern in her voice.

"Why didn't you tell me you needed money?" Lennon looks hurt, like he can't believe I didn't come to him with the need for more.

"Son, how much are you paying her?" My father's angry look turns accusatory, like if given the tiniest provocation he would murder Lennon right here on Marilyn Monroe's face. There's a colorful mosaic of the actress's profile on the main floor, the top of her head beginning beside the cash register and her bare legs stretching nearly to the front door. I don't know if Lennon put it in or if the building came designed this way. I've never asked, and now just doesn't seem like the right time.

"I still don't see why he was touching you. He's...he's..." My father takes in Lennon, his lips pursed like he's just sucked half a lemon as his eyes roam up and down, pausing on Lennon's forearm and holding there. The largest part of his tattoo is showing—the cross and chains and daggers and, for the love of God, the drops of blood. It doesn't matter that the blood symbolizes something good. Lennon might as well be a member of an underground cult for the look my father gives him.

"What exactly are you son?"

Lennon is an eight-string guitar, and my father is shredding him. While he looked dazed and stunned, I search for a way to save him.

"He's my boss, Daddy. Only my boss, and nothing else."

Beside me, I see Lennon flinch.

My words are a lie, an echo of Lennon's earlier words, but the damage has been done anyway.

"Thank God." My mother says it like a prayer, but I'm pretty sure God doesn't take kindly to giving thanks while disparaging another person. But I know my place; I know the way I was raised. I keep my mouth shut and wish I could disappear.

"If he's just your boss," my father says with a hand around my arm, "you'll have no trouble finding another one. Grab your things, Darby, and let's go."

I want to say no. I want to tell them to go back home and let me live my life. To accept Lennon for the good man he is and not condemn him just for a few pieces of body art. To trust me and to love me and to let their little girl grow up. My mouth is dry. My voice won't work.

That's when I glance at Lennon and know. If my words hadn't cut him enough, my indecisiveness just twisted the knife. Both just cost me everything.

So I nod.

Grab my bag.

And wordlessly follow my parents out the front door.

Leaving behind the best job…the best memories…potentially the best person I've ever met.

No one has to tell me I'm making the wrong decision.

Chapter Seventeen

THE NEXT MORNING my phone rings. I grab it without looking at the caller, hoping it's him.

"I just fried twelve pounds of bacon. Not even kidding."

Avery doesn't bother to say hello, but I can hear the stress in her voice. I haven't exactly been that supportive of her sudden internship, but encouragement, at least from me, is something I've been fresh out of since my parents walked into my work yesterday and silently commanded I leave the only place I've ever really fit.

"My parents showed up and dragged me out of the tattoo parlor yesterday. Right in front of Lennon," I say on a sigh into the phone.

"Oh crap, you win. Where are you now?"

"In a hotel room outside of Los Angeles waiting for my dad to get here and announce it's time to head home. Why do I always get stuck in these situations?"

My words hang for a minute, long enough for me to notice there's an extended pause on the other end. I pull the phone away from my ear to see if the call was disconnected.

"Avery?"

"I'm going to tell you something," she says, "and you're going to listen."

I swallow. Avery does this thing. Of our little group of four friends who've stayed close since kindergarten, Avery is the self-appointed mother. The one to give an occasional lecture. The one who listens when we cry and empathizes when we're depressed and wallows with us when we're down—and then slaps us on the head and tells us to get up, brush ourselves off, and find a new attitude.

"Okay." I scoot back on the bed and lean against the headboard, bracing myself.

"You're in this situation because you allow yourself to be. Look, your parents love you. And I know you love them, right?"

"Right?" I have no idea where she's going with this.

"Fine, at least that's established. But it's possible to love someone without controlling them. It's possible to accept that the best for someone might not necessarily be what we have in mind."

I look up at the ceiling. "You know my parents. How am I supposed to get them to believe that?"

She clears her throat. Sniffs. Then sighs. When all three happen, you know she's ready to wrap up her lecture and go back to just being your friend.

"You're supposed to sit your parents down, tell them how much you love them, and then nicely tell them to butt the heck out of your life. It's time, Darby. Now grow a set and do it."

In spite of my depressing circumstances, I laugh. Avery is wise. She's caring to a fault. And she has a way of explaining things that gives you a new perspective on an old situation.

I hang up with her and sit on the hotel room bed to wait. And while I wait, I think of the day I left home with money in my pocket, a dream in my mind, a desire to see the world, and no idea what came next. But I made it to Los Angeles, found myself a job, auditioned for part after part even though nothing materialized, and made a new friend. A new friend who, in seven short weeks, has given me a different way of thinking and a new way to dream.

Lennon.

If I leave now, I may never see him again.

But if I stay, my parents might be angry for a while…maybe even longer.

I stare at the wall, wrestling with the two realities in front of me, doubt and insecurity fighting for the most prominent space in my mind. But there's one thing I've never doubted: my parents love me. They've never given me a reason to believe their love will fade with time. There's no reason to believe it now.

"*Grow a set,*" Avery had said. "*Tell them.*"

And she was right.

So when my parents walk in twenty minutes later from a Wal-Mart gas and grocery run to prepare for our long drive home...

That's exactly what I do.

Chapter Eighteen

I WALK INTO the tattoo parlor later that night without telling him I'm coming. He looks up from across the room, a broom in his hand and Coldplay blasting over the speakers. It's an interesting choice for him, different from the alternative bands I'm used to hearing. From the look on his face he's both surprised and annoyed, but there is a smile behind his eyes. I see it...I can always see it because despite his devil-may-care attitude, his feelings are transparent.

Lennon says nothing when he sees me and neither do I. Sometimes more than enough can be said in silence, especially if no one is around to interrupt the conversation. Thank God the place is empty. The fact that I'm here tells us both everything; I'm not leaving again, not unless he fires me. He's threatened it so many times, I no longer know if it's even a real possibility.

"Hi," he says. "You took an awful long lunch break."

I feel myself smile. "Well, I was starving, plus I had a few errands to run."

"Did you get them all taken care of?" His meaning is clear. *Are you sticking around? Or are you going to leave me without a word again?*

"I did. Everything has been straightened out."

He studies the wall. "Permanently?"

I look around the room. Is anything in life really permanent? We grow, we change, we love, we leave. But we all have a choice about who we ride the adventure with. For now, my choice is here. Because my friend is here. Because my dream is here. And because something tells me those last two are closely tied together, maybe for a very long time.

"Permanently. At least for now." I say.

He finally smiles, so big it fills his face. "That's good enough for me," he says, tossing the broom in my direction. It flies through air and lands in my left hand.

For the next twenty minutes we clean in silence, me feeling a little like Cinderella after she came home from the ball.

When I catch Lennon watching me, I almost feel like singing.

⁓

"JUST HOLD MY hand. I promise I won't let go." Lennon says two days later. I'm in a chair surrounded by glass and mirrors, and my face is pale. So pale it's like I'm doused in baby powder from forehead to neck, except I smell like sweat. Sweat and nerves and an overactive imagination, the worst combination. I hate that I can see myself at so many angles, because it's there, plain as this very long day, and there's no way to escape it. So I look straight into Lennon's eyes, and focus only on him.

Fear is a powerful thing, but courage is stronger. And it doesn't hurt if you are lucky enough to find someone you trust enough to help absorb your weakness.

Lennon offered to absorb mine, so I let him. "I'm holding your hand, but can you please squeeze tighter?"

He raises an eyebrow. "Do you want it to hurt?"

I nod, up and down, up and down. "Yes, and then maybe I won't notice when—"

I scream. Give a little whimper. And then I wait.

And wait.

And wait.

"Is it over?" I blink at him. Blink a few more times at the lady in front of me.

She smiles. "It's over. You were very brave, Miss."

"Thank you." I ignore the condescending wink and subsequent

grin she and Lennon give each other and look at my reflection. They can make fun of me all they want, but nothing is going to ruin this moment for me. Nothing.

"I can't believe I did it," I say, in awe of my own reflection.

"You did it." He sounds proud. Sincerely and completely proud. "I especially like the Hello Kitty ones you picked out. Very mature. Should go nicely with all your outfits. And by outfits, I mean pajamas."

I backhand him in the stomach and stand up, placing the mirror on the table in front of me. "Look, if you had waited your whole life to get your ears pierced, you would pick these out too." I walk around him and pay the lady. "And as for my *yoga pants*," I say, emphasizing the word as I tug on the black pair I'm currently wearing, "you know you like them. So suck it, Lennon." I stick out my tongue, further sealing his low opinion of my maturity level. Whatever.

We make our way out of the store, walking side by side in the California sunshine, me practically skipping and unable to keep my hands off my newly pierced ears. I can't believe I finally did it. I can't believe it hardly even hurt. What was I so afraid of? Why did this take me so long?

When I glance over at Lennon, he's smiling. "Pretty proud of yourself, aren't you?"

I can't help beaming like a fourth grader. "A little. I got my ears pierced!" I shout up to the sky and do a little spin. "Thank you for talking me into it. And for going with me. And for hurting my hand."

He laughs. We walk a little further before I feel it. His hand touches mine, his fingers spreading wide until each one of ours is linked together. I pull them tighter, palm to palm, as close as they can be. So close I might never let go.

I don't say anything, but when I look over at him he's thinking about something. Something important. Something he wants to say, so I wait. Lennon always says what's on his mind if you give him a minute. And always...always...the words are worth the wait.

"Do you have an answer for me yet?"

I take a deep breath. The moment of truth. I know it would come eventually, but I'm still unprepared.

"I don't know, Lennon. It's just—"

"You're good, Sparky. I wouldn't ask you if I didn't really believe that. Do not spend another second thinking I'm asking you out of pity or that you're some sort of charity case on my part."

I don't tell him I've struggled with those thoughts since he asked me yesterday.

Lennon said yes to the gallery. By this time next month, all of his creative works will be on display at the Museum of Contemporary Art, one of the most prestigious art galleries in California.

But here's the kicker.

He wants me to write the stories behind the pictures. Not all of them, but his favorites. Which means that for the first time since I began writing my private little stories before my tenth birthday, someone besides myself—and now Lennon by default—will read them. And critique them. And love them. Or hate them and mock them and criticize them in front of the entire California population and maybe the whole world.

It's a struggle. Maybe not a real one and maybe only in my mind, but whatever.

I take a deep breath and tell him before I can change my mind. "Fine, I'll do it."

He jerks us both to a stop and looks at me. Really, really looks at me.

"You will?"

When I see the half-smile on his face, I know I made the right decision.

"I will."

He doesn't say anything right away, just watches me with that same expression I've seen from him before. Like he is contemplating something, weighing things in his thoughts, battling himself for an answer he never seems to find. He almost always surrenders, almost always walks away without a resolution or final conclusion, almost always leaves me wondering what he's thinking.

This time is different.

It takes me a second to realize what's happening. Just a few seconds after, he reaches for my waist, pulls me flush to him, fans his fingers across the back of my neck. After my hand collides with his chest, the other traveling up toward his hairline. After he gives me a lazy grin, tilts his head in a question, moves forward to lightly touch his lips with mine. It takes me a second.

But then I get it and pull back before anything good has a chance to begin.

His chest is ridiculously chiseled. I peel my eyes away from it and look up at him.

"I thought you were my boss? The other day, you said—"

"Technically I still am," he says with a gleam in his eye, one finger tracing the waistline of my jeans. "But since you agreed to the gallery, now we're more like partners. Right?"

"Right." I smile right back at him. "We are like partners. And now I want a raise. A fifty-fifty split on everything."

He kisses me again, longer this time. Long enough to know that his tongue tastes like mint...that he is insanely skilled at more than just tattoo-giving.

"Don't push it, Sparky." He laughs against my mouth as he goes in for more, his hot breath against my lips warming me like no blanket ever could.

"Fine," I say. I intend to say more, to protest more, but when he kisses me again...and again. When he kisses me longer...deeper. When his hands find my spine and travel lower...lower.

I can't think of a thing to say.

Talking is overrated anyway.

But kissing.

Kissing is different.

And different is definitely good.

The End

About the Author

Author Amy Matayo is the Amazon bestselling author of *The Wedding Game*, *Love Gone Wild*, *Sway*, and *In Tune With Love*. She graduated with barely passing grades from John Brown University with a degree in Journalism. But don't feel sorry for her—she's super proud of that degree and all the ways she hasn't put it to good use.

She laughs often, cries easily, feels deeply, and loves hard. She lives in Arkansas with her husband and four kids and is working on her next novel.

Other books by Amy Matayo:

In Tune With Love

Sway

Love Gone Wild

The Wedding Game

Follow her on:

Instagram: @amymatayo

Twitter: @amymatayo

Facebook: www.facebook.com/amymatayo

Keep reading for Avery's Summer adventure in Sugar Creek!

Wild Heart Summer

By
Jenny B. Jones

Chapter One

I HAD SO wanted this year to be different.

Hadn't I done everything I could to put that into motion? Eaten black-eyed peas on New Year's—with watering eyes and gag reflexes fully engaged. Made a wish over my twenty-first birthday cake, a wish so lovely, so dotted with audacious hope, not breathing until every dancing flame surrendered. And every time I'd eaten Chinese food in the last six months? I'd basically won the fortune cookie lottery. I'd also won a few rounds of indigestion, but it's not like that should've canceled out anything.

And still here I was. Living yet *another* day of catastrophe on this first afternoon of June. As if fate got a sick thrill from spitting all over my fiery better intentions.

My mother said I'd been born under an unlucky moon, when Venus was in retrograde or giving Mercury the bird—something like that. But she'd also said my biological father was a NASA astronaut who'd sacrificed himself to live on the moon and start a new colony. By the age of ten, I'd changed my mind on which statement I actually believed.

"Joss, can you hear me?" I'm checking in with my friend, holding my phone to my cheek with my shoulder and walking down the tiniest airport concourse, en route to get my luggage. I speak louder over the din. "You gotta see this airport. It's cute and all, but I'm pretty sure it's in the middle of a cow field." I know we flew over barns and cattle. I have pictures to prove it. "Tell me again where you said you're going."

"I said I'm spending the summer at the cabin," Joss says.

"You have no idea how much I want to be there. Do your parents know you're going by yourself?"

"We're not talking about me. We're talking about the fact that you're losing your mind."

"I'm not losing my mind. I'm visiting Arkansas."

"Same thing."

I feel a tiny stab of annoyance on behalf of the state I'd just landed in. It wasn't like I was from here. Well, technically I was born in Little Rock, Arkansas, but a few months of residency did not a bond make. I'd moved all over the country, finally landing in the state of Washington in middle school, where I met the three girls who were still my best friends, sisters even. This is the first summer we weren't spending a few weeks at Joss's cabin, our retreat away from it all, and I'm more than depressed about that.

"I don't understand," she says. "I thought you were doing your culinary internship at a fancy restaurant in Chicago."

"It got cancelled at the last minute." And if I wanted to pass my program and be eligible for the senior year in France, I had to take whatever the school offered me. "The only internship open was the Shadow Dude Ranch."

"You've got to be kidding me. The one your grandfather owns?"

I prefer to refer to him as my Mother's Former Father. "The one and only."

"And that job just came up? Just like that?"

"I guess he's been keeping tabs on me lately and contacted my school about the opportunity. I'm desperate here. I'm just going to complete my eight weeks, cook for some ranch hands, and stay out of Mitchell Crawford's way."

"This is a lot to take in," Joss says.

"I know." I walk down a set of stairs. "I've had to eat a lot of Cheetos over this."

"I meant for *me* to take in. I can't keep up with your drama. First,

John Mark cheats on you and now this?"

"We're not talking about John Mark. Ever." Two weeks ago I'd been on top of the world, dating the student government president at Bethel College in New York, only to find out his election motto of "I will do all I can to serve the student body" was being put to good use on a blonde and busty Kappa Delta. Never trust a sixth-year poetry major.

"You still haven't given us all the details," my best friend reminds me.

"I'm aware of that. It's not worth mentioning. I need to put it out of my mind, ignore every college guy on the planet, and throw myself into—"

"Avery Crawford?"

At this unfamiliar new voice, my phone-carrying hand drops. I'm intercepted at the bottom stairs by one tall, dark, and newly declared off-limits member of the male species.

"Yes?" Somewhere it registers that a plaintive voice streams from my phone, but I manage to power the device off. It's hard to do anything but stare into eyes as blue as sea glass and full lips that smile with a dimpled promise of sweet church picnics on Sunday and roving hands in the backseat the night before.

His smile deepens, and I inwardly sigh. I just decide to give up men, and of course, the cover model for *Southern Hot Gents* purrs my name.

"I'm from Shadow Ranch." Mr. Dimples sticks out his hand. "Owen Jackson."

"Hi." It's hard not to smile back, but I mostly accomplish it. I give him a polite stretch of the lips, but nothing flirty, nothing that says I think he's, unfortunately, quite beautiful.

"Did you have a good flight?" Owen's accent hearkens back to days of cowboys and front porch sitting.

"I did. I got a lot of work done." Like reading three *People* magazines, eating two candy bars, and composing my own poem to my ex titled, "I Hope You Get a Rash That Rots Off Your Naughty Bits."

"Your grandpa mentioned you were in a culinary program at school." Owen says. "He's really proud of you."

I have no trouble not smiling at this bit of ridiculousness. Sweet twang or not, Owen's words could not be further from the truth. "Mitchell Crawford is not my grandfather," I manage. "He's my temporary boss."

Beneath a University of Arkansas baseball hat, Owen's face goes still and neutral, as if I've just requested a stop for tampons on our way out. "Well." He tilts his head and looks down at my five-foot-six form as if he wants to say more. But doesn't. "I'm your ride to the ranch. Why don't we get your bags?"

Great idea. The sooner we get this started, the sooner it will all be over.

Chapter Two

"ARKANSAS IS NOT what I'd expected." I gaze out the passenger window of Owen's Ford truck and take in the mix of city and country. We'd passed chicken houses. We'd passed a Pottery Barn.

"This part of the state is really booming." Owen navigates the black truck over a bridge, and I read the sign that welcomes me to Sugar Creek in strong, bold letters. "The ranch is about ten miles from here on the outskirts of town. Really not even in the Sugar Creek city limits."

I know from things my mom told me that Mitchell's property is large enough to be its own settlement. "How many acres did you say he has?"

Owen gives a two-fingered wave to a woman pushing a stroller on the sidewalk. "About a thousand where you'll be."

"You mean there's more?"

Owen takes his eyes off the road to look at me. "You really don't know much about him, do you?"

"What I know about him really isn't too redeeming. I'm here to work and to get credit for my internship. This isn't going to be some happy family reunion." I instantly regret the bitterness in my tone. Between the drama I left behind in New York and this, I can't seem to tamper it down.

"Give Mitchell a chance." Owen turns the radio station to a song that's as country as the boots he's wearing. "I'd hate for you to miss out on something just because of old mistakes. You never know what the summer might hold."

Old mistakes? Old mistakes were side-ponytails on picture day and not giving the computer nerd in seventh grade a second glance. Old mistakes were sneaking out the house with the captain of the football team or eating strawberries before you realized they made your lips swell like an aging, plastic Hollywood diva. What Mitchell Crawford had done went so far beyond that. "Cooking and getting credit for a college class," I say. "That's all this summer will hold."

In a matter of minutes, the smooth, paved road gives way to dirt and gravel, and clouds of dust billow behind Owen's truck. Or maybe it was clouds of my anxiety, chasing our vehicle down, swirling around us and entreating me to turn back.

Owen taps his fingers on the steering wheel to the beat of the music as we amble down a long drive with fencing running on either side of us.

"What's that?" I point to a newer-looking structure, a sprawling two-story cedar cabin large enough to house an NFL football team. Six or seven smaller cabins surround it.

"The big building is the lodge. That's where the main kitchen is, where a lot of our activities are held. The others are the dude ranch cabins where people stay."

"Is one of them yours?" Owen had already told me he lived on the ranch. He alluded to being a manager of some sort, but of what exactly, I'm not sure. "Do all the employees live here?"

"No." Owen frowns, his dark brown brows slanting low. "Did you read the information I sent you on the ranch?"

"Of course I did." I mean, in the last-minute rush, I'd read the names and addresses on the envelope the information had been mailed in. That had been all I'd really needed to know.

"Then you're totally clear on what you'll be doing?"

"Clear as spring water." See, I was already hip to this Southern slang.

"How many guests will you be feeding?"

"Guests?"

He gives me the side eye. "Tell me what happens every Friday night."

"You go out with a local lassie and share a burger and fries?"

Owen brakes the truck, and my body lurches forward.

Gone was the sweet, amiable guy who'd picked me up at the airport. "Do you seriously not know what you've gotten into?"

Is he going to make me walk the rest of the way if I don't get this question right?

"Mitchell is a cattle rancher with some horses." I try to recall what my mom had once said. "My advisor mentioned he has about twenty-five people on his payroll, so I'll be cooking for them. For you. For you hard-working cowpokes." What was a cowpoke? Did I want to use that term? Was it now offensive to the farming community who might not want their good names associated with poking?

Owen settles his hand on the back of my headrest and leans my way. I can't help but inhale his scent of spice and outdoors. Mixed with a little *eau de frustration*.

"Mitchell expanded his property into more commercial pursuits five years ago." Owen's eyes hold mine steady. "Are you tracking with me?"

"I really intended to read that packet of info you sent me, but in all fairness I only received it a few days ago." I'd seen Mitchell Crawford's name on the envelope, and it had just added to my depressive descent. "I'm still highly qualified to do this job."

"You don't even know what your job is. You're not just cooking for a bunch of ranch hands. You're the main chef and primary overseer of the kitchen for our dude ranch property."

"What does that mean?"

His lightly-stubbled jaw tightens. "It means we open up the ranch to guests. Lots of them. They go out every day for different activities, and you feed them."

"Like a rustic B&B?"

Owen's lips twitch like he's tasting a bitter berry. "We're not some frilly bed and breakfast."

"How many people am I feeding?"

"Twenty-five to thirty guests every day and about twenty employees. Three meals a day, sometimes taken in the dining hall and sometimes on the road. In the mornings, you have an additional twenty ranch hands who stop in for breakfast. It's one of the perks Mitchell offers them before they go out and tend to his other assets."

That's a lot of people. I've never cooked for that many folks at once.

"Look, Avery, if you can't do this, tell me now. Pearl, our retiring cook, is only sticking around two or three more days to train you, then she's done. We'll have no one until Pearl's replacement arrives after you leave."

"I'm not bailing." I'm trying not to be offended at Owen's bothersome frown, but I'm pretty sure I have a similar expression myself. "Okay, I can do this." It's only two months. "I have my own recipes, I emailed someone my grocery lists last week, and I'm familiar with the kitchen equipment." I pat Owen's knee. "Your Pearl sent me photos of the kitchen." I had noticed it was a little on the big side.

"You didn't read one thing about the job, but you requested pictures of your stove?"

"Pretty much."

Owen is not impressed.

"A few weeks out of each summer we have some very special guests—kids. They might have specific dietary requirements. You do know about that, right?"

I twirl my long, black ponytail. "Of course."

My handsome driver is not buying it.

He jerks the truck back into drive and put us into motion. One hundred more fence posts, and we arrive at what could only be called a mansion. No rustic wooden siding here.

"Here we are," Owen says. "Are you ready for this? I'm not going to find you at midnight climbing out your bedroom window on a rope made of bed sheets, am I?"

I stare at the main house, with its two stories of red brick, more windows than I can count, and four giant columns that hold it all together with mortar and Southern pride.

This was the home my mother had grown up in. Had told me about.

Then she'd escaped. And never looked back.

Mitchell made sure of that.

Inside that house was my grandfather. "Maybe we could just sit here a minute." My voice wavers.

"We could." Owen unbuckles his seatbelt. "Or we could go inside. I promise I'll be right beside you."

I shut my eyes and let those words repeat in my head because I'm a little weary of doing everything by myself. Weary of a lot of things.

"He knows you already," Owens says. "He's got your picture plastered all over his office."

"I've never even met him. He and my mom . . . " I press my lips together, silencing the rest of the story. Something about those eyes of Owen's just make a girl want to tell him her every care. "Never mind. Let's get this over with."

"That's exactly what I told the pigs yesterday when I took them to the sale barn."

I pull my worried gaze from the house. "I'm not really up on my farm humor."

"It was in the packet."

Before I can unbuckle and grab my bag, he hops out of the truck and opens my door.

"This is really not necessary," I say.

His warm fingers close over mine as he helps me down. "Welcome to ranch life, Avery. And unless I want your grandfather to skin me"—he tips the brim of his ball cap—"manners are always necessary."

I can't help but smile at that.

But a mere three steps later, my smile disappears, and my feet halt on the gravel drive.

"You'll be staying here with your grandfather in the main house," Owen says.

"This little thing?"

"You'll have the entire second floor to yourself."

"Can't I sleep in one of the guest cabins?"

"Not unless you want to bunk with me."

Good heavens, his accent is adorable. Especially when he uses it to say things like that.

I look up at the house and feel my resolve drift away on the breeze that warms my face.

"He's a nice man." Owen stands beside me, his arm brushing against me. "Mitchell can be a little gruff, but he's got a pretty big heart."

"A big heart? I guess that's a new development." I push a pin right into that balloon of esteem Owen holds for my grandfather. "Because that's not the man I know."

"Give him a chance."

He hadn't given my mom a chance. He'd kicked her out, disowned her. Dueling waves of anger and apprehension threaten to send me back to the truck.

I don't want to do this. I don't want to do this.

And yet I have to. If I want to be on track to graduate in two years, there's no choice.

"Avery." Owen's voice is soft and patient, as if he has the time to stand there all day and humor an emotional wreck of a female. "It's going to be okay." He nudges me, gently bumping his side into mine. "Come on. I'll go with you."

Great. A few hours of knowing Owen, and I'm already co-dependent.

But I follow him, my unease tapping maniacally on my nerves. He opens the oversized front door, wipes his feet in what is probably a farmer's habit, and pulls his hat off his head, revealing chestnut hair that falls in short waves. Thick hair meant to run your fingers through.

Which I have also sworn off.

We traipse down a hall and around a corner.

"This is Mitchell's office." Owen raps his knuckles on a door before pushing it open. "Got someone to see you, sir," he says, walking in ahead of me.

This is it. My grandfather. The man who cut all ties with my mother. And me.

And yet here I am—working for him.

Out of desperation.

"Avery?" Owen pops his head back into the hall where I still stand. "Are you coming in?"

I lower my voice to a whisper. "Maybe you could just describe me to him, let him know I'm here, and find out which room is mine?"

"Where's your backbone?"

"It wouldn't fit in my suitcase. It was either that or my hair dryer."

"We're going in." He grabs my hand and pulls me inside.

Mitchell's office smells like cigar, cedar, and leather. Dark wood paneling lines the walls, while two chandeliers made of antler horns dangle from the tall ceiling. A TV in the corner scrolls the stock report.

And my grandfather sits behind a giant oak desk, his eyes steady on mine.

"Avery Clare." He stands, and I'm taken aback by how young he is. How tall and handsome. Mitchell Crawford has a head full of gray hair and a matching mustache. A few thin lines crinkle at the edges of the green eyes so like my mother's. And like mine. He's slender, but clearly a life of manual labor has given him muscle and a posture to command a room.

"Hello." I hate the uncertainty in my voice. Is this the point I should lash out at him with my carefully prepared speech over his treatment of my mother? In another practiced scenario, I overwhelm him with my stunningly cold indifference, dismissing him with my steely glare. My final option included taking my work contract out of my purse, lighting it on fire in front of him, and telling him exactly what he could do with his summer job.

But when I tried that at home, I burned my fingers, set off the smoke alarm, and put a small hole in my roommate's wool rug.

"You look just like Courtney."

A pinprick of heat stabs through me hearing my mother's name on his lips.

Mitchell walks toward me, his intensity swirling around him thick as fog. My grandfather blinks rapidly, as if trying to dislodge something in his eyes, then smiles. "You're pretty as a new Charolais calf."

I turn to Owen for translation.

He laughs. "That's a compliment."

Of course it is. "I, um, appreciate the opportunity to work in your kitchen," I say. "Maybe someone could show me to my room, and I could get started."

"Oh, now, plenty of time for that." Mitchell claps me on the shoulder, but drops his hand when I take a step back—right into Owen.

"Mr. Crawford—"

"At least call me Mitchell."

Okay. "Mitchell, I need to be straightforward with you. I'm not here to catch up." The man has to know where I stand. "I just want to do the job you hired me for."

"I see." Mitchell straightens. "Right." He glances at Owen. "Son, why don't you take Avery to her room upstairs, get her situated, then you can give her a quick tour of the ranch."

"Yes, sir."

I turn to go, but Mitchell calls my name.

He pauses to take an audible breath. "I know you're mad at me," he says. "You have every right to be. I can't change the past."

No, he certainly can't. This was exactly the conversation I wanted to avoid.

"But if you'd let me," he says, "I'd like to get to know you. I've missed out on your whole life. We've been given this wonderful opportunity, and it would be nice to spend a little time together. We're family, aren't we?"

"We might be related by blood." Anger makes my tone sharp as knife points. "But you and I are not family."

"I can't bring her back, Avery. God knows I wish I could."

Lies. He was standing in front of me, a face pinched in sorrow, feeding me a bunch of lies.

"Owen, can you please show me to my room?" I swipe a tear and walk out of Mitchell's office.

Grief has been my ever-present companion these last two years, and any hopes of it not following me to Arkansas evaporate with my every step.

I miss my gypsy of a mother.

I can still hear her voice, see her face. But she isn't here.

She's in a cemetery in Washington.

And I'm now living with the man who hadn't even bothered to show up for her funeral.

Chapter Three

"**I** WANT YOU to know I don't make a habit of crying."

I dab at my eyes with a tissue gallantly provided by Owen as he drives us over a tire-worn path in some super-sized golf cart contraption. Tall grass smacks the sides of the vehicle as we rumble through the fields.

"I'm sorry nobody warned you you'd be staying in your mother's old bedroom," Owen says.

I turn my head away from him and sniffle. "It's fine."

Except it isn't. Though the room has been redecorated since my mother's teen years, some of her things remain, reminders of a life lived and left behind. Seeing her room, I'd instantly burst into tears.

"I don't cry at all," I say as Owen drives. "I mean like hardly ever. I mean yes, I tear up when I watch those Hallmark movies. And commercials with soldiers or puppies, but other than that, we're talking never. Like ever." In my head, I'm vaguely aware of the fact that I'm still talking . . . and Owen isn't. "Not even during certain times of the month when—"

"Avery?" He turns left toward a giant barn then slides me a look. "You've been through a lot. It's understandable you're upset."

"I just don't want you to think that I'm this weak thing who dissolves into tears at the smallest bit of stress."

"You're Mitchell Crawford's granddaughter. I doubt there's very little about you that's weak."

"I'm only his granddaughter by—"

Owen laughs. "You're more like him than you can imagine."

These are not charming words coming from his lips.

Upstairs in my mother's bedroom, I'd traced my hand over a collection of horse racing trophies bearing my mother's name, her senior picture hanging in a frame on the wall, and a Crayon-stained Cabbage Patch Kid sitting in a nearby chair. With heartache swimming in my eyes, I'd picked up the doll and held it to my chest, breathing in the scent of its yellow yarn hair and wondering why my grandfather had kept it after all these years. Had it been my mom's favorite?

"Are you okay?" Owen now asks over the roar of the motor. "You went quiet on me."

He's probably grateful for that. "I'm fine."

"This ATV you're riding in is Dolly Parton. She'll be your best friend for the next eight weeks. I'll leave the keys with you, and any time you need a ride on the property, she's yours. If you need to run to Sugar Creek for supplies, Mitchell has a work truck for you."

"Do you name all your vehicles?"

He grins and pats the steering wheel. "Dolly's no spring chicken, and she's had a lot of work done. But she never lets us down."

"And she has a lot under the hood?"

"Only here an hour, and you get us already."

He spends the next few minutes pointing out various elements of the ranch and doing more than his share to keep the conversation going. I learn Owen doesn't have a lot of family nearby, and he turned twenty-four last month. His smile seems to be a constant fixture on his tan face, and every time he looks at me, my skin warms. And it shouldn't. It just shouldn't.

Clearly I need to extend the age of my Man Ban to at least thirty. Maybe even forty. I might as well cast a wide net and make this male boycott really effective.

"Now over to the left—" Owen continues his tour—"we have Mitchell's prized Black Angus cattle. He's got about two thousand of them right now. They're all named, so make sure you get familiar with who's who. You can expect a quiz at the end of the week, though sometimes I'll admit it's still hard for me to tell the difference between Mable and Sable."

Every single cow looks the same.

I smile, despite my nerves. Despite my heart that's been flip-flopped for the past two weeks.

The sun begins its slow slide down into the hills, but it's still hot enough to encourage sweat on my forehead. I swat away a bug as Owen continues to drive, make small talk, and brake Dolly Parton at various sights along the way. He gives a little trivia about the cows, the duck pond, the newest addition of organic crops Owen planted himself, and the windmill energy they're trying out.

"So what prompted Mitchell to go all commercial and open the dude ranch?" The dude ranch that I'm completely unprepared for.

"Tourism is really starting to pick up in the area. He thought it would be a good investment to cash in on it. Turns out he was right."

"And what's your job here? Besides picking up girls from the airport."

"I guess I'm Mitchell's right hand man."

"You're kind of young to be running the place, don't you think?"

Owen glances at me from behind shiny Ray-Bans. "Nobody runs the Shadow Ranch but Mitchell. I just help pick up some slack. Oversee the employees at the dude ranch, keep an eye on the livestock, and handle some of the trail rides and events."

"It's still a big responsibility."

"I've worked on this property since I was twelve. My grandpa and Mitchell are friends, and I practically grew up here."

I want to ask more questions, but I hold back. I don't need to collect details for some mental Owen Jackson file. I need to keep it just business and nothing more.

Owen makes a U-turn, sending our little vehicle over grassy, gravely mounds like a bouncing space rover. "Hang on, there." He reaches out a strong hand to my shoulder, as my body rocks with the uneven terrain.

His hand lingers. His fingers brush the ends of my hair.

The nerves along my skin come alive like they're caught in a storm of static electricity.

My wide eyes search Owen's face, but if he felt anything, he isn't showing it.

"Sorry." He gives my shoulder a squeeze before returning his hand to the wheel. "I forget you're not used to all this."

All this? As in meeting my grandfather for the first time? Blazing a trail on thousands of acres of a ranch? Or wishing my every girl-cell wasn't fanning herself and calling for the smelling salts in the overwhelming presence of this cowboy?

"New York is pretty different," I finally manage.

"Let's go check out the lodge." He swats my knee with his hand. "You know, the place you knew nothing about."

"I'm a quick learner."

His laugh is low and barely audible over the engine. "I'll keep that in mind."

⌒

"YOU LOOK A little overwhelmed," Owen says as we wrap up our tour of the lodge and head back to Dolly Parton.

That's putting it mildly. Owen proved to be a thorough tour guide, briefly showing me his cabin, which was just like the others. It was sparsely decorated and tidy with a cute front porch and a clear view of the lodge. The other cabins were all currently occupied, each one filled with paying guests who expected three meals a day, snacks, and the ranch to entertain them every hour of their stay.

"It's been a long day," I admit, ignoring the feel of Owen's hand covering mine as he helps me into my seat. Reminding him I don't need assistance is futile.

"Pearl's glad you're here," he says of the current doyenne of the kitchen.

The woman had hugged me and gushed over my resume, then given me a lengthy tour of *her* kitchen. With her youngest daughter due to have a baby any day, Pearl was retiring. Though the woman was sweet as ice cream on a blackberry cobbler, it was *my* kitchen this, and *my* kitchen that. And she quizzed me over cooking things even Betty Crocker wouldn't bother to ask.

"She seems kind of territorial," I say as we drive on.

"Are you talking about the photos on the wall? The ones where she's posing with her stainless steel appliances?"

"I'm sure it's totally normal to kiss your refrigerator."

"She does love its French doors."

I lean my head against the seat and let the warm breeze blow my hair like a Beyonce video. Only with sweat. And bugs. And the smell of cow manure. But other than that, *just* like it.

"This ranch could have its own zip code," I say when Owen is still driving past pastures ten minutes later.

"It's beautiful, isn't it?" Owen slowly brings us to a stop, slips off his sunglasses, and looks out over the land. As I watch man survey creation, I study the profile of Owen's face. His nose that has a slight bump as if once broken. The strong jaw that dares girls to trace it with their hands. The work-earned tan that covers every bit of visible skin. The sense of satisfaction and contentment lighting those eyes.

"You love this place, don't you?" I ask, almost afraid to interrupt his holy reflection.

"I do." He drawls the words and turns to me. "I hope you grow to love it too."

I open my mouth for a quick rebuttal, but Owen beats me to it.

"It wouldn't be a complete tour without showing you Mitchell's prized horses." He hops out, his boots hitting the ground. "Come meet the kids."

I smile at the affection in Owen's voice, but something black and heavy curls in my stomach.

"That's Jasper Johns. And there's Newton's Apple. We have a few named after First Ladies—Hillary, Michelle, Barbara, and that beautiful one right there is Jackie. That older man there is our best trainer, Roger Parsons." Owen leans his tall body on the fence and watches a man working with a Thoroughbred. "Those horses are Mitchell's pride and joy."

"I know." I stare at the animals and try to see what could be so important. "He picked them over my mom."

Shoot. There it went again—the words. They just keep pouring out. I didn't mean to get into it, to unpack one thing from the suitcase I'd stuffed away called "Mom's Past." But I'm so angry for her. For what could've been. "When Mom got pregnant with me, she quit racing."

Owen watches a younger ranch hand approach a skittish foal. "I hear she was the best female jockey in the state."

"One of the best period." At only eighteen. "I guess that's when things imploded. When he cut her off and Mom left." With some guy who wasn't my dad, but who'd made a faulty promise to take care of us all the same.

Pulling his eyes from the training, Owen studies me for a long moment before finally speaking. "Mitchell loved your mom, Avery. Don't doubt that."

"He disowned her. All he cared about was his precious reputation, his horses, his name."

"Maybe he was a different man then."

I shrug, feeling the weight of Owen's stare.

"I know it has to be hard to be here." He steps closer. "Why did you come?"

"I didn't have a choice. I needed an internship, and this one became available."

"And with our cook retiring, it was perfect timing."

"My advisor tells me the ranch started offering the internship only a few weeks ago. It's not exactly divine coincidence."

"Mitchell's been trying to reach out to you for years."

I push back my warring thoughts as the young man in the Shadow Ranch t-shirt reaches for a foal with a halter. The wild thing bucks and scrambles away. He walks after her and tries again, but the foal wants none of that and neighs in protest.

"I guess it's not the kitchen you thought you'd be managing," Owen says.

I laugh ruefully, grateful for the shift in topic. "I was thinking more French restaurant. Not dude ranch. But I guess it gets me credit all the same."

"It's an opportunity to check a box for your program," he says, "but it could also be an opportunity for more."

"Leave it alone, Owen. There's not going to be some happy reconciliation. I don't want to get to know a man who wrote his own daughter off."

In sullen silence, I see Roger Parsons speak to his younger help a few moments before gently walking to the foal, cooing so quietly, I can't make out a word. He rubs her face and body, taking his time as the pony smells his shirt, his hands. Roger lets her sniff the halter, and using tediously slow movements, he circles his arms around the foal and carefully slips it over her.

Owen pushes his sunglasses back on, covering up those eyes steady on me. "I guess with enough time and care, anything is possible."

Chapter Four

I WAKE UP the next morning with dread in my heart, knowing I can count the time spent sleeping in minutes instead of hours. When I emerge from my bedroom showered and no longer looking like I require a hangover remedy, I walk downstairs ready to do whatever I have to do to get coffee. Even talk to curmudgeonly grandfathers.

Like the one perched on a stool at the large island in the center of the kitchen.

Mitchell holds his coffee cup in one hand and a page of the newspaper in the other.

"You kids get your news from the internet," he says, not bothering to look up as I near. "But I still like the routine of the morning paper." He flips a page, takes a sip, then lifts his eyes over his silver bifocals. "I know it's going to be at my front door by four-thirty. I know the news will tick me off. And I know I'll see someone I recognize either in the police report or obits. I can count on it."

I guess now isn't the time to tell him the closest I get to news is the Celeb Crazy gossip site. Somehow I don't think my grandfather really cares about the royals or the latest boy band breakups. "I just wanted to grab some coffee before I headed out to the lodge."

Mitchell rises from his stool with intention, flooding the room with even more awkwardness.

"Don't bother, sir. I can get it."

"Nonsense. The least I can do is serve you some coffee. This is my kitchen." He frowns. "I mean it's your kitchen as well. You make yourself home here. What's mine is yours. I just meant that I could darn well wait on my guest. That is to say—oh, never mind."

I watch him walk to the fancy coffee maker, mumbling under his breath.

He's nervous too.

I file this away under "Things I Have No Idea What To Do With," which I shall refer back to later. When I'm not so anxious myself.

"Sugar and cream?" Mitchell asks.

"Actually, do you have any butter? The real kind?"

"To put in your cup?"

I nod. "It's strange, but good."

Mitchell's head disappears into the stainless fridge, and he quickly emerges holding a small container. "Grass fed butter from the Pittman family's dairy a few miles east. Cows treated so humanely, they get their own stockings at Christmas."

"Perfect."

He finds me a spoon, and I stir the butter in my black coffee.

"Sit down." Mitchell pats the stool beside him as he resumes his seat.

I blow on my mug. "I should go."

He glances at the clock on the microwave. "It's four-thirty. Pearl won't be at the lodge 'til at least five."

The dueling voices in my head argue so loudly, I'm surprised Mitchell can't hear them. I don't want to stay. But it's the polite thing to do. He did offer me a job.

"The least you can do is plop some of that butter stuff in my coffee." He holds out his full mug. "Let's see what this is all about."

Tentatively, I oblige him, stirring his cup until it's just right and passing it back. Mitchell takes a drink, quietly considers it, then commits to another sip. "Not bad. Not as good as my vanilla creamer, but it has merit."

This is way too cozy.

"I better go," I say. "I want to get a jump start on breakfast." And get out of this kitchen.

"Avery?" Mitchell calls as I'm nearly out the door.

I stop and warily turn to face him.

"You'll do great." He lifts his mug in salute. "Go get 'em, cowgirl."

I refuse Mitchell's offer of a ride to the lodge and walk. The sun is still asleep, that lucky girl, and I use my phone to light my way. About a fourth of a mile in, I realize my tired face is smiling.

Cowgirl.

Just like my mom called me when I was a kid.

"LOOK WHO'S UP before the roosters." Pearl wipes her hands on her 'Kiss My Grits' apron. "Are you ready to get cooking?"

"Yes, ma'am." I plop my beloved recipe binder on the counter. "I thought I'd make a quiche with sun dried tomatoes, chives, bacon and—"

"Whoa, whoa," Pearl says like she's trying to stop a galloping horse. "Hon, these folks want eggs, bacon, biscuits, and gravy. And that's what they'll get."

"Every morning?"

"Well, of course not. Some days we add pancakes." She hands me a carton of eggs. "Now get to cracking."

"But my quiche is good enough to end world wars."

"Which is what we'll have if you don't give our folks what they expect. The ranch hands like routine, while the guests just want down-home cooking."

But this is so boring. I love bacon as much as the next human with a pulse, but the chef in me wants to create, to design, to experiment. To at least serve something they can't get at the gas station grill.

Pearl sighs. "Mitchell did tell me to let you do whatever you wanted. The place will be all yours by Wednesday anyway."

"Wednesday? I thought you were staying all week."

"No, my daughter called, and she's been put on bed rest. She needs help with the other two kids. Three-year-old twin boys. They're like dueling tornadoes. Anyway, I suppose if you want to fix your frou-frou breakfast, then you go right ahead. I got all those groceries on the list you emailed us." Pearl sweeps her arm like she's Vanna White. "This is your kitchen, hon. Do with it what you want, and I'll just occasionally butt in."

I study the lined face of the retiring domestic dominatrix and have to admire her. I know she's cooked for Mitchell—first, just his house, then later, the staff and guests—for thirty years; and according to Owen, has only missed a few days here and there to birth a child or bury a parent.

Pearl knows her stuff. I guess I don't need to change everything all at once. "Can I cook what I want for lunch?"

"Naw, folks are heading out on their own for some sight-seeing in Bentonville."

"Dinner then?"

"Sure." Her voice is noticeably lacking conviction. "Maybe I'll learn a new recipe."

"I was thinking a nice kale lasagna."

"You're pushing it, city girl."

I laugh and help myself to one of the commercial refrigerators, which truly is a thing of beauty. Not only can I check my lipstick in the shiny exterior, but I could fit a month's worth of food and a small family within.

"Grab some more eggs while you're in there," Pearl calls.

I dutifully obey and rejoin Pearl at a nice, large granite counter. With a flick of my wrist, I crack egg after egg into a bowl.

"Did your momma teach you to cook?" Pearl crosses to the gas range and twists knobs until flames dance beneath multiple skillets.

"No." The eggs swim in a pool of yellow. "I did. My mom was gone a lot. Worked a few jobs. I kind of had to fend for myself." Rachel Ray and the internet taught me to cook, and I quickly pro-gressed from being able to toast a Pop Tart to flaky perfection to putting a four-course meal on the table for dinner. My cooking made people happy, took my mind off the lonely hours when my mom worked second shift, and stirred something in me that energized and excited.

"You know, I came to cook for Mitchell when his wife died." Satisfied her bacon is efficiently frying, Pearl pushes up her sleeves and grabs a mixing bowl the size of a small planet. "He was all alone with that little girl—your momma. He worked so hard and did the best he could, but your mother was a pistol, for sure." Pearl shakes her head as if seeing flashes of memories she'd rather forget. "If I had a dollar for every time I caught her teenage-self sneaking back in the house about the time I'd get here. That was one wild child." She smiles. "But a sweet one."

I blink back tears as I put a little cream in the eggs. My mother passed away the summer after my freshman year of college, and flighty as she was, I miss her. Sometimes I still pick up my phone to call her, only to remember. . . she's not there. I thought being at the ranch would upset me, and while it's no easy thing with Mitchell, I feel closer to my mom. Like pieces of her are here, waiting to be found. Last night I flipped through her senior yearbook and discovered she'd been voted best dressed and most likely to become a band groupie.

"Good golly, Courtney liked the boys." Pearl hoots with laughter. "Are you like that too—boy crazy?"

"Maybe a little." I sniff and blink the sad away. "But they don't seem to be crazy about me in return." Just crazy in general. "I'm not the magnet my mom apparently was."

"It's better to attract a few of the right ones than scads of the wrong ones. Your momma had the worst judgment." She checks on her bacon. "No offense to your father."

"It's okay. I barely know him. I guess he turned out to be exactly what everyone warned her about."

"Her running away broke your granddaddy's heart."

"Is that right?" I say blandly. "Apparently not enough to help her out when she got pregnant."

Pearl's weathered hands still. "Your momma passed on a lot of things to you, but her hurt shouldn't be one of them. Maybe you should talk to Mitchell about those days."

"I think I know all I need to." I inhale the scent of the butter melting in my frying pan. "But he was right about my dad. I'll give him that."

"Do you ever see him? His name was Bobby Kirk, right? Didn't he become a player for the Dodgers?"

"Yep. He was their third baseman for about two months." When I was twelve, I got to meet him for the first time. He'd waltzed back into our lives, fresh off a minor league baseball season, bearing signed baseball gloves and promises of frequent visits. My parents briefly reunited, but Bobby's career soon withered, and so did their relationship. He spent a few months with us, but soon went back on the road chasing that dry, empty dream. He didn't find big success out there, but he did find a Sheila in Cincinnati, a Linda in Topeka, and a Denise in Detroit. By the time my mom died, I was living on my own at college and knew I couldn't rely on my dad for more than an occasional call on Christmas.

"I hope your Man Picker is better than your momma's," Pearl says.

"Not much." I grab a large knife. "My last two boyfriends cheated on me." My blade slashes through some cheese. "I'm kind of over men."

Pearl snorts. "I said that when I was your age. Then I found myself a good one. Some days, I'm over him too." She laughs. "But I keep him anyway. You'll find a good one. You just gotta learn how to look for them."

Clearly my Good Dude Radar is broken.

A nearby phone bursts into an old Garth Brooks tune, interrupting our chat.

"I better get that." Pearl wipes her hands and grabs her cell. "Hello?" Her eyes widen. "You're what?" She listens intently, her hand holding her forehead, as if the conversation is just too much. "Okay, we'll be right there. You keep me posted, you hear? Dad and I are on the way." Pearl slips the phone into her back jeans pocket. "Avery, I gotta go."

"Now?" Panic hits me cold as a bucket of ice over the head. "You'll be back though, right? I mean, it's just breakfast. I can do this, but what about later when—"

Pearl brackets my shoulders with her hands. "My daughter's going into labor right now—wasn't due for two weeks. I gotta grab my bag, grab my husband, and get on the road."

"Will I see you tomorrow. . . or the next day?" I know the answer, but I ask anyway.

"No, hon. This is it for me. Looks like my retirement starts now."

Oh, crap.

"But you give me a call anytime if you need some help, okay?"

Oh, right. A phone call will fix everything. Yeah, ten minutes of cracking eggs with the pro Pearl, and I have all I need to cook for the ranch.

Is she insane? How can she leave me at a time like this?

"Sorry to drop the ball." Pearl whips off her apron with the skill of a Chippendale's dancer and slips her purse over her shoulder. "You'll be fine. This is what you're here for, right? You just feed the folks the basics, and it will be super."

Yeah, super. As in super disastrous.

Pearl gives me a smacking kiss on the cheek. "Have a good summer." Her warm palms cup my face, and she smiles. "You're Mitchell Crawford's granddaughter. You can do anything. From taking over a commercial kitchen to finding you a good-hearted feller."

This is not happening. "Right now I just want to focus on one of those."

She pats my cheek. "I say you can do both. Oh, and you have help coming at six."

My first taste of relief. "I do?"

"Yep, Elizabeth arrives at six most mornings to serve."

"Can she cook?"

"Not if you don't want the health department involved." And with that Pearl floats out of the kitchen, throwing out final tips and instructions like rose petals before a bride.

Chapter Five

*T*HE NEXT HOUR passes in a frenzy of pots, pans, sweating, and one tiny grease fire I put out with my baking soda and dirty words.

Just as predicted, Elizabeth, shows up at six. A high school senior, she's full of blondeness, perkiness, and a breathy voice that would've had my ex-boyfriend pledging endless love and boob grabs. I'm fully prepared to dislike her, but when Elizabeth gets the tables set in record time and tells me her paychecks help her disabled, single father, I decide she might be my most favorite person ever.

"The food smells great," Elizabeth declares, as she walks between the dining room tables. "They'll love it." Her head turns toward a window at the sound of voices. "Here they come. You ready?"

I nod dumbly.

The Shadow Ranch staff files in, wearing their uniforms of jeans, boots, and blue company t-shirts.

I follow Elizabeth's lead and visit each table, offering coffee and a cheerful good morning. Owen catches my eye and nods his head in greeting. He looks like a pinup for a Hot Farmers calendar. He would be Mr. June—full of sunshine and heat. His shirt stretches over the contours of his hard-earned muscles and his eyes pop in that coordinating blue. He wears scuffed work boots, and the hem of his jeans fray where they rest on the scarred leather. I look away, redirecting my attention to anyone but Owen, but not before I see his smile that packs enough voltage to light up the whole city. And all the dead parts inside me.

Not that I'd let it.

"Owen Jackson is totally checking you out," Elizabeth whispers later as I pass her en route to another table.

I nearly drop my tray of food refills. "No, he's not."

"Looking at you the same way he looks at bacon." She laughs and nudges me with a friendly elbow. "Which means he thinks you are some kind of sexy."

I just got compared to a pork product.

It's strangely flattering.

"Do you know him well?" I ask casually.

"Known him for most of my life. He's a good friend of my family." Elizabeth holds out a basket of warm biscuits. "Take this to his table. They're already running low."

"Actually I need to get back to the kitchen and—"

She adds the basket to my tray and gives me a push.

I turn toward Owen's table and suck in a breath when I find his eyes trained right on me. I also suck in my stomach. I've spent the last few weeks consoling my sorrows with a lot of bitterness and ice cream. Apparently at least one of those is very fattening.

"Good morning." Owen's rich timbre greets me as I reach his table and unload my tray.

"Everything taste, okay?" I address the entire group, which consists of Owen and five other people in ages ranging from college to silver-haired. Two girls who have to be in their early twenties occupy part of the table, and I wonder if either one is dating Owen.

Not that it's my business! And not that I care. Because I don't. "More eggs?" I all but slam down the bowl.

"Guys, this is Avery Crawford, Mitchell's granddaughter," Owen says. "She's running the kitchen this summer."

The table erupts in kind welcomes and polite greetings. Owen introduces everyone around him, and my brain seizes at the information overload.

"Can I get you anything else?" I ask them.

"I think we're in good shape," says an older man at the table. "Glad you've joined us."

"Thank you." I scurry away, with too much to do. Like avoiding Owen and all the tingly feelings seeing him causes. I do not want one *single* thing tingling this summer.

Though the kitchen is hot as the flames of hell, it provides a refuge for a quick break to calm my anxious pulse. I throw back a glass of orange juice and shoo away the hair that's escaped from my melting ponytail.

Elizabeth pops her head in the doorway, staying only long enough to bark an order. "Need more bacon!"

"My goodness, these people eat like they're never going to get another meal," I mutter.

"That's because they work it off in a few hours," says a male voice that does *not* belong to my helper.

I turn and find Owen in the spot where Elizabeth had just stood.

He walks on in, wearing that easy grin and the confidence of one who knows this place like his own. "You look tired."

"Does that line usually work with the ladies?" I throw some bacon on a serving plate. "Because it's not exactly doing anything for me."

"Who needs pickup lines? Usually my offer to show them the barn loft is all I need."

Guys. They're all the same. "Cute. Now move out of my way so I can get some more bacon."

Owen glances at the stove. "Is that all you have left?"

"It's under control." Actually I'm a little concerned it's not. Who knew these people would eat so much?

"Do you want some help? I'm not a total slouch in the kitchen."

"No." I push him toward the door, but he grabs my hand and holds it, his skin light on mine.

"I'm serious about helping," Owen says. "Mitchell told me Pearl left early. We pull together around here, so don't try to be a hero."

Nobody has ever helped me—except my three best friends. But

even they knew I had my limits. My mom had been good to me, but she'd been gone more than home. I'd learned early that it was better to insure it was done right the first time and do it myself.

"I've got this under control." I pull my hand out of his. "Now let me work."

"How much rest did you get last night?"

"I don't know." I squirm under the concern in his voice. "An hour or so."

"You're never gonna make it on the ranch like that."

"I rarely sleep more than a few hours every night. I seem to have done okay so far."

"I've got just the thing for that insomnia of yours," he drawls.

"Oh, I'm *sure* you do."

He laughs, a deep, melodic sound that makes me want to fan myself even more. "I meant a little late-night star gazing."

"Is that what you Southern boys call it?"

Owen leans against the doorjamb, patient as you please, blocking my way. "I don't know what kind of guys you've been dating in the big city, but around here, we're a little more gentlemanly than that."

Good heavens, his eyes are hypnotic. "I. . . I have to get back out there."

"Your grandpa told me to look after you."

"Did he now?" An angry heat spreads up my neck. "I've been taking care of myself for years. I don't need a keeper now. Feel free to pass that on to Mitchell."

"There's nothing wrong with having people concerned." Owen says it in such a way that I instantly feel churlish.

"You haven't seen the ranch until you've seen it at night," he adds. "They've forecasted a clear sky, and I promise you, it will help you shake off some of that stress."

"I don't—"

"You don't need to. Right." He takes the serving tray from my hands and opens the door. "I'll pick you up at ten." And then Owen proceeds to serve bacon to the tables, as if it's his job.

Elizabeth finds me standing in the doorway watching him.

"The answer to your question is yes," she says.

"And what question is that?" I drag my attention from Owen, who's laughing with his coworkers as he stops by each table.

"You were wondering if Owen really is as good as he seems." She sticks a piece of bacon in her mouth and takes a noisy bite. "The answer is yes."

Chapter Six

THE REST OF the day is a total catastrophe. Like hurricane followed by tsunami, torched with wildfires, then capped off with a plague of locusts *disaster*.

"Avery?" Elizabeth knocks on the pantry door a half hour before dinner. "How long are you going to be in there?"

I lean my head against a shelf of bagged rice. "I just need a moment." When I open my eyes, maybe it will be yesterday. Maybe God will give me a do-over.

"I'm sorry you didn't know about the ranch guests. I guess that's a pretty important detail."

Flinging open the door, I glare down my helper. "As if breakfast wasn't bad enough, not *one* person thought they should tell me that this is a ranch for children with cancer?" When I'd stepped out to serve our first table of breakfast guests after the workers left, I'd noticed a young boy who clearly wasn't well. But then each family trickled in, and the heartbreaking pattern just repeated. Adorable, beautiful children of all ages who were clearly here to get away from a brutal bully of a disease.

And I hadn't known.

"It's just a few weeks of the summer. Most of the kids are patients at the Children's Hospital," Elizabeth says. "I think Mitchell might be on the board."

I can do this. I know nothing about feeding kids, but I'd been one once. That had to count for something. "Let's just get through dinner.

Then I'll scrap my menus for this week and come up with a new strategy."

Elizabeth looks at the dinner ingredients on the counters and her worried face offers me little encouragement.

This morning I completely underestimated the amount of food everyone required, and most of it had gone to the ranch hands. Elizabeth and I spun into turbo mode, scrambling, frying, and serving as fast as we could. My helper received a quick lesson in egg preparation, but even that hadn't ended too well. The lodgers missed their short morning trail ride before they loaded a ranch bus and went into nearby Bentonville for shopping and sight-seeing.

I spent the rest of the afternoon prepping for dinner. Though Pearl had sent me some texts with lots of exclamation points recommending I stick with the original dinner menu of pork chops and stuffing, I wanted to redeem myself from the breakfast disaster. It was time to break out the Avery's Awesome Recipe Book and show them what I was made of. I was here to run a professional kitchen, and that's what I would do.

"What is this?" Elizabeth holds up a chilled plate, her ponytail now as droopy as mine.

I check the clock. Already families were trickling into the dining room. "It's a fresh pear and fig salad over a bed of greens." I catch Elizabeth's scrunched face. "Trust me. This menu's a huge hit every time it's served."

"Those families are going to starve on this. They've been out all day." Elizabeth's help was on an as-needed basis. She didn't always assist with food prep, but worked elsewhere on the ranch and only showed up five days a week to serve meals. The other days were covered by another woman I'd yet to meet. And right now I needed both ladies plus a whole cadre of chefs.

"The salad is only the first course." I open one of the ovens so Elizabeth can get the full aromatic effect. "Then we serve them lamb chops in a balsamic reduction with bacon-wrapped asparagus on a bed of quinoa."

"What's quinoa?"

"Something they don't serve in the nacho line at your school cafeteria."

"Those nachos have seen me through some dark times." Elizabeth fills the pitchers with iced water. "Besides, Pearl is gonna flip."

"Pearl isn't here." I garnish the salads with my homemade croutons. "We are."

"You know people come here expecting soul food, right?"

My culinary skills are so not being appreciated. "It's time to break ties with gravy."

Elizabeth takes a water pitcher in each hand. "That's one breakup I don't ever want to be a part of."

In a matter of minutes, the frenzy begins anew. The dining room fills, the chatter swells, and folks take their seats in hungry anticipation.

"They're not eating their salads," I say to Elizabeth as we load the trays with the main entree. "Are they waiting for a prayer or something?"

"Those short people out there? Those are kids. And they're born hating salads. Maybe if we gave them some ranch dressing? Got any of that?"

A plate nearly slips from my fingers. "I am not letting *anyone* put ranch on my salad. It's much too delicate for that."

Elizabeth's eye roll is hard to miss as she carries out her first tray of lamb chops. "By the way, add two more plates," she says as she pushes the door with her hip. "Mitchell and Owen are here."

"What?" My hair is a total mess. Would it be too obvious to put on lipgloss? "Why are they here?"

"Mitchell always eats here in the lodge, but Owen? He rarely does." Her smile taunts and teases. "How interesting to see him tonight."

I check my hair exactly five times in the reflection of the refrigerator door before going back out and approaching Mitchell and Owen's table.

"Hi, there." I fill their glasses with water. "Can I get you guys anything else to drink?"

Mitchell picks his salad with his fork. "Unique blend of flavors here. What is this—a raisin?"

"Fig." I catch sight of Elizabeth carrying a tray of uneaten salads back into the kitchen. "Fig and pear."

"Very healthy," Owen says. "We could all use some more fruit and veggies."

But I notice he hasn't touched his either.

Elizabeth joins us, offering both men their lamb chops.

"What a nice presentation," Mitchell says. "Very Cordon Bleu, right Owen?"

"Looks great." Owen smiles at me. Not some leering lift of the lips, but a smile meant to bolster, to encourage. I don't know what to do with it. So I escape back to the kitchen.

Over the next hour, Elizabeth and I scurry like squirrels in a grove of oaks. And by the time the last family leaves, it's clear my dinner was a complete, utter flop.

Pearl and Elizabeth had been right.

Sure, some guests cleaned their plates and even requested seconds, which I happily obliged. But given the amount of food we put in the scrap bucket for Mitchell's pigs, there are probably going to be a lot of hungry kids later.

I've failed once again.

WHEN THE LAST dish is washed, I bid Elizabeth a good night and shoo her out the door.

I collapse onto a bar stool in the kitchen and flip through one of Pearl's worn recipe books. This collection is more like a binder, with hand-written recipes stuck in plastic sleeves that have lived through spills and spatters. When I get to the spaghetti and meatballs, it's nearly scratch-and-sniff.

I prop my chin in my hand and turn another page.

Meatloaf.

I'm an honors culinary student, and I've been reduced to serving blue plate specials. It just isn't fair. I want to flex my cooking muscles, try some new dishes, show off my favorites, and create a few new masterpieces to take back to school. Instead I'll be spending my summer breading and gravy-boating.

"You still here?"

I look up and find my grandfather standing in the doorway.

I straighten my spine. "I have a few more things to do."

He walks toward me, approaching like I'm a wild animal he's not convinced won't suddenly bite.

"I know I screwed up today," I say as Mitchell pulls out a stool and sits down.

He laces his leathery fingers together on the granite counter and the room is so quiet, all I hear is the hum of the fridge.

"Your grandma Clare was an excellent cook," he finally says. "But it wasn't always that way." A wistful smile lifts his lips. "We got married young . . . too young. Didn't have five dollars between us, so I took a job on a ranch in Texas. It didn't go well. To get the job, I'd lied and told them Clare could cook. We went as a package deal, but your grandma couldn't fix anything more than a bowl of cereal. I pretty much threw her to the wolves. She was so mad at me. Cried the first month we were there. So, at night, we'd come dragging in after work and stay up late in our little kitchen with the two-burner stove, and we learned to cook together. I'd bought her a Betty Crocker cookbook at a garage sale, and we'd try two recipes every evening." Mitchell chuckles, as if he's right back in that little kitchen once again. "I almost regretted when she got good and our late night cooking sessions stopped. I missed watching her open a bag of flour, and it exploding all over us. Or the time we attempted a whole chicken and thought it would get done faster if we doubled the oven temperature. About burned the place down with that one."

I don't want to, but I find myself smiling. "Grandma Clare sounds like she was wonderful. Mom never said much about her."

Like I pulled a switch, the light in Mitchell's expression dims. "I guess your mom was about ten when Clare passed away. Too young to lose your mother, and too young to hold on to many memories."

Though I was nineteen when my own mother died, I know what it's like to feel robbed of time and memories. The first year after Mom's death, I frantically wrote in a journal every night, making furious lists of every moment with her I could recall, desperately afraid time would slowly steal it all away. I didn't want to forget funny things she'd said, the way her hair smelled, the horrible advice she'd given me, or the Southern lilt she never lost.

"You'll learn quickly," Mitchell says. "Just like your grandma did. It just takes some trial and error."

"This morning I didn't have enough food, and tonight the slop bucket could feed every pig in the county."

"The guests will be fine. Their rooms are stocked with snacks. Tomorrow they'll get up and eat a good breakfast and forget about the whole thing."

I drum my fingers on the cold countertop and look at my grandfather's face, searching for features that match my mother's face. But other than his eyes, Mom must've favored his Clare. "How come you didn't tell me you open the ranch to sick children?"

Mitchell shrugs a shoulder. "Pearl said she took care of it. She said it was in Owen's information packet. I'm sure it was mentioned. And it's just a few weeks in June. It's not like it's the whole season."

Right. The packet. "It's a nice thing you do here."

"I don't do anything. My ranch hands do it all. I simply let the families use my land. God knows I've got plenty to spare."

This benevolent facet of my grandfather sticks in my conscience like a splinter, an irritation that's small, but impossible to ignore. "Well." I seemed to lose all communication skills around this man. "I'll do better tomorrow."

He studies me for a moment and slowly nods. "I know you will. Say, do you want a ride back to the house?"

"No, thank you. I need to get tomorrow's sack lunches ready."

"Good night, then." He hesitates, as if he's considering a hug, but settles for a light pat to my shoulder instead. "You could call me Grandpa, you know."

The air stills around us, and I struggle to draw some into my lungs. "I don't think I can." I study my hands, the ever-present cuts and marks a testament to my hurried work. "Do those families pay to be here?"

"Money has never been my first priority, Avery." Mitchell settles his cowboy hat back on his head and rises to his feet. "I pray one day you can believe that."

Chapter Seven

I'M SO TIRED, you'd think I'd roped doggies and chased cattle all day.

Or whatever people on a ranch did.

I unwrap another loaf of bread and sigh. My aching back craves a plush, comfy bed to fall into, but I know despite my fatigue, sleep will elude me. If sleep were a friend, I'd send her a nasty text with lots of frowny faces.

"Are you standing me up?"

At that unexpected voice, I whirl around, grabbing the nearest thing as a weapon.

Owen strolls into the kitchen, wearing a faded Razorback t-shirt, jeans, and what I'm guessing are his nicer work boots. And by nicer, I mean ones that rarely meet cow poop.

He lifts one amused brow. "You gonna take me out with that package of Wonder Bread?"

My heart pounds faster than a Shadow Ranch racehorse. "Why are you sneaking up on me like that?"

"I said your name twice. You were probably too caught up in your Owen fantasies to hear me."

I consider beaning him with the bread anyway. "What are you doing here?"

"We have a date."

A date? "No, we don't."

"Yep. You, me, and some stars."

"I never said I'd meet you." My gosh, he's cute. Dangerously cute. "You just assumed."

Owen closes the distance between us until he stands right beside me, and I'm not too exhausted to miss the scent of his evening shower.

He looks at the sandwiches perfectly lined up on the counter like little carb-stuffed soldiers. "Is this for tomorrow's trail ride?"

"Yes. I need to have them ready by morning. I'm not finished packing the lunches, so that outing I never agreed to will have to wait. I can't afford to screw up one more thing."

Owen reaches into a bag and pulls out two slices of bread. He slaps on a few pieces of ham and cheese. "Don't be mad about supper."

"I'm not mad." My vision fogs with the tears I'm absolutely not going to shed. "It's just been a rough day. And I'm worn out."

His arm slides over mine as he grabs a sandwich bag. "Your dinner was good."

I sniff indelicately. "You're just saying that."

"Mitchell liked it."

"He did?"

"Ate it all."

"He was just being nice." Which apparently he's occasionally capable of.

"Mitchell doesn't do anything he doesn't want to."

"The other guests didn't eat it." I smack the ham onto the bread like it needs to be roughed up.

"Avery." Owen pulls the beaten sandwich from my hand and sets it on the counter. "This can wait."

"No, it can't." The whine in my voice could crack a window or two. "I have to get this done tonight."

"You need a break."

"What I need is to be left alone so I can get this finished."

He tugs my hand, bringing me closer to him. "Come outside with me." His gentle eyes hold mine. "I promise I'll have you back in an hour."

"I don't have an hour to—"

"And when we get back, I'll help you with this. We'll get it done in no time. But right now, you're missing the most beautiful moon to ever graze an Ozark sky. One of those super moons."

"I live next to a frat house. I've already seen way too many super moons."

"Come on." He holds my hand to his chest, like he's not going to let it go. My traitorous hand doesn't seem to mind. "You've been going since before dawn."

"No, Owen."

"If you go, we'll come back and work. We can knock this out in five minutes."

I guess a few minutes to sit down really would be nice. And I'm too fatigued to argue. "A half hour. That's it."

His lips curve. "I'll take it."

The humidity jabs us with both fists as we walk outside to Owen's truck, and my tank top does little to protect me from the hovering mosquitos. Crickets chirp, frogs sing in the overgrown grass, and a cow moos in the distance, providing a little evening serenade.

He opens the passenger door, his hand on mine as he helps me up, his body a little too close.

"Hey, Owen?" I click my seatbelt in place.

"Yeah?" He smiles and leans in, his hand bracing the top edge of the cab.

"I don't know much about ranch life, but I figure there are only two reasons to take a girl out to the middle of nowhere at this time of night. And that's either to make the moves on her or to throw her lifeless body in the deep end of the pond."

"My body count's pretty low."

"For which option?"

He gives a slow wink that sends tingles spiraling through me and wakes up my every nerve-ending.

I'm in so much trouble.

THE DRIVE TAKES less than five minutes, but long enough for me to recognize I'm a total fool for going out with Owen. I don't need a guy in my life, especially one who could only be temporary. And even though he's not a poetry major who likes to rhyme his text messages and take pensive, angsty-faced selfies, he's to be off limits.

But Owen draws me in with his easy conversation, from ranch trivia to a charming story about the winter night he kept a calf in his cabin. I find myself laughing, letting the cool air from the truck's vents blow away some of my tension.

The dirt from the road plumes behind us, and finally he pulls over and parks.

"You're just going to leave your truck here?" I ask when he gets out. "We're practically in the road."

"Yeah, but it's Mitchell's road, and there's plenty of room for someone to pass." He holds out a hand and helps me down. "Besides there's nobody out here but us."

His words send an unexpected thrill zinging through me.

Owen reaches behind the seats and pulls out a blanket and a flashlight.

"Wow. You come prepared. You must do this often."

He flicks on the light. "Never with a girl from New York City." His fingers clasp mine, and he smiles. "Follow me."

Old fashioned as it is, there's always something about a guy holding my hand. Something that makes me feel treasured, loved, protected.

I tell myself that I'm allowing Owen this liberty so I won't fall on my face as we walk through the dark field. But I'm too tired to pretend I don't like it. I do. I like it too much.

"You did a good job today," Owen says as we walk up an incline.

"Can we not talk about today?" I stumble over a rock and Owen's hand tightens around mine.

"Sick of us already?"

I watch the ground where his light shines. "I worked my butt off for dinner and nobody liked it."

"I wouldn't say that. It just wasn't what the guests expected." His thumb sweeps across my hand. "I guess sometimes we miss the best things when our expectations are low."

"Did you learn that on the ranch?"

"A marketing class," he says.

"As in a college marketing class?"

"I have a degree in business administration."

I didn't expect that. "There seems to be a lot I don't know about you."

"Maybe you should spend some more time with me." Owen's grin could be a weapon of mass destruction. "Add that to your extensive to-do list."

The incline gets steeper, and he slows, watching to make sure I'm safely keeping up.

"Just a bit farther," he says. "A few steps more and . . . ah, here we are."

We reach the top of a hill, where the trees are cleared, as if they stepped back to make room for the view. This beautiful, spectacular view.

"It's incredible," I breathe.

Stars. All around us. Bright, shiny, wish-making stars dot the sky. And a full moon watches us from its perch in the inky heavens.

"You can see for miles." Owen points to my left. "That's Whitney Mountain on Beaver Lake. It's a good thirty minutes away at least. My ancestors lived there." He gestures to the right. "That's Bentonville, where you see more city lights. But the best lights are those." He looks up at the stars.

"I don't see too many clear nights in New York."

Reverence slows his voice. "It never gets old." He drops my hand and unfolds the blanket onto the ground. "I have your front row seat right here."

He sits beside me on the blanket, the denim of his jeans touching my leg. His arm close enough I can—

Do absolutely nothing but watch the sky.

Focus, Avery.

"Did you work on the ranch while you were in college?" I pluck a few blades of grass beside the blanket.

Owen leans back on his arms and lolls his head toward me. "I didn't think a degree was in my future. It was important I work to help out in my house, but Mitchell and my grandpa made sure I went. Mitchell said if I could finish in four years, he'd fund it. And so I did." His eyes are intense on mine, as if he wants me to hear more than his words. "I owe your grandpa a lot."

I think of my own scholarship, the one that pays for my board and tuition. I don't know that I could be in college without that help. "I feel like you're on a one-man campaign to change my mind about Mitchell." Does my voice sound bitter? Because I am. "I'm glad he's so philanthropic now, but—" I've got to stop rehashing this. I don't want to think of my mom's father anymore. "Let's talk about something else. Like whether your girlfriend is okay with you bringing girls out to the lookout point." Oh, no. Did I just say that? I couldn't pick a safer topic? Like politics?

Owen's lips move into a rakish grin. "There's no girlfriend. And I've never brought a girl here. Until you."

Oh.

He shuts off his flashlight and lies back on the blanket, one hand behind his head. "Get comfortable," he says. "You're as tightly wound as a cow on vaccination day."

I bite my lip. "Can I give you some female advice?"

"Does it involve making out?"

"No."

"Not interested." He pats the space behind me in invitation.

"Girls are not really into bovine comparisons."

He gives my hair a light tug. "I guess this means sow metaphors are out too?"

I fall back beside him. "It's a good thing you're cute."

"You can use my classically chiseled chest as a pillow if you'd like."

I press my lips against a giggle at his dry tone. "I'm not going to date you, Owen." As the words tumble out, I don't know if they're for his benefit or mine. "I'm only here for the summer. Cute as you are, you're still a member of the male species, a class I'm actively boycotting."

"Now, that is just a shame." He rolls over on his side and looks at me. "On behalf of all my Y chromosome brothers, can I ask why you're rejecting us?"

"I've had two serious boyfriends in my life, and neither one of them worked out."

"Now the rest of us have to suffer for their stupidity?"

"I am genetically predisposed to attracting losers."

He leans in close enough I can clearly see that frown. "I think that might've been more offensive than my cow reference."

"Why? You're not in the loser camp—because I'm not attracting you."

Owen's pause is that heavy stillness before lightning splits the sky. "Think again, city girl."

He's so near, it seems automatic to put my hands on his shoulders. His head lowers, and those full lips draw closer, as my heart thumps a wild tempo.

I shouldn't want this.

I just said I didn't.

And we both know I was lying.

Owen's thumb traces across my cheekbone, and I lose all ability to breathe.

I close my eyes and part my lips.

"Make a wish," he says.

I wish he'd hurry up.

I pop my eyes open as Owen leans back on his elbow. "Hurry. Shooting star." He points overhead, and my dazed gaze follows.

The star arcs, and my wits return. Just in time to send one of the hopes faintly penciled on my heart.

Owen's fingers find mine on the blanket. "Did you make your wish?"

"No." My second lie for the night. But he suddenly feels too close, like he can see inside where all the wistful, ridiculous dreams hide. "No wish for me." I get to my feet with clumsy limbs, as one does when awkwardly exiting an incredibly romantic moment. "I, um. . ." I brush grass from my shorts and swat another mosquito. "I need to get back."

He stands. "Avery—"

I hold out my hands, as if to push away anything Owen might say to pull me back under his spell. "You and I are not going to happen, Owen. I'm here to do a job, then go back to New York. One day I'm going to be open to dating again, but not for a very long time. And it's definitely not this summer. When I leave here, I don't want any ties to the Shadow Ranch."

He grabs his flashlight from the ground, as if he needs to see my face, to see my decision there. We watch each other in the quiet of the country night. Me, with my heart pounding hard against my chest with every confused, frightening beat. And Owen, putting a neutral mask in place.

But not before I see the concern, the frustration. And the want.

"I'll take you back," he finally says.

We ride to the house in silence.

That night I fall asleep within minutes of my head hitting the pillow.

And dream of a dark-headed cowboy who asked a girl to wish on a falling star.

Chapter Eight

*O*WEN IS MISSING.

I haven't seen him in three days. Not since our near-kiss.

Oh, he's been here working the ranch from dawn to dusk, just like always. Everyone else apparently has seen him. But not me. He hasn't shown up for one meal in the lodge, so God only knows what he's eating.

While he's spent the time working like a dog, I've stayed busy as well. I've cooked and organized the kitchen, planning and baking and roasting and chopping. Not to mention, making our menu more kid-friendly.

And thinking about Owen and that night beneath the stars.

I'd almost kissed him.

I could blame it on the exhaustion or the rejections that brought me down that first day. Surely it was some subconscious desire to stick it to the Cheater Ex.

Never mind that Owen makes me smile. And laugh. And want to be held in those strong, hard-working arms.

I barely know him. And it needs to stay that way.

But reminders of him are everywhere.

Owen had taken me straight to the house that star-watching night, and I'd set my alarm early to finish packing those lunches. Yet when I'd arrived at the lodge kitchen that next morning, the brown bags were finished and waiting in the fridge.

Borrowing some of Owen's avoidance techniques, I'd managed to steer clear of Mitchell. I got up and scurried out of the house before him, bypassing morning coffee time in the kitchen. And I made Elizabeth serve him all his meals. Except for a few run-ins, it had gone fairly well.

But now, as the evening rain pummels against the lodge windows, I spy Mitchell at the head of his table, waiting for dinner. Like a captain of a cruise ship, he sits with the Jessen family, which includes two rowdy young boys. Levi, the six-year old, looks just like his older brother, John, except thanks to leukemia, Levi wears a ball cap to cover his bald head. The boy has a thing for puns and chocolate, and his family has become my favorite so far.

In need of a little information, I deliver dinner to Mitchell's table myself, balancing my serving tray over my head away from prying eyes. "Who's hungry?"

"Me!" Both Jessen boys raise their hands high.

"Well, guess what the first course is?" I set my tray on the table. "Dessert!"

At Mitchell's request, every Saturday night kicks off with something sweet before transitioning to the main dish. I don't know if it's more for Mitchell's benefit or the kids.

As the kids fight over the biggest ice cream sundae, I hand one to Mitchell.

"How are you, Avery?" he asks.

"Good."

"I hear you're adjusting well. The food's been excellent."

"Thank you."

Thunder rattles the windows, and I know the night of S'mores will now be replaced by craft time with Elizabeth in the Great Room of the lodge.

"I haven't seen Owen in a while." I'm about as subtle as a torpedo. "Is he okay?"

Mitchell frowns and checks his phone. "Been waiting for a text from him. We can't find a calf, and Owen's out in this weather looking for it. I told him I'd go, but he insisted." He slides the phone away and shakes his head. "Haven't heard anything yet. Maybe you could take dinner to him later?"

"I would like to talk to him."

Mitchell glances at the window beside him and grimaces. "He's gonna need something to eat for sure."

"Keep me posted." I turn to go.

"Avery?" Mitchell calls.

"Yes?"

"Owen's a good man. I've known him since he was born, and there's no finer person. But he's seen some heartache too."

I move in closer, as if I don't want the entire table to hear of Owen's past. "What do you mean? Did a girl treat him badly?"

"Yeah," Mitchell says. "His mother. She left when Owen was about ten and never came back. I think he still occasionally sends her money like some sort of reverse child support. He helps a lot of people around here." Mitchell dabs his lips with a napkin. "No one finer than Owen Jackson."

⌒

WITH RAIN SPATTERING behind me, I step onto Owen's porch and pause before knocking on his door. Should I go with two knocks or three? Was one any sexier than the other?

I settle on four.

And when I get no response, I add two more.

I know he's in there. At eight o'clock, Mitchell texted me that Owen had returned. It couldn't have taken me but a handful of minutes to make Owen a plate, grab an umbrella, and run across a few puddles to his cabin.

I knock again. Harder.

The door swings open, revealing a shirtless Owen in dark jeans and a wilted towel draped around his neck. "Yes?" He's probably given warmer welcomes to rabid skunks on his porch.

His hair still drips, and he lifts the end of the towel to scrub it over the back of his scalp. The muscles in his shoulders flex, revealing sharp angles honed by years of heaving hay bails and wrestling cattle.

"Did you need something, Avery?"

I pull my eyes from the water beads on Owen's chest and try to think of an answer that's half-way appropriate. "I, um." I clear my throat and try again. "I brought you dinner." There. A complete sentence and everything. Holding out the foiled-covered plate, I force my lips into a pleasant smile, as if I'm just a friend stopping by for a chat.

Owen regards my offering warily.

"It's steak, potatoes, and a salad. Nothing weird here, I promise." Except me.

Like a dog trying to sniff out danger, he hesitates before taking the food. "Thank you."

"Can I come in?"

Refusal is all over his face, so I utilize those Crawford genes, assume an air of confidence, and walk right past him into his cabin. He closes the door behind us as I step into his small living room. A beige couch sits beside a leather recliner, both pointing toward a TV that takes up almost the entire wall. The little kitchen is too cozy to ignore, so I follow the wood floor to check out the gleaming gas stove and matching refrigerator. The granite countertop is clutter free, though two bar stools made of saddles are tucked beneath it. Feeling emboldened, I open the fridge and peek inside. I've been in so many kitchens that I can tell a lot by the contents of a person's perishables. Inside I find water, six brown eggs in a bin, a bottle of Coca-Cola, a package of hot dogs, and half a gallon of what appears to be raw milk.

"You don't cook much." I close the door and turn, only to bump right into Owen. *Shirtless* Owen.

He doesn't smile. "I don't have time. And I can eat at the lodge any time."

"But you didn't today. Or yesterday. In fact, you haven't been there in three days."

"I've been busy."

"Busy avoiding me?"

"We have lots of baby calves right now. It's one of our busiest seasons."

The kitchen is nearly too small for the both of us, and every attempt at moving out of Owen's way just nudges me against him. His frustration at my presence all but hums in the air, and his face looks unfamiliar without that smile.

"Owen, I wanted to apologize for—"

"You don't need to apologize." He tunnels his fingers through his damp hair and contemplates the ceiling for the space of three heartbeats, like he's editing his words before letting them slip off his tongue. "If anyone owes an apology here, it's me. You made your position clear, and I pushed the boundary anyway. So. . . I'm the one who's sorry."

"I don't want you to avoid me."

"I had a lot of work to do."

"How did this morning's trail ride go?"

He sends a pointed glance toward the door. "Fine."

"Bad night to be working outside."

"It is."

With a huff of frustration, I squeeze past him, pull out a saddle bar stool, and sit down. I'm going to make this boy talk to me. "Did Levi get the horse he wanted? How did Hannah do? She looked kind of tired this morning." Owen crosses his arms and says nothing. "I want to hear about it."

"I'm kind of busy."

"Doing what?"

Owen grips the ends of his towel. "You're really confusing me here, Avery."

"I've missed you, okay?" My cheeks go up in flames as I squeeze my eyes closed and pray when I open them, I'll be back in the main house—where I should've stayed.

But no such luck. I'm still in Owen's kitchen, and he's still half-dressed, though now wearing a hint of a smile.

"Missed me, did you?" He stands on the other side of the small counter, his hip pressing against the black granite.

"In a friendly sort of way."

"It's a start."

"We can be friends though—right?"

He rubs the back of his neck, eyeing me cautiously. "I'm not getting manis and pedis with you, but yeah, I guess we can."

"It's strange not seeing your face around here, and I haven't had anyone to talk to the last few days." And then there's the inconvenient realization that it wasn't just *anyone* I wanted to talk to. It was Owen. Sweet, funny, *so-gorgeous-I-lose-all-train-of-thought* Owen. It had been mere days, and yet I found my eyes constantly scanning for him when I stepped outside. My ears stayed alert for his deep laughter in the lodge when I served meals. I missed our conversations, his teasing, and his every thoughtful gesture.

And now finally here he is.

Oh, my, he smells amazing.

"If you need someone to talk to, you could always find Mitchell," Owen says, pulling me from my errant thoughts.

I leave that alone. "Dinner was a hit tonight." I smile sheepishly over my own boasting. "I made burgers and snuck in some garlic mashed potatoes. The kids were asking for seconds." I gesture to his plate. "Sit down and eat before it gets cold."

"Let me get a shirt."

Additional clothing seems so unnecessary.

Owen returns, snapping the pearl buttons on his plaid shirt. He scrounges in the fridge for two water bottles and hands one to me. His knee jars mine as he pulls out the other bar stool and sits beside me.

Owen lifts the tinfoil lid. "You made a steak for me?"

"Mitchell said you've been out in the rain all night looking for the calf. I thought you needed something more than a cheeseburger." I take a sip of water and watch him cut into his first bite.

His eyes close for a brief second as he chews. "This is good."

I did so admire a man who can appreciate good food. "Did the calf make it?"

He stabs at a carrot in his salad. "No."

I slide my hand across the counter and rest it on his. "I'm sorry."

Owen stares at our hands. "It's just part of it."

"That doesn't make it any easier."

"Those animals are important to me. This whole ranch is."

"Do you want to talk about it?"

"Yes." His lips curve in a smile. "We can talk about our feelings then maybe read each other's horoscopes."

"Don't forget the homemade facials while watching *Pride and Prejudice*."

"I don't even know what that is."

"A novel about a witty girl who wears cool dresses and falls hard for this dashing man even though she tries not to."

Owen slices another piece of steak, his eyes hot on mine. "She probably should've cooked for him. That would've gotten her an instant marriage proposal."

"You're not going to drop to one knee over a steak, are you?"

"I only pop the question if dessert's included."

I reach into my bag and pull out a baggie of chocolate chip cookies. "They're still warm."

Owen laughs, a sound that makes my soul lighten, then wraps his arm around me, hugging me to him. "Thanks, Avery."

He begins to move away, back to the safety of his space, but I hold him fast. "Can we just stay like this for a sec?"

Owen stills. "Is this what friends do?"

I nod against his chest. "Can we talk about the other night?"

His hand trails down my arm. "You did bring me cookies."

"I just want you to understand. The last few years have been bad."

My resistance for staying away was diminishing by the minute. "And every time I think it's getting better, the rug gets yanked right out from under me. I like you, Owen. I do." Way too much, too soon. "But I'm coming off a bad relationship, and we both know I'm leaving next month. My heart can't take another fracture."

"Aw, Avery." He wraps both arms around me and presses his lips to the top of my head. "Who says I'd break it?"

Chapter Nine

*T*HE NEXT WEEK passed with the galloping speed of one of Mitchell's racehorses. I worked from sunup to sundown, and like Owen predicted, my bone-tired exhaustion soon defeated my insomnia. Any evening the weather cooperated, Owen picked me up after my dinner shift, and we'd go back to the hill to talk and watch the stars dazzle above us in the sky.

Still just friends, as he frequently reminded me.

But yet my hand occasionally found Owen's. And his arm sometimes curved around my shoulders. And sometimes I'd catch him looking at me, and my heart swelled like a balloon filled with helium.

Tonight we have a new group of guests, and an evening temperature low enough that Mitchell ordered an outdoor movie for the families. There are five new families, and as I stir the popcorn in the fancy popper Owen wheeled out, I watch Mitchell stop and chat with each guest. There's nothing plastic about the way he interacts with them. He's in no rush to leave, and I know from Owen that Mitchell will know the name of each guest before the night is over.

"How's that popcorn coming?" Owen sniffs appreciatively before sticking his hand in the popper and tossing a piece in his mouth.

"Hey." I swat him away. "Where's that hand been?"

"Up a cow's hind quarters." I squirm and laugh as Owen wraps his arms around me tightly. "But it's mostly hygienic." He releases me and steps back, his teasing grin firmly in place on that handsome face. "The movie starts in a few minutes. Want to make out in the back row?"

"Is this what you're offering me in exchange for popcorn?"

"If you give me extra butter, I'll make it worth your while."

I glance at the rows of seats—hay bales lined up in front of a white barn serving as a projector screen. "I think I'm going to have to pass."

"Afraid of getting a little hay in your hair?"

"And scaring children."

"Good evening." Wearing a cowboy hat and looking every bit the part of rancher, Mitchell joins us. "What's this about hay?"

"Just trying to convince your granddaughter to sit with me during the movie," Owen says, his face as pure as a tent revival.

Mitchell laughs. "Why don't you two turn the popcorn over to me and go start the fire for the S'mores? Those are my favorite."

"Maybe Avery could stay here and help you with the popcorn," Owen suggests. "I can grab Elizabeth or a few of the kids."

I send Owen warning messages with my eyes, my mind, and my foot lightly mashing onto his. "I've never made S'mores, so I'd love to see that."

Owen smiles. "I like to work alone."

"That's all right, you two kids go ahead," Mitchell says. "I've got this covered."

This is where I should feel badly.

And I do. It's hard to be around Mitchell all the time and maintain my bland demeanor.

"Oh, say, Avery." Mitchell waves to a family across the way. "There's a barn warming dance this Friday night at the Pickens' place. Everyone at the ranch is invited, of course. I figured it would be your first barn warming, and I'd love for you to go. The ranch will provide the food as our gift to them."

"Sure," I say. "So how many people am I catering for?"

"None." Mitchell hands me a bag of popcorn. "It's already taken care of."

"You're hiring someone? But I can do it." It would look impressive on my résumé and give me a new challenge.

"I want you to have a good time at the event. Not work."

"Don't you think I can do it?"

Mitchell straightens. "Of course. But I've hired—"

"Then let me handle it. I'll cater the dance."

Mitchell considers this. "All right. The job is yours."

"Thank you." I turn to Owen. "Why don't we go see about those marshmallows?"

"I think you should reconsider catering the barn warming," Owen says as we walk to the fire pit.

"Why?" I sidestep two kids playing tag with water guns.

"Because Mitchell wants to spend time with you. He can't do that if you're working the event."

"My job this summer is to get as much culinary experience I can. Do you realize my classmates are currently serving in fancy kitchens all over the globe—Paris, Rome, New Orleans. And where am I? On a farm in Arkansas."

"It's a ranch."

"You're missing the point."

"No, Avery." Owen stops and snags my hand. "You're the one missing the point. Mitchell's trying to get to know you, but you go out of your way to avoid him. He wants you to enjoy yourself at the barn warming, and he wants to be able to see that. To maybe even have a conversation with you."

"Was I hired for this internship to manage a kitchen or build a relationship with my grandfather?"

"Can't it be both?"

"He screwed up years ago, and I can't fix that for him. I'm not his daughter. I'm not his do-over. And that's what he wants."

"He's quite aware of the fact that you're not your mother."

I picture Owen and Mitchell sitting down and talking about this—about me—and I don't like it. "Stay out of this, Owen. I know you think the world of Mitchell, but you don't know him like I do."

"It's only fair to both of you that you get to know the man he is now." Owen gestures to where Mitchell passes out popcorn to a mob of kids. "Does it matter who he was?"

"Two years ago, I buried my mom by myself," I say. "It matters."

Chapter Ten

"ELIZABETH, I NEED that jalapeño dip on the table with the pita chips. And see if we need to put out more mini-cheesecakes."

"Yes, boss."

I ignore my helper's teasing sass and check the heat beneath the chaffing dishes. Some of the food I'd been able to prep days before, but I'd stayed up all last night putting everything together. Mitchell hired a few extra hands, including some of Elizabeth's friends, to help set up, serve, and be ready to take any of my commands.

As I pause long enough to survey the large barn and all the people in it—laughing, dancing, eating—I know it's all been worth it. The night is a success. Nobody's throwing away plates full of food. Even the kids are coming back for seconds and thirds.

A bluegrass band plays from a makeshift stage, and in the spaces not covered by hay bales for eating and talking, people dance, two-by-two.

"Would you like to dance?"

I set down my platter of spring rolls with my special peanut sauce and smile at the appearance of Owen. "You look . . ." Gorgeous, beautiful, breath-stealing, heart-stopping, hotter than the Shadow Ranch branding iron. ". . . great."

His smile packs more wattage than the hundreds of fairy lights hanging from the rafters above us. Owen takes my hand and spins me around. "And you look beautiful. New dress?"

"Maybe." A few days ago I'd been walking in downtown Bentonville, checking out their restaurant scene, when a dress in a shop window caught my eye. A sleeveless cotton dress the color of the raspberries I'd just bought at the farmer's market, with a flouncy skirt that stopped below my knee. It was a dress made for a Friday night out. Or a waltz across a hay-scattered dirt floor.

"I like the boots." Owen maintains his soft hold on my hand.

I glance at the new cowboy boots on my feet. "They were sitting on my bed when I got back to my room last night. Do you happen to know anything about that?"

He reaches for a lock of my hair, curled into a loose wave. "Ranch girls need the right shoes."

No gift from Tiffany's or Rodeo Drive could've touched me more. "Thank you." I lean in and lightly kiss his cheek. "I love them."

I forget I have a hundred things to do as Owen captures my hand and brings it to his lips, his blue eyes smoldering. "Save a dance for me?"

"I . . . " My heart trills with a song I'm growing powerless to deny. *I am crazy about this boy.* "I don't dance." Wallflower memories use pointy elbows and shove their way past any dreamy thoughts.

"We can fix that."

I don't know how to dance, and in this barn where every person seems gifted with rhythm and sure-footedness, I definitely don't want to be the odd cowgirl out.

Even Mitchell has moves. I watch as he strolls across the dirt floor with Jasmine, one of our ten-year-old guests, a girl with a blonde wig cut in a flattering bob that looks like it could be her own hair. But those of us at the ranch know it isn't. Just like we know she loves to dance. And that her single mother is scared. But tonight, with lips curved in joy, Jasmine's mom watches her daughter standing on Mitchell's toes and two-stepping to some song about tractors.

Owen sees it, too. "Mitchell wants to give the families chances to forget about all the bad stuff," he says, still holding my hand. "Just a week where there's no concerns about bills, diagnoses, doctors, and what-ifs."

"It's a nice thing to do." My compliment is about as generous as reaching past the twenty to drop a quarter in the church offering plate. What Mitchell does is more than nice.

"You're trying so hard not to like him. But admit it, Mitchell's winning you over."

"He's really not." Though I have taken to serving his table every meal myself. Just to be polite and get in my daily hellos. "I'm glad you think he's a changed man, and I hope you're right. But it doesn't really matter. I'll be gone soon, and Mitchell and I will go back to being absent in each other's lives."

"It doesn't have to be that way," Owen says. "And you're his only heir. You could be a part of it."

"Whoa, slow down." Like I would want anything from Mitchell. Does Owen think any of my grandfather's assets are important to me? "I don't want his property or his money. Why would you even suggest—"

"Don't you two make a fine pair." As if conjured by my shrewish tone alone, Mitchell walks to us. Like most of the men here, he wears his cowboy hat, casting his face in a slight shadow. "Avery, the food is wonderful. No catering company could've compared. Thank you."

"Glad to do it," I say lamely. But, in truth, his compliment is sunshine to my heart. It matters what Mitchell thinks. Whether we have a relationship or not, I want him to be proud.

"Tell me how you made those puffy crab things. And there's something special in those sausage rolls, isn't there? Some rogue ingredient." Brows raised, eyes bright, Mitchell looks as interested as he does when talking cattle.

I can't ignore a fellow foodie. "Special olives are my secret for the rolls." Minutes pass, and I realize I'm still talking, my hand rests on Mitchell's arm, and Owen is watching it all with a gentle smile on his face.

"I guess I've rambled on." I have food to monitor. People to serve.

"I need to get back to work."

"There's enough help here," Mitchell says. "The hard work is done, and now it's time to let your hired help do their thing."

"But I really need to oversee the—"

"I insist." Mitchell uses the same voice he employs with unruly horses. "You're officially off the clock."

"But—"

"Don't argue with the boss." Owen is clearly on Mitchell's side in this.

"How about you take a spin across the floor with an old man?" Mitchell holds out a hand. "What do you say? Then I'll return to you to this fine fellow here."

"I . . ." I don't know what to say. My mother would not approve. She wanted nothing to do with Mitchell. She definitely wanted me to have nothing to do with him.

But my mother isn't here.

Panic is a kick drum in my head. I can't dance. I don't like to dance. People will be watching. And then there's Mitchell. Who will expect me to talk. Or worse—listen.

"Oh, shoot." Mitchell makes a grab for the chirping cell phone in his denim pocket and reads his text. "I need to take a rain check on that dance. Got an issue at one of the corrals that's gonna require a vet."

"I'll be right there," Owen says.

"No, son." Mitchell claps him on the shoulder. "Your orders are to stay here and make sure my granddaughter has a good time and see her safely home. I'll take care of the ranch." He looks to me. "No more work. It's covered, you got it?"

"Yes, sir. Good night."

I watch Mitchell walk away, a slow process, as he speaks to everyone he passes.

Owen slides his arm around my shoulders. "You weren't going to dance with your grandfather, were you?"

I consider telling him a pretty lie. "No. I wasn't." It's a mix of pity and disappointment that looks back me. "I've only known him for three weeks, Owen."

"Three weeks?" His eyes soften as he strokes a hand down my arm. "I think that's plenty enough time to care for someone."

Chapter Eleven

*B*E STILL MY heart and every other fluttery part of me.

Owen slips his hand to the nape of my neck where my hair covers the goose bumps on my flesh. My skin warms beneath his caress.

He leans in, his breath a feather brushing my ear. "Would you like to dance?" he asks.

I close my eyes and sigh. He just had to go and ruin it. "I don't really know—"

Owen ignores my protest, laces his fingers with mine, and pulls me toward the floor. We weave in through two-stepping couples until he finally stops right in the middle of the makeshift dance floor.

"I don't know how this works." I stand there feeling like Cinderella, one minute after midnight—a little hopeful, a little shamed.

"Didn't you go to dances as a teenager?"

He pulls me closer with a light grip on my hip. If only dancing were no more than this—bodies pressed together and hands in all the right places.

"Of course I went to dances," I say. "And I used that time to artfully arrange the cookies and add shots of vanilla to the punch." Vanilla that I kept in a vial in my purse. "The boys kind of looked over me."

"I don't believe that for a second."

"Can we just not do this?" Everyone around us seems to know what to do. They're scooting, spinning, swaying. It's like the Ice Capades. In a barn. "Let's go back to the lodge." I stare deeply into his eyes and bat my eyelashes. "I'll let you get to second base."

He lifts a brow. "Someone really does have bad dance memories."

"Yep. So I think I hear the crab pot stickers calling me and—"

My words die on my lips as Owen slowly slides his fingers down the length of my bare arm, his touch sending a fever right through me.

"This hand goes on my shoulder." His voice is a light whisper against my ear. "Then this hand, I get to hold." With a palm at my back, he draws me closer.

I revel in the feel of being in his arms—the safety, the comfort, the heat. I want to close my eyes, lean my head on his chest, and just forget we're surrounded by people. This force that is Owen—it's too much and not enough. I find myself thinking of him relentlessly, wondering what he's doing, wondering if I cross his mind half as much as he crosses mine.

"Are you paying attention?" Owen's lips tease as they hover temptingly close to mine.

I realize he's been talking. My cheeks flush pink, and I meet his knowing eyes. "Yes. I'm listening."

He proceeds to show me the basics of the two-step. While he's surprisingly fluid and graceful as he moves, I'm stiff and choppy. Owen continues with the lesson, even coaxing me into trying a spin. I crash right into his abs—a wonderful consolation prize, if I do say so.

"I'm terrible at this," I huff a few songs later as I step on the foot of a lady beside us.

"You're overthinking it."

Owen runs his hand up and down my back, sending shockwaves of electricity jolting through my limbs.

"There are so many people here." And I've bumped into most of them.

"Forget them." Owen stops. His eyes search mine as he gently tucks a stray piece of hair behind my ear. "It's just you and me here."

I want to write his words down and forever save them like a keepsake flower.

"There's nothing fancy about this," he says. "Put that perfectionist brain of yours on pause and just have fun."

The band begins another song, this one about finding love in unexpected places. And Owen, keeping his gaze locked on mine, draws me to him and begins again, quietly counting for us.

"You're doing good."

We have two more stops and starts, but I tune out everyone around us and focus on the beat of the music, the light pressure of Owen's hands as he leads us, and the luxurious feel of being in his arms. Because Owen's unlike any guy I've ever known before. He's protective, loyal, and totally alpha.

And I like him entirely too much.

"I'm going to twirl you," he says, pulling me from my wayward thoughts.

He gives a quick explanation, then counts it out, spinning me under his strong arm.

I'm a beat too late.

And crash into the wall of his chest.

Owen's arms hold me to him, steadying me from a fall. His laughing smile fades as I lift my eyes to his face, my hands on his beating heart. The music mutes in my ears, as my thundering pulse intrudes. My skin tingles, and I know—I *know*—he's going to kiss me.

I'm afraid one kiss will open a Pandora's Box of hurt.

But I'm even more terrified of what I'll miss if he doesn't seal his lips to mine.

He dips his head, and his nose rubs against my cheek. "Avery?"
"Yes?"

"I'm going to make you forget about that jerk in New York."
Yes, please.

Owen sweeps his lips against mine, a tentative taste, an exploration. Then his hands cradle my face, and he kisses me like I'm a long-lost love, someone he's been waiting for, longing for.

Like someone he cherishes

His kiss is slow and sweet, with just enough pressure to make me want more. I curl my arms around his neck and thread my fingers through his hair, fire rocketing through my veins. While I cling to him with a reckless urgency, Owen seems in no hurry, taking his precious time.

My mind empties of all thought but *Owen.* This moment fills my heart with a warmth that hasn't been there in years. I lean deeper into him, suddenly tired of carrying it all, and for this time, I know he's got me. No concerns about keeping grades afloat for scholarships, grocery money, or missing my mom. No anger, no resentment over Mitchell.

It's just me, just Owen.

And a kiss that's a spring thaw to my wintered heart.

On a night I never want to end.

Chapter Twelve

THE NEXT FEW weeks floated by light and fragile as dandelion petals in the wind. I wanted to hold on to each day, to beg it to last longer, but time marched on with a rude indifference. My days were spent on kitchen duty, but as soon as the dinner dishes were finished, I'd hang up my Shadow Ranch apron, liberate my hair from its ponytail, and find Owen. He made the most of our limited hours, from a candlelit dinner in his cabin to a dip in the creek beneath an Ozark moon. Some nights we were both just too tired to do anything besides curl up on his couch and watch a movie.

Or pretend to.

It was hard to focus on a plot when Owen's lips found that sensitive spot on my neck. Or when my hands traced the muscled geography of that body and all thoughts of movies and conversation disappeared.

I told myself I'd be able to walk away from this in two and a half weeks.

Lots of people had summer flings. It was very progressive and *Grease* of me.

But the longer I stayed at the ranch, the harder I was falling.

I lift my phone and check the text as I walk down a sidewalk on the Bentonville square. I smile at Owen's face on my screen.

Lunch at the Station? Grab us a table. I'm almost there.

With a rare day off, I came into Bentonville for another supply run at the farmer's market, and Owen promised he'd try to get away to meet me.

I pay a friendly vendor for my spinach and tomatoes and walk toward the Station, a cafe with a long history of good cheeseburgers and conversation. A teenager pedaling a small ice cream cart smiles as we both pass a group of food trailers. The sun shines hot overhead, and a group of tourists takes a photo in front of the Wal-Mart museum. The town is a larger version of Sugar Creek, and like everything within this part of Arkansas, I'm unexpectedly charmed.

I open the Station door and am immediately greeted by the scent of deep fried temptations and the swell of lunchtime chatter. I stop a moment and catalog the scene. This is a restaurant that thrives and nurtures, holds a history and a place within the community. It draws young and old, the corporate executives and the blue-collar heroes.

And Mitchell Crawford.

He sits at a table on the far left wall and throws up his hand in a wave. He gestures to the empty side of his booth in invitation.

The Station might be a hot spot, but I know it's more than a coincidence that Mitchell's here when I'm supposed to meet Owen.

I quickly order for Owen and myself at the front, then make my way to Mitchell's booth.

"Mitchell." I slide into the other side and set down my lemonade. "Funny running into you."

"Owen invited me." Mitchell empties a packet of sugar into his tea and stirs. "He thinks we need to talk. . .and I agree."

It's like I've stepped on a land mine of awkwardness, and I know there will be casualties. "About what?"

"Your mother."

I press my back into the padded seat. "Why?"

Mitchell takes off his glasses and slips them into his pocket. "Because I owe you an apology."

"I don't really want to talk about this."

"Well, we're going to."

"Mitchell—"

"You've got to stop calling me that. It kills me. I'm your grandfather."

"No, you're not. You're my mother's biological father, but you and I have no ties other than—"

"I loved your mother. She was my only child. The apple of my eye."

"Yes, when she was a successful jockey for you."

Mitchell's eyes flash with anger. "Is that what she thought?"

I wait 'til a couple passes by and lower my voice. "She gets pregnant at nineteen and goes from being your darling daughter to kicked out and disowned."

"There's more to it than that."

"You told her to leave and never come back."

Mitchell doesn't deny it. "I said it in the heat of the moment. We'd had a big argument. In the space of a few minutes, I learned she was pregnant *and* intended to marry her joke of a boyfriend. The very one I'd warned her about. She never listened to me."

"She lost everything that night. Her future as a jockey was over and now she had no job, no way to pay for college, and no family support."

"I tried to contact her multiple times—calls, letters."

"It wasn't enough." I need to calm down. I also need that waitress to serve my fries so I can stuff them in my purse and go. "Mitchell, you're my boss, and I appreciate your reaching out to me and offering me this internship. But that's as far as it goes. If you lured me here to connect—" I shake my head and push through—"it's not going to happen. I lived the effects of your decisions. You want to know what life was like growing up? It was hard. We never had any money, so Mom worked two jobs. She married two losers who promised to take care of us, but neither one could." I dash away the tears slipping down my sun-kissed cheeks. "And after that wreck, it was me the police delivered the news to. You weren't there. You were never there. For every meager Christmas, for every school event she couldn't attend because of work, you weren't there. And when we lowered her in the ground, where were you?" I stand and jerk my purse over my arm. "I've practically raised myself, and I've done a pretty good job. So, you'll excuse me if I find your offer to be my grandfather to be at least twenty years too late."

Propelled by fury, I scoot out of the booth and storm away.

Who does that man think he is? That he can just show up in my life now and win me over?

My hands slap against the door, and I shove it open.

And nearly take out Owen.

"Whoa—hey." He swiftly dodges the powder keg door, then reaches for me.

I sidestep him and march down the sidewalk.

"Avery?" Owen runs behind me, his boots thunking on the warm concrete. "Wait."

"Leave me alone." Shoppers spill out of a boutique store, and I don't even bother to turn down the volume on my crazy. I can't get back to the ranch truck fast enough.

Owen's hand latches onto my upper arm. "Hey, stop. Please." He moves in front of me and blocks my path. His sky blue eyes search mine. "Talk to me."

"You set this up today, didn't you? You had Mitchell meet us for lunch—the one you were conveniently late for."

He takes a visible breath, like he knows he's just a few wrong words away from me going off like a bottle rocket.

The ones he settles on light the first match. "I'm just trying to help."

"Help? I just made a scene in front of all those people eating their burgers." And did I get my shake and fries? No. I did not.

"You've been avoiding Mitchell since day one, and it's not fair to him."

Like a red scarf waved in front of a bull, I'm ready to charge. "Fair to him? Are you hearing yourself?" He can't possibly be serious. "What about me? What about my mom?"

"That's the past. For God's sake, how long are you going to hold onto that?"

I want to punch Owen in the nose. Why does every man in my life have to be from some planet where logic and reason don't exist? "He doesn't deserve my forgiveness. And I don't deserve what you did today." My eyes mist, and I blink to hold off the tears. "You manipulated me. You didn't even *ask* me. You just threw me in there unaware."

"Okay." Owen's so quiet and calm, like I'm one of his ailing cows. "You're right. I probably should have asked you."

"Probably?"

"You wouldn't have met with Mitchell."

"It was my decision to make, Owen."

"I care about you both. I want you to patch this thing up."

"What he did can't be fixed with a Band-Aid. Do you know how hard our lives were?" How hard my life *is,* I want to say. But I don't. I can't. I will not be pitiful. "You don't get it."

"If you'd just talk to him—"

"Stop." My voice quivers, and that angers me even more. "I can't discuss this with you."

"All I'm asking is that you hear him out."

I stare into the face of the boy I care about so much.

But all I feel as I look at him is betrayal. Hurt.

"You're asking too much," I say. "You're paid to be loyal to Mitchell. But I'm not."

"That's low."

"Is it?" I know my words are invisible slaps. "He's got you so under his thumb, you can't see the truth. He used you today—and you let him. And then you used me."

Owen's face hardens, his expression furious as a newly bridled Mustang.

But I walk away.

Leaving part of my heart behind.

Chapter Thirteen

N EVERY BATTLE, a girl has the option of exercising her greatest war tactic—the silent treatment. And that's exactly what I did.

Until now.

Exactly twenty-four hours after I stood on a city sidewalk and went off like a tea kettle, I feel the anger making an unwelcome comeback. Like the flu. Or poison ivy.

Or a boy band.

While our newest round of guests amble toward the lodge thirty minutes late for lunch, I stand on the front porch, tapping my foot, eyeing my watch, and ready to ring the proverbial chow bell one more time. Owen brings up the rear, wearing a ball cap, jeans that hug in all the right places, and just enough sweat to separate the men from the boys.

I break my vow of silence as he walks by. "You're late."

He stops, his face grim. This is a man who knows if I avoided his repeated attempts at communication, I'm sure not in the mood to put up with anything he's bringing now.

"The roping lesson ran late."

"You could've let me know. Their food's getting cold."

"Yeah, I guess I could've sent you another text—for you to ignore."

I really hate it when men make sense.

"You ready to talk this out like civil human beings yet?" he asks.

"Not really."

"You ready to admit I could be right?"

"You ready to admit you acted like the back end of a steer?"

He runs a hand over the light stubble on his chin and steps closer. Too close. "I think you're afraid I'm right. And you're afraid of letting go of that old hurt because it's been your anchor."

Can't breathe. Can't pull my eyes from his.

"Mitchell loves you."

I could topple over with the weight of his ridiculous words. "Mitchell loves himself."

"You have no idea what he'd do for you."

What does that mean? "I don't want anything from him. I want to finish this job and go back to New York."

"And us? What about us?"

My mind whirls with my choices, my answers. But I can't verbalize a single one of them.

How did one person get under my skin so quickly?

"Owen." Mitchell's voice pushes us off the tightrope and brings us back to this front porch. My grandfather nods at me and regards his protégé. "Did you update her on the changes in the itinerary?"

"What change?" Those are my first words to Mitchell since yesterday's lunch.

"We have some weather moving in," Mitchell says. "Forecast says we're getting a cold front and some storms, with the biggest chances in a few days. We're moving the Civil War battlefield camping trip to tomorrow tonight. Might get still some light rain, but it shouldn't have an impact."

"Okay." I speak to a spot near Mitchell's shoulder. Because I'm mature like that. "So I need to have the dinners and breakfasts packed tomorrow morning?"

Mitchell's forehead wrinkles in a frown. "Didn't you tell her, Owen?"

Owen inspects his calloused hand. "Seems like I left her a message or two last night."

"You're not just sending food, Avery," Mitchell says. "You're going on the camping trip to cook. I assumed Pearl reviewed this with you when you got here. We provide fresh, fire-cooked meals. We want the campers to rough it like it's the 1800s."

Owen nods. "Except with waterproof tents and portable cell phone chargers."

"Let me make one thing straight." Mitchell gestures toward the lodge. "These people show up every year. You got thirty Civil War enthusiasts in there who travel the South looking to trace the steps of Confederate soldiers, do a little reenactment, and have a nice time. You two will put aside your differences long enough to give them just that. They'll get their historical hike along Sugar Creek, set up camp, and eat a few good meals. They will not hear any fighting or see anything but two Shadow Ranch employees dedicated to their jobs. Am I clear?"

Owen and I both respond with a dutiful "Yes, sir."

"Good." Mitchell studies my face for a beat before walking inside.

Leaving Owen and me standing there.

"You couldn't have told me about this?" I ask, with a stomach full of mad.

"Why don't you check one of the twenty messages I left on your phone?"

Even angry, he's so darn sexy. It infuriates me even more. "I needed at least another day to prepare."

Owen's voice is dry as wheat straw in a drought. "I can help you."

I yank open the door. "You've helped more than enough."

Chapter Fourteen

*I*F WINNING THE Civil War came down to who was the better camper, Owen would've been an all-star general. While I was the rotten corpse the company threw daisies on and left behind.

I stayed up late last night Googling important items such as tent pitching, camping necessities, and how not to become coyote bait. Surprisingly, there wasn't too much on "camping with guys who make you mad but also turn you on."

"I don't need your help, Owen." I stand on tiptoe and make another reach for my tent. "I can do this myself."

"I'm just getting it out of the truck for you," Owen says, with all the exasperation used on a tiresome child.

"I can get that."

He spins around to face me, removing his sunglasses so I get the full effect of those storm-cloud eyes. "I get that you're mad at me, but let me do my job. I'm pretty sure my carrying your tent isn't going to shred your independence or lessen the impact of your grudge, especially with so few witnesses."

"Fine." My eyes narrow. "But I'll put the tent together."

His brows raise with obnoxious doubt. "Have you ever done that?"

"No." I cross my arms over my chest and lift my chin. "But it's not like we're constructing three-story houses here. I think I can manage." I point to a flat spot on the ground a few feet away. "Just throw it there."

"Is that where you're making camp?"

"Yep."

"Well, enjoy your alone time. Because the rest of us are hiking five miles into the woods and setting up somewhere else. I just assumed you'd want the food and water we brought, but I don't want to interfere with your *expert* skills."

Darn him. Darn that boy to Dixie and back.

"I guess I could join you." I sniff. "For the good of the ranch."

He wisely says nothing.

I, on the other hand, am not so smart. "But I will take my tent."

He looks like he's ready to throttle me and write it off as a camping casualty. "Did you catch the part where I said we're hiking five miles?"

"You think I can't do it?"

Owen moves close to me, plying his anger and body against my skin. "It's not a question of my belief in your skill or intelligence, something I believe you possess a lot of. What this is about is your questioning everything I say, every small attempt at helping you. We agreed we would put aside our differences until we got back to the ranch. If you think you aren't going to be able to follow through on that, tell me now so I can get a replacement."

I know I'm being ridiculous. All I'm doing is poking the beehive and waiting for new stings.

"I can be civil." I turn my head so he won't see me roll my eyes. "But give me the freaking tent."

Muttering a curse that could split the surrounding trees, he pushes the bag into my waiting arms.

And I nearly drop it.

"Can you carry that?" His shirt stretches across his back as he reaches in the truck for his own equipment.

"Yes."

"Because this is my last offer."

"You're not my caddy." I heave the awkward, oversized bundle higher into my arms, my shoulders already complaining. "Piece of cake."

An hour later, I want to cry. Owen hadn't mentioned that the terrain would be rocky and hilly, with absolutely no path, cutting across three ditches, one ravine, and some shallow bit of Sugar Creek that involved strategically hopscotching onto mossy rocks to avoid stepping right into the water.

I want to go back to the lodge.

I want to go back to New York.

I want a number four Value Meal at McDonald's.

"You okay back there?" Owen has made his way to the end of the line of campers, waiting patiently on the other side of the creek for the last person to cross. And that would be me. I can't even see most of our party, they're so far ahead.

Those rude overachievers.

"I'm fine." I don't bother to make eye contact as I pass Owen. At least not until I feel the weight of a hundred elephants leave my back when he snatches my tent away.

"You are so damn stubborn." He balances my tent with his, glaring behind those shades. "Just like your grandpa."

"I'd like to carry my own stuff."

"And I'd like to get to the battlefield before morning."

He doesn't even wait for a response, just turns and continues his hike. I'm so overheated and tired, I can't think of a single quality comeback. All I can manage is a lip snarl as I follow.

"Okay, guys, we'll set up camp here," Owen says when we reach a clearing a mile later. He gives instructions for where he wants the tents, some additional how-to tips, and makes his rounds, assisting each person.

The campers, dressed in everything from shorts and t-shirts to one couple in authentic wool period costumes, seem to know what they're doing. It's like the Tent Pitching Olympics. And not only do I not bring home the gold, I don't even qualify. But the folks around me have their blessed shelters up in no time, and of course, they look perfect. No lean, no wobble, no person shaking her fist and kicking the canvas that simply will not cooperate. I consult the pamphlet of instructions, which seems to be written by someone with a PhD in being as vague as possible.

Owen starts my way, but I hold up a hand. "I got it."

He inspects my progress, his head tilting one side, then the other. "Clearly you have it covered."

"Clearly." Did I need all those tent spikes? "I'll have dinner going in no time."

"Pretty good chance of rain tonight." His accent is buttermilk dipped and sweet tea anointed. "But don't worry. This baby's water proof." Owen walks right on by and pats my tent. "Unless you don't put it up right."

Chapter Fifteen

PLOP. PLOP. PLOP.

My eyes spring open as drops of water ping me in the nose. I brush them away and notice my face isn't the only place that's wet. The entire bottom half of my sleeping bag is soggy.

Thunder rumbles outside the tent, and I sit up and look around, though I see nothing. Nothing but my own stupidity in not accepting Owen's help in assembling my tent.

Surely the rain will stop. Because I will crawl naked across that battlefield in broad daylight with a smoking musket between my teeth before knocking on the door of Owen's tent.

I stand up with the resolve of a thousand bra-burning feminists just as a clap of lightning illumines my tent.

And the whole sorry structure buckles.

The heavy top collapses, nearly knocking me to the wet ground. I throw out my hands and swim in the canvas like I'm caught in a riptide. My heart races, and I struggle to catch a good breath.

I'm dying.

Death by Crappy Tent.

The rain, falling in sheets, slaps against me like some weatherly dominatrix. Arms flapping, I throw out a judo kick in vain, only to slip and pitch backward right on my butt.

I'm drowning in a puddle of water and humiliation.

Just as I lie back, uncertain if it's to amp up my fight or cross my arms prettily over my chest and die, there's a *whoosh*.

And the water-heavy tent lifts from my shaking form.

"Avery?" Owen's voice is loud and urgent.

He holds up the reject teepee with one muscular arm, standing over me like an avenging god, ready to do battle with Poseidon, Zeus, and whoever else can do the cool party trick of shooting a lightning bolt on command. "What in *the* world are you doing?"

I shield my face from the rain. "Just hanging out. Getting closer to nature."

He drops to his knees, impervious to the downpour. "Are you hurt?" His hands are suddenly everywhere, feeling every nook, crevice, and cranny of my body. I inhale a breath to protest, but when his fingers graze my sides, I forget where I packed my complaints.

"Are you hurt?" he repeats in a yell.

I finally remember to use my words. "No."

Before I can say, "You have five minutes to stop touching me," Owen lets the tent go, scoops me into his arms, and pulls us from the heaping mess in a move worthy of a Marvel hero. He runs us right into his own tent, where he deposits me on his sleeping bag. A lantern flares to life, casting a faint glow all around us.

"Don't say it." I wrap my arms around myself—cold, soaked, and not wanting to offer a one-woman wet t-shirt contest. "Do not say I told you so."

"I'm not." Water drips from his hair onto his cheek. "What I *am* saying is to get out of those clothes."

I blink twice. Because that sounded fifty kinds of hot.

"Here." He rifles through a duffle bag as the rain continues to hammer at his tent. His very sturdy tent. "Put these on." Owen holds out a t-shirt and pair of shorts, his eyes traveling the wet outline of my form.

"Thanks." My hand touches his as I grab the offering. "Any chance you have a bra in there?"

He doesn't smile. "You could've been hurt. That tent could've made you a human lightning rod and nuked you like a burrito. Is your pride really that important?"

I clutch the clothes to my chest as wind howls outside. "I'm sorry."

"I don't want you to be sorry." He swabs his forehead with a dash of his arm. "I want you to come to me if you need help. I want you to trust me. I want you to get that I'm not your enemy. So your ex-boyfriend was a loser—his loss. So your dad and grandpa wimped out on you—it was never about you. Not every guy on the planet is going to screw you over."

I plant a hand on my hip. "Like when you decided I'd have lunch with Mitchell this week? Without asking me, without so much as a word?"

In one swift move, Owen peels off his wet shirt, exposing an upper body perfected by manual labor, the Southern sun, and angel-kissed genes. He digs into his bag again and pulls out another pair of jeans.

"All Mitchell wants is ten minutes to have more than a surface level conversation with you. Is that asking too much?"

"Yes." So is being in this small space with a half-dressed Owen while still keeping my wits.

"He's a nice man, Avery. He made some serious mistakes, and he wants to make up for them."

"He can't undo them." My eyes widen in the dim tent. "What are you doing?"

"Changing into dry pants. You can stand there dripping wet all night if you want to, but I'm not."

I turn and face the entrance. "You could've asked me to look away."

"You're awful bossy for someone who doesn't have a place to sleep."

I hear him shuck out of his water-tight jeans and imagine the view. The skin. The muscle.

"You can turn around now."

My fantasy is interrupted way too soon.

Owen holds out a large white towel. "Your turn."

"Can't you just be a gentleman and turn around?"

"It's three a.m., and I'm running on four hours sleep in two days. My word that I won't peek is as gentlemanly as I can manage."

"Losing sleep over work?" I step close to his make-shift curtain, as Owen holds the towel high enough to give me a questionable amount of coverage.

"Work and one frustrating female."

His words flood me with a bold happiness. "I'm changing clothes now."

Owen lowers his head, his eyes covered from sight. "Go for it."

"Here goes the shirt."

"Hurry up, Avery."

I toss my top at his feet. "Shorts are kind of sticking. So hard to peel off. Did you have that problem?"

He whispers a curse. "You have two seconds to finish."

"This bra is a total lost cause. Maybe I should go next door and ask Mrs. Mathis if I can borrow her replica from 1865."

"One. . ."

I laugh and quickly shimmy into Owen's shirt. It falls softly over my skin and smells just like him.

"Two. Time's up." Owen lowers the barrier and finds me standing in my bare feet, completely clothed.

"Disappointed you didn't get to see anything?"

His low chuckle follows his first smile in days. "I deserve a nomination for sainthood. Are you cold?"

I inch closer. "A little bit."

He wraps the fluffy towel around me and reels me in. His arms encircle me, warm and tight. "I've missed you, Avery." He kisses my cheek, my temple.

I lean back in his embrace, sliding my hands up his chest, before finally holding his face. "I've missed you, too."

He nips at my bottom lip. "I'm sorry I was a jerk."

"Me, too." I press closer. "Let's not fight again."

"Deal."

"So you promise to stay out of this thing between Mitchell and me?"

His lips pause in their exploration of my neck. "I don't think I can do that."

It doesn't get more honest than that.

I know I'm at a fork in the romantic road. If I stay with Owen, he comes with a fierce loyalty for Mitchell.

Or I can walk away. With nothing.

I have no idea what to do about my grandfather. And I'm tired of trying to gauge his guilt or innocence.

But the man in my arms is the truest thing in my life. Somehow in a matter of weeks, he now holds my heart in those rough hands.

"I choose you, Owen." The words scare me as much as they thrill. "I choose you."

I seal his mouth with mine, and we sink to his sleeping bag.

"When you go back to New York, you're still mine." Owen lays me down gently and slides his thumb over my lip. "We'll make it work."

"I don't want to talk about the end." My lips find the tender spot beneath his ear. "I don't really want to talk at all."

Owen answers with a searing kiss, his mouth exploring, teasing, and branding me as his. Our limbs entwine, and I hear my own sighs as each kiss takes me higher, deeper. Seconds stretch into minutes, and I'm lost. Unable to do anything but cling to him and pray he doesn't stop.

But eventually he does. Leaving the both of us short of breath and hovering near a point of no return.

"We have to get some sleep tonight." Owen lifts his head and looks into my eyes. He combs back my bangs with his hand and kisses my forehead.

He's right. I know it.

But that doesn't make it any easier.

My pulse still a wild staccato, I trace my fingers across the heavy stubble on his chin. I could stare at this face for a lifetime. "Thanks for saving me tonight."

He smiles. And with one final kiss, he rolls to his side and pulls me to him.

"You're a good man, Owen." I burrow closer.

His arm around me tightens, and I close my eyes and listen to him breathe.

Until finally sleep finds me—a little cold, a little wet.

A little in love.

Chapter Sixteen

I DON'T WANT to leave Shadow Ranch.

Ever.

This is the thought that's been playing on repeat in my head ever since that wonderfully disastrous camping trip last week.

I know that New York is where my life is—my dorm, my college, my future.

But Manhattan doesn't have Owen.

Funny, smart, sexy Owen, who works ten and twelve hour days, then spends his evenings with me before driving me back to Mitchell's house later than he should. I want time to slow down and summer to hold tight. The days and nights are rolling by much too fast, as if they're conspiring to rush the moments that remain. The moments where Owen has some romantic date planned—like a pontoon ride on the lake or an evening carriage tour through Sugar Creek. Or the equally sweet times that involve no plan at all—like last night. Just the two of us curled up on his couch, each of us reading a book, content to do our own thing—together. Or two evenings ago when I sat in the barn with Owen and watched as he helped a troubled mama cow deliver her baby. Seeing that strong man cooing gently to the wobbly calf nearly made me call the university and tell them I was never coming back.

"I've got this." Elizabeth loads the last plate into the large dishwasher. "Get out of here. You've been going since four-thirty."

I survey the kitchen, pleased that it's nearly spotless after a chaotic dinner. It's been a full day of showing our new guests a good time of cattle work, a trail ride, and an afternoon game of baseball. And now all the guests were headed out on a late night hayride, while I was on my way to see my favorite cowboy.

"You've had a long day, too," I remind Elizabeth.

"Yeah." She pours herself a tall glass of sweet tea. "But you don't get paid overtime like I do." She lifts up her glass in salute. "Go do whatever it is you do with Owen."

"Bible study." I grab my phone.

"Right."

I walk through the dining hall, giving it one last inspection before stepping outside. I rub my arms against an unusually cool evening and make my way to Owen's cabin. The porch light shines overhead like a welcoming beacon as I knock on his door.

No answer.

I try again.

He's probably in the shower.

I ease the door open. "Owen?"

Walking inside, I find an empty living room. Except for a white piece of paper taped to the floor—with my name on it.

Frowning, I pick it up and turn it over.

GO CHECK THE REFRIGERATOR.

"Owen?" I call again.

Still no response.

I follow his directive and wander into the kitchen area, opening the fridge.

And smile.

There on the top shelf is a bottle of white wine with another note brandishing my name.

I pluck this note off and read.

BRING THE WINE AND RETURN TO THE LODGE KITCH-
EN.

What is this boy up to? The bottle under my arm, I trudge back to the lodge. The lights are on, but Elizabeth is suspiciously nowhere to be seen when I step into the kitchen.

But on the counter sits a beautiful bouquet of wildflowers, a gorgeous mix of purples and reds and yellows, tied together with a big burlap bow. Laughing, I lift them to my nose and sniff. A card falls out.

HOP IN YOUR TRUCK IF YOU WISH.

JOIN ME FOR DINNER AT A PLACE WE LIKE TO FISH.

At this rate, I'm never going to be able to get Owen Jackson out of my system. And who would want to?

Some way, some how, we're going to make this work. There is no way I'm letting this guy go.

I set the flowers and wine on the seat beside me and buckle up in the truck. Lights on bright, I drive carefully down a dirt road, stopping only to open and close a gate like a pro, then jostle across an empty pasture to the pond where Owen taught me to fish.

If my heart weren't tethered inside my body, it would surely float away. I rest my hand over my chest, just in case.

Because there on the bank, overlooking the pond is Owen's truck. His lights shine a spotlight on a table and chairs a few feet away. Owen stands next to it all, hands in his pockets, those full lips curved, and the way he's looking at me has me wanting to write some poetry of my own.

I barely get the truck in park before I bail out, flowers and wine in each hand.

"What have you done?" My bewildered laugh fills the country air. *And what are you doing to me?*

Owen pulls out a seat as bluegrass music plays quietly from his truck. "A little candle lit dinner." He glances about the table. "Except battery operated candles." He shrugs. "We're under a burn ban."

"Owen, it's beautiful. The flowers, the wine, the table." I shake my head in wonder. I can't stop staring at it all—at him. I go up on tiptoe and give him a kiss. "I can't believe you did this for me."

He pulls me to him, deepening the kiss, making my head whirl. "I haven't seen you all day."

I press my lips to his chin. "I guess now I know why you weren't at dinner."

"You smell amazing."

"Spaghetti," I say. "I wear it well."

His smile is crooked and adorably hesitant. "Ever had a date by a pond?"

"No," I say. "Those Manhattan girls have no idea what they're missing."

He gestures to a chair. "Let's take care of that bottle of wine."

I sit down, watching as Owen pulls out his trusty pocketknife capable of dismantling a bomb or slicing a piece of twine. He flips out the corkscrew utensil and makes quick work of unsealing the bottle. He fills two glass goblets then sits down himself.

"To a beautiful night." He holds up his glass, his eyes on me. "And a beautiful girl." He clinks his goblet to mine and takes a sip. "What are you looking at?"

"You. I like you very much, Owen Jackson."

"You're just saying that because I brought fried chicken."

"I'll admit your sexy quotient is incredibly high right now." I take a drink, letting the sweet Moscato slide across my tongue.

The table is set with real plates and silverware, as well as cloth napkins. Fluffy biscuits sit in a basket right next to a plate of golden, fried chicken. A small mound of potatoes occupy a blue dish, and white gravy stands watch nearby. I spy coleslaw and bacon-laced green beans.

I take another sip. "Did you make this yourself?"

Owen loads my plate, filling it with more food than I can ever eat. "I wanted to impress you." He adds some more potatoes. "Not give you food poisoning."

Under a canopy of stars, we eat and talk between laughter and refills of wine. It's all I can do not to pull out my phone and take a hundred photos because I want to capture this moment forever, lock it in my mind and never forget it. I know I'm experiencing a once-in-a-lifetime memory in the making. A dinner date beneath the moon, a man who looks at me like I'm all he could ever want, and this pressing reality that my summer is little more than a week from being over.

An hour later we lay in the back of Owen's truck on a pallet of soft blankets. I'm curled into his side, and we try to pick Cassiopeia from the thousands of sparkling stars above.

"Don't you wonder what your mom was like as a kid?" Owen asks.

My hand stills its roaming path on his chest. "I think I have a pretty good idea. She talked about her childhood a lot."

Owen runs his fingers along my back. "Mitchell has lots of stories. She sounds like she was a spitfire."

"I guess it would be nice to hear about Mom from her own parent sometime."

"He even has pictures," Owen says. "I know he'd be glad to show you."

I lift my head and study Owen. "Did you bring me out here to sweet-talk me into having a heart to heart with Mitchell?"

"No," he says. "But it is on my mind a lot."

Though I'm weary of the conversation, it's hard to be angry at Owen's intentions. "I love that you have such a big heart."

"But. . . ?"

"But I need some more time to think about this Mitchell thing, okay?"

Owen smiles. He knows my resistance is weakening. "I actually brought you out here to just be with you." He gently pulls me down for a kiss. "And to talk to you about next week."

"No." I want to stay in my romantic bubble where summer never ends and life makes me smile and I'm right here with Owen. "I don't want to even think about that."

"My agenda for that day says I'm to drop you off at the airport."

That wonderful dinner now sits heavy on my stomach. "It seemed so far away when I got here."

His arm around me tightens. "Long-distance relationships are really hard."

"Pretty much impossible."

His gaze softens. "Guess we'll be an exception."

My relief is headier than the wine. "We'll show everyone how it's done."

Owen kisses my forehead. "Where was this can-do attitude when I tried to get you to ride Mustang Sally last week?"

"Mustang Sally has a death wish for black-headed girls who frequently smell like bacon."

"My favorite kind of girl."

We lapse into a contented silence, watching the glittery sky. My words are hushed by the beauty around me and the sad pull of my thoughts.

"Owen?"

"Yes?"

I close my eyes and smile. "Let's stay like this forever."

Chapter Seventeen

⁓⁓⁓

*T*WO DAYS UNTIL my time on the ranch is over.

Less than forty-eight hours left to spend with Owen.

I reach into the oven in the lodge kitchen and take out a spiral ham. Using a recipe Mom had claimed was her own mother's, I had basted the ham with brown sugar, pineapple, and a few ingredients of my own. The scent fills the kitchen as the fading sunlight pours in through the windows, and I move on to slicing potatoes.

"Ham, fried potatoes, and some sort of pie," Owen had said last night as we'd walked downtown Sugar Creek with ice cream. "That's Mitchell's idea of the perfect meal."

So that's what we would have tonight. The other guests would dine on homemade pizzas and salads, but I invited Mitchell and Owen to a dinner for just the three of us afterward at the main house.

Yep. I'm taking that step. Reaching out to my grandfather in the way I communicate best—food.

I open the refrigerator and take out a chocolate cheesecake I made yesterday. Without bothering with a plate, I grab a fork and sneak out a few bites. The dark chocolate ganache makes me sigh in happiness, but even that is short lived.

I was leaving the ranch. Returning to New York.

This thought requires three more bites.

On the bright side, no more waking up while the rest of the world still slept, no more cooking meals for people who wanted hamburgers and hotdogs over my gourmet offerings, and no more working days so long there wasn't a makeup product created to cover up the fatigue.

But it also meant no more going out to check cattle with Owen, sitting beside him in the truck, his hand on my knee. No more late nights in his cabin, kissing and laughing until we both fell asleep.

And no more Mitchell, the man I still didn't know, but who offered me a job when my summer plans derailed.

Joss, Sydney, and Darby have been my family, especially after my mom died. They'd laughed with me, cried with me. They'd come into my life when we were all awkward, giggly ten year olds, having no idea how much we'd truly need each other. But our lives are changing, taking us in different directions. Mitchell is my only blood family, a connection to my mom and my history.

So tonight, with the bolstering presence of Owen, Mitchell and I would talk. And if that failed, I would just eat more cheesecake.

"Got any left for me?" Elizabeth enters the kitchen, her usual cute blonde self in a school t-shirt and shorts that show off her tan legs.

"Don't you have the afternoon off?"

"I'm on my way out. I had to finish up some paperwork for Mitchell." She hands me an envelope. "For you."

"What is it?" I rip into it and find a check. "Five hundred dollars?"

Elizabeth grins. "For catering the barn warming."

"I can't take this."

"You have to—the boss said. Besides, he would've paid a caterer anyway. Might as well keep it in the family."

I stare at the check in my hands as the tears press against my eyes. "This is kind of a big deal." I can use this for books next semester, go visit my best friends, or buy a plane ticket back for a fall break in Sugar Creek.

"I get it." And she does. Elizabeth is my sister in scraping to get by and having to work for everything you have. "Don't spend it all on cheap booze and lottery tickets." She gives me a quick hug. "Mitchell's up at the blue barn if you want to thank him."

After seeing to my food and packing up some chocolate chip cookies to go, I go find Dolly Parton. "I'll miss you, too, girl." I give the hood a little pat before jumping in and rambling down the dirt road. I drive by the horse training area and wave at the families gathered there for a lesson. Next week there will be thirty new guests.

And I'll be gone.

The July heat sears through my shirt, and the only breeze stirring is an atomically hot one. I make a right down a well-worn path and spot two familiar trucks. Grabbing the foil-covered plate of chocolate chip cookies, I hop out, my new boots swishing through the grass.

Cows gather in the nearby field, and two birds give chase over a giant oak. This place has become just a little piece of heaven.

With a smile on my lips, I enter the barn, inhaling that now familiar scent of hay and animal. Following muffled voices, I make my way toward a row of stalls. The guys are going to love these cookies. I even added pecans just for—

"You need to tell her."

My entire body freezes at the sound of Owen's voice.

"She deserves to know," he says.

"Why?" Mitchell asks. "So she'll have something else to hate me for?"

"Maybe at first, but she'll understand."

Tell me what? I inch forward to the edge of the third stall, close enough to hear, but still out of sight.

"You think she's not going to figure it all out? You think she's not going to eventually piece it together—the scholarship, the dorm, the funeral?"

I lean into the wall, my knees turning to liquid. Suddenly gravity can't hold me, and I fight to stay upright.

"Her college won't say a word," Mitchell says. "I donate too much money for them to screw that up."

I press my hand to my heart, wondering if it's still beating. My grandfather's words echo in my pounding head, denial screaming within me. Surely he hadn't bought my way into the university.

Hadn't I earned that?

But the truth is right there.

All this time I've been such a fool.

My college scholarship has been a lie. I've been so arrogantly proud of that. I'd gotten into my top choice of schools, gotten into the culinary program. And it was all a lie.

"Avery needs to hear about her mother," Owen says. "From you."

"What about her?" I step in the stall, my pulse skittering triple-time. Owen and Mitchell stare wide-eyed like two thieves caught in the act. "What about my mother?"

"Avery—" Owen steps toward me.

"Don't." I hold out my hands to stop him. "Don't touch me."

"Avery," he repeats, his voice so full of pathetic compassion.

"Is that all you can say?" The barn magnifies my voice. "Because it sounds to me like there's a lot more you should be telling me." I turn to Mitchell. "Isn't that right?"

His eyes briefly lower to the dirt floor before returning to mine. "What do you want to know?" Mitchell asks calmly. Always so unflappable. "I've tried talking to you dozens of times, and you wouldn't listen."

"You were going to talk to me about my mom. But you had no intention of telling me you've been bankrolling my life." Tears cling to my eyelashes. "Why? Why would you do that?"

"Because I love you. You're my grandchild. You may not know me, but I've kept up with you your entire life."

"You've *bought* my entire life." I direct my anger toward Owen. "And you knew, didn't you? How many times did I talk about college and my life, and you kept his secret?"

"I wanted to tell you," Owen says.

"But you didn't. Because Mitchell Crawford said not to. And what Mitchell wants, he gets. It's the very thing my mom tried to move away from."

"It wasn't like that," Owen says. "Your mother—"

"That's enough." Mitchell's voice slices through Owen's words like a whip.

"What about my mom, *Grandpa*? What else is there I don't know?"

Mitchell crosses to me, his mouth grim. "I loved your mother. I would've done anything for her. Yes, I blew up when she told me she was pregnant."

"And you disowned her."

"For all of one day. I went to her boyfriend's apartment to talk to her, to bring her back home, to tell her I'd support her no matter what. But they were already gone. That's when I hired someone to track her down. I called, sent letters. I even showed up at her job. And when they'd move, I'd just find her again. But she didn't want anything to do with me."

My chest shudders as I try and catch my breath. "I don't believe you."

"Why would I lie about this?"

"Nothing in my life has been the truth. You let me live so many lies, so you'll pardon me if I have trouble accepting your word."

"All I ever wanted to do was help you and your mother."

"With money."

"I would've preferred a relationship, to be a family," Mitchell says. "But your mother wasn't interested."

"I'm sure it angered you that she didn't want your money."

"But she did," Owen says. "You said she worked two jobs, and you were poor, but Mitchell sent her money for years."

"That's enough," Mitchell snaps.

But Owen won't be quieted. "I saw the checks myself when I was a kid. Mailed out on a regular basis."

I shake my head in denial. "She couldn't have cashed them." All those years of struggle. There was no way.

But Mitchell only watches me in silence.

"Did she cash them?" I yell.

His nod is almost imperceptible. "Yes."

I open my mouth to ask where the money went.

But the horrible answer hits me before I do. And with it, comes shame.

The two husbands. The idiots she dated. The trips they took, the things she said they bought her. The new cars they drove.

She'd given it all away, floundered it in her vain attempt to get them to love her. To get them to stay.

But what about me?

I close my eyes as hot tears track down my face.

"Your mother loved you." Owen slowly walks toward me. "No matter how she spent Mitchell's money."

"Well, it wasn't on me." I rub my hand across my dripping nose and glare daggers at my grandfather. "Unlike her, I don't need your financial support. I don't need anything from you. Do you have any idea—do either of you have any idea—how humiliated I am? To learn that everything I thought I'd achieved on my own was just my grandfather coming along behind me and paying people off?"

"You got into that college all on your own," Mitchell says.

"I'll never believe that." My laugh is brittle as a fall leaf. "It was such a long shot when I applied, and I believed my grades and my interview had just wowed them. But it was you, wasn't it?"

"I might've talked to some people, but you earned it, Avery. I didn't give the school money until you got accepted. I didn't want you to struggle anymore than you already had. How could I live with myself when I sit here with all this money, and my granddaughter can't afford one single class at the school of her choice?"

"That's not how it works!" I smack the wall with my hand. "I want to make it on my own. Not be some ranch heiress. Those people at the college must laugh when they see me coming, when they hand over that refund check every semester. *Look at her, she thinks her scholarship is bigger than her tuition.*"

"They have no idea," Owen says.

"Well, now, *I* know. And the Mitchell Crawford Scholarship ends today."

"How are you going to cover that insane tuition?" Mitchell asks.

"I guess I'll have to quit and go somewhere else."

"Don't be ridiculous."

"And I'll pay you back for the funeral. Every dime."

"That was *my* daughter." Mitchell's voice raises and his cheeks flush red. "And I was her father, and by God, nobody is taking that away from me. Her funeral is not yours to pay for."

"You didn't even show up."

Owen decides to jump back in. "Your grandfather—"

"Just stop," I say. "Stop making excuses for him." I can barely speak past the lump in my throat. "You asked me to trust you, and I did. I've never let my guard down like I did with you. And this—" I sweep my hands and gesture to them both—"this is where it got me. You owed me this information, Owen."

His expression hardens. "It wasn't mine to tell."

"It sure wasn't yours to keep—and I guess neither am I." A thought slivers in my head, a black, thorn-covered thought. I turn to my grandfather. "Do you know anything about the French restaurant I was supposed to work at this summer?"

Mitchell says nothing.

"You arranged for me to lose that internship, didn't you?"

"I'm not proud of that," Mitchell says, as if that erases it all. "But I don't regret it. I wanted to spend some time with you. To get to know you."

The only words that come to mind are vile, crude things that would only bring me to his level. I take three heavy breaths before I can speak. "I will not be manipulated like my mother. Because that's not love." If looks were bullets, each man would be writhing on the ground. "I'll be off this ranch within the hour. And that's the last I ever want to see of either one of you."

My world crashing around me, I walk out of the barn.

And out of their lives.

Chapter Eighteen

"AVERY! AVERY, STOP and talk to me."

Owen continues to call my name, but I don't turn back.

I can't. I know if I pause for even a second, my heartbreak will spill over, and I'll flood this ranch in tears.

Faithful Dolly Parton seems miles away from me, but I walk like the hounds of hell are nipping at my feet.

"Avery!"

Finally, I reach for the vehicle and dive in, the plate of cookies taking a tumble to the floorboards. I turn the key and put the thing into motion, but Owen positions himself right in front of me, arms outstretched, like he's either offering himself up as a sacrifice or daring me to mow him down.

"Move it, Owen." I lay on the horn. "We're deep enough in the South that I can exercise vigilante justice."

"Not without going to prison first."

I eye him like road kill. "It might be worth it."

"Stop that thing and talk to me."

"You've had two months to talk to me. Two months to tell me all that crap I just listened to. But you didn't. And you wouldn't have if I hadn't walked in on your conversation."

"The one that involved me telling Mitchell to tell you the truth?"

"Yes, your boss. You know, the guy who pays you and orders your every move."

He walks closer and slaps the hood. "You're making a mistake,

Avery."

"Coming here was a mistake." I inch the vehicle forward, and Owen retreats. "And so was falling for you."

He rips off his sunglasses. "That's big talk coming from the girl who's running away—again."

My foot nearly slips off the brake. Blood thunders through my veins. "What did you say?"

"I said you're running." Owen says it loud enough for every rooster, cow, and chicken to hear.

"Were you even *in* that conversation in there?"

"I was." He plants his hands on Dolly Parton. "You want to tell me what your relationship with Mitchell has anything to do with ours?"

Dear God, give me patience. Because I'm about to run over one of your most beautiful, but clearly dumbest *creations.* "Are you *insane?* It has everything to do with us."

"You want to cut Mitchell out of your life, that's your business. It's a mistake, but it's yours to make."

"Is this the part where you're trying to win me over? Because you are miserably failing."

"I get it," he says. "You're scared."

My fingers clench the steering wheel. "Scared of how much of a mess this is gonna make."

"You're not just running from Mitchell, Avery. You're running from us."

"There is no us."

"You're using the fallout with Mitchell to leave me, too. It's convenient, isn't it? I mean, you've been waiting for me to screw up. That's what you think all guys do. That's what they've done before."

"Owen, you better move yourself out of my path before—"

But he doesn't. Owen walks right up to the driver's side and leans dangerously close. "What I feel for you is real. It's not anything your grandfather orchestrated. It's not another lie. I'm sorry I kept things from you, but I did not have a choice."

"Yes, you did." I jab my finger toward him. "You could've chosen me."

"I am. Right now." Owen puts his hand over mine. "Caring for someone means you don't leave when it gets rough. You stay and work it out. You're not the only one who didn't get that from a parent." His voice lowers. "You think I'm not scared at how fast this is moving? I've never felt anything like this before. But I'm not running away from it."

"I'm not hearing this. Don't make this about me when you screwed it up."

"You want to bundle me up with Mitchell, you go ahead. But we both know what's at the heart of your walking away from me. You're afraid. And instead of staying and fighting this out, it's just easier for you to take off."

"I'm not going to stay for someone I can't even trust."

"I would never intentionally hurt you, and you know it."

"Really?" Because I'm surprised I'm not bleeding all over the ground. "I think you hurt me pretty good." I shake off Owen's hand. "This whole time, you knew *all* of that, and you never said a word. That's not caring for someone."

"No? Then what do you call it?"

"Being Mitchell's puppet."

His expression turns thunderous, and I see those eyes lose all warmth. "Is that all you think I am?"

"Owen, I don't really have time to figure out who the real you is."

He slaps his hand on the frame above us. "You go ahead and run, Avery. Go back to your big city and your poetry-writing boyfriends. And when all that leaves you cold, you remember what you left. What you were too scared to fight for."

"And you go back to Mitchell," I counter. "He's the one you really love."

I peel away, great puffs of brown dust covering the view behind me like a curtain on the final act.

I turn around one more time and see Owen standing there, framed by the dust. Watching me leave.

But there's no going back, no turning this thing around. I'm getting off this ranch and back to freedom. Back to life before Owen, and way before Mitchell.

I drive that jaunty vehicle down the miles of dirt road, passing two milk trucks, a Ford, and one very confused man in a Chevy. With one hand on the wheel and one on my phone, I call Elizabeth.

My friend answers on the third ring. "Hello?"

I promptly burst into tears. And inhale a bug.

"Avery? Avery are you okay?"

"No." I spit indelicately.

"What's going on?"

"I need—" I sputter on a sob—"a favor."

"Anything."

I wipe away my very last tear. "Take me to the airport."

Chapter Nineteen

"**W**HAT DO YOU mean there are no flights out to New York? What about Newark?" Sitting in a gas station parking lot, I hold the phone to my ear and watch for Elizabeth's car. Dolly Parton doesn't come with an air conditioner, so sweat trickles down every part of my body like a final insult. "Nothing until tomorrow?" I needlessly repeat the words of the customer service agent in my ear. "But what if—no? Okay, but if you looked for a Red Eye flight to—" I let her interrupt me one more time because her story is the same. There are no flights out of the small local airport today. I slump lower in the seat, taken down by heat, defeat, and an abundance of anger. "No, I don't need help purchasing a ticket for tomorrow. Thank you." I click the phone off and stare at the convenience store doors. From the signs posted, the place sells beer, frog legs, and live bait. Perfect for a deep-fried fishing afternoon. Not so great for a complete life meltdown.

Just as I'm considering going in to trade someone my sob story for a slushie, Elizabeth's old Ford sedan wheezes and grunts into the parking lot. Even though my friend wears hot pink sunglasses big enough to cover most of her face, I can see her worried frown from here.

"What happened?" She hops out of her car and approaches Dolly Parton and me. "You look like death."

"Thanks."

"You got mascara running down your cheeks like leaky marker and—" She waves her hands in my general direction—"you're covered in sweat."

"You took your sweet time getting here."

"It's happy hour at the dairy barn. Had to stop for a half-priced shake. I bought one for you, but then I ran into the captain of the football team and—"

"Can we please get out of here?" My bottom lip quivers, my throat tightens, and I know I'm not through with the water works after all.

Elizabeth pushes her glasses on top of her head. "How about we start with you telling me why you're going to the airport."

"Because everything fell apart. My whole life is a lie."

Her head tilts with pity. "Last time I heard that my cousin James asked to be called Juanita."

"I walked in on Mitchell and Owen talking in the barn." I fill her in, stopping long enough to wipe my drippy nose and swat away two mosquitos.

At the end of my story, Elizabeth's face is grim. "That moron."

"I know." I don't know if she's referring to Mitchell or Owen, but either way she's spot on. "I can't get a flight out until tomorrow morning. Unless you want to drive me to Dallas."

Elizabeth glances back at her rusted car. "Not unless you want to push us all the way there." She envelopes me in a quick hug. "Get in the car. I'm taking you to my house. There's someone I want you to meet."

"Someone with a jet?"

"No," she says. "But he does have wheels."

Chapter Twenty

*S*TORM CLOUDS BEGIN to move in and follow us, as if my horrible day conjured them into existence. Elizabeth drives us through Sugar Creek, winding through a neighborhood of ranch-style homes that probably saw their better days when Reagan occupied the Oval Office and hair bands ruled the FM airwaves. She pulls into a cracked driveway leading to a red brick home. The yard needs a good mow, but otherwise the house is tidy and ready for its close-up with freshly painted shutters, landscaping that lines the front walk, and a pristine, white mailbox bearing Elizabeth's last name.

"Come on in inside," Elizabeth says.

I schlep behind her as we step into a living room with sunny yellow walls and a giant TV blasting a soap opera.

A man sits in a wheelchair, his frame thin, his posture bowed. "Hey, Lizzie, girl."

Elizabeth leans down for his kiss on her cheek. "Brought you a chocolate shake."

"Extra chocolate?"

"You know it." She fusses with the sparse hair on top of his head. "Avery, this is my dad, Ben."

"Nice to meet you." I stick my hand out, but find he's not reciprocating.

"My arms are a little numb today," he says. "But it's nice to put a face to the name. Elizabeth's told me all about you. Our meals around here were good, but they've sure improved since she's been working with you."

My first ray of sunshine today. "Thank you."

"She says you're dating our Owen."

"I'm actually going back to Manhattan tomorrow." I'll spare Ben the gory details. "So I don't think Owen and I will be seeing each other again." This seems more polite than saying, "I want to claw Owen's eyes out, forget Mitchell exists, and walk all the way back to New York."

"Well." Ben gives his daughter a none-too-subtle side-eye. "I'm sure everyone on the ranch will miss you. I know Elizabeth will."

"Speaking of Owen," Elizabeth says to her father. "He said to tell you he'll be by to mow tomorrow on his day off."

"That boy takes good care of us," Ben says.

Elizabeth gestures toward the TV. "What's the latest with Anna and Rafe today, Dad?"

He sighs. "Anna's demon-possessed evil twin is back, and Rafe just found out he accidentally fathered those two kidnapped children."

"This love stuff." I plop my body onto the couch. "It's just never easy, is it?"

We finish watching *Malibu Longings* with her father, then Elizabeth pulls me back to her bedroom.

"You and your dad seem really close." I settle into a chair by her desk.

"We've had to rely on each other." She sits on her quilted bed and pulls her legs beneath her. "He has MS. We have lots of good days, but occasionally we have a bad one. We couldn't make it without the help of our friends."

"Like Owen mowing the yard," I say.

"Like that," she says. "How are you going to get your stuff from the ranch?"

"I don't know. I didn't really think that through when I drove off in an ATV named after a busty country star." I scroll through my phone searching for tomorrow's flight. "I just know I want to go home." The very word *home* clangs in my spirit like a penny hitting the bottom of an empty well. "Are you sure you're okay with me sleeping here tonight?"

"You can stay as long as you want. But I really think you should talk to Owen." She holds up her phone. "He's texted me nonstop for the last hour."

He and Mitchell had both attacked my number with calls and texts too. "I'm through talking to them. The day I arrived in Sugar Creek, I told myself to keep my distance. I should've gone with that instinct."

"Owen's got it bad for you, you know."

"It's over. And it's time for me to get back to my life." I flick off a small bug stuck to the dried sweat on my arm. "But first, I need to take a shower. Can I borrow some clothes?"

Elizabeth rises from the bed and helps me pick out a pair of shorts and t-shirt. "The bathroom's the second door on the left down the hall."

"Thanks, Elizabeth." I hug my friend tightly. "You saved me today."

"Okay." She gives me a small pat. "You stink."

I muster the energy to smile, and with my change of clothes under my arm, I reach for the doorknob.

And my world teeters and tilts.

My hand drops as I move closer to the bulletin board hanging on the wall before me. It's decorated with photos spanning years and generations. I stare at the faces smiling back at me from their frozen tableaus.

"That's my mom." Elizabeth stands next to me and points to a faded picture. "She and my dad never married. She lives in Los Angeles."

"Do you ever see her?" The words are automatic, polite. Because I'm too focused on the other photos to even hear her answer.

"Nah. She started a new life in California. I've only seen her twice."

Now it's my turn to point at a photo. "This is your dad." The young man stands tall without the assistance of a wheelchair, his smile beaming. "And this looks like—"

"Owen," Elizabeth says. "The one-year-old my dad is holding is me. The lady in the wedding dress holding the bouquet is Owen's mom."

"Owen's your stepbrother? I've been on the ranch all this time and nobody thought to mention this?"

"*Former* stepbrother. Our parents married when Owen was seven, but it only lasted three years. When my dad started getting sick, Maria took off. I don't think anyone even knows where she is now. Owen's dad was never in the picture, so he went to live with his grandpa after that."

My battered heart aches for Owen, even though I'm still furious with the boy. "And then he started working at the ranch."

"Been there since he was twelve. That's about the time we started finding cash under our welcome mat on the first Friday of every month. My dad says when it started, it was just a few dollars. But as the years went on, the amount got big enough that it would come in a cashier's check from the bank."

"The money was from Owen?"

Elizabeth nodded with a wry grin. "I finally caught him when I was about ten. Owen doesn't just send us money though. He comes by all the time to check on my dad, bring us meat from the ranch, or to see if the house needs any repairs. Last week he fixed a leaky faucet." Her pink nail taps another picture. "This one's the day we got our house about six years ago. My dad couldn't work, but he kept getting denied for disability. We'd been living in this one room apartment over someone's garage."

"Owen bought the house?" What kind of money was he making on that ranch?

Elizabeth laughs. "No, take another guess. He refused to get in the photo with us, but he was there."

"Mitchell."

"One day this fancy white Cadillac pulled into the driveway. Out steps Owen and this man in a cowboy hat. Mitchell's pretty much a celebrity around here, so I knew instantly who it was. They came into our apartment, sat down on our ratty couch, and Mitchell told my dad he'd hired an attorney to pursue his disability. Then Mitchell said he had a rent house that was just sitting empty, and he needed someone to occupy it until he found some good renters."

I know where this is headed before Elizabeth even finishes.

"That was a long time ago," she says, "and Mitchell hasn't found his renters yet."

My heart folds in half, and I have to take a step back from Elizabeth. She's standing too close. Everything I feel—it's much too close.

"Why?" I ask hoarsely. "Why would Mitchell do that?"

"Because Owen asked him to. It's an incredible gift Mitchell's given us, but we're just one of many of his recipients."

I blink back the moisture in my eyes. "This doesn't change anything."

"Doesn't it?" Elizabeth asks. "You want to know why Owen never said anything to you about Mitchell's meddling in your life? Avery, he feels like he owes him. Mitchell takes care of us—for Owen's sake. And the man took Owen under his wing, gave him a job when he was too young to be working, trained him to run a ranch. Gave Owen his own cabin when he graduated from high school, so he'd have a place to live while juggling work and college."

"But Owen owed me the truth. They both did."

"We'd all do anything for Mitchell Crawford. *Anything.* My daddy has the best care in the country. I work a job that lets me set my own hours and pays more than I need." Elizabeth rests her hand on my shoulder. "I know you're hurt, and you have a right to be. But maybe Mitchell never knew how to approach you. What he knows is how to help, how to use his money to do good. That man isn't famous around here for his big ranch. He's famous for his big generosity. He obviously made some serious mistakes in the past, but do you know what I think?"

I numbly shake my head.

"If you're going to judge Mitchell, judge his *entire* past. And that includes what he did for me, for my dad, for Owen, for every family that comes to his land with a sick child, and for countless other folks who've benefitted from the owner of the Shadow Ranch."

A tornado of thoughts spin in my head until I'm dizzy with it all. "He completely manipulated my life. I don't know that I can just let that go." My sigh comes from the depths of my weariness. "There are so many things I still don't understand."

"Then maybe you ask Mitchell." Elizabeth grabs a tissue box from her desk and offers it to me. "And as for Owen, he's crazy about you, Avery. I've known him most of my life, and I've never seen him like this about anyone."

She might be wise beyond her seventeen years, but this part she definitely doesn't understand. "How can I just trust him?" I pull out a tissue and blow my nose. "Every guy I've ever dated has lied to me. I really thought Owen was different."

"He is different." Elizabeth looks at her bulletin board before returning her winsome gaze to me. "And that's exactly why you adore him."

Chapter Twenty-One

THAT NIGHT I find Mitchell in his office, sitting in his leather chair at his desk and staring at his laptop screen. He takes a drink from a nearby glass and sits it back down with a thud.

"Did you ever wonder why I called this place Shadow Ranch?" He swivels in his chair and faces me, as I stand in the doorway.

He knew I was standing there. The man misses nothing.

I take a few steps inside. "Tell me."

He eyes me warily as he leans back. "It was my pet name for your mother." The amber liquid in the glass draws his focus, and he seems to go somewhere else for a moment. "From the very beginning, your momma was my girl. Her mother loved her something fierce, but Courtney was just a daddy's girl. She'd go everywhere with me—on the tractor, to the race track, the feed store. She was my little shadow. I was crazy about her. Her momma said I spoiled her. Now I realize she was right, and it was the last thing she needed."

I ease into the high back chair in front of his desk and wait for him to continue.

"I was at her funeral. No power in hell could've kept me from going." He looks away, his eyes glistening. "I stood in the back. Owen went with me. I cried like a baby all the way home, and he never said a word. He just drove the truck and played that twangy music of his."

"Why didn't you say something to me?" My throat is raw from all the talking, all the tears. "I was so alone." I can still feel the weight of that pain, that isolation.

"You had a group of friends around you. I told myself you were better off with them than with me. I knew your momma had told you all about me—her version anyway—and I didn't want to upset you any more. I told myself I'd contact you when things settled down."

"But you didn't."

"No, I didn't. I guess you're not the only one scared of a little heartbreak. If I visited you and you wanted nothing to do with me—well, I don't think I could've taken it."

"So you found a way to get me here. Found a reason for me to need you."

Mitchell runs a hand over his face. "You have every reason to be mad about that, Avery. What you said was right—it was manipulative. I guess desperate people do desperate things." He splays his hands. "I've got all this and nobody to share it with. And there you were struggling all by yourself. It just seemed to me like we should get to know one another." He chokes out a small laugh. "I hoped if you got to know me, you might like me."

"I do like you." The words come from a place that's been kept under lock and key. But they're true. "And I have been so alone." All the nights I cried myself to sleep, praying for God to send me some help. And here was Mitchell, waiting for me. "But you can't treat me like my mother. You can't orchestrate my life and step in and take over. I had an amazing internship lined up for this summer. It could've really opened doors for me."

"I can open doors for you."

"I want to make it on my own. I don't want your money to make opportunities happen. I've got to know I've accomplished everything on my own abilities."

"Well, of course you will. You're smart like me. And a wonderful cook like your Grandma Clare." His voice warms. "And spirited like your mother."

I give him a watery smile. He made us sound like a family. One I could belong to and a lineage I could proudly claim as my own.

My mother had chosen to cut ties with her father forever, and it changed our lives.

Tonight I was choosing to return to Mitchell Crawford like the prodigal she could've been.

And lives would change once again.

"I'm going to need some time," I say. "I still have a lot of questions. And I'm not sure I'm through being mad."

Relief lights his face. "You let me know when you're done. I'll be here." His smile lifts his cheeks. "I'll always be here, Avery."

Chapter Twenty-Two

O WEN WASN'T IN his cabin.

He didn't answer his phone.

And he wasn't in any of the barns.

So Dolly Parton and I make the jostling, bumpy trek down a few more dirt roads until I see Owen's truck pulled to the side.

I know exactly where he is.

With my phone as a flashlight, I walk through a field, stubbing my toe twice on invisible rocks and nearly falling on my face when I trip over a squishy mound of something I'm afraid to inspect. But when I finally get to that hill, my breath catches and my heart whispers one solitary word.

Owen.

Holding a lantern, he stands with his back to me and his face turned up to the sky. One rugged, beautiful man against the backdrop of the land he loves.

He slowly turns to face me. "If you've come to yell at me some more, I'm fresh out of fighting words."

"Good." I walk to him, the grass swishing against my legs. "Because you can just listen."

It's not so dark that I don't make out the resignation on his face.

"You lied to me," I say.

"I think we've established—"

"I said I would do the talking." I see that dark brow lift, and I plod on. "You knew important information about me, about my life, and about my mother. I needed to know that. I realize you love Mitchell like a grandfather, and you were in the middle. Maybe I would've done the same thing. I don't know. Because I've never had someone pour into my life like Mitchell has yours. And tonight I met Ben. And I know, Owen. I know all about the money you left for them when you were just a little boy." My word, I love him for that. I want to take that twelve-year-old boy and just hug him until he squeals.

"I'm not going to talk about Elizabeth and her dad."

"Of course you're not. Because Mitchell raised you by his example. But Elizabeth told me what you did for her family, and I happen to think you're incredible. And I know you were at my mother's funeral."

"You've talked to Mitchell."

I nod my head. "All this time, my anger at my grandfather was all I had left of my mom. I was raised on that venom, and I thought if I let it go, I'd lose a part of her." It's still such an unsettled thing in my heart. "I don't know why my mom never forgave him and never came back home. But I don't want to live like that."

A warm breeze blows, ruffling Owen's hair. "What are you saying, Avery?"

I inhale deeply, ignoring the humidity teasing my skin, the bugs biting my bare legs, and the fear roaring like a caged lion. "I lied, too." I take his hand, letting my fingers slide over that familiar rough skin. "The night you first brought me here, a star shot across that dark sky. And you asked me if I'd made a wish."

His fingers wrap around mine. "And you said no."

"I made a wish. I watched that star shimmy over me, and I closed my eyes and gave it the desire of my heart."

Owen tucks a strand of hair behind my ear. "Tell me what you wished for."

The word sticks to the tip of my tongue, but I push it out. "Love. I wished for love. I wasn't sure what I was even asking for. All I knew was that I was alone. And then I got to know you. And my grandfather." The grass dances around our legs as I step closer. "People have let me down. They've rejected me, cheated on me, and gone away. But I can't live on all that disappointment. You once said we can miss the best things when our expectations are low." I reach a hesitant hand out and cup Owen's cheek. "I don't want to miss one more thing. Even if it's hard and complicated and messy."

Owen's pause stretches painfully long. But then he turns toward my hand and presses a kiss right in the center. "You sure about this?"

"Yes," I say. "Mostly. Pretty much. Minus a few areas of doubt. But the good kind. So, back to yes. Absolutely. At least ninety-percent."

Owen snakes his arm around me until my body is flush with his. "Let's go with yes."

My laughter bubbles over. "Why don't we?"

"I love you, Avery." His smiling face lowers, and his lips find mine.

"Never stop saying that." I slide my hands around his neck and kiss Owen with a reverence and freedom I've never felt.

I would be going back to New York. And even though Owen and Mitchell won't be there, I'm no longer alone.

My mom might not have had enough to come back to.

But I certainly do.

I have a grandfather. And a boyfriend who has stolen my heart.

And more wishing stars than one girl can count.

The End

About the Author

Award-winning author Jenny B. Jones writes romance with sass and Southern charm. Woefully indecisive, she writes YA, New Adult, and women's romance. Since she has very little free time, Jenny believes in spending her spare hours in meaningful, intellectual pursuits, such as watching bad TV, Tweeting deep thoughts to the world, and writing her name in the dust on her furniture.

Want to Be the First to Know When Jenny's Next Books Come Out? Sign up for Jenny's Book News.

Other Books by Jenny B. Jones

In Between

On the Loose

The Big Picture

Can't Let You Go

A Sugar Creek Christmas

Save the Date

A Charmed Life Series

Just Between You & Me

And More!

Website: JennyBJones.com

For Information Contact: Jen@jennybjones.com

Follow Jenny on Facebook: facebook.com/jennybjones

Follow Jenny on Twitter: @JenBJones

Instagram: @JennyBJonesAuthor

Special Thanks

Writing is a process. Sometimes that process involves swear jars and dry cereal eaten by the handful. But no matter what, the writing process will *always* include a round of editing...or several rounds. *cough* Every well-told story has a brilliant editor rooting for the hero and heroine from behind the curtain. And in the case of *Just One Summer*, we were fortunate enough to have *two*.

Thank you to Kristin Avila for your fearless brainstorming, thoughtful comments, and round-the-clock availability. You're a fiction rock star. We've been blessed by your geniusness. That's a word, right?

Thank you to Christa Allan for your expertise, your witty notes, and your sharp attention to detail. You've enriched each one of our characters and saved us all from the deadly grasp of the grammar police. Hugs to you!

Made in the USA
Charleston, SC
20 November 2015